"Long time no see, Curtis."

He was about to reply when she came closer and the words evaporated on his tongue.

Barrie's tan canvas winter coat was open in the front, and her belly swelled under a loose cream-colored sweater. She sauntered down the aisle toward him, her vet bag slung over one shoulder, and stopped at the stall.

"You're—" He wasn't sure if he was allowed to point out the obvious, but he'd never been a terribly diplomatic guy. "You're pregnant."

"I am." She met his gaze evenly.

"Congratulations." He wasn't sure what else to say. Somehow, in all of his considerations surrounding seeing Barrie again, he hadn't considered this one.

"Thank you." For the first time, her confidence seemed to falter, and color rose in her cheeks. "You look good, Curtis."

His jeans were mud smeared and he hadn't shaved in several days, but he'd take the compliment. He allowed himself one more glance down her figure before he locked his gaze firmly on her face and kept it there. Her body and her baby weren't his business.

D0558610

HOME ON THE RANCH:
MONTANA HOLIDAY PROMISES

⚒

PATRICIA JOHNS

ANN ROTH

Previously published as *Montana Mistletoe Baby*
and *A Rancher's Christmas*

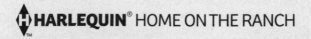

PLEASE RECYCLE
THIS PRODUCT IS RECYCLABLE

Recycling programs
for this product may
not exist in your area.

ISBN-13: 978-1-335-44565-0

Home on the Ranch: Montana Holiday Promises

Copyright © 2019 by Harlequin Books S.A.

Montana Mistletoe Baby
First published in 2017. This edition published in 2019.
Copyright © 2017 by Patricia Johns

A Rancher's Christmas
First published in 2013. This edition published in 2019.
Copyright © 2013 by Ann Schuessler

This edition published by arrangement with Harlequin Books S.A.

For questions and comments about the quality of this book,
please contact us at CustomerService@Harlequin.com.

® and TM are trademarks of Harlequin Enterprises Limited or its
corporate affiliates. Trademarks indicated with ® are registered in the
United States Patent and Trademark Office, the Canadian Intellectual
Property Office and in other countries.

Printed in U.S.A.

HARLEQUIN®
www.Harlequin.com

CONTENTS

Montana Mistletoe Baby   7
by Patricia Johns

A Rancher's Christmas   225
by Ann Roth

Patricia Johns writes from Alberta, Canada. She has her Hon BA in English literature and currently writes for Harlequin's Love Inspired and Heartwarming lines. You can find her at patriciajohnsromance.com.

Books by Patricia Johns

Harlequin Heartwarming

Home to Eagle's Rest

Her Lawman Protector
Falling for the Cowboy Dad

A Baxter's Redemption
The Runaway Bride
A Boy's Christmas Wish

Love Inspired

Montana Twins

Her Cowboy's Twin Blessings
Her Twins' Cowboy Dad

Comfort Creek Lawmen

Deputy Daddy
The Lawman's Runaway Bride
The Deputy's Unexpected Family

His Unexpected Family
The Rancher's City Girl
A Firefighter's Promise
The Lawman's Surprise Family

Visit the Author Profile page at Harlequin.com for more titles.

MONTANA
MISTLETOE BABY

PATRICIA JOHNS

To my husband, the love of my life.
Life with you is never dull!

Chapter 1

Curtis Porter was too old to be a bull rider, and right about now, he felt like a failure at ranching, too. When he'd moved away from Hope, Montana, for good, he'd left behind a soon-to-be ex-wife and a whole heap of memories. He figured if he ever came back, he'd show her just what she missed out on. He didn't count on coming back washed up.

Curtis hunkered down next to the calf in the barn stall. The calf was having difficulty breathing and looked thin. It obviously hadn't been eating properly. Curtis had been back on the ranch only since Friday, so he couldn't blame himself for not noticing sooner. Bovine illness could be hard to spot at first glance, but the later stages were obvious. He still wished he hadn't missed this one—he hated the unnecessary suffering.

December was a tough month—the days being snipped shorter and shorter, and darkness stretching out well into his work hours. He did chores in the morning and evening with a flashlight while winter wind buffeted him from all directions. It wasn't an excuse to have missed a sick calf, but it factored in.

Curtis rose to his feet and let himself out of the stall. He'd just have to wait for the vet. He was officially out of his depth. Curtis was a recently retired bull rider, and when the aunt who'd taken him in as a teen asked him to come back to help run the ranch while she recovered from a broken ankle, he'd agreed, but it wasn't only because of his soft spot for Aunt Betty. He had other business to attend to in the tiny town of Hope—the sale of a commercial property—and he'd been putting that off for longer than his finances would comfortably allow. He no longer had the choice—he needed the money now.

Curtis's cell phone blipped, and he looked down at an incoming text from Aunt Betty.

The vet passed the house a couple of minutes ago. Should be there any second.

There was a pause, and then another text came through.

Tried to get Palmer, but he's out at an emergency for the night. Had to call Barrie. Sorry, kiddo.

His heart sped up, and Curtis dropped the phone back into his front pocket. Of course. There were only two vets in Hope, and his ex-wife, Barrie Jones, was one of them. At least Aunt Betty had *tried* for the less awkward option.

The barn door creaked open, and Curtis looked up to see Barrie framed in the doorway. From this vantage point, he could see her only from her shoulders up—chestnut-brown hair pulled back into a ponytail, no makeup and clear blue eyes—and his heart clenched in his chest. Her gaze swept across the barn, then landed on him, pinning him to the spot. Fifteen years, and she could still do that to him.

"Betty said I'd find you out here," Barrie said, pulling the door shut behind her. The sound of her stomping the snow off her boots on concrete echoed through the barn. Then she headed past some stalls toward him. "Long time no see, Curtis."

Apparently Aunt Betty had given Barrie time to compose herself, too. He swallowed hard and was about to reply when she came around to the aisle and the words evaporated on his tongue.

Barrie's tan canvas winter coat was open in the front, and her belly swelled under a loose cream-colored sweater. Her walk was different—more cautious, maybe—but other than the belly, she was still the long-legged beauty she'd always been. Barrie sauntered down the aisle toward him, her vet bag slung over one shoulder. She stopped at the stall.

"You're—" He wasn't sure if he was allowed to point out the obvious, but he'd never been a terribly diplomatic guy. "You're pregnant."

"I am." She met his gaze evenly.

"Congratulations." He wasn't sure what else to say. Somehow, in all of his considerations surrounding seeing Barrie again, he hadn't considered this one.

"Thank you." For the first time, her confidence seemed to falter, and color rose in her cheeks. "You look good, Curtis."

His jeans were mud smeared and he hadn't shaved in several days, but he'd take the compliment. He allowed himself one more glance down her figure before he locked his gaze firmly on her face and kept it there. Her body—and her baby—weren't his business.

"You look good, too," he said. "You're doing really well, then. Your veterinary practice, a baby on the way... So, who's the lucky SOB? Anyone I know?"

It was annoying to admit it, but that was his biggest question right now—who'd managed to make her happy? He couldn't say that he wouldn't be a tiny bit jealous. A man didn't marry a girl, vow to love her until death parted them and then watch her move on with some other guy without at least a twinge of regret.

"I doubt it." Her smile slipped, and she turned toward the stall. "Is this the calf?"

So she wasn't going to tell him? How bad could it be? This only made him all the more curious. He unhinged the latch and opened the gate.

"Seriously?" he asked. "All I have to do is ask Betty who you're with—"

"I'm single." She shot him a sharp look, then went into the stall and crouched down next to the calf. "I'll take a look."

Single? So, some idiot had knocked her up and

walked out on her? That sparked some anger deep inside him. He'd walked out, but only after she'd shown him the door, and she most definitely wasn't pregnant when he'd left. So he might be an SOB, too, but whoever had left her alone with this baby was higher on that list.

Barrie put on some rubber gloves, pulled a flashlight out of her bag and checked the calf's eyes. Then she pulled out a thermometer and murmured reassuringly to the calf as she worked.

"So who's the father?" Curtis pressed.

Barrie glanced up again, then sighed. "Curtis, I'm here to do a job. Would you like to know what's wrong with this calf or not?"

"Fine." He leaned against the rail and watched her check the calf's temperature.

She looked at the readout on the digital recorder. "A cow's body temperature rises continuously during the day, so it's hard to get a really accurate idea of how much fever a calf is running…"

Barrie pulled the plastic cover off the thermometer wand, then dropped it back into her bag. She rose to her feet and turned to Curtis. "But this calf is definitely running a fever. I'm thinking it's probably bovine respiratory disease. It's catchy, so keep an eye on the other calves bought at the same time. It can be transferred to adult cattle, as well, so make sure you quarantine the sick ones or you'll end up with a costly epidemic."

"Got it." He nodded. "Treatment?"

"I'll give antibiotic doses for a few days. It's caused by a virus, but the antibiotics treat any secondary illnesses that develop as a result and let the body focus on fighting the virus. If we find the sick cows early enough, they get over it. If not, it turns into pneumonia and you'll lose them." Barrie opened her bag again and pulled out some packaged cattle syringes and bottles of liquid medication.

She was beautiful when she was focused like that. Barrie had always been that way—she could be knee-deep in manure and still look sweet. Curtis cared about the cattle—and about the running of his aunt's ranch—but right now, his mind was still working over the fact that Barrie was both single and pregnant. She'd always been the prim and proper type—so much so that it had driven him kind of crazy—so he knew how hard this would be on her.

"Tell me that you told the father to take a hike, and I'll feel better," he said after a moment.

"I don't need defending, Curtis," she replied. "Least of all from the man who walked out on me."

"You kicked me out," he countered.

"And you *left*." Anger snapped in that blue gaze. Then she shook her head. "This is dumb. It was fifteen years ago. There's no use fighting over it."

She had a point. Their relationship was solidly in the past, and whatever her problems now, at least she wasn't blaming him.

"So, how long are you in town?" she asked, turning to the calf again with a syringe. He wasn't sure if she was asking to see how fast she'd be rid of him, or if this was just small talk.

"For a few weeks to help Betty until her ankle heals," he said.

"I'm sure she appreciates it."

"Yeah…" He cleared his throat. Her current state made his other news that much harder to deliver because he'd be the bad guy yet again. But he'd have to tell her eventually. There was no avoiding this one, even if he wanted to.

Barrie administered the syringe, then stroked a hand over the calf's muzzle comfortingly.

"Poor thing," she murmured.

"Will it be okay?" he asked.

"We'll see," she replied. "You may have caught the symptoms in time."

She tried to stand but stumbled. Curtis stepped forward and caught her arm, helping her up.

"I'm fine." She pulled back, and he felt stung. He'd reacted on instinct—she was a pregnant woman, after all, and any able-bodied man would want to give her a hand.

"Look, Barrie, I'm here for something else, too," he admitted.

Barrie's clear blue eyes met his, one eyebrow arched expectantly. She was so close that he could smell the soft scent of her perfume mingling with the tang of other barn aromas. She looked the same—the big blue eyes, the light eyebrows she always used to complain about, the faint spattering of freckles over her nose. Fifteen years had gone by, aging him beyond his ability to keep bull riding, and she still looked as fresh as the twenty-year-old he'd married. He really wished he could have come back a little more successful to prove that she'd missed out, but he couldn't change facts.

"I'm selling the building," he said.

Professional. In and out. That had been Barrie's plan when Betty apologetically told her that Curtis was waiting in the barn with the sick calf. And seeing him again... He was older, obviously, but he was still the same Curtis who was too ruggedly handsome for his own good. But she was fifteen years older this time around, and pregnant. She had bigger worries than Curtis's ability to make her melt with one of his half smiles. Besides, there was a far higher risk of him irritating her. She didn't have the patience to deal with his boyish whims—her life had been turned upside down with this pregnancy, and she was facing her first Christmas without her mom, who had passed away last February from a stroke. She hadn't seen that heartbreak coming, either.

"Selling the building?" she repeated, slipping past him into the aisle, his words not sinking in.

"The commercial building my uncle left me—the one you lease for your practice."

Barrie whipped around in shock. "Wait—what?"

"I don't have much choice, Barrie."

"Selling it to who?" she demanded. A change in ownership didn't have to mean an end to her ability to lease there... Her mind spun forward, sifting through the possibilities.

"Nothing's finalized," he replied.

As if that made his intentions any different. Anger

simmered beneath the surface. She'd worked too hard for this, for too long, but Curtis had never cared about her ambitions. Fifteen years hadn't changed much between them. What she needed was information—then she could make a plan. She'd had too many surprises lately, and a plan was an absolute necessity.

"But you have an interested buyer," she countered.

"Palmer Berton is interested, but we haven't nailed anything down."

Barrie swallowed hard, her stomach dropping.

"You're going to sell the building that houses my clinic to my business rival," she clarified. "And you think he'll keep leasing to me? I'm going to have to find a new place—move all my equipment, renovate the new space…" She was already tallying the cost of this, and as the tally rose, so did her anxiety. "Why are you doing this?"

"It's not personal," he said. "I need to liquidate."

Not personal? Curtis of all people knew how personal her practice was to her. "You need the money *now*?"

"I'm going to buy a stud farm with my business partner in Wyoming, and I need to sell to get the money for my half of the down payment. I don't have a choice, Barrie."

"So, what happened to bull riding?" She couldn't control the ice in her tone. That had been the cause of their divorce—bull riding had stayed his priority, leaving her in the dust. She'd wanted a real home with him, not to follow after him in a beat-up trailer. She'd wanted to start a family, to pursue her education and become a vet. She'd wanted a life, not a road trip.

"My body can't take it anymore," he replied. "I've broken too many bones. This wrist—" He held up his arm and moved his hand in a circle. "You hear that clicking? Both of my ankles do that, too. I've gone as far as I can in the circuit. I'm officially old."

At thirty-seven. Barrie had seen that coming, too, but he'd never listened to her. A body could take only so much punishment, and every time he'd get thrown and break a rib or dislocate his shoulder, she'd be the one patching up his injuries and begging him to find something safer, something more reliable... How many times had she sat in her parents' kitchen, describing some new injury to her mom, who wisely just listened and offered no advice?

"That's it, then," she said. "You're selling and this is my heads-up."

He didn't answer. She sighed and hitched her bag up on her shoulder.

"Fine," she said. "Thanks for the warning."

Since when had Curtis been stable, anyway? This had always been the problem—Curtis was always on the move. Leasing from his uncle had seemed safe enough, but when he died of a heart attack last year and left the building to Curtis, she'd had a sinking suspicion that her comfortably predictable days were limited. She paid her monthly lease to a management company, and she'd hoped that arrangement could continue for a while.

"You don't know that Palmer will kick you out," Curtis said.

"Really?" she snapped. "Because I know Palmer pretty well. I worked under him for three years after I got my doctorate degree. He was furious when I started my own practice. He hates competition. I'm still under water on my student loans, I owe a good amount for supplies and renovating my clinic… I've only been running my own practice for four years! If you need help with that math, I'm nowhere near financially stable enough to ride this out."

Plus, there was the baby, which complicated everything further. She'd been wondering how she'd run a veterinary practice with a newborn. If her mom were still with them, she'd have a solution, but Mom was gone, and Barrie would have to sort this out on her own. Vets were on call 24/7. That was the way things worked in this field, and she wouldn't be able to afford to take a decent maternity leave. She ran a hand over her belly and the baby squirmed in response. Emotion rose in her chest, and she swallowed against it.

"What am I supposed to do?" Curtis's tone softened. "I own the building, but I can't do a thing unless I sell it. I'm sorry, Barrie. I mean it when I say selling the building isn't personal. I've put off the sale for a year, and there isn't any other way. I can't do the circuit anymore, and I have a chance for a fresh start. I either sell and invest in a business, or I'm washed up. It's as simple as that."

"It's you or me," she said wryly. "Nothing's changed, has it?"

Curtis took off his cowboy hat and scrubbed a hand through his hair. "We always did want different things."

"Yeah." The baby poked out a foot—maybe a hand? She put her own hand over the spot. Would she be forced to give up her dream of running her own practice and work under Palmer Berton again? The very thought put a sour taste in her mouth.

"Barrie, I'm sorry."

"You keep saying that." She shot him a chilly smile. "But let's keep things professional. I'm here as your vet, not as your ex-wife. If you notice any more cattle with hanging heads, lethargy or nasal discharge, call me and we'll treat them right away. We can get this under control if we're careful."

Curtis blinked, then nodded. Had he expected her not to be professional? He'd been gone a long time, and life hadn't just stopped in his absence. He might have wasted his time on the circuit, but she'd made good use of hers. Ironically, he could still pulverize her plans— that had been Curtis's greatest talent.

"Okay," he said. "I'll keep an eye out and give you a call. Unless you'd rather we call Palmer so you don't have to deal with me."

And give Palmer the job? No, she didn't want that in the least. She still had a practice to run, and she'd need all the money she could squirrel away.

"Curtis, I'm a professional," she replied. "And I'm good at what I do. Call me."

He nodded. "Will do."

Curtis—or at least, her feelings for him—had been at the center of all of Barrie's biggest mistakes in life, starting with marrying him and ending with a very un-planned pregnancy. This baby wasn't his, obviously, but he'd been unwittingly connected.

As she headed back to her truck, Barrie let out a wavering sigh.

Professional. In and out. She'd managed it, hadn't she?

One thing was certain—she wasn't going to let Curtis close enough to mess with her heart again. He'd already done enough damage for a lifetime.

Chapter 2

That evening, Curtis sank into a kitchen chair while Aunt Betty dished up a big plate of shepherd's pie and placed it in front of him. She wore a walking cast—cumbersome and awkward, but she still got from place to place. Heaven help her if she tried to get onto a horse, though.

It was only dinnertime, but outside the kitchen window the sky was black. Curtis had more work to finish up before he was done for the day; this was just a food break. He'd forgotten how much work a ranch was. Bull riding came with training and practice, but running a ranch was the kind of work that never ended—there was no night off.

"Barrie says the virus is containable," Betty said, flipping her gray braid back over her shoulder. "That's a relief. I should have kept a closer eye on those calves myself."

"Now we know," Curtis replied. "I've got the other ranch hands keeping an eye out, too, so we should be able to keep it from spreading."

Betty dished herself up a plate of shepherd's pie, as well, then deposited it on the table with a clunk. His aunt's shepherd's pie was amazing—spicy meat, creamy potatoes and a perfectly cooked layer of green peas.

"You didn't tell me Barrie was pregnant," Curtis added. He'd been thinking about Barrie all day after seeing her in the barn. He'd known he'd run into her eventually, but he'd halfway hoped he'd have some control over that. Might have made it easier, too, if his aunt had given him more than a minute's warning.

Betty pulled her chair out with a scrape and sat down. "Any chance the baby is yours?"

Curtis shot her an incredulous look. "Of course not."

"Then it was hardly your concern," Betty retorted.

That sounded real familiar, and he shot his aunt a wry smile. "Fine. Point made."

They both started to eat, and for a few moments, Curtis thought the conversation might be over, but then his aunt said, "This town has been gossiping something fierce, and I wasn't about to be part of that. Everyone has a theory on who the father is, and Barrie isn't saying."

"I noticed that. I asked her about it, and she pretty much told me to mind my own business." He reached for the pitcher of milk and poured them each a glass.

Betty's expression softened. "She's not yours to worry over anymore, Curtis."

"I know that." He took another bite and glanced out the window again. Snow swirled against the glass.

"Do you?" Betty asked.

He sighed. "I'm not here for Barrie, Aunty. I'm here to take care of my business, help you out and be on my way."

Betty didn't answer, but she got that look on her face that said she thought she knew better.

"I told her that I'm selling the building," he added.

"And how did that go down?" Betty asked.

"Not well, I have to admit." Curtis sighed. "She says that Palmer will push her out of business."

"And he will."

Curtis put down his fork. What made everyone so certain? "Palmer isn't the devil. Maybe he just wants a real estate investment. That isn't unheard of."

Betty shrugged. "She's a better vet."

"Is she?" Curtis had never seen Barrie in her professional capacity until today, and while he'd been impressed by her competence, he couldn't judge much. Back when they'd been married, she'd wanted to go to school, but that hadn't happened yet. Her life—everything she'd built for herself—had come together after he'd left town. It was slightly intimidating. She'd become a talented vet, and he'd become...too old to bull ride.

"Palmer has more experience, obviously," Betty said, "but she's got better instincts. Working together, they were a great team. On her own, Barrie has more potential. Palmer has already peaked in his career. She's still climbing."

"So you think he's threatened," Curtis concluded.

"If he's smart, he is."

An unbidden wave of pride rose up inside him. Barrie had always wanted to be a vet, and she'd not only achieved her dream, she was better than the established vet here in town, too. He'd always felt proud of Barrie when they were together. She was smarter than he was, in the book sense, at least. That had been frustrating when they'd argued, though. When she got mad, she got articulate. When he got mad, it all just balled up and he went out to ride until it untangled. Even their fighting hadn't been compatible.

"So she's doing well, then," he said.

"Besides her mother passing away last winter," his aunt said. "I told you about the funeral, right?"

"Yeah." He sobered. Gwyneth Jones had never been his biggest fan, but she'd been a good woman, and he'd been sad to hear about her passing. This was a hard year for Barrie, and he hated to contribute to her difficulties, but he didn't have a whole lot of choice.

"She's done really well in her practice," Betty went on. "She's still single, though."

"So are you," he quipped. "We aren't still judging people's worth by their marital status, are we?"

"Of course not," Betty said. "It's not like I'm one to talk. But I'm more of the saintly single type," she replied with a small smile. "It suits me."

Curtis chuckled. "And Barrie isn't?"

"She's more like you," Betty said, reaching past Curtis for a dinner roll. "Damaged."

"Ouch." Was that really how Betty saw him?

"You don't count on me for flattery," she replied, taking a bite. "You count on me for honesty."

"Fine." That was true. Betty had always been a rock in that sense. "So, we both know why I'm a wreck. Why is she?"

"In my humble opinion? It's because of you."

Curtis's humor evaporated as his aunt's words landed. "What do you mean?"

"She never did bounce back, dear."

Barrie had always been tough, beautiful and definitely desired by the other guys in town. He'd tormented himself for years thinking about the cowboys who would have gladly moved in to fill the void he left behind. Over the last decade, he hadn't called his aunt terribly often. When he did, and when he'd asked about Barrie, there was normally a boyfriend in the mix somewhere.

"I know she dated," he countered. "You told me that much."

"Oh, she dated," Betty said with a nod. "She's always been a beautiful girl. But she never did get anywhere near marriage again."

Neither had he, for that matter. As a bull rider, women had come to him, and he hadn't had to put a whole lot of effort into it. But he hadn't gotten serious. He told himself it was because he'd been married before, and he wasn't the romantic type anymore. Marriage was a whole lot harder than he'd anticipated. He'd done everything he could think of to make Barrie happy, and he still hadn't been enough for her. He wasn't a glutton for punishment, but he'd never imagined that she had ended up just as jaded as he had.

"I have to tell you, Curtis," his aunt went on, "the gossip has been vicious about Barrie."

"She isn't the first person to have a child outside wedlock in this town," he pointed out.

"No, she isn't," Betty confirmed. "But she won't say who the father is, and people's imaginations can come up with a whole lot more scandal than is probably the case."

"Like what?" he asked.

"Some suggest she's had an affair with a married guy around town. I know one woman who has an itemized list on why she's confident that the mayor is the father. Others say she's given up on finding love and went to a sperm clinic—" Betty paused. "Does it even matter? My point is that this isn't an easy time for Barrie. And maybe you could…consider all of that."

"When selling the building, you mean," he clarified.

"Yes."

"Aunty," he said slowly. "If I'm going to buy that stud farm, then I'm on a timeline. I need to liquidate and come up with my half of the down payment by Christmas Eve, or the deal is off. I feel for Barrie— losing her mom, all of it—but we've been researching this business venture for two years now, and this sale is not only an excellent price, but it would be a future away from bull riding. This is no whim—it's a plan."

"I know that," his aunt replied.

"So you can see that I don't have a lot of options here," he said. "Barrie has her practice. She's built a life for herself. It's been tough—I can see that—but she's got a life put together. I have to do the same thing."

Betty sighed. "I know. I just... Be as kind as possible, okay?"

"I'll do my best."

But what his aunt expected of him, he had no idea. None of this was his fault. If he didn't invest in something soon, he wouldn't be able to provide for anyone, let alone himself. If he didn't sort out his own life, no one else was going to do it for him.

Except providing for someone else hadn't even entered his mind until this moment...and along with the thought was an image of pregnant Barrie. He pushed it back—Barrie wasn't his to worry about anymore. Besides, while she'd lost her mom, she had the whole town of Hope to back her up. The locals might enjoy some salacious gossip, but when it came right down to it, they took care of their own. He ate his last bite and rose to his feet.

"I've got more cattle to check on," he said. "Thanks for dinner. Delicious as always."

"Thanks for helping out," Betty replied. "I mean that, Curtis. From the bottom of my heart."

Curtis wiped his mouth with a napkin and deposited the plate in the kitchen sink. Shooting his aunt a grin, he headed for the door.

Barrie was independent. She'd fought him every day of their marriage and then proceeded to get her education and build a veterinary practice on her own. She was a force to be reckoned with, and while he understood his aunt's concern about Barrie right now, he'd be smart to follow his carefully laid plans and start a life away from the circuit. That's what Barrie had always wanted him to do, wasn't it? And she'd been right. Better late than never.

He stepped into his boots and looked out at the ranch truck, snow accumulating over the hood in a smooth sheet. Snow was floating down in big fluffy flakes, and his mind was skipping ahead to the cattle. Curtis pushed his hat onto his head and trudged out into the cold.

Short days and long nights. This time of year brought the solstice, the shortest, coldest days before daylight started pushing back once more…

He glanced over his shoulder at the cheery glow of indoor lights shining through the windows. He was back in Hope for Christmas, and it wasn't going to be a cheery homecoming. But he'd get through it and hold out for spring and new beginnings.

The next morning, Barrie awoke three minutes before her alarm went off…and her feet were already sore. Her Great Dane, Miley, stood at her bedside, soulful eyes fixed on her. She'd never had trouble with her feet before, but pregnancy seemed to be changing the rules on her, and she hated that. When she'd first found out that she was pregnant, she'd promised herself nothing needed to change until the baby actually arrived. Some women nested when they were pregnant, but Barrie was going to control that instinct. These last few months would allow her to build up her practice enough that after the baby came she could scale back to clinic hours only, cut out the after-hours emergency calls and still keep her business afloat. But her body seemed to have other ideas.

"Morning, Miley," she said, reaching from under her cozy comforter to give the massive dog an affectionate ear scratch. He'd started out as a regular-sized puppy with paws like dinner plates, and he'd grown past even ordinary Great Dane proportions. He was a huge, jowly, slate-gray lap dog—at least, that's how he saw himself. He was a big baby, and absolutely worthless as a guard dog, but she loved him.

Barrie rolled out of bed and ran her hand over her belly. The baby stretched inside her. She didn't know if she was having a boy or a girl yet. She'd tried to find out at her last ultrasound, but the baby's legs were firmly crossed. She'd try to find out again—planning was key, and she didn't have the luxury of sweet surprises.

She pulled her bathrobe around her body and cinched it above her belly. She was ever growing, and as she passed her full-length mirror before she padded out into the hallway, she caught a glimpse of a rounded, bed-headed stranger with a colt-sized dog trailing after her. There was no getting used to this, but she did enjoy it. She'd always wanted kids—the nonfurry kind—and while the timing wasn't great, she was finally going to be a mother. It wasn't quite how she'd imagined it happening... At least she'd get a chance at motherhood, and still being single at the age of thirty-seven, she'd started to give up hope.

Barrie lived in a single-level ranch house on the north

end of Hope. She looked out her kitchen window at the pristine snow from last night's storm. The neighbor kid she paid to shovel her driveway was already at it, metal scraping against asphalt. This morning, she had plans to organize her presentation for Hope's 4-H club. She'd been invited to speak about a woman's contribution to agriculture, and that was a subject Barrie was passionate about. Girls needed encouragement to step out and become leaders in ranching and animal care. If there was one thing Barrie knew, it was that a woman couldn't wait for a man to define her future.

"You hungry, Miley?" She pulled down his food dish—which was really a medium-sized mixing bowl—took out the bag of dog food and filled the bowl to the top. Miley hopped up, paws on the counter, and snuffled his nose toward the bag.

"Miley!" she said reproachfully, and he dropped back down to the floor. He didn't need his paws on the counter to see over it. When she put his bowl on the floor, he immediately dropped his face into it and started to gobble.

While Miley ate, she headed to the fridge to find her own breakfast. She felt just about as hungry as the dog. She grabbed a bag of bagels from the fridge and a tub of cream cheese. Then her cell phone rang, and she picked it up from the counter and punched the speaker button.

"Dr. Jones, veterinary medicine," she said.

"Barrie?" She knew his voice right away, and she froze in the middle of cutting a bagel. Why did he have to sound like the same old Curtis? Her heart clenched, and she had to remind herself to exhale. Miley looked over at her, sensing her tension, no doubt.

"Curtis," she said, resuming what she was doing and attempting to keep her voice casual. "Everything okay over there?"

"We have another sick cow."

Bovine respiratory disease could spread quickly in the right conditions, and it could decimate a herd if left unchecked.

"A calf?" she asked.

"No, this is a full-grown heifer," he replied. "It's out in the south field. I saw it this morning on my rounds, and she's too big to just tip into the bed of a pickup and bring back to the barn, so I was wondering what the best course of action is in this kind of situation."

Barrie sank a butter knife into the cream cheese and began spreading it onto her bagel. This was going to be a breakfast to go.

"I'll leave in about ten minutes," she said. "I'll go with you to see her in the field. We might be able to leave her where she is, depending on how sick she is."

"Great." He paused. "You sure this is okay? Not too early?"

Barrie rolled her eyes. She was pregnant, not an invalid. She hated the kid gloves men used with her now that she was expecting, but there didn't seem to be any avoiding it. Perhaps this could turn into a nice little anecdote for her presentation to the 4-H girls.

"I'm a vet, Curtis," she said wryly. "This is the job."

"Of course." His tone softened. "See you soon."

Barrie hung up the phone and took a jaw-cracking

bite of her bagel. "Eat up, Miley," she said past a mouthful of food. "We're leaving."

Ten minutes later, Barrie was dressed, Miley had finished his breakfast and she had her own breakfast in a plastic container on the seat beside her. Her veterinary bag and other portable equipment were in the bed of the truck, and Miley was in the back seat, breathing dog breath over her shoulder. He was the worst back seat driver.

"Miley, give me some space," she said, pushing his jowly face away from hers. "Miley!"

He ignored her until she pointed and said, "Lie down, Miley."

Miley heaved a sigh and folded himself into the seat, his nails scratching against the vinyl. Lying down back there was no easy feat for a dog Miley's size.

"Good dog," she said with a smile. "You're my boy, aren't you?"

Miley made a conversational growling noise. It was his way of giving a verbal reply without getting into trouble for barking in the vehicle, and Barrie put her attention into driving.

Betty Porter's ranch was about forty minutes outside Hope. Barrie had done some work with Betty's livestock in the past few years, but her most vivid memories of the place would always be from when she'd been married to Curtis. They used to go to Betty's place for dinner sometimes, and it had always been so warm and cozy. Curtis used to slide a hand up her leg under the table, which had embarrassed Barrie to no end. It amused Curtis just as much when she'd blush and Betty would give her a quizzical look. Barrie pushed the memories away.

She'd been in love with the soft-hearted rebel in Curtis, but that rebellious streak also made living with him difficult. Curtis was better at sneaking out to see her than he was at coming home to see her. He'd been better at seducing than he was at supporting.

And he was back. Seeing him again stirred up a confusing cocktail of old feelings. She'd married a bull rider but hadn't been successful in taming him. That was how wisdom was earned—through mistakes—but even if she hadn't married him, she'd have lived to regret it. Curtis Porter was a no-win situation.

The miles and minutes clicked past as she ate her breakfast one-handed, and before too long, she came up on the side road that led to the Porter ranch. She signaled and turned, scanning the familiar landscape. This mile marker, the copse of trees at the edge of the first field…she knew this area like the back of her hand.

Dealing with her memories of Curtis was hard enough, but adding the real man into the mix seemed foolhardy, even now. Why couldn't he have just stayed away? The timing was awful—she was already off balance with the baby coming and her mom's recent death. If it weren't for her pregnancy, she might have been able to deal with all of this more easily…maybe.

Miley started scrambling again as he tried to get up.

"Hold on, Miley," she said as she turned in to the gravel drive. "Almost there."

Barrie took Miley with her on veterinary calls quite often. Not only was he good company, but she felt safer with him at her side, too. Not every ranch was equally well run, and some of them housed some rather slimy employees who stepped just a little more carefully around her with a dog Miley's size staring them down. He'd never been tested to see how far he'd go to protect his mistress, and that was probably for the best.

Barrie pulled to a stop next to the ranch house and turned off the engine. The front door opened almost immediately and Curtis came outside. He was already in a coat and boots. He'd always been a tall man, but he looked broader and bulkier now that he was firmly in his manhood. If only he'd aged a little less attractively…

"Alright, Miley," she said quietly. "Let's go."

Barrie pushed open her door and hopped out, then opened the back door for Miley, who followed her. Curtis's step hitched just once as his gaze landed on the dog, and she couldn't help the smile that twitched at her lips at his reaction.

"You rode bulls," she said wryly. "This big old baby shouldn't be a problem."

"He's almost as tall, too…" Curtis put out a tentative hand, and Miley sniffed him.

"Meet Miley," she said. "He's my right-hand dog."

"Hey…" Curtis let Miley sniff him again, then stroked the top of Miley's gray head. "You're a big fella."

Miley rolled his eyes back in ecstasy and nuzzled closer to Curtis like the big baby he was. She heaved a sigh. When Miley looked back at her, the dog froze for a moment, his eyes locked on his mistress.

"You're a traitor," she said with a low laugh.

Miley, reassured that there was no actual danger, turned his attention to sniffing the ground and finding a place to pee.

"So, are you ready to head out to the field?" Curtis asked.

"Absolutely. Let me get my bag." Barrie went around her truck and opened the back to get her supplies. Then she met him at the ranch truck they'd take out into the field.

"Is...*he* coming?" Curtis asked dubiously.

Betty opened the side door at that moment, and when she spotted Miley, her face crinkled into a smile.

"Oh, you handsome young man!" she exclaimed. "Come over here, Miley. Betty has some treats for her boy!"

Curtis shot his aunt a look of surprise and Barrie chuckled. "They're already acquainted."

"Looks like," Curtis replied with a shake of his head.

Betty disappeared into the house, Miley joyfully bounding behind her. The screen door slammed shut, and Curtis faced her with one side of his mouth turned up in a smile.

"Lead the way," she said, jutting her chin toward the rusty red Chevy. She wouldn't be softened by him. At this point, she was immune to his charms. Besides, Curtis Porter was selling her out. He might not owe her a blasted thing anymore, especially when it came to that particular piece of property, but he still had the uncanny ability to turn her entire life upside down just by waltzing into town. And she hated that. His fingerprints were still on her life, and she couldn't ever quite scrub them off.

So Curtis was back, and he was screwing her over, but in the meantime, he was a paying customer and Barrie couldn't afford to be choosy.

Chapter 3

Curtis opened the passenger side door and held out his hand. Barrie stepped smoothly past him and awkwardly hoisted herself up into the seat without his aid. He shook his head. Just like old times.

"It's a hand up," he said with a wry smile, "nothing more."

And he meant that. He wasn't foolish enough to try something with her again. He already knew how that ended, and he was no longer a twenty-year-old pup looking to belong somewhere. The last fifteen years had solidified him, too. He'd learned about himself—his strengths and weaknesses, as well as what he wanted out of life: a job he could rely on, a place where he could make a difference and earn some respect. Just once, he wanted to be called Mister.

"I'm fine." Barrie met his gaze with a cool smile of her own, and he adjusted his hat, then handed her the leather veterinary bag. She'd never really needed him for anything, and that had chafed.

Curtis slammed the door shut and headed around to the driver's side. The south field was a fifteen-minute drive. Earlier he'd brought the cow some hay and a bucket of water and tossed a saddle blanket over its back to keep it warm until he could bring Barrie out there. He started the truck and cranked up the heat.

"That's some dog you've got there," he said as he turned onto the gravel road that led past the barn and down toward the pasture.

"Miley's my baby," she said, and he noticed her rub a hand over her belly out of the corner of his eye. He was still getting used to this—the pregnant Barrie. She looked softer this way, more vulnerable, but looks were obviously deceiving, at least as far as her feelings for him were concerned.

"Until you have this one, at least," he said, nodding toward her belly.

"Miley will still be my baby," she replied, then sighed. "But yes, it'll be different. I honestly didn't think I'd end up having kids, so I may have set Miley up with some grand expectations."

"You always wanted kids, though," he countered.

"I know, but sometimes life works out different than you planned," she replied. "Exhibit number one, right here." She patted her belly.

According to Aunt Betty, he'd been the reason she stayed single and childless, and he didn't like that theory. So their marriage hadn't lasted. The rest of her life's choices couldn't be blamed on him any more than her successes could be attributed to him. He stayed silent for a few beats.

"What?" she said.

"Betty kind of—" How much of this should he even tell her? "She said I'd done a real number on you."

"You did," she retorted. "But like I said, I'm fine."

"So you don't blame me for…anything?"

"Oh, I hold a grudge, Curtis." She shot him a rueful smile. "But you'll just have to live with that. Divorces come with grudges built in."

Curtis nodded. "Alright. I guess I can accept that."

Besides, from where he was sitting, her life hadn't turned out so bad. And as for the kids—she was having a baby, wasn't she?

"So, you're done with bull riding, then?" she asked.

"Yeah." She'd been right about the longevity of it. "It's tough on a body. I can't keep it up. Besides, it's time to do something where I can grow old."

"Like a stud farm," she said.

"Yep. As half owner, I'll be managing the place, not doing the physical labor."

She nodded. "It's smart. I'll give you that."

"Thanks."

"Will you miss it—the bull riding, I mean?"

He rubbed his hand down his thigh toward his knee, which had started to ache with the cold. There was something about those eight seconds in the ring that grew him in ways Barrie had never understood. It was man against beast, skill against fury. He was proving himself in there—time after time—learning from mistakes and fine-tuning his game. He never felt more alive than when he was on the back of an enraged bull.

"Yeah," he admitted. "I will miss it. I do already. My heart hasn't caught up with my age yet, I guess."

"It never did." Her tone was dry, and she cast him one unreadable look.

He chuckled. "Is that the grudge?"

"Yep." And there wasn't even a glimmer of humor in her eye.

But that wasn't entirely fair, either. They'd been opposites, which was part of the fuel of their passion. She was almost regal, and he was the scruffy cowboy. She came from a good family, and he came from a chronically overworked single mom who'd consistently chosen boyfriends over him. Barrie had been the unblemished one, the one life hadn't knocked around yet, and he'd already been through more than she could fully comprehend by the time he'd landed in Hope at the ripe old age of sixteen. If anyone should have been the obsessive planner at that point, most people would have assumed it was Curtis—just needing a bit of stability—but it had been Barrie who wanted everything nailed down and safe. And she had her untainted life here in Hope as her proof that her way was better than his. What did a scuffed-up cowboy like him know about a calm and secure life?

Curtis had known exactly how lucky he was to have her in his life, and his heart had been in their marriage. The problem, as he saw it, was that she hadn't trusted him enough to risk a single thing after those vows. He'd wanted to make something of himself, and she'd dug in her heels and refused to budge. Her safe and secure life was here in Hope, and he was welcome to stay there with her, but she hadn't trusted him beyond those town limits. So he had a grudge or two of his own.

"How is your dad?" he asked, changing the subject.

"As well as can be expected since Mom passed away. He's looking at retirement in the next couple of years."

"He isn't retired yet?" Curtis asked. "He's got to be, what, seventy?"

"Sixty-nine," she replied. "And who can afford to retire these days?"

Sixty-nine and still working as a cattle mover—that would take a toll on a body, too, but Steve Jones didn't have the luxury of a career change.

"I'm sorry about your mom," he added. "Betty told me about her passing away when it happened, but I didn't think you'd want to hear from me."

"Thanks." She didn't clarify if he'd made the right call in staying clear, so he'd just assume he'd been right. He was the ex-husband, after all. Not exactly a comfort.

"That must have been a shock," he said.

"Yeah." She sighed. "You don't see that coming. This will be our first Christmas without her."

"I'm sorry, Barrie."

"Me, too." She was silent for a moment. "I guess you'll have Christmas with Betty, then."

"I need to have the sale finalized by Christmas Eve," he said. "Betty says she could do without me by then, so, yeah. Christmas with Betty, and then I'm leaving."

"So I'll be screwed over by Christmas." Her tone was low and quiet, but he heard the barb in her words.

"Barrie, this isn't personal!" He shook his head. "You, of all people, should appreciate my situation. Your dad is in the same boat—working a physical job that takes a toll on a body—"

"Leave my father out of this."

Curtis had crossed a line; her dad's plans were none of his business, and he knew that. It was hard to come back to Hope and pretend that the people he'd known so well were strangers again just because he and Barrie had broken up. Mr. and Mrs. Jones had been a huge part of his life back then, but obviously, her father would feel different about him postdivorce.

"Like I said before, you were right," he said. "Bull riding was hard on my body, and this isn't a matter of choice anymore. I simply can't keep going. My joints are shot, I've broken more bones than I can count, and I couldn't get on another bull if I wanted to. You told me all those years ago that this would happen, and I said I was tough enough to handle it. And I was—until now. So… I don't have a lot of choice here, Barrie. I have to establish a new career and get some money in the bank so I can retire at a reasonable time."

She sighed and adjusted the bag on her lap. "I always thought saying I told you so would feel better than this."

Curtis smiled ruefully. Yeah, well, he'd always thought hearing it would sting more. But fifteen years had a way of evening the scales, it seemed. She used to be the one with all the cards, and now he was getting his turn at being the one with the leverage. Still, tilling her under hadn't been the plan…

"You worked with Palmer before," Curtis said. "Would it be so terrible if you ended up working together again? You've got some loyal clients—"

"I worked too hard to get my own practice to just cave in like that," she interrupted. "And no offense, Curtis, but I don't need you to solve this for me."

"Just trying to help," he said. Which really felt like the least he could do considering that he was selling the building to her direct rival.

"Well, don't. I'll figure it out."

The same old Barrie—single-minded, stubborn as all get-out and perfectly capable of sorting out her own life. That's what their married life had been—her way. And if you just looked at what she'd done with herself in the last fifteen years, it could be argued that the best thing he'd ever done for her was to get out of her way. He'd never been a part of her success—and she hadn't been a part of his. From this side of things, it looked like a life with him had only slowed her down.

The truck rumbled over the snowy road, tires following the tracks from that morning. Fresh snow drifted against the fence posts and capped them with leaning towers of snow. Beyond the barbed wire, the snow-laden hills rolled out toward the mountains, the peaks disappearing into cloud cover. He'd learned to love this land those few years he'd stayed with his aunt, and having Barrie by his side as he drove out this way was frustrating. Curtis might be a constant irritation to Barrie—even now, he was realizing—but he wasn't useless, either. So if he and Barrie were only going to butt heads, he might as well focus on the work ahead of them.

"We're almost there," he said. "Around this next corner."

Barrie sat up a little straighter, her attention out the window.

"I left the cow with some feed and a blanket—you know, just in case. I wasn't sure how sick it was, so—"

"That was a good call," she said, glancing around. "How far out into the field is it?"

"A few yards," he said. "Not too far. I found it when I was filling feeders this morning."

He pulled up to the gate that allowed trucks access to feeders in the field, and got out to open it. The cows looked up at him in mild curiosity—an older calf ambling over as if interested in some freedom beyond the fence.

"Hya!" he said, and the calf veered off. Curtis jumped back into the cab and drove into the pasture, then hopped out again to close the gate behind them. By the time the gate was locked and he'd come back to the truck, Barrie was standing in the snow, her bag held in front of her belly almost protectively. Her hair ruffled around her face in the icy wind, and her breath clouded as she scanned the cattle that were present, her practiced gaze moving over them slowly. She was irritatingly beautiful—that was the first thing he remembered thinking when he'd met her in senior year. She was the kind of gorgeous that didn't need what he had to offer, but he couldn't help offering it anyway.

"The cow's over—" he began, but Barrie was already

walking in the direction of the cow about twenty yards away now. The cow had shaken off the blanket, and the rumpled material lay in the snow another few yards off.

"I see her," Barrie said over her shoulder.

Once—just once—couldn't Barrie be a step behind him? But whatever. They were here for a cow, and not their complex history. If she wanted to know why he needed a new start so badly, here was a prime example.

"Lead the way," he muttered. It's what she'd always done, anyway.

The cow was definitely ill; she could tell by the way the animal stood. As she got closer, she could make out nasal discharge, the bovine equivalent of a runny nose. The snow was deep, and she had to raise her feet high to get through it, something that was harder now that she was pregnant. Her breath was coming in gasps by the time she approached the cow. She had to pause to catch her breath, and she glanced back to see Curtis's tall form close behind.

It felt odd to have Curtis in town, and something had been nagging at her since she'd seen him in the barn last night—how come this was the first she'd seen of him in fifteen years? Betty was in Hope, and she'd been like a second mother to him. He'd walked out of town and come back only once—to finalize their divorce. Did he hate Barrie that much by the end of their marriage?

She looked around the snowy field, gauging the cow's flight path. When handling cattle, it was important to make sure they had a free escape route, or the cow might panic, and two thousand pounds of scared bovine could be incredibly dangerous. She couldn't allow herself to be distracted.

"You never visited Hope," she said as he stopped at her side.

"Sure I did."

She looked over in surprise. "When? I never saw you."

"A few Christmases. I didn't call friends or anything. I just had a day or two with Betty and headed on out again."

"I didn't realize that." She licked her lips. "Why the secrecy?"

"It wasn't a secret visit, just streamlined. I didn't really keep up with people from high school. I came to see Betty."

She eyed him speculatively. "You weren't avoiding me, were you?"

His lips turned up into a wry smile. "Why would I avoid you?"

Barrie sighed and turned back to the cow. She felt the cow's belly. It hadn't been eating much—like the calf—but the belly wasn't completely empty, either. The cow shifted its weight from side to side, and she took a step back.

"Maybe the same reason you left in the first place," she replied, her voice low.

"You really wanted me dropping in on your family Christmases?" he asked.

"No." She sighed. She wasn't sure what she wanted— absolution, maybe. She hadn't been the wife she'd tried to be back then, but now, as a mature woman, she wasn't sure that her image of perfection had been realistic. It certainly hadn't included the fights they used to have...

Barrie liked the challenge of taming a wild spirit when it came to horses and cattle, but she resented that same wild spirit when it came to her husband. Marriage meant hearth and home to her, but to Curtis, it had been a beat-up trailer parked wherever he was bull riding.

But he'd come back for Christmas with Betty a few times, and somehow that stung.

"I meant well, you know," she added. "I only ever tried to make a home for you."

"I was a bull rider," he replied. "You knew all of that before you married me."

"Most men settle down when they get married," she countered. "A wife should change something."

"Not my identity. You wanted me to act like a different man."

"I wanted you to act like a *married* man!"

The old irritation flooded back, and she hated that. She'd come a long way in the last fifteen years, and it felt petty to slide back into those old arguments. She wasn't the same person anymore, either.

"I never cheated on you," Curtis countered.

"There is more to marriage than monogamy," she said. "You had a *home* with me, Curtis. You treated it more like a hotel room."

"In all the best ways." He shot her a teasing look, and she rolled her eyes in response. They might have shared a passionate relationship, but that hadn't been enough. She'd been the fool who'd married a man based on love and her belief in his potential.

"Forget it," she said with a sigh. "It was a long time ago. I'm sorry to have brought it up." This was exactly why they hadn't worked out. They talked at cross purposes, but maybe he was right—she'd been trying to change him. She was wise enough now not to try that again.

Barrie turned her attention back to the cow. She checked its temperature, and while she couldn't tell exactly how sick the animal was by temperature alone, it had a low fever. All the signs were here—the illness was spreading, apparently. She patted the cow's rump, and it didn't move.

"We wanted different things, Barrie," he said. "You wanted that white picket fence that would please your parents and give you some respect around here. I didn't care about Hope's respect. I wanted some adventure. We just…clashed, I guess."

Barrie dropped the thermometer back into her bag, and pulled out a fresh syringe and the bottle of medication. Yes, she'd wanted a respectable home, and she'd worked hard to create it. A garden in the backyard, flowers in the front… He'd never cared to put down his roots where she'd turned up the soil.

"Quite simple, really," she said with a sigh. "And we'd been young enough to think it wouldn't matter." She turned back toward the cow. "I'll give the antibiotic shot. It'll boost her recovery."

"You're the expert," he replied, and she glanced back to see Curtis standing there with his hands shoved into his jacket pockets. The wind had reddened his cheeks, and she had to admit that he had aged. In a good way, though. He wasn't like some of those boys from high school who were bald under their baseball caps and sported beer bellies now that they were creeping up to forty. Curtis was in good shape.

Barrie prepared the syringe, then felt for the muscle along the flank. Her feet were cold in her boots, and the wind stung her fingers. Just as the needle hit flesh, the cow suddenly lunged, knocking Barrie off balance as it heaved forward.

The cow stepped back so fluidly that she wasn't able to pull herself out of the way quickly enough. But just before she was trampled, strong hands grabbed her by the coat and hauled her backward so fast that her breath stuck in her throat.

Barrie scrambled to get her feet underneath her, and Curtis lifted her almost effortlessly, then pulled her against him as she regained her balance. She was trapped in his strong arms, staring up into a face that was both achingly familiar and different at the same time.

"You've aged," she said feebly.

"Yeah?" He chuckled. "Is that how you thank a cowboy?"

"Thanks…" Her stomach did a flip as she straightened and pulled out of his arms. "I'll be fine."

Curtis cast her a dry look.

"What?" She smoothed her hand over her belly.

"How many times have you told me now that you're fine? I'm calling BS on that, Barrie. You aren't the least bit fine right now."

"The cow missed me—"

"That's not what I'm taking about, and you know it."

Barrie bent down to collect the syringe that had fallen into the snow. The cow had wandered off a couple of yards—maybe this particular cow had a bad experience with an immunization or something. Whatever had happened was all perfectly within the realms of normal when it came to a vet's daily duties. Granted, if she weren't pregnant, her reflexes might have been a bit faster...

"Curtis, you don't actually know me anymore."

"Hey," he said, his voice lowering. "You might not have liked the kind of husband I was, but I *was* your husband. I knew you, and I can recognize when you're freaked out."

Curtis might know some of her deeper characteristics, but that didn't mean he still knew how she thought and what could get a rise out of her. He'd missed fifteen years of personal growth. Besides, she hadn't been enough for him, so he could take his insights into her reactions and shove them.

"I'm not freaked out." She shot him an irritated look. "I'm *fine.*"

She looked toward the cow again and adjusted the syringe, getting it ready for one more try.

"I don't need rescuing." Her fingers moved as she spoke. "So do what you have to do with that building, and I'll sort things out. I always have."

"Fair enough."

Barrie didn't want him to sell that building, but he'd already made it clear that he was out of options. If their divorce had taught her one thing, it was that she was better off facing facts and dealing with them. Hoping and wishing didn't help. She'd focus on her future with her child.

"And you'll need to quarantine that cow," she added.

"Yeah, I know. I'm not new to this, Barrie." His smile was slightly smug, but arguing with Curtis Porter about just about anything wasn't a great use of her time. *Professional. In and out.* What had happened to that excellent plan?

She headed toward the cow that had wandered off. She might be pregnant, and her life might be spinning right out of control at the moment, but she'd get through this by standing on her own two feet. Curtis was a cautionary tale—that was all.

Barrie took a deep breath, and let her tension go. The cattle could feel it. She patted the cow's rump, then inserted the needle into the tough flesh. She slowly depressed the plunger, then pulled the needle out and firmly rubbed the injection site.

"Done." She turned around and gave Curtis an arch look. "Like I said, quarantine that cow, and any others that appear sick. That's the fastest way to curb an outbreak."

Curtis might know her weaknesses, but she also knew his, and he was the furthest thing from reliable. She needed a plan and blinders, because with a baby on the way, she didn't have the luxury of being knocked off balance a second time by the same cowboy.

Chapter 4

The next morning, Barrie ran her hand over a golden Lab's silky head. This was Cody, the beloved pet of the Hartfield family, and he'd broken his leg while running on the ice. He was still unconscious from the sedative she'd given him, but his leg was set, the cast was in place and he'd recover just fine. His mistress, thirteen-year-old Melissa Hartfield, stood anxiously to the side. She wore her winter coat, open in the front, and a pair of puffy boots. She was a town kid—her dad was the mayor.

"Will he be okay?" Melissa asked. She looked younger than her age—her hair pulled back in a ponytail and her large eyes scanning the equipment. She glanced up at the IV inserted into a vein in the dog's leg, then down at the catheter Barrie had introduced to keep the dog comfortable while she worked. The catheter was out now.

"He'll be fine," Barrie reassured her. "It's not a bad break. I've put a cast on, and he'll have to wear a cone so he leaves the cast alone, poor boy. The cone is the worst part for them—it hits them in their dignity."

Melissa smiled faintly. "Will he be in pain?"

"I'll give you pain medication and some antibiotics. He'll need to take both daily—they're very important to help him rest more easily and to keep infection at bay."

"The IV—" Melissa looked intrigued. "How did you find his vein through his fur?"

"By touch." Barrie caught the girl's eye. "You're interested in veterinary medicine?"

Melissa's cheeks colored a little. "I want to be a vet like you when I grow up."

Barrie grinned. She never tired of talking to young people who wanted to follow in her footsteps. "That's great. And you can be. Just make sure you stay focused on school, because it's a long haul. And you can't let yourself get sidetracked by boys, either."

"That's what Mom always says," Melissa said with a roll of her eyes.

"Your mom is right," Barrie replied.

The front door to Barrie's clinic opened—she could hear the soft chime—and Melissa looked toward the door. Her mother, Jennifer Hartfield, would be arriving anytime now to pick them both up, but Barrie couldn't see the waiting room from where she stood.

"Is that your mom?" Barrie asked.

Melissa nodded.

"Let's bring Cody out to the waiting room, then," Barrie said. "You can take him home before he wakes up all the way. He'll be groggy for a few hours, but when he does wake up, you need to make sure he stays off this leg, okay?"

Melissa nodded. "Dr. Jones?"

"Hmm?" Barrie removed the IV and pressed some gauze over the puncture.

"I was wondering if you might need some help. I'm not asking for a job—I know I'm not old enough for that. But I could help out, and I'd really like to learn…"

Barrie shot the girl a smile. "I'll give that some thought, Melissa. I might be able to find something for you to do. And you'd have to get your mom's permission, of course. I'm going to be talking to the 4-H girls next week, so I'll see you then, too."

"Are you really?" Melissa asked. "That'll be cool."

"I'm looking forward to it."

Barrie set aside the last of the equipment and they wheeled the dog into the waiting room. Barrie was surprised to see both Jennifer Hartfield and Curtis standing by the line of chairs. He stood there like a tank—hat off but legs akimbo as he looked around. That dark gaze still gave her pause, even after all these years, and she shoved back those familiar feelings. Attraction had never been their problem. She gave Curtis a nod.

"Is there a problem with Betty's herd?" Barrie asked.

"Nope. Just came by." That dark gaze warmed, and she swallowed. Why did he have to do that? They weren't married anymore, and he had no right to go toying with her emotions when she was trying to work. She turned a smile to Jennifer.

"Cody is going to be fine," Barrie said, and she began explaining the care he'd need at home while his leg recovered. Jennifer and Melissa listened as she finished her explanation, and after Jennifer had paid the bill, they prepared to transfer Cody to the back of their SUV.

"Mom, Dr. Jones says that I might be able to help her out some time," Melissa said.

Jennifer's smile tightened. "Oh, did she? We'll talk about that later."

"But I could learn about being a vet, Mom, and—"

"Melissa..." There was warning in Jennifer's tone, and Barrie glanced between them. It didn't look like Jennifer was on board with this.

"Mom, you said that if a vet were willing to have me around—" Melissa started.

"I said if *Dr. Berton* were willing to have you around," Jennifer said, her gaze flickering toward Barrie and then back to her daughter. "But we couldn't get in to see Dr. Berton, so you'll just have to wait."

Barrie knew exactly what this was about—her pregnancy. Jennifer was a church lady through and through, and this pregnancy offended every sensibility she had. But now was not the time to offend a paying customer. Besides, there was more to Jennifer's story than simply being the mayor's wife and a Sunday school teacher... There was a whole story there that most people didn't know—but Barrie did. She and Jennifer had been close friends when they were fourteen-year-olds in the eighth grade, and when Jennifer disappeared for the rest of the school year, Barrie might have been the only one who knew where she really went.

"It's okay, Melissa," Barrie said. "Dr. Berton is a very nice man."

"But I don't want to go with Dr. Berton," Melissa said with a shake of her head. "I like Dr. Jones. She's a girl. And she'd know stuff about being a female vet, Mom."

"I said no!" Jennifer cast Barrie a pointed glare. "Could you just leave my daughter alone?"

Jennifer's expression wasn't angry, it was scared, and Barrie understood exactly why. Melissa was her only child…that most people knew about. And this was a delicate situation.

"Why?" Curtis's deep voice reverberated through the room. They both turned to find Curtis standing there, arms crossed over his broad chest, steely gaze trained on Jennifer.

"Excuse me?" Jennifer slammed a hand on her hip and shot him an icy look.

"Why is Barrie such a bad choice?" Curtis asked. "As your daughter pointed out, she's a female vet. She's incredibly good at what she does."

"If you must know, she isn't the kind of influence I want for Melissa. As if that's any of your business."

Melissa blushed pink in embarrassment and Jennifer looked between her vehicle, visible out the window, and Cody, who was starting to wake up a little on the wheeled table. Barrie put a hand on Cody's head and gave him a reassuring stroke.

"Curtis, leave it," Barrie said quietly. He glanced at her, then shook his head.

"She's probably the most moral person in this town," Curtis went on. "So your husband is the mayor, and you think you're better than the rest of us? Sometimes babies happen."

"Curtis—" Barrie repeated, trying to keep her voice moderated. "Shut up!"

Curtis shot her an incredulous look, then shook his head. His expression was one of disgust—but she'd been used to that.

"You're going to accept that?" he retorted. "I've been married to you, and I know firsthand what a Girl Scout you are. You're just going to roll over and accept the scarlet letter with a smile?"

"Mrs. Hartfield is my customer," Barrie retorted, her anger rising. "And as my customer, she is owed a certain level of respect! I don't need you to butt into this, Curtis, so kindly leave it to me!"

Jennifer and Melissa were both watching Barrie and Curtis, and Barrie felt heat rise in her cheeks. She'd *been* in control until Curtis had decided to get all protective of her reputation around here. About fifteen years too late for that! And now she wasn't the smooth-faced professional that she wanted to portray—she was red-faced and fighting with her ex. Nice. This was a delicate situation as it was without Curtis's bumbling attempts to defend her.

"If you could just get the door, Melissa, your mom and I will carry Cody out to your vehicle," Barrie said, forcing a smile.

The girl did as Barrie bid, and Barrie and Jennifer lifted the dog carefully, doing their best not to jostle the leg. He had enough pain killers in him that he should be okay, but still…

As Barrie eased past Curtis, she caught him eyeing her irritably. As if he had any reason to be annoyed!

"Back off, Curtis," she murmured icily. "This is *my* life."

Curtis watched as Barrie loaded the dog into the back of the SUV. She moved with confidence and tenderness as she adjusted everything to make sure the animal would be comfortable. That had always softened him—watching her with animals. Something calm and almost angelic radiated from her when she was helping a wounded animal. Everything around her seemed to hush, leaving just her and the creature in her hands. When she turned all her attention on him, it had been like that, too. It was like being in a pool of sunlight when she smiled into his eyes.

But that was long ago, and he'd had to let his fantasies about her go when he was faced with the reality of married life. Being her husband didn't mean that he could bask in that sunlight, because every time he disappointed her, it would turn off, and he'd be more alone than he'd ever been in his life—right next to her.

He'd come by to make peace with her today. He didn't want to leave things like they were after her last visit to the ranch—testy and tense. He'd promised his aunt that he'd be kind, and he was trying to make good on that. Obviously he hadn't done much to repair things, though.

Once the Hartfields' SUV pulled out, Barrie stomped back into the clinic and fixed him with an angry stare.

"What?" he said.

"Did I ask you to jump in and defend my honor?" she snapped. "I had everything well in hand! You're here for, what…a few days…and you think you have any idea of all the tensions around here?"

"Apparently you're one of them," he quipped. "And I'm sorry if I couldn't stand by and have some prissy woman slut-shame you."

"What do you know about my virtue?" she asked, raising one eyebrow. "And how is whoever I sleep with your business?"

So now she was turning this around on him. Curtis barked out a bitter laugh. "I'm in no mood to fight with you. I came by to make peace, but if you're not interested—"

"If I'm not interested, you'll just leave." She shrugged. "Seems like your MO."

"That's not fair." Curtis turned back to her. "I was *defending* you."

"You were making a tense situation even worse," she countered. "Jennifer isn't indignant about me being pregnant out of wedlock. She's scared for her daughter. Jennifer got pregnant in the eighth grade, and her parents pulled her out of school to go have the baby. She gave it up for adoption, and she hadn't even turned fifteen yet. Well, her daughter just turned thirteen, and misguided as her techniques may be, she's trying to make sure that her daughter doesn't end up in the same position."

Curtis blinked. "Jennifer Hartfield?"

"Sunday school teacher, advocate for chastity and purity county-wide…and yes, teenage mother. She wouldn't talk about that baby. She wouldn't say if it was even a boy or a girl, but I knew Jen back then, and giving up her child would have torn her heart out."

He'd never realized that Jen had that kind of tragedy in her past, and he eyed Barrie skeptically as a question rose in his mind.

"How come you never told me that?" he asked.

"I told Jen I'd never breathe a word," Barrie replied.

"I was your husband," Curtis retorted. "And I had more than one run-in with Jen and her high-and-mighty attitude, and you never filled me in…"

What else had she hidden back then? But it had always been like that. Barrie's loyalty was first and foremost to that blasted town!

"What does it matter now?" Barrie shook her head. "I'm trying to keep my clinic together here. So get off your soapbox and butt out of my business. Hope is my home, and you'll drive on out of here in a week or so, but I'm staying. My life is here…my practice is here! So the next time you have the urge to pipe up and put someone in their place—don't!"

Curtis closed his eyes. She didn't need his help. She never had—this town had been her stomping grounds, and she'd always had a better handle on all those conflicting relationships than he ever did. Now he felt stupid standing here…stupid for having thought any of this would change.

"My intentions were sound," he said quietly.

"Just…" She sighed, and didn't finish.

"They always were," he went on. She'd had the last word—always! But not this time. "You thought I was selfish and egotistical, but everything I did was for you."

"Not anymore," she said.

"Of course not!" He shook his head in exasperation. "We're divorced! I'm putting my own plans first, as I should. What would you have me do, take a hit to make your life easier?"

"I didn't ask you for anything," she snapped.

And standing there, her blue eyes flashing into his, her lips parted as if she were about to come out with another cutting remark, he was reminded so vividly of the old days that he had to hold himself back from shutting her up by kissing her. He knew what those kisses felt like—the softness of her lips, the way her eyes would widen in surprise as he pulled her hard against him…

But this wasn't fifteen years ago, and he wasn't about to do something so stupid as to kiss his ex-wife into silence. Those days were long gone.

"And why do you care if I resent you or not?" she added, turning her back on him as she picked up the cloth that the dog had been lying on.

"I promised my aunt I'd be kind," he said.

"So you're trying to smooth things over for Betty."

"I'm doing it for you!" He was sick of this—the bantering, the constant attempt to get the upper hand. "You might not believe me, Barrie, but I still care about you. I want you to be happy. I want—"

He didn't know how to finish that. He wanted to leave her with a better memory of him than she'd been carrying around for the last fifteen years. He wasn't the same immature kid he used to be, and dumb as it was, he cared how she remembered him.

Barrie slowly turned and eyed him uncertainly. "You care."

"Yeah."

"And you show this by selling my office out from under me."

There it was—she always did have the last word, didn't she?

"I'm heading out," he said, turning for the door. This was why they'd never lasted. She was better in a fight, and she knew how to back him into corners. More than that, he'd stupidly hoped he could be her knight in shining armor. But she had no need for a knight. She took care of her own business—always had. He was the idiot standing off to the side.

Barrie didn't answer him, and he pulled open the door and marched out into the watery winter sunlight.

She'd chosen this town over him back when they were married. She could have come with him on the circuit. It didn't have to be forever. Would a few months have killed her? But this town—and visions of her future inside it—had mattered more to her than an adventure with him. She'd counted on this blasted town to catch her, not him.

He glanced over his shoulder as he headed toward

his truck, and he saw Barrie through the window, staring after him. She wasn't angry anymore. She looked like she wanted to cry.

And maybe that was hardest of all, because she didn't need his comfort and he couldn't make things easier on her. Loving Barrie had turned out to be the most painful experience of a lifetime, and he'd be wise to shake those feelings off for good.

Chapter 5

That evening, Curtis came back inside from the last of his chores. His body ached in that pleasurable way that meant he'd put in a hard day's work. He stomped the snow off his boots and shook off his coat.

He'd been thinking about Barrie all day as he worked, and he'd come to a few conclusions—namely, that he was better off taking care of his own affairs and letting her do the same. She was perfectly capable, and if he lost this opportunity to better himself, what solace would it be that his ex-wife had been spared some inconvenience? She'd made herself abundantly clear that morning at her clinic, and he was still stinging from it.

He hung his coat on a peg next to his hat, then paused, standing in the quiet of the house. It was still so much the same—the smells, the one creaky floorboard… This ranch had been a place for transitions in his life: back when he was a teen starting fresh in the country, and now again, starting fresh away from the circuit.

He was still wrapping his mind around his current life changes. Bull riding was the one thing he'd been really good at, and as a bull rider, he knew who he was. As a joint owner of a stud farm, he'd be nailed down to one piece of land, and if he worked hard enough, he'd have some financial success to lean on. He still didn't know what that would make him, though. Who was he now that he was too old to work the circuit?

Curtis pulled his boots off one by one. The warmth felt good, and the house was scented with freshly baked bread. He clipped his gloves to the clothesline hung above the heat register so they'd dry out before morning.

"Curtis, I was waiting for you to do the honors." Aunt Betty's voice filtered out from the living room.

Curtis headed out of the mudroom and into the kitchen. The leftovers from supper had been put away, but there were still some dinner rolls in a bowl on the counter. He grabbed one and bit into it on his way through to the living room.

The room was softly lit by a couple of lamps and the lights on the Christmas tree. Betty stood next to the window, the curtains drawn.

"Do the honors for what?" Curtis asked as he came in.

"The outside lights. I finished them up this afternoon."

"With your cast?" he asked incredulously. He'd broken an ankle, too—twice, actually—and he knew just how painful that recovery was. He'd wanted his aunt to rest and put that cast up for a couple of weeks. That was why he was here to help her out, after all. The women in this town were notoriously stubborn.

"I didn't push it," she said with a bat of her hand. "But go ahead—flick the switch."

Curtis did as she asked and flicked the switch on the wall next to the front door. Tiny lights wrapped around the top rail of the fence that encircled the yard blazed to life. They were plentiful, like a cloud of fireflies out of season.

"Now it feels like Christmas," Betty said quietly.

"Yeah…it does."

Except this Christmas wasn't just a little break from the ordinary with his aunt. It was a complete break from everything he'd built up to this point in his adult life. He'd always thrived on adventure and change, but this new step, while a change, would give him a completely different lifestyle…something closer to the nailed-down home that Barrie had tried to give him fifteen years ago. And seeing Barrie again had unsettled him, too… She was just as stubborn as she'd always been, so why wasn't he keeping clear of her? He should know better. He had a chance at some success of his own, and he should be enjoying this.

Curtis headed back to the couch and sank into it. From his position, he could see the lights outside glowing in the darkness.

"What's the matter?" Betty asked.

"Hmm?" He roused himself from his thoughts. "Oh, just thinking about the stud farm."

"So why the frown? I thought you wanted this," she said.

He hadn't realized he'd been frowning, and he shrugged. "I do want this. I hate giving up bull riding, is all. But I recognize that I need to sort out something more stable, and this is a great opportunity."

"But it's no eight seconds," Betty concluded.

He chuckled. "It's no eight seconds," he agreed.

"Not everything worthwhile risks your hide," Betty said.

"I know," he said with a quick grin. "Like making some good money. If I can't ride bulls, I'll settle for a lucrative income. This stud farm is already performing well."

"What does your mom think of all this?" Betty asked. "Have you talked to her lately?"

"I texted with her last night," he admitted.

"And?" Betty's tone seemed a little too carefully indifferent. The sisters were as different as night and day. Both women cared about each other, even if they didn't understand each other. And when it came to Curtis, they both were protective of him in their own ways. It was like being stuck between a rock and a hard place, except the rock and the hard place were slightly judgmental of each other.

"You know Mom," he said. "She can appreciate a fresh start."

His mother had thrown her life into a struggling

singing career, so she was the one person who could fully understand his adrenaline junkie ways.

"What's she doing for Christmas?" Betty asked.

"She has a singing gig at a local country club."

"At her age." Betty shook her head.

"She's fifty-four," he countered.

Betty raised her eyebrows as if nothing else needed to be said, and Curtis shook his head. His mom had aged well, so while she was in her fifties, she could pass for her midforties, and she could sing a country ballad that could break a heart in two. Sure, she hadn't gotten her big break, and maybe never would, but there were plenty of singers who made some money on the side doing what they loved, and Noreen Porter was one of them.

The fact that his mother had sent him to Betty's ranch in the first place spoke of just how desperate Noreen had been, because going to Betty for help would have given her pride a hit.

"She's not alone, if that's what you're worried about," Curtis added with a short laugh.

"What's his name?" Betty asked.

"Scott. He seems to be a nice guy."

Betty raised an eyebrow, then shrugged. "I shouldn't judge. As long as she's happy."

Betty didn't mean that, and Curtis knew it, but he appreciated her saying it anyway. His mom had worked through a fair number of men in her life, and Betty... hadn't.

"But what about you, Aunty?" Curtis asked, moving the conversation away from his mother. "Any guys in your life?"

"Just the bovine variety." Betty's gaze turned toward the window and the twinkling lights along the fence.

"You obviously know a few human males," he pressed.

"Several." Betty shot him a smart-alecky look, and he laughed.

"Any of them remotely your age and single?"

"Nope. Married. Every last one." She paused, then pressed her lips together. "Well, except for one. But he's widowed, so it's just about the same thing."

This was new. Curtis far preferred needling his aunt about her personal life to listening to her gripe about his mother. "Who is he?"

"Dr. Berton."

Curtis sobered. The man who was seriously considering buying that commercial building from him. He'd been intending to tease his aunt about a possible romance, but Curtis hadn't realized that Palmer Berton's wife had passed away, and the humor seeped out of the moment.

"What happened to Louise? I didn't realize she'd died."

"It was a brain aneurysm last summer," Betty replied. "Very fast and tragic. Like I said, it's the same thing as being married. Berton is still grieving."

Palmer and Louise had been a fixture around Hope. They had two sons, both in the army.

"He never mentioned Louise passing when we talked about the sale," Curtis said.

"He wouldn't," Betty replied. "He's private that way. He keeps his grief to himself."

"He talks to you, though," Curtis said. She seemed to know a fair bit about how he grieved, at the very least.

"Sure, we talk. Sometimes people need someone to talk to, especially after a loss like that. I've known Palmer since we were kids, and he's been my primary vet ever since I inherited this place," Betty said. "We have history."

There was so much history in this town that Curtis had never guessed, but people born and raised here—like Barrie—were connected to the rest of Hope at the roots. Curtis had always seen himself as an outsider in Hope, but he had his own history here, entwined with a woman who still drove him nuts.

"You still think Dr. Berton will use the building to push Barrie out of business?" he asked.

"Louise gave him balance," Betty said. "She tempered his more aggressive nature. And now that she's gone, he's got a lot of time on his hands that he'll be putting into his work. It's only natural."

Curtis sighed. "Do you have any clout with him?"

Betty shot Curtis a sharp look. "Having second thoughts about that sale?"

"No." He sucked in a deep breath. "If I don't sell that building, I've got nothing. I might not like it, but that's a fact. I just wish it could be smoother…for everyone."

For Barrie. That's what he meant. He wished his step forward didn't have to impact her quite so much. He wished all of this were simpler and he could arrange a sale and walk away without any nagging guilt. The shared histories in a small ranching community weren't always a comfort.

"Some Christmas…" Curtis said after a few beats of silence.

"It might not be a merry Christmas for all of us," Betty said softly. "But Christmas comes all the same."

True enough. Dr. Berton was widowed, Betty had a broken ankle, Barrie was pregnant and facing her first Christmas without her mother… Here Curtis was in Hope, working alongside his pregnant ex-wife, who he'd never really gotten over, making her life more difficult in order to scrape a future together for himself. It wasn't exactly a merry Christmas, but Christmas came once a year whether they were in the mood for it or not.

The next morning, Barrie pushed Miley's face away from her shoulder and turned her vehicle onto the Porter ranch drive. This would be a busy day. She had the Porter cows to check on, then a visit to the Granger ranch, where she had some calves to immunize. The truck had given her some trouble starting that morning, and she couldn't even blame the cold. Fourteen degrees wasn't exactly balmy, but it wasn't cold enough to shut down a vehicle, either.

She'd been thinking about her mother a lot lately. She hadn't been gone long, and this Christmas loomed. It wasn't just the thought of merriment without Mom. It was all the questions she wouldn't be able to ask her, all the advice she'd miss out on. Until she got pregnant, she hadn't realized how much she still desperately needed to be mothered herself.

Mom would have had something to say about Curtis's reappearance, and she wished her mother were here to say it all. "Love is one thing, Barrie. And being man enough to take care of a family is another. You can love a man heart and soul and still not be able to live with him."

That was what her mother had said a few weeks before Curtis took off. She'd said it again in the weeks that followed. Love wasn't enough... Somehow, it had given her permission to let go of him. It didn't mean she hadn't loved him, it just meant it hadn't worked. But now he was back, and she found herself unsettled about the muscular cowboy. She needed her mother's wisdom to set her straight. Gwyneth Jones had always had an uncanny ability to see through the smoke screen and get right down to basics.

"I love you, but I need some personal space, Miley," she said, and Miley snuffled at her ear instead of obeying. She nudged his nose back again as she followed the drive around and pulled up in front of the house. She gave a short beep of the horn to let Betty know that she was here, and Betty emerged a moment later in the doorway, a sweater pulled around her shoulders. Barrie lowered her window.

"Dr. Jones!" Betty called with a smile, hobbling up to the driver's side. "Curtis is down in the barn already, so you might as well drive through."

"Thanks." Barrie raised her voice over the sound of her truck's engine. "I'll keep you posted on the situation down there."

"Sounds good," Betty replied, and she gave a final wave before she disappeared back into the house. Barrie put the truck in gear and hit the button to put up the window. It was cold out there, and she cranked the steering wheel to head down the drive toward the barn.

Why couldn't seeing Curtis again be easier? She hadn't meant to give him any kind of reaction yesterday. That had happened on its own, and she'd regretted it. It showed weakness. She'd made it seem like she hadn't dealt with their divorce, when she had. How many hours had she and Mom talked it out? Barrie had made her peace with having done her very best, and it not being enough. That hadn't been easy. But seeing him again had opened a few old wounds.

Why couldn't he have lost some of that magnetism with age? That would have been more fair. He'd come back to town to find her single and pregnant. At the very least, he could have come back with a bald spot and a pot belly to match the other guys from their class. But having him be all gentle and sweet with her out there in the field was irritating. Having him standing up for her as if she needed the pity was even worse. If it weren't for her pregnancy, would Curtis still be this sweet? Not likely. She didn't need his special treatment.

The red of the barn's sides contrasted with the snow on its roof. Icicles hung off the eaves, glittering in morning sunlight. She liked these early morning rounds, at least when she wasn't going to be running into Curtis. But she had a job to do, and her practice needed the income. She couldn't afford to recommend that Curtis call in Palmer Berton just to give herself some space.

Barrie parked in front of the barn's main doors and hopped out of the truck. She opened up the back door and Miley poured himself out of the back seat, then gave himself a shake, his tags jingling.

"Come on, Miley," she said, giving the dog's head a stroke. Then she pulled open the passenger side door and grabbed her vet's bag. "You be good now, okay?"

But Miley knew the drill. When Barrie opened the barn door, Miley followed her in, his head staying by her side. She let her eyes adjust, then scanned the barn. She spotted Curtis near the back. He was leaning over a rail, looking into a stall, his face in the shadows. She knew that stance—she couldn't see his feet, but she could tell he'd hooked a boot over the bottom rail. He straightened and tipped his hat.

"Morning," she called.

"Morning." He pulled off his gloves. "Two more quarantined since last night."

Barrie nodded. "Four in total now?"

"That's right."

Miley's nails clicked against the concrete floor as Barrie headed down the aisle toward the back of the barn, where Curtis waited. She had antibiotics to administer and temperatures to take. The baby shifted, and she gave the side of her belly a rub. The movements were getting stronger as the weeks passed, and she could feel a good hard jab to the bladder now and again. That was irritating when she wasn't near a washroom, but it was also reassuring. If her baby could wake her up several times a night with wriggles and stretches, then all was well—at least in the baby's world. The outside world was a little more complex.

When she arrived at the stall where Curtis waited, Barrie pointed to the floor.

"Miley, lie down," she said. Miley complied, his eyes fixed on her. "Any improvement with the first calf?" she asked, turning to Curtis. He'd shaved since she'd seen him yesterday, and he held a pair of gloves loosely in one hand, his shirt sleeves rolled up to reveal muscular forearms. He was definitely a more solid man now—the years had hardened him in a way she'd find appealing if she didn't know him better.

"He seems to be getting better," Curtis said. "He's eating more and he's less lethargic."

Both good signs. She turned her attention to the newest quarantined cows and inspected them with an expert eye. She let herself into the first stall and opened her bag. She wasn't wasting any time here this morning—the Grangers were waiting.

"Last night I found out that Louise Berton passed away," Curtis said, and Barrie glanced up.

"This year. She had an aneurysm," she confirmed. "Mom died in February, and then Louise passed in June."

"It's been a tough year," he said.

Barrie turned her attention back to the calf. She pulled out a syringe and the antibiotic. "Miserable."

There had been no warning when her mother died. Dad came back from work and found Mom on the floor. He called an ambulance, but when they got her to the hospital, they'd pronounced her already gone. One day, Mom was her usual bright, funny self. And then... Barrie blinked back a mist of tears. The pain was still fresh.

Curtis was silent while Barrie administered the medication and rubbed the spot to relieve the sting. She pushed herself to her feet, then took her bag and headed to the next stall over. Miley raised his head.

"Stay," she commanded.

"How are you holding up?" Curtis asked.

"If I say that I'm fine, you'll say I'm lying," she said as she squatted next to the other calf. "And if I say I'm not fine, what are you going to do about it?"

Curtis sighed. "I'm still not allowed to care?"

"No. You aren't. You lost that right when you left me."

"I'm sorry that your mom is gone, all the same," he said. "Your mom might not have thought I was right for you, but she was a good person."

Her mom was more than a good person. She'd been a great mom, too. She'd been full of advice and hard-won wisdom. She'd been a silent listener when necessary, and a ferocious ally. She'd made the best shortbread cookies and decorated them for every single occasion possible from Christmas to baby showers. She'd even made Barrie some postdivorce cookies—pink hearts with icing Band-Aids.

"It'll get better, Barrie," her mother had told her.

"What makes you so sure?" Barrie had asked bitterly. *"You've never been divorced."*

"I don't have to know divorce," Gwyneth had retorted. *"I know my daughter. And you're strong and beautiful. You'll get through this. Life is long, and you have so much more ahead of you..."*

Barrie administered the shot, then rose to her feet. She glanced over to find Curtis still watching her.

"Betty's worried about you," he said.

Somehow that got past her defenses. Maybe because Betty was close to her mom's age...

"And Betty is allowed to worry," she snapped. "You know why? Because she's a friend and a customer. She's a part of my life. You aren't anymore. You didn't want this life, this town...or *me*. You made your choice. Do I resent you? A bit. But that doesn't mean you have anything to fix or make right. I have a job to do. So do you. Let's just keep it on those lines."

Barrie opened the stall door, and Curtis took a step back to let her out. He didn't retreat further than one stride to allow the gate to swing open, however. He closed the clasp on the gate and she shot him a cool smile, then slid past him toward the stalls of the other two cows that were recovering. Miley rose to his feet, clicked over to the stall where she was working and sat down on his haunches. Barrie administered the antibiotics quickly, checked the calves' vitals and was pleased to see some improvement.

When she let herself out of the last stall, she found Curtis eyeing her with a thoughtful look on his face.

"What?" she asked testily. She'd told herself that she'd be professional and contained this time, but there was something about Curtis's attention that irritated her.

"It's nice to see you again, that's all."

His thorough appraisal made her skin tingle. He'd always had that effect on her, but she wasn't dumb enough to succumb to it anymore.

"Let me ask you this. If I weren't pregnant, would you feel this way?"

"What way?"

"Whatever this is." She shrugged. "This urge to make sure I'm okay. You've always had far too much testosterone coursing through your veins, and that factored into all of our problems. But right now, you aren't reacting to *me*. You're reacting to my belly. I'm no longer Barrie, the woman who drove you nuts. I'm now… this…" She spread her arms. "Curtis, it's still me. We don't have anything to sort out. Our marriage is history. I'm the vet. You have sick cows. It's pretty simple."

Barrie patted her thigh and Miley rose to his feet and immediately tagged along after her. When he got to her side, the dog cast a mournful look back at Curtis, and Barrie grit her teeth. Even the dog was softening to that frustrating man! She reached over and gave Miley's head a scratch all the same. The poor dog couldn't be blamed for his good temper.

Barrie pushed open the door and headed out into the bright sunlight. She tossed her vet's bag onto the passenger side front seat, then opened the back door to let Miley up. He clambered onto the seat, and she slammed the door.

How did Curtis Porter always manage to get under her skin like that? Why did she even allow him to bother her? They were ancient history. They'd never had children together. There was nothing tying them to each other, save a few memories. But then he'd look at her in that way he had, and she'd see red. It was stupid. She knew it.

As she angled around to the driver's side and let herself in, Miley was still scrambling about, trying to get comfortable. Barrie put the key into the ignition and turned it. There was a grinding sound, but the engine didn't turn over.

"Blast." She shut her eyes, willing the engine to cooperate, then turned the key again. Nothing.

She sighed and looked back at Miley. Miley whined and gave a low growl—his form of commiseration—and she ran her hand through her hair. For all of her bravado back there in the barn, all she wanted was to get out of here—get onto open road, away from him.

"One more try," she muttered, and turned the key again, but instead of hearing the engine, there was a tap on her window. She grimaced, then glanced over to see Curtis. Her plans to be through with the man as quickly as possible seemed to be slipping through her fingers. She lowered the window.

"You have a problem there?" he asked.

She sighed. "It won't start. I'll call a tow."

"Want me to take a look?" he asked.

"Since when do you fix trucks?" she demanded. "You rode bulls. You were no mechanic."

They weren't here to reinvent history, or for him to play hero. Whatever he had on his conscience, he'd have to sort out without her.

Curtis crossed his arms over his chest. "So what's the plan, then?"

"I'll get towed to the garage," she said. "And I'll have to call the Grangers and tell them I can't make it."

"So you have another call," Curtis clarified. He

looked away for a moment, chewing the side of his cheek, then back at her. "What if I drove you?"

"To the Grangers'?" She frowned. "Why?"

"Why not?" he shot back. "Do you need a reason? How about guilt? I'm selling that building out from under you and I feel like I owe you something. Is that reason enough?"

It was the most honest thing she'd heard from him yet. She couldn't afford to be sending business to Palmer Berton, and a ride would allow her to do her job while she waited for a mechanic to fix her truck.

Barrie eyed him for a moment, then nodded. "Alright. Thanks. I'd appreciate the ride."

He was right; he did owe her.

Chapter 6

Curtis stepped back as Barrie pushed open the door and slid slowly to the ground. He hadn't been sure if she'd accept his offer of help, but he was glad she had. His aunt's ranch wasn't too far from the Granger ranch. Besides, there was a part of him that didn't want to see her leave. It was a stupid part of him, but it was still there. Barrie had always drawn him in like that, whether it was good for him or not.

Barrie's pregnancy slowed her movements, but right now he knew better than to offer her a hand. She wasn't about to let him in close, and he couldn't entirely blame her. She was right—fifteen years was a long time, and he wasn't a part of her life anymore. What *was* he feeling for her, exactly?

Barrie adjusted her jacket over her hips, and he refused to allow himself to appreciate how well her jeans fit. She'd always been slender when he'd known her, but pregnancy had rounded her from behind as well. Was she right—was he reacting to her pregnancy or to her as a woman? Because she *had* driven him crazy back then...

Barrie circled around her stalled SUV for her black bag, and opened the back door. The dog unfolded himself and scrambled down to the ground. That was one huge dog. He stood as tall as a colt, and stayed protectively close to his mistress.

"We'll walk up to my truck at the house," Curtis said. "You okay with that?"

"I'm fine," she said. "I'd better call a tow truck, though."

Curtis waited while she dialed the local towing company, and within a couple of minutes, she'd given the crucial information.

"Alright," she said as she hung up. "Let's go."

So competent—not that she shouldn't be, but even though she'd accepted his offer of a ride, he had the feeling that she didn't really need his favors. Miley trotted next to Barrie, but when Curtis fell into step on the other side, Miley fell back for a pace, then nudged between them, the warm bulk of his shoulder shoving Curtis over. The dog was definitely making a statement here.

"Miley doesn't like me?" Curtis asked with a short laugh.

Barrie looked down at Miley, then shrugged. "If he didn't like you, you'd know it."

What did that mean exactly? He wasn't sure he

wanted to find out. The Great Dane was a friendly enough breed, but Miley was still two hundred pounds of solid muscle. They found their stride as they headed up the road toward the house, and after a couple of minutes of walking, Miley seemed to lose interest in protecting his mistress and bounded ahead.

"Traitor." Barrie chuckled.

"Is he a good guard dog?" Curtis asked.

"He's awful," she replied. "You can buy him off for a treat."

Curtis shrugged his coat higher on his neck to fend off the probing cold. "He makes a good impression, though."

"Which is why I keep him around." The old joking glint was back in her eyes, despite the lack of a smile on her face. She walked at a brisker pace than he expected, but then, she was used to marching through fields to find injured cattle, so this was nothing, even with her pregnancy.

"So, what's your history with Palmer?" Curtis asked.

"I told you. I worked for him for a few years before I started my own practice."

"Betty told me you're the better vet," he said.

Barrie shot him a quizzical look. "Why would she say that?"

"She says he's more experienced, but you have better instincts," he replied. "She says that he's peaked in his career, and you're still climbing."

"Not that Dr. Berton would ever admit it," she quipped.

"So you didn't work well together," he said.

"He was a micromanager. He wanted me to do everything his way, not mine. I'm a good vet—Betty's right. I don't know…" She sighed. "I thought he'd be glad to get rid of me when I opened my own practice, but he was furious. He said I was ungrateful."

"Maybe he recognized the competition," Curtis suggested.

Barrie shrugged. "Maybe."

She'd always been talented. Barrie didn't do anything unless she could be the best at it, and when he knew her, she'd never taken anything less than seriously. Curtis was different, though. He liked to go with the flow for the most part, and his competitive streak only came out in the bull riding. For all the good that had done him.

"So you butted heads a lot, I take it," Curtis clarified.

"He wouldn't trust my way of doing things," she replied. "I have the same education he does—more current, even. But that's Dr. Berton for you—it's his way or the highway."

"You want to know what I think?" he asked with a small smile.

"I'm not sure I do," she retorted.

"I think Aunt Betty might be sweet on him."

Barrie's attitude evaporated and she looked at him in shock. "What?"

There she was—the Barrie he remembered. He felt a surge of satisfaction at having shocked her into a more natural reaction. He knew he shouldn't be gossiping about his aunt, but it felt good to get past the icy veneer.

"Hey, I'm not saying it's a fact. Just a…feeling, I guess. They're friends. So don't pass that around."

"Your aunt has better taste than that," Barrie replied, but her tone had warmed.

"They're both single, and the same age," he countered. "I always thought Betty would have liked to get married. She just never seemed to find the right cowboy."

"So that's why she never married?" Barrie asked. "Just bad luck?"

"Or bad timing." Curtis shrugged. "And there could be worse matches."

"He's impossible," Barrie countered.

"You're impossible, Curtis!" How many times had she muttered that over the course of their short marriage? And he felt a strange urge to stick up for Dr. Berton in spite of it all.

"He was married for what…thirty-five years?" Curtis raised his eyebrows. "Louise handled him. And if Betty can wrangle cattle, I don't see Palmer being too much for her."

"Some cowboys aren't worth the trouble," she retorted.

And he was obviously one of them. But he'd won her over once… Her refusal to deal with difficult cowboys shouldn't be sparking up his competitive streak. He pushed the thought firmly away.

Miley came bounding back toward them in joyful abandon. While Curtis had ridden bulls in the ring, he still found this massive dog slightly unsettling. At least a man knew a bull's intentions, and he could brace himself for it. Miley's jowls flapped with each leap. Barrie cracked a smile for the first time that morning as

Miley fell into step next to her again—standing solidly between Curtis and her mistress.

"You're back, are you?" she asked the dog, stroking his head, which came up to her chest.

Miley turned to look at Curtis, and he could have sworn he saw a challenge in the dog's eyes. Or was that his imagination?

Curtis's truck was parked in front of the house. As they approached, Betty poked her head out of the screen door. While Barrie went over to talk to Betty, Curtis sauntered over to his truck and started clearing out the back. Normally the back seat wasn't put to use, but that dog was going to need all of it. He covered the leather seats with a woolen blanket, tucking it in at the head-rests. It would have to do.

Soon enough, Barrie returned with Miley at her side, and Curtis opened both doors—one for Barrie and one for Miley. The dog hesitated, watching his mistress.

"Let's go, Miley," Barrie said. "Get in."

Miley did as he was told, and Curtis inwardly grimaced at the sound of dog toenails against leather seats as the blanket was pushed aside. He slammed the door. He held out his hand for Barrie, and she gave him her bag of veterinarian supplies and carefully hoisted herself up into the passenger seat. Then she reached for her bag.

"You are one stubborn woman, Barrie," he said with a short laugh.

"One of my many strengths."

And looking at her life now, maybe she was right, because his way hadn't exactly panned out. He swung her door shut and headed to the driver's side. When he hopped into the truck and started the vehicle, he heard panting close behind his head, and he glanced back to see Miley staring him in the face.

"Hello, Miley," Curtis said uncertainly. "Want to sit back a bit?"

"Miley," Barrie said reproachfully. "Personal space!"

The dog retreated a few inches, but the smell of dog breath was still rather close. Curtis pulled out of his parking spot and headed down the drive that led to the main road.

"He's a bit of a back seat driver," Barrie said, adjusting her bag on her lap. "Thanks for doing this, Curtis. I appreciate it."

"What do the Grangers need?" he asked.

"I'm doing some calf immunizations," she replied. "We've had this appointment scheduled for a couple of weeks now, and it takes some preparation to get the calves all in the barn, so canceling would be a real headache for them..."

And as she talked about the different types of immunizations and the reasons behind them, Curtis noticed Miley's gray face creeping up next to his once more. Curtis looked over, and his face connected with the dog's jowls. He planted a hand on Miley's nose and pushed him back.

"Miley..." Barrie reprimanded him. "Go back! Now!"

Miley retreated once more with a low growl that sounded more like a complaint than a threat, and Curtis started to laugh. It was ridiculous—this massive dog that wanted to be as close as possible to the humans around him.

Curtis eased to a stop at the main road.

"Miley!" Curtis commanded. "Come here." The dog's face appeared over his shoulder again, and Curtis gave him a thorough scratch behind the ears. "You're a good boy," he reassured the dog. "Aren't you?"

Miley cocked his head from side to side to get the best pet possible, and when he was through, he retreated on his own. There was the scramble of toenails against seat as he got comfortable once more. Barrie was looking at Curtis in surprise, and he ignored her.

Curtis signaled his turn and pulled onto the main road. As he looked both ways, he caught Barrie watching him still, her expression softened, less guarded.

"I'm a nicer guy than you think," he said, his voice low.

There was a beat of silence as he accelerated a little past the speed limit.

"I know," she said with a sigh.

"Are you agreeing with me?" He shot her a surprised look.

"Of course. You're a nice guy, and you do mean well. I don't think you're some heartless SOB trying to till me under. I never thought that. You put up this tough front, but under it all you have a lot of heart." She paused. "I never should have married you, though."

That stung—not quite the reaction he'd expected. "Okay…"

"You know what I mean," she said. "You aren't the devil, Curtis. And neither am I. We just want different things—always have. We never should have run off to Rickton and eloped. That was the biggest mistake we ever made."

"You really regret what we had that much?" he asked. Because he didn't. She was still his biggest adventure to date.

She sighed. "I regret having to get over you, Curtis. That was misery."

Had it been that hard on her? He'd wondered over the years. It had been agony for him—starting fresh, his heart in shreds. It had taken him two years to ask another woman out, even with all the girls willing to throw themselves at him on the circuit.

"What do you mean?" he asked cautiously, not even sure he wanted to hear this, but he probably should. He'd had an effect on her, and he should take some responsibility for it.

"Lying in bed at night—our bed—and knowing you weren't coming back." There was a tremor in her voice. "Or the day I packed away that white summer dress I wore for our wedding. I know I said I wanted a dress I could wear again, but how could I? I'd married you in that dress. Or facing the onslaught of questions from everyone who wanted to know where you'd gone. And I had to tell them that you'd left. We were over."

"Did you tell them you kicked me out?" he asked.

"Of course." She laughed bitterly. "I had to save face."

He was silent, her words rattling around inside him. He'd hurt her more deeply than he'd suspected. He'd always imagined that he'd left her behind furious. Maybe it was easier for him to think of her as angry instead of gutted.

"It was bad for me, too," he admitted gruffly. But he didn't want to enlarge on that. He'd had his own sleepless nights, and it had taken him a few weeks to finally take off his wedding ring...

"So we're agreed," she said.

"That I'm not the devil?" He shot her a wry look.

She smiled faintly, then rolled her eyes. Back when he was nothing more than a kid, he'd loved the challenge of winning her heart, and while he wasn't the same naive sap he used to be, there was still a small part of him that liked the challenge of changing her opinion about him.

"Yeah, we're agreed," he said after a minute.

He was a nicer guy than she thought. He stood by that. But she was right—they never should have married to begin with. That divorce had been both inevitable and the worst pain he'd ever endured.

The Granger ranch was about thirty minutes away from the Porter land, and by the time they arrived, Miley was antsy in the back seat. Curtis was more patient with her dog than Barrie had thought he'd be, and she had to admit that had softened her a little toward her ex-husband—very little. And she was grudgingly grateful to him for taking her to this appointment with the Grangers.

They parked beside the Grangers' house. The twin boys, who were about three years old now, were playing outside in the snow, and Mackenzie was standing in the window with the baby on her shoulder. She waved and disappeared from the window, and a moment later the side door opened. She still had the baby on her shoulder, but there was a blanket over the baby's head now to protect her from the chill.

"Hi, Barrie!" Mack called. "Where's your truck?"

"It broke down at the Porter ranch. Curtis kindly offered to shuttle me around this morning," she replied. Mackenzie Granger was one of the few people who hadn't been around during Barrie and Curtis's short marriage, and for that, Barrie was grateful. She was tired of dodging explanations. "Should I just head down to the barn?"

"I'll text Chet and Andy to tell them you're here," Mack replied. "But yes—just head on down. Thanks, Barrie." She turned her attention to the boys in the snow. "Jayden, no snow in the face!"

"Mack!" Barrie leaned out the window again. "Which barn?"

"The Granger barn." Mackenzie grinned. "Sorry, I should have specified."

Barrie waved and put her window back up. Curtis eased the truck forward and raised his eyebrows.

"Which barn is that?"

"Just follow the road down," Barrie said. "It's the first one."

Mack had her hands full with three kids now, and Barrie felt a wave of anxiety. She'd be the mom with a new baby soon enough, but she wasn't as ready for all of this as Mackenzie had been. Mack was in a solid, supportive marriage to a great guy. She owned half this ranch, and there was a certain amount of freedom that came with that, too.

Barrie was still grieving for her own mom, and while she'd always wanted children, she'd envisioned that happening with her mother in her life.

The truck bounced over a rut, and Barrie winced, bracing herself.

"Sorry," Curtis said. "Didn't see that one coming."

"It's okay…" But the more her pregnancy progressed, the more painful jolts like that got. Curtis slowed down and eased around a pothole.

"So that's Chet's wife?" Curtis asked.

"Yes. Mackenzie is Helen Vaughn's granddaughter. I don't know if Betty told you, but she passed away a few years back and left Mack the ranch. She and Chet got married and joined their ranches. It's a profitable outfit."

"Strange to see old buddies with families and kids."

"Andy is Chet's ranch manager," Barrie added.

"Chet's brother, Andy? I thought he was in the city."

"No, he came back. He ended up marrying Dakota Mason—Brody's sister."

Curtis shook his head. "Wow. Time marches on."

It did, indeed. Barrie rubbed a hand over her belly. This was the easy part, she'd been told. Pregnancy was hard, but once a newborn was in the world, everything would be infinitely more complicated. She wouldn't have the luxury of staying home with her baby like Mackenzie did, and her heart ached at the thought of handing her newborn over to someone else while she went tramping out into fields as the local vet. She had no safety net to catch her, which was a position she shared with a lot of hardworking women.

The Granger barn was down a sloping road that bent west, within sight of the Vaughn barn. That was a vestige from the days when people wanted their neighbors within shouting distance. It made sense, because emergencies came up, and people needed each other. It was a simpler time. Before the two ranches were joined, a fence had separated the barns. But that fence had been torn down when Chet and Mack got married, and the two barns were both put to use.

The truck rumbled to a stop next to a rusted blue pickup. Barrie eased herself down to the ground and opened the back door to let Miley out.

"Come on, Miley," she said. The dog hopped down, his long legs reaching the ground more easily than she had, and stretched. Curtis came around the truck just as she grabbed her black bag. A few yards off, a white goat regarded them cautiously.

"Don't even think about it, Miley," Barrie warned. "You stay put."

The barn door opened, and Andy Granger stuck his head out. "Butter Cream, you little scamp. Get back in."

The goat sauntered lazily toward the door, gave one backward glance at the new arrivals and disappeared inside.

"Curtis Porter? Is that you, man?" Andy asked, turning his attention to them.

Curtis headed over and the two men shook hands. They'd been friends in high school.

"Are you two—" Andy hooked a thumb in Barrie's

direction, and Barrie lifted one eyebrow. The inference was obvious. As much as she liked being talked about in front of her face, rather than behind her back, she had no patience left for the curiosity of this town.

"Curtis is my ride today," Barrie said with a small smile. "And I'm your vet. Shall we?"

Andy chuckled and shook his head. "Hey, at least I'm the kind of guy who asks instead of gossiping with the neighbors."

Barrie laughed. "I'll give you that. But there's nothing to wonder about. Curtis is back in town long enough to sell the building I'm leasing. Then he's leaving."

"Oh, yeah?" Andy shot Curtis a questioning look. "You have something going on?"

"I'm buying a stud farm with a business partner," Curtis replied.

"Have you seen anyone else from the old days?" Andy asked as they headed toward the barn door.

"Not really planning on sticking around for a reunion," Curtis said with a short laugh. "Are any of the guys still in town?"

"A few."

"Whatever happened to Dwight Petersen?" Curtis asked. Andy frowned, then caught Barrie's eye.

"Drank himself into oblivion," Barrie answered for him. "You can find him at the Honky Tonk pretty much any day of the week."

"Anyone try to help him out?" Curtis asked.

"Who hasn't?" Andy replied. "I've personally driven him to AA several times, but it never seems to stick.

People have pretty much given up." Andy pulled open the barn door. "Fifteen years changes a lot."

Barrie had to admit that Andy had probably tried harder than most people to get Dwight some help, which was magnanimous considering the history his wife, Dakota, had with the guy. But Dwight was one of those people who, faced with two choices, would pick the wrong one every time.

Andy went into the barn first, and Curtis held the door for Barrie. She glanced up as she passed in front of him, the faint smell of musk tickling her nose. His dark gaze followed her, and he moved in close behind her as the door shut. Andy moved on ahead, and Curtis's hand pressed against the small of her back, nudging her forward. She could feel the warmth emanating from his body, and his touch softened, turned more gentle and pliant...

She knew that touch... Her breath caught, and she shut her eyes for a moment, pushing back her familiar physical response. Why couldn't fifteen years have changed *that*? She missed those warm touches, the smell of his cologne.

"Don't do that," she murmured, glancing back.

"Do what?" His dark eyes glittered in the low light, and her heart gave a flutter. His hand was still on her back, warm and solid.

"That. Be all gentlemanly."

She had no right to miss him. He belonged in the past, and she'd worked too hard to get where she was to let herself romanticize a doomed relationship. Like Andy said, fifteen years changed a lot around here.

Curtis's warm touch dropped away. "Sorry about that. Habit, I guess."

Habit… They'd had a good long time to break those habits, but she understood what he meant. Curtis coming back seemed to conflate the time in some ways, bring back memories so solidly that they ached.

She picked up her pace and sucked in a deep, stabilizing breath. She'd rather do this job without Curtis here to distract her, but she'd take what she could right now.

The barn was warm and smelled of tangy hay. The white goat, Butter Cream, was now in a stall with a couple of new kids. The low moo of weaned calves echoed against the walls, and Barrie followed Andy's lead toward the west side of the barn. Dakota was waiting, filling feed pails for the calves. When she turned toward them, Barrie was surprised at how large her belly had become. Petite Dakota was pregnant, too, but much further along. She was carrying the baby all in front, it seemed.

"Barrie!" Dakota shot her a grin. "Look at you! I haven't seen you since you started to show. How far along are you now?"

Barrie glanced down at her own belly—much smaller than her friend's.

"About five months," she replied. "You?"

"Eight months. Ready to be done with this already." She looked tired and a little wan.

Andy arrived at his wife's side and reached for the pail of feed she held. Dakota shot him a look of warning. "I've got it, Andy. I'm fine."

Andy put his hands up in retreat. "Just trying to help."

"I don't *need* help," Dakota snapped. Then her cheeks flushed. "Sorry, I'm testy."

"She is," Andy confirmed. "But since I contributed to this pregnancy, I still keep trying to help."

Andy grinned at his wife, and Dakota looked ready to smack him. It was the hormones—Barrie could recognize that straight away. Barrie was feeling the same way—irritable and ready to lambaste whoever tried to help her out. She knew it wasn't a wise approach, but she couldn't seem to help herself, either. Wasn't motherhood supposed to soften her? Instead she was getting more frustrated, and the only way to make herself feel better was to prove that she didn't need extra help. Judging from Dakota's reaction, maybe she wasn't alone in that.

Andy and Curtis moved off to check some of the new calves, leaving the women in privacy.

"So… Curtis?" Dakota asked quietly as Barrie set down her bag and opened it.

"Your husband already asked," Barrie said with a bitter laugh. She pulled out some syringes and the bottles of vaccine fluid. "There's nothing to tell. He's selling the building I'm leasing and then leaving town. He feels like he owes me something. And he does."

Dakota eyed her questioningly. "Is he the father?"

Barrie rolled her eyes. "No, he's not the father. He's just the idiot ex-husband who's going to sell my office space to Palmer Berton."

"Ouch." Dakota shook her head. "'Idiot' is right."

Barrie sighed. Except she could grudgingly understand why he was doing it—it just wasn't convenient for
her right now. But this pregnancy was her own fault...
well, hers and the married vet who wanted nothing to
do with her.

"Andy's driving you crazy, is he?" Barrie asked.

"Oh, I'm going nuts..." Dakota sighed. "He keeps
trying to take things out of my hands, or he'll hand me
little bites of food like I'm a squirrel or something—"
She gritted her teeth. "It sounds stupid when I say it,
but I feel huge, and my hormones are soaring and..."

"Yeah, I get it." Barrie chuckled. "He's a good guy,
though."

"I didn't say I don't *love* him," Dakota said with a
shake of her head. "I just want to kill him half the time.
I really hope this improves once the baby arrives, because I don't know how much longer he'll be able to
stand me."

Barrie looked over to where Curtis and Andy stood
together. Andy's gentle green-eyed gaze was focused
on his wife. Curtis's dark gaze drilled into Barrie. He
wasn't flirting or teasing—she was well accustomed
to both with Curtis. This was a different look, something slightly guarded but filled with painful longing.
Her heart sped up, and she swallowed, breaking the
eye contact.

"Andy still seems pretty smitten to me," Barrie said.

"You sure Curtis's only here to sell that property?"
Dakota asked softly.

Barrie sighed. "I'm positive. We aren't all as lucky
as you are."

Except that look he'd given her—he missed all of this, too. She knew better than to think it changed a single thing, but whatever it was that had drawn them together in the first place hadn't gone away.

Barrie pulled her attention back to the job at hand. None of them had time to waste. This ranch wouldn't run itself, and neither would the Porter ranch.

"Okay, so let's get started," Barrie said. "I've got the first vaccines ready. Let's begin with this stall here, and we'll work our way back."

For Barrie, doing her job helped to soothe that rising anxiety inside her. She might not know how to balance everything as a single mother, but she did know how to give animals medical care. Sometimes it helped to just stick with her strengths and sort out her other feelings when she could be alone.

Chapter 7

The mechanic had assured Barrie that her truck would be finished by noon the next day, and she was going to keep him to that. While she didn't have any scheduled appointments, there was always the possibility of an emergency call. She needed her truck. Curtis had been kind to help her out yesterday, but she couldn't allow that to get out of hand. She was still attracted to him—frustrating as that was—and the memory of his hand on her back warmed her. They'd always had chemistry, and that had been the problem. She hadn't been thinking straight when she married Curtis; it had been a heady mix of passion and defiance that she'd lived to regret.

Earlier in the morning, Barrie's father had called her during his break at work. She always had been Daddy's girl, and even at the age of thirty-seven, she liked it when her father checked in.

"Just calling to make sure you're okay, sweetheart," he'd said. "And to see if you need me to talk to the mechanic for you."

"Dad, I can do that alone." She'd chuckled. "I'm not sixteen."

"If you need me, though—"

"Dad, I'll always need you," she'd reassured him. "But not for the mechanic today. I'll be fine."

He'd grudgingly let her go and headed back to work, but she appreciated the thought. Her dad made her feel safe in that elemental way that fathers had.

When noon approached, Barrie locked up her clinic and headed down the street toward the garage. The day was overcast and little shards of snow spun down from the sky. The temperature had dropped overnight and she wrapped her scarf a little closer around her neck.

Hope's downtown shops were decorated for Christmas, the lights in the windows glowing comfortingly into the snowy street. Their radiance was especially welcome since the low clouds kept the day darker than normal. Barrie walked past the drugstore's display window, which had a faux fireplace with stockings hung. Some wrapped boxes sat in the far corner beside a plate of half-eaten cookies. The bookstore had books wrapped in colorful paper stacked in the shape of a Christmas tree. The bakery next door had chocolate yule logs on display, as well as plates of elegantly decorated shortbread cookies, and she paused at that window, her heart filling with sadness.

Mom, I miss you so much...

Barrie had been trying her hand at shortbread cookies for weeks now—a connection to her mother that she just couldn't get right. They always ended up brittle and tasteless, and her cookie icing skills were amateur at best. Her fixation on recreating her mom's cookies had been taking over her free time. She knew that she couldn't replace her mom's presence in her life with a plate of perfectly turned out shortbread cookies, but she had such cozy memories associated with them that she wanted to be able to do the same for her own child. Then she could say, "My mom used to bake these, too," and Gwyneth wouldn't be quite so far away...

Barrie's veterinary practice was on the east end of Montana Avenue, and Hope Auto was on the west end, so her walk was a direct one—straight through downtown. Her toes were chilled through her boots by the time she reached the auto shop, and she pulled open the main door with a shiver.

No one was in the office. She let the door shut behind her, listening to the soft chime of the motion detector that let the mechanic know someone had come in. She shook the snow from her coat and waited for a few moments before the side door opened and Norm Reed came in, wiping his hands on an oil-stained cloth.

"Morning, Dr. Jones," Norm said. "You here to pick up your truck?"

"I am," she replied.

"I've got some bad news there," Norm said, and her stomach sank.

"Is the fix worse than you thought?" she asked.

"No, not that," he replied. "Brent's kid is sick, so he couldn't come in today. I'm on my own, and I haven't gotten to your truck yet."

"Oh…" She sighed. "Norm, I can't run my practice without my vehicle."

"I know, I know. And it's top priority. I'll have it done by morning. That's a promise. I'll stay here all night if I have to. Is that fair enough?"

"It'll have to be," she said with a tired smile. "Thanks, Norm. I appreciate it."

Norm hooked a thumb toward the garage. "I'll get back to it, then. I'll call if it's done early."

Barrie exited the shop and started back down Montana Avenue. Everything seemed to be slipping lately, and that was part of her dedication to those blasted cookies. She was cautious by nature, and she didn't do anything without a proper plan in place—she'd done well following that rule. But this baby hadn't been planned, and neither had Curtis's arrival in town. She'd worked so hard to get her life safe and orderly, and Curtis had breezed in, determined to sell her building. So yes, she needed to feel in control of something that mattered, something she could pass on.

Barrie's stomach growled. She was always hungry lately, and she might as well stop at the Vanilla Bean for a Danish and a coffee. There wasn't much else she could do today. At the very least, she could enjoy a few minutes in Hope's only coffee shop.

When she got to the Vanilla Bean, she could smell the sweet scent of coffee from the sidewalk. Her stomach rumbled again, and she pulled open the door and stepped into the welcome warmth. The shop had a few patrons scattered inside, and as Barrie approached the counter to place her order, someone called her name.

She turned to see her good friend Mallory Cruise sitting by the window, her four-year-old son, Beau, opposite her. Barrie waved.

"I'm coming right over," she said. "Let me just order."

Mallory gave her a thumbs-up, and Barrie ordered a decaf mocha latte with a cherry Danish on the side. Then she crossed the room to Mallory's table.

"How are you doing?" Mallory asked, moving her purse from the chair next to her so that Barrie could sit.

"I'm fine," Barrie said. "How are you all?"

"Katie's in school," Beau, the four-year-old, announced. "And I'm having a treat without her."

Barrie got herself settled, her latte and Danish in front of her. "You're lucky, Beau."

"Yup," Beau agreed, biting into his chocolate muffin.

Mallory was married to Mike Cruise, one of the cops on the force here in Hope. She'd arrived in town only a few years ago, but she was already a solid part of the community. Barrie and Mallory had hit it off almost as soon as they met.

"We're all fine," Mallory said, answering her earlier question with a smile. "We're going to Disneyland next month."

"Are you really?" Barrie said, taking a sip of her latte. "When did this happen?"

"Mike surprised me for my birthday. Or he tried

to…" Mallory chuckled. "The travel agent called our home to clarify which room we wanted yesterday."

Barrie laughed. "He tried."

"And I'm not complaining," Mallory said with a grin. "You're still coming to the Christmas party, aren't you?"

The party… Barrie grimaced. She'd completely forgotten. She wasn't in the mood to dress up and make nice—not with everything on her plate lately.

"I have nothing to wear," Barrie said. And that was the truth. "I have some jeans, and I've got a few big sweaters, but I'm in no way set up for a party, Mal."

"Let me take you shopping." Mallory's eyes lit up. "I never got to do that stuff, either. I was hiding the first half of my pregnancy and then I was on bedrest for the last half of it, so there were no cute maternity outfits for me."

"I don't know…" Barrie had never been into fashion, and shopping for new clothes had always been mildly intimidating.

"Trust me," Mallory said. "You'll feel better once you own something that fits properly. Let me take you shopping, and there's no pressure to buy."

"This is more for you than it is for me, isn't it?" Barrie asked with a small smile.

"Maybe." Mallory chuckled.

Barrie's phone rang, and she glanced down at the number. "Oh, it's Leanne from 4-H. I'd better take this."

Mallory nodded and turned her attention to Beau, who had slopped some hot chocolate onto the tabletop.

"Hi, Leanne," Barrie said. "How are you doing?"

"Not too badly," Leanne replied, but she sounded slightly nervous. "I needed to speak with you."

"Oh?" Barrie turned away from the table and ducked her head for a bit more privacy. "What's going on?"

"It's delicate," Leanne said, and there was apology in her tone. "First of all, I need you to know that this has nothing to do with me. When we voted, I voted for you, but a lot of the mothers have been raising concerns."

"About what, exactly?" Barrie asked, misgivings rising up inside her.

"About you speaking to the girls next week," Leanne said. "They're concerned that your pregnancy might be a distraction."

"From what?" Barrie couldn't help the flatness that entered her tone. "I'll be talking about veterinary care. I'm not doing a belly dance."

"They're young and impressionable," Leanne said. "And your pregnancy has been the talk of the town for weeks now."

"So I'm an unwed professional who happens to be pregnant, and that makes me a danger to their morals?" Barrie wasn't even trying to hide her irritation now. They'd asked *her* to talk to the girls, and she'd agreed. She hadn't gone looking for this.

"It's not me!" Leanne insisted.

"Is it Jen Hartfield?" Barrie asked with a sigh. For all of her compassion for Jen's history, she was getting really tired of being the target around here.

"Not only her," Leanne said. "I got outvoted. I don't think it should be an issue, but the other mothers do. They think you're a bad example."

Barrie had put herself through veterinary school, had set up her own practice and was serious competition to the only other vet in town. But her pregnancy seemed to be more important to these women than her professional accomplishments.

"So you're canceling," Barrie clarified.

"I'm afraid so."

"Thanks for the call," Barrie said curtly.

"No hard feelings, Dr. Jones," Leanne said. "We wish it could have worked out."

"Of course. Take care." Barrie hung up, and her cheeks burned. When she turned back toward the table, she found Mallory's eyes pinned to her.

Mallory winced. "Is that what it sounded like?"

"Probably." Barrie pulled a hand through her hair. "Leanne says I'm a bad influence on the girls, and they're canceling my talk."

"That's downright insulting." Mallory shook her head. "What is this, 1950?"

Mallory had been pregnant when she'd arrived in Hope. Her boyfriend had left her for her best friend, and when he discovered Mal was pregnant, he offered to pay for the abortion. That baby was now sitting across from them, slurping hot chocolate. Mallory was now married, but some of the bigger prudes in this town hadn't forgotten.

"How bad are the rumors about me?" Barrie asked.

"You don't want to hear about that," Mallory replied. "It's just stupid talk."

"I do," Barrie pressed. "I mean, if I'm getting treated

like the scarlet woman around here, I should probably know why. What are they saying?"

"People's imaginations are far worse than reality," Mallory said. "Most of the time. They make up the worst stories possible."

"Like what?" Barrie asked.

"Like you're pregnant with a married man's child," Mal replied with a sigh. "And they've been finger-pointing at a few candidates around town..."

"Oh, for crying out loud!" Barrie shook her head. They were right, ironically enough, but the married man wasn't from Hope, and she'd had no idea he was married to begin with. But Leanne's husband had cheated on her twice in the last five years, so maybe Leanne wasn't quite so supportive of Barrie as she claimed, if there were stories circulating that Barrie was a homewrecker. No hard feelings, indeed.

"Why don't you just tell the truth about the father of the baby?" Mallory asked quietly. "I'm sure it can't be as bad as people imagine. It'll stop the tongue wagging, at least."

"No." Barrie turned her latte slowly in front of her. If she kept quiet, at least she'd have deniability. And some semblance of privacy. Her mistake at the veterinary convention was humiliating enough without offering it up for public chatter.

"I'm here if you want to vent," Mallory said. "And you can trust my discretion."

"Thanks, but I'm not ready to do that." Barrie didn't feel the need to vent; she needed to solve her own problems and set up her life so that she could raise her child on her own. Besides, as soon as she told one person, the story would get out. It might be overheard, or a text might be seen. Someone might see Mallory's face when they suggested some theory... The possibilities were endless. A secret was no longer a secret once she told the first person.

"Okay." Mallory didn't look offended, to Barrie's relief. "But I'm here for you, Barrie. You know that."

Barrie reached over and squeezed her friend's hand. "Absolutely."

"Miss Barrie?" Beau said quietly.

"Yes, Beau?" Barrie turned her attention to the boy.

"Are you going to eat that?" He pointed at her Danish.

"Beau!" Mallory chided. "That's rude. Don't ask people for food. Good grief!"

"It's okay," Barrie said with a low laugh. "I'm going to eat most of it, but I'll give you a piece, okay?"

Beau seemed pleased with this option, and she tore him off a chunk of pastry. Right now, Barrie might not have a husband, the conception of her child might be her biggest embarrassment so far and she had no idea how she was going to balance everything once this baby arrived, but she'd heard somewhere that all a person could do was take the next right step. She'd try that, because she couldn't see the bigger solutions for the life of her.

Curtis loaded bags of dog food, salt licks for the cattle and several bags of ear tags into the back of his truck in the parking lot of Hope Ranch and Supply. His mind had been on Barrie all morning, no matter how hard he tried to distract himself with work. It wasn't just memories from their marriage that had left him uncomfortably preoccupied. It was her as a mature woman, and not just her pregnancy like she'd suggested. She was the kind of woman who'd grown more beautiful as the years went by—and more interesting. He liked having an excuse to be around her, and he knew he was playing with emotional fire here. It had taken him years to get over her, and falling for her again would be a terrible idea.

His cell phone rang just as he slammed the tailgate shut, and he rooted out his phone with a sigh. He glanced down at the number.

"Betty?" he said, picking up.

"Curtis, I'm at the barn, and there's another sick cow," his aunt said. "I don't have Barrie's number in my phone, only Dr. Berton's, but Barrie has been dealing with this outbreak, so I think we'd better stick with her for the time being. Can you give her a call and get her to come by?"

Curtis had Barrie's business card in his wallet, so contacting his ex-wife wouldn't be an issue. "Aunty, what are you doing in the barn?"

"If you hadn't noticed, this is still my ranch!" she quipped. "Now quit trying to babysit me and give the vet a call, would you?"

"Sure thing," he said. "Don't break anything new."

"Har har," his aunt replied, and hung up without a farewell.

Curtis smiled wryly, then pulled out the business card. Betty might have asked him to help out, but holding her back from running her ranch wasn't even a possibility. He paused before he dialed Barrie's number.

He was actually looking forward to calling her, and he recognized the problem there… He was starting to get attached again, and he needed to stop this. He was leaving town, and her life didn't include him. If only his feelings could catch up with his brain.

"Dr. Jones," she intoned as she picked up.

"Hi, Barrie, it's Curtis." He cleared his throat.

"Oh…hi. Everything okay?"

"Betty just let me know that there's another sick cow. They have it in the barn, but she needs you to come down. Are you free?"

"My truck is still in the shop," she replied. "I'm sorry about that. You might want to—"

Call Palmer Berton… Yeah, he could, but he didn't want to.

"Where are you?" he interrupted.

"Downtown. The Vanilla Bean," she replied.

"Great. I'm at the Ranch and Supply. I could pick you up, if you want. You're the one who's been dealing with this outbreak, so you're our go-to for this."

"And I'm happy to do it," she said.

"Would you be ready in ten minutes?"

"Not a problem," she replied.

"See you soon."

Curtis hung up and hopped into the cab of his truck. He could still make out the soft scent of her perfume in the vehicle from yesterday. It was the same scent she used to wear when they were married, and a long-forgotten memory surfaced of her standing in front of their dresser in a pink summer dress, spritzing some perfume onto her wrists… But somehow in that memory, he aged her into the woman she was now.

He started the truck and pulled out of the parking space. The Ranch and Supply was located on the west end of town along the highway, but Hope being as small as it was, he was only five minutes away from downtown and the coffee shop. When he turned onto Main, he could already see Barrie standing on the street, waiting for him. The wind blew her straight hair, and she hunched her shoulders. He wasn't going to get used to seeing her pregnant. She was right. Her condition certainly did soften him toward her, but it wasn't just a testosterone reaction to a pregnant woman. She was vulnerable, and whatever it was that set Barrie Jones off balance sparked a protective instinct inside him. It just so happened to be a pregnancy.

Curtis pulled up to the curb, and Barrie crossed the street. He leaned across the cab to open the door for her, and she climbed inside.

"We'll need to stop by my clinic for my bag," she said as she fastened her seat belt.

"Hi," he said, and her cheeks colored.

"Sorry, hi."

Curtis signaled, pulled a U-turn and headed back down Montana Avenue toward her clinic. The last time he'd been there, she'd told him to back out of her life, and it was like she'd put up an emotional fence around that place. It had worked—he didn't feel welcome anymore.

Curtis glanced over at her, and Barrie's expression was grim.

"You okay?" he asked.

"Huh?" She forced a smile. "I'm fine. So, tell me about the cow."

Was it him making her so uncomfortable? Or was there something else?

"The same as the others, I'm assuming," he said. "Betty just called and asked me to get you, so I haven't seen it myself... But you're not fine."

She licked her lips, then sighed. "I'll figure it out. It's not that big of a deal."

"Is it me?" he asked. "Have I crossed a line, or ticked you off?"

"Not everything is about you, Curtis." She gave him a smile.

"Good. I'm glad it's not me," he said. "So, what is it?"

They were approaching her clinic, and he slowed and put on his turn signal. Another pickup passed in the other direction, and Curtis waited until the road was clear before making the turn.

"It's just gossip around town," she said as he pulled into the parking lot in front of her clinic and chose the spot near her door.

"So, what's fueling the gossip this time?" He put the truck into Park and turned toward her.

"They're trying to guess at the father of my baby."

Curtis eyed her, watching for her reaction. She looked away. "That's kind of insulting, but not surprising, right?" he said. "You've got to ignore them."

"And I was," she replied, pushing the door open and letting in a rush of cold air. "But now my talk with the 4-H girls has been canceled because of it."

Barrie eased herself down and slammed the door behind her. He watched her head to the clinic and unlock the door. She disappeared inside while her words spun through his mind. He remembered Hope's tenacious gossip, but could it really have gone so far? That pissed him off. Barrie deserved better from this town.

A couple of minutes later, Barrie emerged with her black bag in hand. Curtis leaned over and pushed the door open from the inside, then grabbed the bag to give her room to get in. Once she was settled, he headed for the highway.

"What happened?" he asked.

"Leanne Perkins called a few minutes ago and let me know that my pregnancy was a distraction, and they worried for the impressionable girls."

"Girls who've all seen cows inseminated and calves born," he retorted.

"I'm a scandal."

He caught the quiver in her voice. This was no joke to her—this had hurt her, and he felt a rise in that old protectiveness.

"You're a professional and a good person," he shot back. "Leanne Perkins is an idiot. Wait…is this because of Jen Hartfield?"

"Leanne insists that it wasn't only her," Barrie said. "The mothers voted."

Curtis sighed. There had been a time when Hope had turned on him—but he'd had the luxury of leaving.

Still, he knew what it felt like to have an entire town make up its mind about him.

"How much does this presentation matter to you?" he asked.

"I cared about it," she said. "I want to encourage girls to work in agriculture. We need women in this field, and if I can encourage just one girl to become a vet—"

"They'll be encouraged by you simply being a vet," he said. "You show them that it's possible. Like the Hartfield girl."

Barrie was silent for a moment, and then she said, "I'm not used to being the cautionary tale, Curtis."

He slowed at the intersection and signaled a turn onto the highway. It was a straight drive out to the Porter ranch from here, and he settled back into his seat. The telephone lines looped past the truck window, and he glanced at the fences sagging in snow drifts. The clouds hung low, threatening more snow.

"You might consider stopping the gossip by just telling people who the father is," he said after a moment.

"You aren't the only one to suggest that, but it isn't their business," she replied. "This is my body, my baby, my mistake!"

"No child is a mistake," he said. "Not every family starts the same way. My mom was a teenager when she had me, and we still count as a family."

"I'm not calling my *baby* a mistake," she said, tears misting her eyes. "But I messed up. I'm not the kind of woman who goes around having one-night stands. I know that consequences matter and that they can dog you for a lifetime. I was the responsible girl who studied hard. Even after you, I made sure that my choices were solid so I could have a bright future. I'm not the irresponsible sort!"

"I know." Did he ever know. She'd been cautious and proper from the start, and that had been part of her allure. He liked the idea of teaching her a little bit of fun.

"Do you? Because apparently, the entire town now questions that." She shook her head. "I'm a professional. I work hard. I got myself through school, and I built something for myself. That should count."

"So it was a one-night stand?" he asked.

She'd said more than she'd planned, he could tell. She shot him a cautious look. "It doesn't matter."

"You're right," he said. "It doesn't. What you do romantically isn't anyone else's business."

"Thank you."

And yet he still wanted to get his hands on whatever moron had done this to her… But who was he to get on a high horse? He'd walked out on her, too. Had she been shaken—like this? But she'd kicked him out. He never would have left her otherwise. He just hadn't fit into her responsibly planned life anymore.

"If you ask me, you were always too careful," he said.

"Since when?" she asked, irritation in her voice.

"Since always," he said. "The biggest risk you took was marrying me, and then you shut down. You wouldn't risk anything, and maybe it's time you did."

"I'm thirty-seven," she said. "I have what…twenty-five years left to work? I have to pay off my house. I have to get ready for retirement—"

"You've got twenty-eight years left to work," he retorted, "and you're having a baby. You always liked to plan everything, and this wasn't planned. Well, the best things are a surprise. I say, enjoy it. Quit beating yourself up, and ignore the people who are going to judge you, because I have news for you, Barrie—if they're judging you now, they were doing it before, just a little more quietly."

"You think?" she asked.

"I'm pretty certain," he replied.

The highway was plowed clean, but some spots on the asphalt shone wet. Seeing as the temperature was well below freezing, it was ice. He let up on the gas and slowed down a little. He had a pregnant woman with him in the truck, after all.

"Curtis, how do you do it?" she asked. "I mean, how do you just see what happens, and not worry?"

"I have faith in my own abilities," he said. "I'm relatively certain that I can handle whatever comes."

She sighed. "I don't bounce back as well as you do."

"You think I did?"

"You're the one who left," she replied. "I'm assuming you did."

He sighed. "I left because I was constantly disappointing you. You married me because you loved me, but you expected things I couldn't deliver."

"I didn't."

"Sure you did. Like money," he replied. "You knew I was a bull rider when we got married. That was no surprise, but once we said our vows, the things you used to accept about me were no longer okay with you. You wanted a certain income, a certain life, and you had an image of what you wanted me to become, but you never stopped to ask if I wanted to be that guy."

"I wanted you to be my husband!" Barrie shook her head.

"Yeah, but you seemed to think that me following my dreams meant I wasn't committed."

"It wasn't that," she said.

"No? Then what was it?"

Barrie sighed. "I had dreams, too. You didn't seem willing to compromise. When I told you to leave, I was just so tired. I was tired of fighting and being hurt and wondering what you were thinking or feeling. I was just so tired of it all."

"And I can understand that," he said. "Now, at least. But do you know what it's like to look into your wife's eyes and see disappointment, maybe even a little regret?"

Barrie was silent.

"It hurts. A lot. When I married you, I wanted to give you everything. But I was only good at one thing, and that was bull riding. I'd made promises to you about how I'd provide, and then you didn't want me to use my one skill to do that."

"There were stable jobs—" she started.

"There were, but I was…me." He cast her a sad smile. "I wasn't cut out for that stuff, Barrie. I'm a bit of a lone wolf in a lot of ways. If you'd married some other guy, he'd have been able to give you all the stuff I couldn't afford yet, and I knew that. I wanted to give you all of that, but… I had to do it my own way."

"You sound like I wanted a certain lifestyle," she

said. "I wasn't expecting money, Curtis. I wanted time with you. I wanted some regularity, something I could count on."

"You could count on my love," he said gruffly.

"Until you left." Her voice was low, but the words stabbed.

He'd left, and he'd never live that one down, would he? Curtis sighed. "Yeah. I left, but you no longer wanted what I had to offer. Everyone has their limits, I guess. I couldn't change who I was, and you wouldn't be happy with what I could give. There didn't seem to be any way to fix that."

She was silent.

"You said I bounced back, but I didn't," he went on. "I'd given you everything I could—all I had—and it wasn't enough. That gutted me. So I looked in your eyes, and I saw the way you looked at me—the way you saw me... You saw a loser, someone lower than you, someone you couldn't respect. I didn't bounce back from that. Ever."

"I didn't think you were a loser," she said quietly.

"Did you trust me to provide for you?" he asked. "Did you trust me to take care of you, or did you think you needed to fix me first?"

She didn't answer, and he glanced over at her. Her expression was somber.

"Don't worry about it," he said. "I didn't mean to say all that, anyway. I just wanted you to know that I didn't waltz off and forget you. I crawled off and licked my wounds for a really long time. If that helps at all."

He was supposed to come to town and take care

of his business with as little fuss as possible. This—whatever he and Barrie were doing—hadn't been part of the plan.

"It does help a little bit," she said after a few beats of silence.

He wasn't sure how he felt about that, but whatever. He wasn't supposed to be getting attached. He'd have to be more careful—and put a lid on whatever he was feeling. He hadn't been enough for her when he was an able-bodied bull rider, and he wouldn't be enough for her now. He'd do well to remember that.

Chapter 8

When Barrie arrived at the barn, another two heifers were ill besides the one Curtis knew about. Barrie's work was cut out for her. One of the original calves had taken a turn for the worse, and Barrie set the calf up with more heat and an extra shot of antibiotics. One of the goat's kids wasn't getting enough milk, so they bottle-fed the little thing. By the time Barrie had finished in the Porter barn, the sun had set and her whole body ached.

She'd been thinking about Curtis's words in the truck that morning. She'd never realized what he'd been feeling back then, but it was still hard to pity him. He'd left, and that had ended everything. He could have talked to her—actually put those feelings out there! He could have explained his position. They could have gone for couple's counseling. Anything! Walking away wasn't the only option. She hadn't backed him into a corner, and in her defense, she'd had something to offer to their relationship, too, if he'd only stopped to look. Their marriage wasn't about him taking care of her. It was about two people loving each other and going after their dreams. Both of them. Not just him.

But his question had been plaguing her: had she trusted him to take care of her? If she had to be utterly honest, the answer was no. She hadn't. She'd wanted to stay in Hope because while she loved Curtis, she needed the security of her home and family close by. He'd been right—she'd wanted more than he was offering, and she was afraid to take her eyes off the shore.

Barrie followed Curtis out of the barn into evening twilight. A sliver of a moon hung low, and the strongest of the stars were but pinpricks on the gray velvet of the sky. In the west, the horizon still glowed red.

Her feet and back ached, and Barrie felt like her body was betraying her. If this was how her body handled a pregnancy at five months, what was it going to be like at eight or nine? She put a hand into the small of her back and straightened.

"You okay?" Curtis tossed a plastic bag of salt blocks into the back of his pickup truck.

"Fine."

"Yeah, you don't look fine," he said. "Come on, I'll drive you home. Thanks for all of this today."

"It's my job," she said.

"And I'm still grateful." He arched an eyebrow.

Barrie smiled, then shook her head. "You're welcome."

Curtis pulled open the passenger side door, then headed around to the driver's side. Apparently he'd learned not to offer any more hands up, but she secretly appreciated the gesture of the opened door. The baby moved inside her as she hoisted herself up into the cab with a sigh. She slammed the door shut and stretched her legs out, giving her feet a much-needed rest.

"Can I get you a burger or something?" he asked.

She was hungry—there was no denying that—but her body was sore and all she wanted was to get back to the house. She wanted to sink into her couch, put her feet up and eat something microwaveable.

"I'm exhausted," she said. "But thanks anyway. Besides, Miley has been home alone all day."

"No problem. Straight home, then."

Curtis put the truck into gear and pulled away from the barn. The headlights sliced through the darkness, but Barrie's attention wasn't on the road ahead of them—it was on the fields out her window. Moonlight sparkled over the cold-hardened snow, and there was something so peaceful in the scene that she could feel the tension seep out of her shoulders and back.

"So, what are your plans for Christmas?" Curtis asked.

Barrie glanced toward him, but Curtis's eyes were on the road ahead, and he changed gears as they drove past Betty's house and headed toward the main road.

"What I always do," she said. "Dinner with my parents. Well, I guess just Dad this year."

"That's it?" He shot her a quick look. "You were always more into Christmas than that."

"It was different then," she replied. "I was married."

Curtis chewed on the side of his cheek, and she inwardly winced. She was tired and achy and apparently her filter wasn't working as it should. She remembered all the love she'd poured into their two Christmases together. From the cooking to the decorating, she'd done everything she could to make their home glow for him.

"You did make a nice Christmas, Barrie," he said.

For all the good it had done... "Do you have any idea how hard I worked at our marriage?" she asked, adjusting herself in her seat so she could see him better. "I poured everything I had into making our home warm and special." She shook her head, unsure of how to encapsulate it all in words.

"There was nothing wrong with our home," he said.

"Nothing wrong with it..." Tears misted her eyes, and it was the exhaustion, she knew, because this pain was so old that it shouldn't logically matter. "Curtis, I was aiming for something a little better than that."

"You know what I mean." He sighed.

"No, I don't!" She pulled a hand through her hair. "I did everything I knew to make our home into a place where you'd feel...at home! I planted the garden, I canned fruit, I made those orange peel scents for our drawers, I—" She stopped, feeling exhausted even remembering it all. "I did that for you, and you never seemed to notice. And I was the idiot who never saw that you'd have one foot out the door no matter what I did."

"I noticed." He shook his head. "I just didn't care about those things like you did. I thought you were doing it for you."

"Like Christmas," she confirmed bitterly.

"Yeah, like Christmas! I don't know. I never really did too much for Christmas at home with Mom. She usually had a gig over the holidays, and I could go watch her sing, or I could stay home and watch TV. I mean... Whatever. It wasn't that big of a deal."

"Christmas is *always* a big deal," she retorted. It was supposed to be, at least. Traditions held a family together.

"Not to you. At least, not anymore," he shot back. "You're having dinner with your dad as usual, I thought."

She didn't like having her own words tossed back at her, especially by the man who had no right to even ask about her personal plans.

"Well, it's different now," she replied. "When I had you, I had someone to create some traditions for. I wanted to make a home for you that would always call you back..." Emotion tightened her throat, and she stopped talking.

"There was nothing wrong with our home," he repeated, and she heard sadness in his voice. "But you were so stuck in it. It was just an old house with some used furniture. And you made the most of it—don't get me wrong—but it wasn't about that for me. It never was."

Barrie swallowed hard and leaned her head back. "I know. It's okay. It doesn't matter."

"No, let me say my piece," he countered. "You keep saying that you poured yourself into making a home for us, and I know you did. I saw how hard you worked on it. But I didn't want a home like that. I wanted a woman by my side."

"And where was that woman supposed to live?" She almost laughed at the ridiculousness of it all.

"With me," he said. "Wherever we happened to be."

"In some ratty trailer," she said. "Or a tent. Or a one-star hotel."

"We were young and in love. What did it matter?" He shot her a small smile—that tempting kind of smile that made her stomach flip. But that had been his way— cajole her into some adventure, and then see what happened.

"It mattered," she replied. "I needed more security than that."

Following her bull riding husband around the circuit wasn't the kind of life she needed. She had plans for her own education, but more than that, she needed money in the bank and a roof over her head. She wasn't the kind of woman who liked uncertainty.

"I know." He sighed. "Matching sheets, scented drawers…that iron skillet your parents got us for a wedding present. You needed that stuff to feel like you were safe. Thing is, Barrie, I wanted you to need *me* to feel safe."

"It wasn't just about our home," she said. "I had dreams and ambitions, too, and I couldn't pursue those if I was trailing along with you on the circuit. On top of which, what is this—the 1950s? It wasn't just about provision. It was about making a life together, and you were really bad at compromise."

"I wasn't against you becoming a vet," he said.

"You just weren't willing to make room for it," she replied.

"And we come full circle again," he said. "We wanted really different things out of life, and we didn't talk about that soon enough."

They fell into silence, and snow began to fall in lazy flakes, blurring their vision through the windshield. They were approaching town, and Curtis slowed as he came to the turnoff.

"Barrie, you did well for yourself," he said as he took the turn. "You've put together a great life here in Hope, and you should be proud. Looking at the results, you made the right choice."

"What choice?" she asked. "Staying in town? Going to school?"

"Kicking me out." He met her gaze for only a moment, but she read sadness in those dark eyes.

"Like I said before," she replied, "I might have kicked you out, but you *left*."

"Yeah. I did." He signaled the last turn onto her road, and she felt a wave of sadness of her own. She hadn't actually wanted to win that one. She didn't know what she'd hoped he'd say...or maybe she did. She wished that just once she could hear Curtis Porter tell her that the life she'd offered him had been the best option all along. But he wasn't going to say that, because even now, fifteen years after the fact, the home she'd poured her heart into creating still wasn't enough to tempt him.

* * *

Curtis pulled into Barrie's drive and leaned back in the seat. He wasn't sure what she was feeling right now, but he knew that bringing up the past had been a bad idea. This was all fifteen years ago, and he was leaving town just as soon as Christmas was over... What use was there in dredging up old hurts? They'd made the choice back then and gotten divorced. It was over.

The snow was coming steadily down now. He turned off the engine, and they fell into that velvety silence. She looked pale in the moonlight—paler than usual.

"Barrie, are you alright?" he asked.

"I'm tired," she said quietly. "And sore."

"You should have said earlier." He unfastened his seat belt. "Come on. Let's get you in."

"I'm fine—"

"Yeah?" He wasn't taking that answer this time. "Well, so am I. And I'm getting you all the way inside." He pushed open his door and hopped out. When he got around to her side, she was just sliding down to the ground, wincing as her feet hit the concrete.

Curtis slammed the door shut for her and took her arm in his. She didn't argue this time, which told him she wasn't alright. He knew nothing about pregnancies—but he knew Barrie, and she'd been putting on a brave face for longer than she should have. He was willing to bet on it.

When they approached the door, the scramble of toenails and a joyous woof greeted them from the other side.

"Miley missed me," she said, pulling out her key.

Curtis followed her in, and after Miley licked his mistress, the dog turned his attention to Curtis.

"Hey, there," Curtis said, holding out his hand. Miley bounced up and planted both paws on Curtis's shoulders. He was a big dog, and about as heavy as a weaned calf, too. He stuck his wet nose into Curtis's face.

"Miley!" Barrie chastised him. "Get down!"

Miley did as he was told, and turned a few circles around the linoleum.

Curtis looked around the kitchen. "Barrie, go sit down. I'll get you some supper."

"Curtis, no—"

"Take this as my apology for being terrible at compromise back in the day," he said. "You're right—I was pretty focused on my own career and didn't bother to see what you really wanted. Well, today you overdid it on my watch. I'm making you something to eat."

Barrie looked ready to argue. Then she glanced at the couch and her expression softened. He'd just won this one. Sort of. She walked toward the couch, her movements slow and cautious. Then she sank down onto the seat and heaved a sigh. As Curtis took off his boots and hat, Miley hopped up onto the couch, too, then settled his massive self onto what was left of Barrie's lap.

"Isn't he heavy?" Curtis asked.

"Like you wouldn't believe." She chuckled. "But he missed me."

"Miley, you want to go out to pee?" Curtis called. He spotted a bag of dog food on the counter, and he grabbed what he assumed was a dog bowl on the floor—except it was more the size of a mixing bowl. He filled it and put in onto the floor. The dog leaped down from Barrie's lap and beelined for the door. Curtis opened it, and Miley headed for the snow and lifted a leg.

"Thanks." She leaned her head back. "And I hate to point this out, but I don't remember you knowing how to cook anything more than toast."

"And I made the perfect toast, too," he said with a low laugh. "But you haven't seen me in a good long while, Barrie. Some things have changed."

Miley came back in and headed for his food bowl. Meanwhile, Curtis poked through her cupboards and then her fridge. He came up with some sausage, a tomato, a few eggs and a loaf of bread. He was good for that toast. In his rummaging, he came across a tin of cookies. Curious, he opened it and found some shards of what were probably meant to be shortbread cookies.

"What happened here?" he asked, shaking the tin.

"Oh, don't ask. I can't get them right," she said.

"I've gotten pretty good at cookies recently," he said.

"What?" She opened her eyes and fixed him with a curious stare. "Since when?"

"I took a class." He met her gaze, then felt the heat rising in his face. "To impress a woman."

"Was she impressed?" Barrie raised one eyebrow.

"She was." He chuckled. "It didn't work out, though."

"I'm trying to figure them out. It seems like a motherly thing to do, doesn't it? Mom made amazing shortbread cookies, and I just don't have the knack yet."

Gwyneth Jones had been a real artist when it came to baking, and he remembered Barrie trying her hand at her mother's cookies… No one could match Gwyneth, though. He set about chopping sausage, onion and some green pepper and tossed them into a pan. As he worked, he glanced again into the tin. They really hadn't turned out. He looked around the kitchen and spotted a wad of yarn behind the fruit bowl. When he pulled it out, he discovered what seemed to be the beginning of some knitting that also wasn't turning out. She was more than trying to get ready for this baby…and she was hitting a wall.

"So, you knit now, too?" he called over the sizzle of frying.

"No, I don't," she called back. "I'm terrible at it."

"What were you trying to make?" he asked.

"Booties. Not that you can tell."

Barrie, who'd longed to make a home for him, was attempting to do the same thing for this baby, and the realization stung. This wasn't just some attempt at a craft. She wouldn't have a whole lot of free time to fill that way. This was her effort to create a home that would…how had she said it? A home that would call her child back again. And she was failing—at least in the ways she was trying to make it work.

Barrie's eyes had closed, and she absently rubbed a hand over the dome of her stomach.

Looking at that little bundle of yarn, and at the shards of cookies in the tin, he wondered how much he had hurt her by not settling into that nest she'd so lovingly prepared for them. Would it have killed him to compliment the matching towels? It just hadn't seemed to matter back then, and he'd cared more about tugging her away from it all. But the more he coaxed, the deeper she dug in.

When the food was finished, he brought two plates out to the living room and handed her one.

"Thank you." She accepted a fork and immediately set into the meal. He watched as she took a bite, then shot him a look of surprise. "This is really good!"

"You aren't the only one who grew up," he said. "I've improved. What can I say?"

She nodded and took another bite. He sank into the seat next to her, and they ate in silence for a couple of minutes, Barrie making little sounds of enjoyment as she chewed.

"You're going to be fine," he said.

She looked over at him, then swallowed. "It's what I keep saying."

"Yeah, but *I'm* telling you," he said. "You're going to be just fine. And you don't have to make shortbread or knit booties, or whatever else you've decided would make you the perfect mom."

"I'm not giving up on the cookies yet," she said, taking another bite.

"No?" He shrugged. "Thing is, kids like cookies, but they don't really care if you whip them up by hand or pass them a box from the grocery store."

"I care." Her voice was low, but he caught the depth of feeling in those words. This wasn't only about her child. This was about her needs, too. Maybe Barrie needed these trappings just as much as she thought everyone else did.

"Your kid will love you for what you are, Barrie," he

said. "My mom made really good toast. She might not have been perfect, but man, I loved her."

Barrie's cheeks flushed and she met his gaze for a moment, then smiled. "Then I guess I have hope."

Barrie speared the last piece of sausage and popped it into her mouth. He took her plate, put it on top of his and set them on the floor. Miley came over and licked every inch his tongue could touch, forks rattling against glass as he gave them his full attention.

"Give me your feet," Curtis said.

"What?" She looked honestly alarmed, and he grinned.

"Give me your feet, Barrie." He bent and lifted them into his lap as she pivoted on the sofa so she could lean back against the arm. He took one foot in his hands and started gently rubbing in slow, firm circles.

"You don't have to—"

"I know. Shut up already." He met her gaze, but he didn't stop working her feet with slow, measured strokes. He was defying her—daring her to turn this down. For a moment, she was tense, and he thought she might pull away, but then she sighed and shut her eyes.

"This is wildly inappropriate," she murmured.

"Probably," he agreed. "But it feels good."

"Hmm…"

With her eyes closed, he could let his gaze wander over the chestnut locks that framed her face, the roundness of her figure and her belly, down to her feet, which lay warm in his hands. He rubbed the arches of her feet, moving down to her toes—they were cute toes. He knew that from before. He could see her body relax, and he had to admit that he wasn't just thinking about being helpful right now…he was thinking about taking this a whole lot further.

He wouldn't. Obviously he wouldn't, but even pregnant and fifteen years older, she still drew him in. He could see the lines around her eyes, and how her lips were fuller with the pregnancy, or perhaps with her age. She was no longer a lithe twentysomething sweetheart. She was a mature woman with the full bust and plump thighs that made him long to slide his hands up them…

But he *wouldn't*. He swallowed. He wasn't the womanizing type. He'd rarely taken advantage of the offers he'd gotten from girls wanting to have a good time with him. But having Barrie lying on her couch with her feet in his hands…how on earth had this just become the sexiest thing he could imagine?

He kept massaging, watching her chest rise and fall in a slower and slower rhythm.

"Barrie," he murmured.

"I'm not asleep," she whispered, as if reading his mind, and her eyes fluttered open. She pushed herself up into a seated position, pulling her feet from his lap, and he regretted having disturbed the moment.

"Okay, well—" He swallowed, because his mind had been going along some dangerous paths there, and he had too many reasons not to mess with Barrie's peace of mind again. He needed to get out of here now before he did something he regretted.

"I'd better get going," he said. "I have an early morning."

She nodded. "Me, too."

"Look, about what we were discussing in the truck—"

"It was a long time ago, Curtis," she said with a faint shrug. "We were both a whole lot younger."

"Even if we hadn't lasted," Curtis said quietly, "I wish I'd done better by you."

"Yeah?" He watched as her lips formed the word, and she was so tempting… She always had been his weak spot.

"Yeah." She was close enough that he could have moved in and caught those lips with his, but instead, he sucked in a breath and pushed himself to his feet. "I'd better head out, Barrie."

"Okay. Thanks for dinner and the foot rub."

Curtis cast her a grin and headed toward the side door, where his boots and hat waited. He knew the limits of what he could endure, and he'd better get out of here before he took some serious advantage. Barrie followed him, Miley padding along behind her, and when he'd done up his coat and dropped his hat back on his head, he turned toward Barrie and found her closer than he'd thought. Her tired eyes widened in surprise, too, but before she could step back, he slid an arm around her waist and tugged her closer against him.

Her belly pressed against his abs, and he looked down at those plump, soft lips, feeling an undeniable hunger rise up inside him. He sucked in a breath. He shouldn't do it—he knew that. He should walk out and not give himself more to apologize for tomorrow. Barrie was pregnant, sexy as anything, but also vulnerable. This wasn't a game—

She rose onto the tips of her toes, and her eyes fluttered shut as her lips touched his so lightly that it almost tickled.

"Ah, hell…" he murmured, and he lowered his mouth over hers, deepening the kiss, pulling her harder against him. The room evaporated around him, and there was only Barrie in his arms and her lips moving against his…

But then Miley gave a yip, and Barrie pulled back. Her cheeks blushed crimson and she touched her fingers to her mouth.

"I should go," he murmured.

She nodded. "Yes. Leave. Bye."

Curtis chuckled. Did she mean that? He doubted it. If he pressed the issue he could probably get her into his arms again…but this wasn't right.

"Okay," he said, pulling open the door. "I'll see you."

Barrie nodded, but her eyes still sparkled with that kiss. She'd felt it, too. He could tell. He stepped outside, and she shut the door firmly behind him. They had no business doing this again—it couldn't end well. But at least that kiss hadn't been one-sided. She'd felt it, too.

Chapter 9

Barrie leaned against the door, shut her eyes and let out a soft moan. What had she just done? She'd started that, and he'd most definitely finished it. Kissing him had *not* been part of the plan!

Maybe it was his consideration in cooking for her and rubbing her feet... That had been the first time since she'd announced her pregnancy that anyone had done something like that for her. She didn't have a boyfriend, and she'd been so determined to prove she didn't need one that she hadn't been prepared for how good it would feel to have someone take care of her for a change. Add to that his way of looking at her, which had always dissolved her reserve...

"What was I thinking?" She opened her eyes and

found Miley staring at her with a look of reproach on his canine face. "I know. It was a bad idea."

And if only that kiss had proved he couldn't still make her feel like she was floating…if only that part had changed. But it hadn't…or more accurately, their level of attraction hadn't changed, but kissing him *had* been different than before… Curtis was no longer the eager twenty-year-old. He was a man who had showed some reserve, some self-control. And when he'd finally kissed her, there was something deeper, more urgent than she'd ever sensed from him.

She didn't get to blame this one on him, either. That was irritating, too. He'd been holding himself back. Sure, he'd pulled her close, but she'd seen the battle on his face, and she'd made the choice for him.

"Stupid, stupid, stupid," she muttered to herself as she flicked the lock on the door and headed toward her bedroom. Was she really so vulnerable right now that a little bit of kindness and a foot rub could empty her head of all logical thought? Curtis was still the same guy he always was. He'd only just stopped bull riding, and it had taken him fifteen years to give it up! This wasn't a different man, just an older version of the same guy who'd never been husband enough.

Barrie sank onto the side of her bed. She had a baby coming, and enough problems of her own that the last thing she needed was more complication… She wouldn't do that again.

Her cell phone rang, and Barrie looked at the number. She heaved a sigh, then picked up the call.

"Dr. Berton?" she said.

"Dr. Jones. How are you doing?"

"Fine, thanks," she replied. "What can I do for you?"

There was a pause. "Can I call you Barrie?"

"If I can call you Palmer." She was in no mood to be patronized today.

"Fair enough," he replied. "Barrie, I have a proposition for you."

"Oh?" She didn't even try to hide the wariness in her tone.

"I want you to work for me again," he said.

"You've got to be joking," she retorted. "We've done this before, Palmer. We don't work well together. I drive you crazy, if you'll recall."

"You're a good vet."

"I'm more than good," she said. "I'm also rather stubborn and do things my own way."

"I'd pay you well, provide health insurance and give you a more regular schedule. With the baby coming, I'm sure that would be helpful."

"Where is this coming from?" she asked.

"I think it would be beneficial for both of us," he replied. "I'm getting older, and I find it hard to keep up with the caseload. But still, I have the most clients, and I have thirty years of experience in this community. You're having a baby soon, and you won't be able to keep up with the emergency calls anymore. We could both benefit from working together."

"Under your shingle," she clarified.

"Yes. I've worked for this longer. I'm sure you can recognize that."

"I've worked for this, too," she said.

"Be reasonable…" Palmer sighed.

"I'm not interested." She covered her eyes with one hand. "I'm sorry."

"Barrie, I'm a father. I know the changes in your life that are coming up. Babies take over everything—"

"I've worked too hard to build my practice to dump it now!" Barrie tried to calm her rising anger. "And what do you care about my work-life balance? I'm competition, that's all."

"You are competition," he said. "And I'd much rather work with you than against you. We're both good vets, Barrie. Together we would service all of this county."

"We could do that separately, too," she replied. "If you were so interested in working with me, you'd offer to be partners—fifty-fifty."

"No." He barked out a bitter laugh. "I've been at this for thirty years. You've been on your own for what… three years?"

"Four."

"Four years," he conceded. "Does that seem fair to you, that I should share everything down the middle after having built up my own practice all this time?"

"I really have no interest in working *for* you," she said. "I'm sorry. I like being my own boss, and I'm not willing to give that up."

"Fine," he said. "Fair enough. Don't say I didn't offer."

There was something both final and cautionary in his tone, and Barrie's senses tingled. This was more than a passing offer. She could feel it.

"Does this have to do with the building I lease?" she asked.

He was silent for a moment. "I'm buying it, Barrie."

"I heard," she said. "So what's the plan there? Are you going to push me out of my office space?"

"I'm planning on opening a second clinic," he said. "I wanted you to be my assistant vet. You'd be able to stay where you are and I'd give you a cut in your current lease."

"Assistant vet..." she murmured.

"Yes."

She sighed. The cut in her lease was tempting, but working under Palmer Berton again...she just couldn't do it!

"Thank you for thinking of me, but it's too hard to go back to working for someone else, Palmer. I'm sure you can understand that."

"You really can't humble yourself to work for me?" he asked incredulously.

"Humble myself?" she snapped. "Would you have given up your practice four years in?"

"I wasn't a single parent," he said, his voice quiet. "Your situation is different from mine. You should give this some serious thought."

She wanted to find her own solution, but she had a suspicion that wasn't going to be so easy. Palmer Berton had confirmed that he was buying her clinic space, which was good information to have, but now she was backed into a corner. She'd have to find a new space to lease and renovate it to suit her purposes all before the baby was born. And then what? He had a point.

None of this would be easy. She'd been hoping to build herself up enough that she could survive without the emergency calls, but what if she couldn't? Dr. Berton expanding to two offices might affect her ability to do so. She still didn't have a solution for all of the changes coming up. Dr. Berton's offer was actually logical. Except she hadn't worked this hard for this long to just give up her autonomy.

"Dr. Berton," she said at last. "I appreciate the offer, and I can see the benefits of your plan. I'm not turning you down because I'm angry or dislike you. This isn't personal. This is about my practice, and that's personal in a whole different way. I'm determined to stay afloat on my own."

"You're sure?"

Was this just a little bit of pride getting in her way? Possibly. "I'm sure. But thank you for the offer."

"Alright then." Dr. Berton sighed. "I'll be in touch when the sale is final, and we can hammer out the details for your exit."

Was she an idiot for holding out, hoping for some solution to present itself? But she knew that she'd regret it more if she agreed to something prematurely and discovered later that she could have kept her own practice intact. That would hurt a whole lot more.

"I suppose there is no way around that," she said. "Have a good night."

She hung up the phone and tossed it onto her bedside table. Miley sat down in front of her and leaned his large head into her lap, soulful eyes looking up at her. Dr. Berton didn't need to do this. He already ran his own practice. He didn't need to expand to swallow her little corner of the business, too, yet he was doing it.

"Blast," she muttered and sucked in a shaky breath. She smoothed a hand over Miley's head and gave him a sad smile.

"I didn't work this hard to lose it, Miley," she said, and Miley looked back at her in silence. She liked things planned and predictable. She liked to know what was coming and be prepared for the worst. Ironically, that was exactly what Dr. Berton was offering her—stability. But she just couldn't work for him. She still had her pride.

The next evening, Curtis stopped off at the Honky Tonk for a beer. It was located in the west end of town—a short, dumpy building with a neon sign that flickered and buzzed in a blacked out window. He didn't come to the bar often; in fact, he hadn't been here since he'd arrived back in Hope, but he needed some space to himself, and the Honky Tonk seemed like the place to get it.

Curtis ordered himself a beer—his limit, since he'd be driving later—and headed toward the back of the bar, which was a little less populated. A few Christmas decorations were up—a faded wreath on one wall, some garland hung in loops along the front counter. A green felt pool table had a few cowboys surrounding it, and across from the pool table were a dartboard and a couple of old guys playing. Their aim was remarkably good for their level of inebriation. The Honky Tonk was the kind of place that was depressing if you weren't already half in the bag, and the last fifteen years hadn't improved it.

In fact, back when he'd been married, Barrie had made him promise that he wouldn't go there. Controlling, his friends had called it, but he'd understood her fear. All too many guys drank away their paychecks in the Honky Tonk, then went home to their wives with their tails between their legs. Curtis had never wanted to be one of them. It had been one of his and Barrie's deals—marriage being full of deals, he'd found out. Sitting here now still felt like a betrayal to her, but he wasn't sure why. He wasn't her husband and he owed her nothing when it came to his leisure time or his paychecks.

Curtis sat near the back, his beer in front of him and his elbows on the table. The jukebox played a mournful holiday tune about a cowboy grieving a lost love, which wasn't doing much for his mood right now. He hadn't expected to feel that strongly about Barrie—not after all these years. He was no longer the hot-headed cowboy with six-pack abs. And she was no longer the slim girl with the shining eyes. They were both older, and in his case, a little more beaten up. But the sensation of her body pulled hard against his was so sharp in his memory that his heart sped up even thinking about it. She was softer now, rounder, and very obviously pregnant. She was attractive in a whole new way that fired his blood up like some young buck. He knew better than to go there again, so what had happened?

Barrie was still the same woman who hadn't been able to trust him with her future. Nothing had changed there. Except, she'd had a point—what about her career? They could have sorted out something between them, but staying with him, she'd never have achieved quite so much. He didn't like that thought—he'd wanted to give her more, not hold her back. If anything, she'd only proved herself right. She was better off without him—definitely more successful than he'd turned out to be. Maybe that should prove something to him, too, but she was also still the same woman who could turn his logical mind to mush just by being close enough to let him smell her perfume.

And he'd kissed her... She'd kissed him first, but he didn't have to take over quite so thoroughly. He could have given her a quick peck and headed on out, but once her lips had touched his, there was no going back. He'd wanted to do that for far too long now. He wished he could say that the kiss had gotten it out of his system, but it had only whetted his appetite.

Curtis let his gaze move around the bar, and he recognized a couple of guys from high school. Dwight Petersen was there—looking scruffy and sweaty. Curtis wasn't in any rush to reintroduce himself—he'd come here for some quiet, after all—but the drunk cowboy's words were filtering across the bar.

"Dakota never loved Andy," Dwight was saying, his words slurred. "She married him for the money."

"I don't know, man," the fellow sitting next to him said with a shake of his head. "They seem good together."

"He was my best friend!" Dwight was getting emotional now. "A guy doesn't move in on another guy's woman!"

"Yeah, yeah..."

The tabletop in front of the two men was strewn with empty bottles. They'd been at this a while. He wondered how often Dwight had gone over this same sob story. Dakota was now happily married to Andy—Dwight might want to let it go already.

"You got to just move on," the other man said, setting his drink down with a clunk. "Just…just…move on!"

Amen, buddy, Curtis thought ruefully. Sage advice from a drunk guy. Moving on wasn't so easy when a guy's heart was in the wringer, though.

The two men hashed over the unfairness of it all for a few more minutes, and then there seemed to be a change of topic.

"You know who I'd do?" Dwight's tone turned slimy. Curtis grimaced. Did Dwight have any idea how disgusting he sounded or how far his voice carried?

"Who?" The friend was all ears now and Curtis looked away.

"That hot little vet." Dwight laughed coarsely. "We were friends a long time ago. Ran in the same circles. She was hot then, and she's hot now. Legs up to here and…" He continued with a lengthy, detailed description of her body—or at least, what he imagined it to look like. Curtis clenched his teeth and glared in Dwight's direction.

"She don't want you." The friend guffawed.

"I say she does." Dwight leaned toward his friend. "I see the way she looks at me. She always did have a thing for me. And the next time I see her, I'm going to—" He made a grotesque motion with one hand and laughed loudly.

This was just drunken talk—at least that's what Curtis wanted to believe, but he didn't like the sound of what Dwight was blathering on about. Barrie never had a "thing" for Dwight, but that wasn't what grated on him. This wasn't just some unknown woman. This was Barrie...pregnant and vulnerable Barrie, who Dwight was promising to manhandle like a piece of meat. The thought was infuriating.

"She's pregnant, though," the friend said. Even drunk, he seemed to have a moral fiber in there somewhere.

"Single, though," Dwight countered. "And I heard what she likes—"

There was more talk that made Curtis's blood simmer—descriptions of all sorts of sordid things that Dwight was positive Barrie would appreciate, and Curtis clenched his fists so hard that he heard his knuckles pop.

"I'm telling you, she'd want it," Dwight went on. "She might say no, but I'd do unforgivable things to that woman—"

That was all Curtis could handle, and he rose to his feet and took three slow steps toward the other table, his boots thunking loudly against the wood floor. He slammed his bottle down on the scratched tabletop with a bang.

"Evening, Dwight," he growled.

Dwight blinked up at him. "Hey."

"You're talking pretty loudly there."

"So?" Dwight snapped. "What's it to you?"

"I don't like how you're talking," Curtis replied,

keeping his voice low. "You mind keeping that filth to yourself?"

"What, about that hot vet?" Dwight asked with a laugh. "What do you care?" The man paused and squinted. "Wait... Curtis Porter?"

"One and the same." Curtis bared his teeth in what he meant to be a chilly smile, but he wasn't sure he managed even that much.

"No offense, man," Dwight said, the color draining from his face.

"I mean it—shut your mouth about her," Curtis growled.

Dwight was silent for a moment, then frowned. "It's not like you want her. What do you care?"

Drunken logic never ran smooth, and Curtis shook his head. "Don't push this, Dwight. You're drunk. Maybe it's time you went home."

"Even if she begs me for it?" Dwight sneered. He lifted his hand in the grotesque gesture once more, and Curtis grabbed the man's middle finger and bent it back until the oily grin on Dwight's face evaporated into a grimace of pain.

"Hey, leave him alone!" the friend bellowed, rising to his feet, his chair clattering behind him. The man pulled out something that glinted in the low light, and Curtis's first thought was of a blade. He couldn't be sure, but he wasn't working with rational thought right now. It was instinct.

Curtis put out an elbow. It caught the other man in the chin with a hollow sound not unlike a dropped melon, and when Dwight jerked his hand free and bounded to his feet, Curtis had no choice. Dwight's fist was already coming toward him. Curtis dodged the drunken blow and landed one of his own.

The fight was on, he realized dismally, and he could either fight back or get himself beaten to a pulp. Considering his mood right now and the way Dwight had been talking about Barrie, he opted for the first choice— much preferable. Besides, on the off chance that Dwight had been serious about assaulting a woman, he'd make sure he dissuaded the moron from ever thinking about it again.

"Call the cops!" Curtis heard someone bellow just as a punch landed on the side of his head, sending him to the ground in a cloud of stars. He was up again a moment later, dizzy, but able to block another blow and deliver a solid punch of his own. He watched his hand connect with Dwight's face in the most satisfying way, and the smaller man crumpled to the ground. That one was for Barrie.

Then something else hit him from behind and there was a blaze of stars once more.

Dammit...was his last thought before he lost consciousness.

Chapter 10

Barrie awoke to the sound of her cell phone ringing from the bedside table, and she shot out a hand and groped around until she connected with it. Her body felt like it was filled with cement, but her mind was already trying to focus. She got emergency calls on a regular basis, so she was already pushing past the fog of sleep, wondering what might be the issue. She opened her eyes enough to see the screen and picked up the call.

"Dr. Jones," she said.

"Barrie, this is Detective Mike Cruise at the Hope sheriff's office. I'm sorry to wake you."

Mike—Mallory's sheriff husband?

"It's fine…" She rubbed her free hand over her eyes. "Hi, Mike. What's the problem? Is everything okay?"

"We have your ex-husband in custody, and he gave us your number," Mike replied.

The detective's words slowly sank into her mind, and she squinted at the clock beside her bed. It was past midnight. "You have Curtis at the sheriff's office?" She was awake now, and she pushed herself up onto her elbow. "What happened?"

"He was arrested in an altercation at the Honky Tonk" came the reply. "Are you willing to pick him up?" There was a pause and a murmur in the background. "Mr. Porter asks that you be told that he wasn't drunk."

That sounded like a drunk Curtis thing to say.

"So *was* he drunk, or not?" she demanded. "What happened?"

"No, he wasn't. His alcohol levels were within the legal limits, but he was arrested for assault and battery." Mike's voice softened. "You don't have to come, Barrie. I can drop him off at Betty's place after my shift tonight. Thing is, he's refusing medical attention, and I'd rather not have him bleed all over my cruiser, if it's all the same…"

Mike had always had a dry sense of humor and Barrie shook her head. Some things didn't change—like the rebel bull rider who lived for adventure. But a bar fight? And here she'd been lying in bed last night, wondering about that kiss, wondering if fifteen years had changed anything in Curtis. Apparently, not enough!

"Is he okay?" she asked reluctantly.

"More or less," Detective Cruise replied. "But I'm not willing to just release him on his own right now.

He needs more TLC than I'm willing to provide at the moment."

So he was roughed up, too. She sighed. "Okay. I won't be long."

"Thanks, Barrie," Mike replied. "I'm sorry about this."

"Is isn't your fault, Mike," she said. "See you soon."

Barrie hung up the phone and swung her legs over the side of her bed. Curtis at the sheriff's office in the middle of the night... He'd always been impetuous, and this was the reason she'd made him promise that he'd never go back to the Honky Tonk—she didn't want this life, and she'd seen it too often in her own extended family. She had an uncle who drank his family into the poorhouse, and a few cousins who did the same. She'd seen it all up close and personal.

Her alarm at being woken up by a call from the sheriff's office was quickly melting into anger as she pulled on her clothes. Miley didn't even move from his spot on the end of her bed. He lay with his head drooping over one edge and his tail flopping off the other, and he didn't look inclined to get up.

"Miley," she said, patting his rear as she passed him to grab her sweater. "Let's go. You're coming with me."

Miley made a groaning noise, then stretched so that his long legs moved into the center of the bed. Yes, it looked wonderfully comfortable, but if Barrie had to go outside into the cold at midnight, then so did Miley. Fair was fair.

"Come on, lazy bones," she said as she pulled the sweater over her belly. "I need your gallant protection."

Barrie headed out of the bedroom and toward the door, and she heard the sound of Miley's reluctant feet hitting the floor mingled with the jangle of his collar. Miley might not like his slumber disturbed, but his loyalty outweighed his comfort. By the time Barrie had her boots and coat on, Miley was waiting by her side.

Luckily she'd picked up her truck that morning—ready just as the mechanic had promised. The drive to the sheriff's office was short, and after she'd parked, she held open the door for Miley to accompany her. If she was being dragged from her bed at midnight, then the sheriffs could deal with a non-therapy dog in the precinct.

"Hi, Barrie," Mike said as she came through the front door.

"Hi." Barrie nodded toward Miley. "I hope you don't mind, but I didn't want to leave him in the cold."

"No problem." Mike held out his hand, and she shook it. "Mallory's going to kill me for even calling you for this."

Barrie smiled wanly. "She might. So where is he?"

"In the interview room."

"Miley, sit." She turned to her dog and took his large face between her hands. "Stay."

Miley lowered himself onto his haunches, and Barrie followed Mike past the desks, where a couple of officers were typing away on their computers, and the coffee machine, which smelled like the last pot had burned. The interview room was toward the back of the station, and her heart sped up as Mike gripped the knob, then turned back to her.

"He's not pretty," Mike apologized. "And that isn't my fault. I wanted to bring him to the hospital."

"Okay." She nodded. How bad was it that Mike felt the need to warn her?

Mike opened the door then stepped back. As Barrie entered the fluorescent-lit room, she spotted Curtis, a towel and an ice pack held to one side of his face. When he saw Barrie, he grimaced.

"Hi," he said.

Barrie dropped her purse on a table and crossed the room. "Let me see."

"It's not too bad," Curtis said.

"Mike disagrees," she replied. "Show me."

Curtis eased the towel off his face, revealing an eye swollen painfully and a gash above it that had already been butterfly stitched by Mike, she assumed. Her stomach flipped, and she looked away for a moment. She hadn't expected to feel like this. She was a vet— she saw gross and painful injuries on a regular basis.

"I'm fine," Curtis growled. "It'll heal."

"You are not fine, Curtis!" A sob rose in her chest. "What were you thinking?"

She'd been prepared for anger, not for the urge to sit down and cry. She was blaming this on the pregnancy.

"I wasn't drunk."

"A point in your favor," she snapped. "Sort of! So you managed this *sober*?"

"There were extenuating circumstances," he replied, pushing himself to his feet. "Thanks for coming, Barrie. I didn't want to give them anyone's number, but

Detective Cruise there insisted, if I wanted to be let out of here."

Barrie glanced back. Mike had left the room, and they were in relative privacy.

"Mike says you should have gone to the hospital," she said.

"Barrie, I've gotten some nasty injuries riding bulls," he said with a sigh. "I have a pretty good sense of when I'm hurt or not. This is cosmetic. It'll heal."

He was just as stubborn as he'd always been—the same old Curtis. So why couldn't she put aside the way he made her feel?

"So, what was this about?" she asked.

"Dwight Petersen," he replied. "You don't want to know."

"I just got up in the middle of the night to pick you up from the sheriff's station. I absolutely do want to know," she retorted.

Curtis picked up his jacket and winced as he attempted to pull it on. So it wasn't just his face. She put a hand on his arm to stop him and felt down his ribs. Curtis grimaced as she got to a puffy place on his side. A cracked rib, too, no doubt. Broken ribs felt the same on animals as they did on people.

"Dwight Petersen had a few things to say about you," Curtis said, catching her wrist to stop her probing. "And I didn't like it."

"What things?" she asked, pulling her hand free of his grasp.

"Things I don't care to repeat," he said, but she

caught the glimmer of disgust in Curtis's dark eyes. Had it been that bad?

"So you started a fight?" she asked.

"I didn't start anything. Okay…maybe I was the first to lay a hand on the slimy twit, but if he ever considered acting on the ugly things he was saying, I wanted him to associate that with a little pain."

"What did he say?" Wariness wormed up inside her.

"He was describing an assault," Curtis replied grimly. "Stay clear of him."

"Oh…" She licked her lips, her bravado slipping away. "Where is he now?"

"He went to the hospital," Curtis replied. "Mike says he'll keep an eye on him. He's definitely on their radar now."

Did that mean that Dwight was in worse shape than Curtis? And was she hoping so?

"For the record, I wasn't the one who beat him so badly. Apparently there were other guys who had a beef with him, too. I was already knocked out cold when they got to Dwight."

That did make her feel a little better, actually. The thought of Curtis beating on some man—deservedly or not—was enough to turn her stomach.

"So you didn't hurt him?" She heard the tremor in her own voice.

"Not very much." He smiled down at her, then grimaced in pain. "I got in one solid right hook. That's it."

"I never liked the Honky Tonk," she said.

"I know." Curtis reached forward and brushed a tendril of hair away from her face. "I'm sorry about this,

Barrie. I had to give them a number or end up in a cell tonight. Maybe I should have taken the cell."

"No." She sighed. "Come on. I'll take you back to my place and get you cleaned up. You can sleep on my couch tonight, if you want."

"I don't need babying," he said. "If you'd just drop me off at my truck, I can take it from there."

Curtis might not want babying, but he hadn't grown up much in the last fifteen years. If he had changed, he wouldn't have been in the bar to begin with, and he'd never have let himself get goaded into some stupid fight.

Barrie shot Curtis a disappointed look as he eased into the cab of her SUV. Yeah, that was familiar. Miley jumped into the back seat, and she slammed the door. He leaned over to push the driver's side door open, and a stab of pain shot through his ribs.

"I always hated this," Barrie said as she hoisted herself into the driver's seat, ignoring his grunt of pain as he pulled himself into an upright position again.

"This is my first bar brawl," he replied with a small smile.

"I hated picking you up with broken ribs, a cast, a split lip…" She turned the key and the engine rumbled to life. "But it was your choice. You loved bull riding, and nothing I ever said could keep you from it."

"This was a little different," he said.

"Not to me." She pulled out of the parking lot and onto Montana Avenue. "This is exactly the same from where I'm sitting. I get a call, and I come pick you up in pieces."

"Barrie, I'm fine." Curtis heaved an irritated sigh. "I get that I'm not pretty right now, but a cold steak on this eye and I'll be presentable."

Barrie didn't answer, and Curtis turned his attention to the streets sliding past. He knew her well enough to see that under that veneer of anger was fear. This had scared her—and, well, it should. A fight hadn't been his intention, but if he could redo tonight, he couldn't say that he'd do anything differently. She hadn't heard the things Dwight had said, and if Curtis had his way, she never would. That would scare her a whole lot more than his mangled mug. They were approaching the turn for the Honky Tonk, but she didn't seem to be slowing down.

"My truck is in the bar parking lot," he said.

"Hmm." She passed the turn without even a glance.

"So you're not dropping me off at my truck," he clarified.

"You're coming home with me," she replied, her tone icy.

"You don't have to do this," he said.

"I really *shouldn't* have to do this!" Barrie shot him an angry look. "I'm taking you back to my place and giving you that cold steak for your eye. If you want your truck so badly tonight, you can damn well walk to the Honky Tonk, but I'm not leaving you there."

Curtis wasn't sure how to answer that—this was a Barrie he'd never seen before. Back in their married days, she'd have yelled and cried. She'd even kicked him out a couple of times. But whatever lecture might have been coming his way back then didn't seem forthcoming now. It stood to reason—they were no longer married. But taking him back to her place was no longer necessary, either.

Barrie signaled the turn onto her street.

"I appreciate the gesture," he said. "But I'm not exactly helpless here."

Barrie pulled into her drive and parked. Then she turned toward him. "So I'm supposed to just not worry about you, then? I should just crawl back into my bed and forget all about you?"

"It's what most exes do."

"I guess I'm not like most." She got out of the truck and slammed her door. Curtis looked back at Miley, who met Curtis's gaze with a mournful look of his own.

"Women, am I right?" Curtis muttered.

Then Barrie pulled open the back door to let Miley out. The dog looked between Curtis and his mistress, then scrambled down and into the snow. Curtis opened his own door and headed around the vehicle. Barrie hadn't waited for him, and she stood with her back to him while she unlocked the front door. Miley was marking a bush at the side of the house.

"Come on," Barrie said, her tone softening, and when he and Miley both moved toward her, he suddenly wondered which one of them she'd been talking to. Whatever. He'd take her up on that offer of a cold steak, and after that, he'd leave her alone.

When Curtis got inside, he managed to ease out of his coat without any help. Those ribs were bruised, not broken—he knew the difference from experience. Bull riding was harder on a body than bar brawls.

"Sit," Barrie ordered, pulling out a kitchen chair.

Miley dropped into a seated position, and the dog shot Curtis a sidelong look.

"He seems to know when you're serious." Curtis chuckled, and he headed for the chair that Barrie indicated.

"Not you, silly," Barrie said, rubbing her hand over Miley's head. Then she went to the fridge and pulled out a bowl of fresh meat cuts.

"So you just have beef in your fridge all the time?" he asked incredulously.

"It's Miley's, so yes," she said, picking through the bowl until she came up with a marbled, gristly piece of meat that looked big enough. Then she came over to where he sat and looked down on him. Her eyes had lost the angry glitter, leaving her looking tired and sad.

"You sure you don't want to just yell at me like the good old days?" he asked testily. Honestly, it would have been easier to tune her out if she'd just tell him off.

"I think we're past that, aren't we?" She carefully laid the meat over his swollen eye. "There."

Miley, still seated, eyed the meat on Curtis's face covetously. Barrie took another couple of pieces of meat to Miley's bowl and dropped them in. Miley followed and gulped them down in two mouthfuls.

"Why did you like it so much?" she asked after a moment of silence. "The bull riding, I mean."

"Adrenaline," he replied. "It makes you feel alive—man against beast." Not unlike a bar fight with Dwight, ironically enough.

"Hmm." She turned on the tap and washed her hands.

"And that was enough to endure the broken bones and concussions and—" she turned the water off "—the pain?"

"I survived." He attempted to turn and look at her, but his side was too sore to allow the twisting motion.

"You never did think of what it did to me, did you?" She pulled out the chair opposite him, then sank into it. "Do you know what it's like to see the man you love in that state?"

"It's part of the sport, Barrie—"

"I know, I know." She sighed. "And it's no longer my business. But all of this—" she gestured to his face "—is a little too familiar."

Her sitting in the kitchen late at night, looking pale and drawn—yeah, this was pretty familiar to him, too. Them butting heads over what he wanted, and what she wanted... It was exhausting.

"I wasn't trying to hurt you back then," he said. "I needed the outlet. I mean, I was no good at school, and bull riding was the one thing that people gave me some credit for. I needed that. You were smart, going places. Everyone said so. I was—" He shrugged, unsure of how to finish that. He was the guy no one thought was good enough for the likes of Barrie Jones.

"You were smart, too," she countered.

Curtis didn't answer. He didn't need to be soothed or mollycoddled. He knew the score, and he'd made his peace with it over the years. Some guys were better at book work, and some guys had better instincts with hands-on work. Curtis was the latter, and that eight-second ride was his proof. That was the one place that his skill set—agility, instinct and bullheaded courage—seemed to matter. Because it sure hadn't been enough to keep him married.

"I loved you, Curtis." She sighed softly. "I really did. And every time you came home with a broken bone or a nasty sprain, it meant that you were choosing an eight-second thrill over me."

"You had me for life, Barrie. You couldn't give me eight seconds?"

"It's my fault, really." Barrie pushed herself to her feet, one hand in the small of her back. "I thought I could tame you."

She started to move past him again, and he shot out his hand and caught her wrist. "You did."

"I thought you'd turn into a family man," she said. "I thought you'd come home to me in the evenings, and we'd talk and cuddle. I thought you'd become a husband and maybe—" she tugged her wrist free of his grasp "—and maybe a father."

Curtis dropped his hand. "I wasn't ready to be a dad back then. I told you that all the time."

"I know."

That had been a source of arguments, too. She wanted a baby right away. That was before she changed her mind and decided she wanted school first. They'd both been young, and she hadn't found her path yet, apparently. For Curtis, he'd wanted to have some fun. Just because they were married didn't mean they had to start with all the heavy responsibilities so soon. They were young and healthy and in love… Frankly, he was more concerned about his time with her between the sheets than he was with starting a family.

"A baby wouldn't have made things easier between us," he added.

"I know that, too." She smiled tiredly. "And you want to know something? I was dumb enough back then to think that a baby would nail you down with us, give you another reason to drop the bull riding and do something serious."

"Yeah?" He'd suspected as much, but he was surprised to hear her admit to it. She went back to the counter and flicked on the electric kettle. Her voice came from behind him, so he couldn't see her face.

"I've done a lot of thinking about it over the years, and I realized that while I loved you for who you were, I wanted to marry you for your potential to be...more. And that doesn't work. I was trying to change you into a different man, and I thought that marriage *would* change you."

Which was why she never should have married him to begin with. He heard that loud and clear. And while he could agree on a logical, mental level, his heart ached.

"I always was too stubborn for my own good," he said.

"Yes, you were." She came back and sat down again.

"I think we both had an idea of what marriage would be, and we never really talked about it," he said. "Or maybe we already knew that if we put all our cards on the table it wouldn't work."

"Maybe," she said. "Everyone told us to think it

through, and we were determined to plow ahead anyway."

More than determined. Desperate. All he'd wanted was to make it legal, claim her as his… If only he'd known how hard marriage would turn out to be. Love wasn't enough when building a life with a woman.

"I might have been a stubborn lout, but for what it's worth, I loved you."

She smiled sadly, then dropped her gaze to the table. "I know."

Of all the tangle of things he wished he could tell her, that was the most important. They might have been mismatched from the start, but he'd been there for the right reasons. The kettle started to whistle, breaking the moment.

"Do you want tea?" she asked.

"No, thanks." He pulled the piece of meat off his eye. "What I want is for you to go to bed and get some rest. I feel bad enough having woken you up."

"I can make you a bed on the couch," she said.

"No." That's where this ended. He wasn't a bedraggled kitten to be cared for by Barrie's big heart. Besides, if he had to spend the night a stone's throw from her bedroom, she'd either end up kicking him out, or he'd convince her to do something they'd both regret the next morning. "I'm going to walk over to the Honky Tonk and pick up my truck."

"But you're—"

"I'm fine," he interrupted her. "Look." He could feel that the swelling on his eye had gone down already.

Barrie put out one hand and gingerly touched his

temple. Her fingers lingered, and Curtis put a hand over hers. Looking at her—her eyes bleary with exhaustion, her hair mussed and her belly domed out in front of her—he wanted to be the one to take care of her, not the other way around. He wanted to pull her into his arms and prove just how "fine" he really was, and that mental image was so strong, he had to shut his eyes to vanquish it. He'd already let things go too far in this kitchen once already, and he wasn't going to do that again.

"I'll get going," he said, and he rose to his feet.

This time when he went to the door, he kept his hands to his sides. "Thank you, Barrie."

He meant for tonight, for fifteen years ago when she'd shared her life with him for just a short while... for enduring the frustration that came with an emotionally stunted bull rider.

"Don't mention it."

Curtis settled his hat back on his head and opened the door. He'd get his truck and go back to the ranch. Chores would be waiting at 4:00 a.m. whether he was ready or not. And he needed to think clearly. Frustrating as it was, Barrie still seemed capable of firing his blood without any effort on her part.

Chapter 11

Barrie stood in her kitchen the next morning, a mug of tea on the counter next to a stack of buttered toast. It was Saturday, and her clinic was closed, except for emergency calls. She was glad for the quiet and the time to herself. She'd slept in after her late night with Curtis, and she'd woken up feeling restless and uncertain.

Curtis was getting under her skin again, and she hated that. They'd always had an unexplainable chemistry. Even when she'd been furious with him last night, she'd felt it—that desire to take care of him, clean him up, give him some comfort.

"Miley, that man isn't my problem anymore," she said, carrying the tea and toast to the table. "You'd think I could remember that."

Miley followed her, his eyes pinned to her plate of

toast. She chuckled and tore off a crust for him, which he swallowed in one gulp.

But Curtis had felt it, too, last night. She'd seen that hungry look in his eye and the dogged determination to keep it in check. She knew his tells, and when his jaw tensed and his gaze grew laser focused, she knew what he was thinking. The realization sent shivers through her. The physical aspect of their relationship had always been amazing. He could coax pleasure out of her that she hadn't even known was possible. But she pushed those memories back. Their sensual connection hadn't been enough to save their marriage, and it wasn't enough to start something up again.

He'd been right to leave instead of staying the night. She'd never have slept properly knowing he was out there on the couch. She was as bad as he was when it came to their attraction. Their feelings for each other had always been intense—both the chemistry and the frustration when they just couldn't seem to get on the same page, and she knew better than to toy with impulses that strong.

Barrie's cell phone blipped, and she glanced down at an incoming text from Mallory:

Mike told me about Curtis. What happened?

Long story, she typed back. Too much to text.

How about a little shopping? Mike will take the kids for the morning.

Barrie sighed. Did she really want to do this? She was already wound up about Curtis, and shopping wasn't exactly relaxing... But this might be good for her—get her out of her head a little bit. She picked up the phone and typed back:

Sure. I'll meet you at the store. What time?

An hour later, Barrie arrived at Hope's one and only maternity shop, Blooming Motherhood. Mallory met her on the sidewalk out front, holding two coffees. Mallory's sandy-blond hair was pulled back in a ponytail, and her cheeks were rosy from the cold. She passed a cup to Barrie.

"Really?" Barrie broke into a smile. "Thanks."

"I had a feeling you could use it after last night," Mallory replied. "So how are you?"

"I'm fine," Barrie said, taking a sip of what turned out to be a hazelnut latte. "He's the same guy he's always been, just a bit older. I don't know what to say."

"What happened after you picked him up from the station?" Mallory pressed.

"I took him back to my place and put a steak on his eye, and then he left." Barrie shrugged. "It was all so familiar—bandaging up my broken cowboy... I can't do it anymore."

"But this was different, wasn't it?" Mallory asked. "He wasn't bull riding, at least."

"When he left, I went to bed, and instead of remembering the good times with Curtis, all I could think about was how shredded I felt when he left me. I still remember waking up the next morning after he'd packed his bag and stomped out, and thinking, 'He'll come back. He always comes back.' And I was planning on punishing him a little bit. Maybe being gone when he finally did. Let him feel some of the pain I felt. But…" Barrie shrugged. "That was the last time."

"What did you fight about?" Mallory asked.

"Curtis was offered a chance to do the bull riding circuit," Barrie replied. "We'd been fighting about everything at that point, and when I said forget it, he said that I was controlling. And that stabbed, because I wasn't trying to control him…" Barrie sighed. "Or maybe I was. I wanted to make him into a stable husband, and that wasn't Curtis. Long story short, we both said things that we couldn't take back, and I told him to get out. And he did."

Barrie's eyes misted and she shook her head. "You see? This is stupid! It was fifteen years ago, but seeing him again has been harder than I thought."

Mallory reached out and squeezed Barrie's hand. "We never quite forget the ones that got away, do we?"

"Apparently not," Barrie agreed. "But it was for the best. If he was going to leave me, better sooner than later, I guess." She hadn't intended to get into all of this on the street, and her cheeks flushed. "Let's go in. I'm cold."

Once they were inside, the shopkeeper called out a cheery hello. Barrie looked around at the various pregnant mannequins and heaved a sigh. She didn't know where to start. Before this belly, she knew what she liked—jeans, fitted tees and the odd sweater. But even her largest sweaters were starting to get snug.

"What about this?" Mallory asked, holding up a shirt.

Barrie eyed it for a moment, not sure what to think. Mallory's expression softened, and she stepped closer. "Do you hate it? Like it? I need a reaction here."

Barrie shrugged. "I don't even know."

"You look like you're hiding, Barrie."

"What?" Barrie looked from the shirt to her friend.

"Your pregnancy," Mallory clarified. "You look like you're trying to hide it instead of celebrate it. And I know all about that. I tried to hide my pregnancy with Beau until the last possible minute. If I could undo that, I would. You deserve to enjoy this."

"This town doesn't want to celebrate this baby," Barrie replied, her voice low. "I'm the scandal, remember?"

"You're pregnant, you're beautiful and this baby is already loved," Mallory replied, meeting her gaze. "Dress like it."

Her friend was right. She might not feel like flaunting this pregnancy, but she did love her baby already, and her child deserved to be celebrated by her, at the very least. Barrie looked around at the various styles of shirts, and she spotted a fitted striped sweater with a cowl neck that looked cozy and soft. "I like that."

"Good." Mallory went and grabbed one from the rack. "What about this one?"

They picked out a few tops together, then snagged a few pairs of maternity jeans that Barrie had to admit looked a whole lot more comfortable than the low-waisted jeans she was wearing now. The saleswoman gladly put everything aside in a changing room.

"Mike couldn't tell me what happened to Curtis, exactly," Mallory said. "Privacy issues and all that. I know there was a fight at the bar, but that's about it."

"Apparently, Dwight Petersen was saying some horrible things about me," Barrie replied.

"And Curtis stood up for you," her friend concluded.

"It wasn't necessary," she said. She wasn't Curtis's wife anymore, and he didn't get to be all territorial about her. Except she'd gotten the impression that this hadn't just been male ego... Curtis had been scared for her.

"And if he'd just sat there and let him?" Mallory countered.

"I'd never have been the wiser," she replied. "And I'd probably have been happier that way."

"Dwight is a scary guy," Mallory said quietly. "He's angry—like, deep down angry. Mike says I need to stay away from him, too, and Mike doesn't say that kind of thing without good reason. I don't know, Barrie. Maybe it's better that Curtis did something."

Barrie sighed. "I'm more upset with myself, Mal. I kissed him."

"Who?" Mallory gasped.

"Curtis." She shot her friend an incredulous smile. "And it was on me. He'd rubbed my feet, and made me a meal and I guess it just felt really good to be cared for—"

"Was this before or after the bar fight?" Mallory asked.

"Before, which is why that fight is so annoying. I'm not his anymore, and he can't act like I am. One ill-advised kiss doesn't change that."

"Is it possible that old feelings are coming back?"

"And what if they did?" Barrie shook her head. "It doesn't change anything. Mal, I'm having a baby. Babies need stability...and so do I. And Curtis was always the kind of guy who thought stability was boring. If I'm going to have a man in my life, he needs to be someone I can rely on, because I don't have enough strength to be taking care of an impulsive man as well as myself and a newborn. Heck, I didn't have the strength for it when it was only me."

"And he hasn't grown up at all?" Mallory asked. "Fifteen years is a long time. Everyone changes."

"See that's my problem—" Barrie tugged her hair out of her face. "I married him the first time for his potential. I could see the man he could be if he only tried. Just because a man could be something doesn't mean he wants to be. I'm not making that mistake twice."

"No, I hear you there," Mallory agreed. "I'm sorry, Barrie. This can't be easy."

"It's just bad timing," Barrie said. "I'm having a baby and I'm trying to figure out how I'll run my practice and be a mom at the same time. Curtis is selling the building I'm leasing, and Palmer Berton is pushing for me to work for him again... If it weren't for these hormones coursing through my system, I'm sure I'd be a lot more levelheaded."

Except she wasn't actually sure of that. Curtis had

always been her weakness, and he still was, despite everything else that was tipping her world.

Barrie stopped when she saw a party dress that was so beautiful she could hardly imagine wearing it. It was crimson, with a satiny crisscross top that would accentuate her bust and a soft, flowing skirt that would swirl around her legs at a tea length.

"For my party?" Mallory asked hopefully. "You've got the legs for it, Barrie. Not all of us do!"

"I don't know…" Barrie hesitated.

"It's on sale, too!" Mallory turned around the tag and Barrie took a closer look. "Try it on…"

Maybe Mallory was right. It would be nice to feel pretty again, put together. Barrie met her friend's gaze, then smiled. "Alright. I'll splurge for your party."

Curtis couldn't get a parking spot in front of Mutt's Fish and Chips on Main Street, and had to settle for a space across the street and south a few yards. His stomach rumbled. He'd expected to eat lunch at the ranch, like usual, but Betty had hurried him off to town to pick up a prescription. Before she'd hustled him out the door, he noticed that she'd put on some makeup.

"Who are you dressing up for?" he'd asked. Her reply was a wrathful glare and a list of items to pick up from town, including her blood pressure prescription, which she'd said she needed because he kept doing stupid things like getting into bar fights. So he'd done what any self-respecting nephew would—apologized once again for his battered face and headed for town. Apparently Betty needed some space.

On his way out, he'd passed Dr. Berton just turning in, and the men had exchanged a somber wave. Curtis rolled down his window.

"Morning," he called.

"Morning," Palmer replied. "You look the worse for wear. What happened?"

"Misunderstanding at the Honky Tonk," Curtis said wryly. "This'll be a hard one to live down."

"Ah." Palmer nodded slowly.

"Just wondering about the inspection," Curtis went on, eager to change the subject. "That happens today, right?"

"They assured me it will," Palmer said. "Don't worry. Everyone is aware of your time constraints for this sale. The lawyers are on it."

"Good to know." Curtis nodded. "Thanks."

"Well, nice to see you." Palmer rolled his window up and, with another wave, drove on past toward the house. Whatever relationship Palmer had with his aunt might not be his business, but Curtis was mighty curious. Their current veterinary needs were being taken care of by Barrie—and his aunt was a stickler for those kinds of proprieties—so was this…social? Betty had mentioned that they were friends, but buddies didn't normally warrant lipstick and mascara…did they?

Curtis had wondered about that all the way into Hope, and after running his errands and tossing a couple of bags into the back of his truck, hunger gnawed at his gut. Since he was apparently not invited to lunch back at the ranch, fish and chips would do nicely. Snow started to fall, big fluffy flakes that spun and drifted on their way down.

He parked his truck and got out, glancing into a shop window as he walked past. It was Blossoming Motherhood—a store he hadn't taken any notice of since his return, but he spotted someone he recognized.

Barrie stood in the shop next to another woman, three plastic bags over one arm. She was smiling about something, and as she spoke to her friend, she started pulling on a pair of gloves. He was frozen to the spot, watching her while she didn't know she was being observed. There was something about Barrie—a sparkle in her eye when she was honestly amused—that he'd always found intoxicating. Barrie and her friend moved toward the door, and it was then that Barrie looked forward and spotted him. Blast. He looked across the street toward Mutt's Fish and Chips, then back at Barrie as she came outside onto the sidewalk.

"Hey…" he said.

"Curtis…" Barrie glanced toward her friend, who perked up considerably when she heard his name. "This is my friend Mallory—Detective Cruise's wife."

"Ah." Curtis shook her hand. "Nice to meet you. So I guess you've heard about me."

"A bit." Mallory shot Barrie a mildly amused look. "Your face doesn't look as bad as I thought."

"Nice of you to say," Curtis muttered ruefully. "I'll be fine. I didn't mean to interrupt. I'm just headed over for lunch at Mutt's."

"You're hungry, right, Barrie?" Mallory asked. "And I'm just looking at the time here. I promised my husband I wouldn't be too long today, so I should probably get back."

Was that a hint? Barrie licked her lips, giving her friend an unreadable look. Had he been the topic of conversation or something? Probably, considering that Mallory's husband had been the one to arrest him.

"Yeah, well, Barrie, if you want to join me for lunch, it's on me," he said.

"It was great seeing you, girl," Mallory said, leaning in to give Barrie a squeeze. "Call me!"

With that, Mallory headed off down the sidewalk. Color rose in Barrie's cheeks.

"She's not too subtle, is she?" Curtis asked with a low laugh.

"She means well." Barrie shook her head. "But don't worry. I'm not going to hold you to that. Have a nice lunch, Curtis. I'll see you—"

"Barrie." He put a hand out to stop her. "I was serious about the offer of lunch. If nothing else, I owe you for pain and suffering last night."

"That was for old times' sake," she said. Then she eyed his face a little more closely. "You don't look half as bad as you did last night."

His eye was bruised around the temple, but the bruises weren't as dark as they could have been.

"Thanks to a timely steak." He smiled. "Look, if you still like fish and chips as much as you used to..."

A small smile tugged at Barrie's lips.

"Come on," he cajoled. "People have been staring at you because of the baby, and now I'm drawing stares for this black eye. Let's give them something to really talk about, and have lunch together." He winked. "What a scandal."

"It's a terrible reason, but Mal was right—I'm starving." She chuckled. "Let's go."

Curtis put a hand on her elbow as they crossed the street. It was only in case she slipped, but he was feeling increasingly protective of Barrie. If she had a guy in her life, he'd have backed off...or would he? He wasn't so sure anymore. Barrie was no longer his, and he knew that whatever they'd been to each other was rooted in the distant past. But seeing her again, fighting with her, standing so close that he could smell her perfume...

"How are your ribs?" Barrie asked, pulling him out of his thoughts.

"A bit sore, but not too bad," he said. "They're only bruised. I told you it wasn't as bad as it looked."

"But you always said that." She ran a hand through her hair. "And you weren't always telling the truth."

Yeah, well, back then he hadn't wanted her to know how bad some of his injuries were—a mixture of male pride and stubbornness. And maybe that hadn't changed. Curtis pulled open the restaurant's front door and suppressed a wince at the jab of pain through his ribs. She passed inside ahead of him. A sign told them to seat themselves, and he spotted a booth next to the front windows.

"Food first," he said, putting a hand on the small of her back and nudging her in the direction of the empty booth. Curtis noticed a few eyes on them as they made their way through the restaurant. A short-lived marriage from fifteen years ago wasn't ancient enough history for the town of Hope to forget. Was it bad that he was enjoying having people jump to conclusions? Barrie lowered herself onto the bench, then slid in and he seated himself opposite her.

"So, Mallory is Mike's wife," Curtis said. He'd known the police officer back when they were all a lot younger, and Mike becoming a cop was pretty surprisingly, actually.

"Mallory was his nanny," Barrie said. "Mike's cousin went to prison and left him with her daughter, Katie. So Mike hired Mallory to help out with childcare, and…" She shrugged. "The rest is history."

"Wow." He nodded. "I'm happy for him. He was a bit of a jerk last night, but—"

"What did he do?" Barrie asked.

"Besides insisting I call someone?" He raised his eyebrows. "Do I have to take all the blame for that late night phone call?"

Barrie rolled her eyes and picked up a menu. "You weren't exactly cooperative about medical care, either, you know."

"You mean not staying put at your place?" he clarified, and her cheeks colored. He'd hit on it. "Barrie, I couldn't… It was a kind offer, but—"

She lifted her eyes to meet his, and the words evaporated on his tongue. How could she still do that? Curtis cleared his throat.

"I'm still a red-blooded male, Barrie," he said.

She smiled slightly, then dropped her gaze. "I wasn't offering anything more than the couch."

"I know that," he said. "But I wasn't going to be

able to lie on that couch and know that you were just down a hallway…" He wasn't sure if he should say anything more, but whatever. He wasn't here for much longer anyway. "Whatever it was that had me hooked on you back then hasn't changed. I look at you and…" He heaved a sigh, searching for a way to explain that didn't sound crude. "I can't look away."

She met his gaze once more, but this time her confidence had slipped and he saw uncertainty swirling in her eyes.

"I'm not twenty-two anymore, Curtis," she said quietly. "I've aged. The body that you knew and loved is pretty much gone." She gestured toward her belly. "Pregnancy will do that, even if fifteen years didn't. So yeah, we still feel that draw toward each other, but this is different."

What she didn't seem to realize was that he no longer craved a twenty-two-year-old. He was no young buck, either, and he wasn't scared off by the softening of a few years. She was still gorgeous, and if she saw the accumulation of scars on his body, she might be set at ease. The allure that Barrie wielded wasn't just physical, though. The vows he'd taken on their wedding day had tied him to her in a way that he hadn't fully appreciated as a twenty-year-old kid. He'd walked away and signed those divorce papers, but it hadn't severed everything. He missed *her.*

"I know," he said soberly. "I'm sorry, Barrie. I'm not trying to cross any boundaries, or—"

"But yes." Her words were so soft that he almost didn't hear them.

"Yes?" He leaned forward.

"Yes, I feel it," she said with a small smile. "And from now on, I'll be smart enough to curb it."

Chapter 12

The waitress arrived, and Barrie turned her attention back to the menu. The truth was, regardless of their attraction for each other, Curtis was doing what he'd always done—exactly what was best for him.

Curtis ordered a Coke and a plate of fish and chips. His voice was low and familiar, and she hated how her heart tugged toward him. Familiar wasn't necessarily a good thing—he was still the same guy!

Under the table, Curtis's leg stretched out and rested against hers. That was something he used to do years ago—she felt her cheeks warm.

"And for you?" The waitress turned toward her.

"Um." Barrie moved her leg. "I'll have the same, thanks."

The waitress smiled and whisked off again, leaving

them in relative privacy. Barrie needed to get this back into safer territory.

"Curtis," she said, keeping her voice low. "There was something that's bothered me all these years."

"Yeah?" He frowned slightly, and his dark gaze met hers.

"You left." Barrie sighed. "I know I kicked you out for, like, the fourth time. I know that was childish on my part, but what…" She swallowed. "Why was that time different?"

Because she hadn't seen it coming. She'd known how much Curtis loved her, and she'd honestly thought that after he'd cooled down, he'd be back and they'd sort something out like they always did. How was she to know that he'd stay away?

"Nothing…" Sadness welled in his eyes. "I know that's hard to hear. I guess it just finally clicked in my head—you didn't want this."

She was silent, her heart pounding. Nothing had been different? So, had their entire marriage been borrowed time?

"When I married you, I had this image of what kind of husband I'd be." His boot scraped as he pulled his leg back. "I'd take care of you. I'd make you proud. I'd make enough money to keep you comfortable, and crawl into bed next to you at night and know that I was home."

That sounded wonderful, but she was afraid to say it. "And…"

"It wasn't like that," he went on. "I felt like a failure, I guess. I gave you everything I had, and when I tried to stretch a bit so I could give you more, you'd get so angry. That night, when I told you I wanted to go on the circuit—go together on that circuit—you got this look on your face like I was nuts, and I suddenly saw myself through your eyes."

"I never thought you were a loser," she said earnestly. "I promise you that."

"I wasn't a provider, though," he said with a shrug. "Not enough of one. You were used to more. And I certainly wasn't measuring up. When I suggested doing something together away from Hope and away from your parents and all those expectations, I could see in your face that you didn't trust me. You needed this town to feel safe, because you didn't feel safe with me."

"I was scared," she said.

"It was more than that." Curtis licked his lips. "I wasn't what I wanted to be... I wanted to be the guy who soothed away your fears. I wanted to be the guy you looked to... I wanted you to hitch your wagon to my star."

Barrie was silent. Had he really wanted all of that? It sounded beautiful now, but their reality hadn't been so idealistic.

"It was a risk, though," she said.

"Yep." He nodded. "And I'm not saying you made a mistake there. I mean, look at you—you've got your life together."

"But you're saying you left because I didn't trust you enough?" she clarified.

"I left because I didn't like who I was with you. I didn't want to be the petty guy who kept pissing you off. I wanted to be a better man, and I just couldn't seem to figure it out." He met her gaze. "And I'm sorry for that. Really sorry. I had to go—we couldn't carry on like we were. I was suffocating."

That word stung, and she winced. Had all of her attempts to create a home for him—for them—been sucking his breath away? If she were honest with herself, she had been trying to tie him down. It hadn't been healthy for either of them, had it?

"I was smothering you…" she whispered.

"I don't blame you, Barrie," he said. "I just wasn't the kind of husband I knew I should be, and I didn't know how to fix myself. I thought if we could get away and do something together, we might find our stride, but I saw the look on your face when I suggested it, and I knew what it meant. I wasn't the man you needed, either."

In a way, he was right—she'd needed more stability, and Curtis had refused to be tamed. He craved adventure, and he wanted her to drop everything and go with him. But a life wasn't built on impetuous choices and seeing where they landed. Lives were built with purposeful steps—at least, that was what she'd always thought.

"I'm sorry," she said quietly.

"Hey—" He cleared his throat. "Me, too. I was too young to recognize that I couldn't be that guy for you."

"So…" She sucked in a breath. "Enough about the past. Tell me about this stud farm."

"You really want to hear about that?" he asked.

She shrugged. "Why not? You obviously believe in it."

"I'm going in fifty-fifty with a friend of mine. He

found the listing, actually, and we went out to Wyoming to take a look. It's a pretty new setup, and my buddy knows a thing or two about stud services. The owner is anxious to sell. A nasty divorce, apparently. Anyway, we're the only ones interested, which kept that price affordable. It's a once-in-a-lifetime opportunity."

"You'd be nailed down," she pointed out.

"I'd be in a position to make some good cash." He met her gaze. "And a man needs that."

"Did you ever think of just…keeping my building and sticking around here?" she asked.

"I can't afford it. Your lease only covers some upkeep. That building is a drain. It's only worth something if I sell it. Thing is, if I stick around here, Barrie, I'm just some washed-up bull rider. In Wyoming—"

"Yeah." She could see that. In Wyoming, he'd be someone. Finally. "You deserve that."

"You sure?" He smiled ruefully. "I'm making your life harder."

Barrie was well aware of that, but wasn't this their tension from the beginning? It was him or her. Always had been. The waitress returned with a platter that had several dishes on it. She put their plates on the table in front of them, then moved on to the next table. Barrie looked down at the crispy breaded fish and then back at Curtis.

"I know I said otherwise, Curtis, but I don't regret it."

"Marrying me?" he asked, then laughed softly. "You sure about that?"

"It hurt when it ended," she said. "Horribly. It was the worst thing I've ever endured, and before seeing you again, I would have said that I wished I hadn't married you at all, that I'd skipped that whole experience. But now that I see you again..."

He was silent, and she tried to collect her thoughts. How could she explain this?

"I think we've both come a long way," she said at last. "And we're okay. We got through it, and we're both capable adults. Sometimes it's a good thing to know how much you can survive."

"I don't want to be the guy you survived," he said, his voice low.

"I didn't mean it like that."

He nodded. "I know. But...for the record."

She smiled and said, "Okay. How about we both survived the marriage? Not each other. We were young and idealistic, and had no idea what to expect. We were victims of romance."

Curtis chuckled. "It's thin ice, but I'll take it."

Barrie picked up a fry and dipped it into her tartar sauce. She was hungry, and they both started to eat. The fish was flaky and moist, and the batter was fried to perfection. The background music was the local radio station, and a jaunty Christmas carol medley came on that brought a smile to Barrie's face.

"Do you think we're mature enough to be friends by now?" Curtis asked, popping a fry into his mouth.

"I think so," she said. "Fresh starts. Forgiveness. Isn't that what Christmas is about?"

He angled his head to one side and plunged his fork into a fish stick. "So you forgive me for having to sell?"

"Not entirely." That was her honest answer.

"What if I did you a favor?" he asked.

"What kind?"

"I'll teach you how to make those shortbread cookies."

"You really know how?" She eyed him skeptically.

"I really know how." He raised an eyebrow. "A truce. A goodbye."

Was he feeling guilty about the sale? Probably, as well he should.

"Alright, that would be nice." Barrie paused. "As for our chemistry—"

"I'll behave." He shot her a grin, and when she didn't answer, he said, "It's possible, you know."

But she wasn't only worried about Curtis... This mature version of the boy who'd stolen her heart was more dangerous. If she let herself feel too much for him, she'd fall again...and if there was one thing Barrie had learned, it was that she didn't bounce back very well. She crawled out and clawed her way forward, but there was very little bounce and a lot of pain. This time, she had a child to consider, and she had to keep her heart firmly in check.

"Are you free tonight?" Curtis asked.

Tonight was Mallory's Christmas party, and she was glad to have an excuse. She needed some distance from Curtis, some space to get her emotions untangled again.

"I can't," she said. "I've got plans."

Curtis picked up another fry. "Fair enough. But before I leave."

Barrie cut into the flaky fish with the side of her fork. He knew how to tempt her—but those cookies were about more than time with him. She wanted to master that recipe to feel in control. And yes, she recognized that he was her weakness, but she needed this. Curtis was on his way out, and she and her baby would be on their own. At the very least, she'd be able to bake a delicious buttery cookie and decorate it for every occasion. Then she could feel more confident that she was ready to be a mom.

That evening, Barrie put on her new party dress and styled her hair in a glossy updo. A string of pearls set off the dress's crimson luster, and as she looked at herself in her bedroom mirror, she was glad she'd taken Mallory's advice.

"What do you think, Miley?" she asked, and Miley stared at her silently from his spot on her bed, big eyes fixed on her with that look of adoration she never tired of. "Do I look presentable?"

Barrie turned back to her reflection. She looked pregnant…and in a different way than she was used to viewing this pregnancy. She didn't look scandalously or inconveniently pregnant, but beautifully, roundly, lovingly pregnant. She looked the way she'd imagined she would after she was already married and the pregnancy was planned.

"I look like a success," she murmured.

Funny how big a difference a dress could make— Mallory had been right after all. Barrie leaned closer to the mirror, smoothed on some lipstick and pressed her lips together. Turning to the side, she surveyed the effect with satisfaction. She might like to plan her life down to the last detail, but surprises happened—and this baby was a shock. She might be forced to work under Dr. Berton again, but that didn't mean she'd never set up her own shingle again, either. Barrie couldn't control all of it, but she was still okay.

The snow from earlier had stopped, so the streets were clear when Barrie drove down to the Cruises' place. They lived about fifteen minutes south of Hope on a rural road that gave them a fair amount of privacy. Mallory seemed to have it all—the doting husband, two kids, a cozy house where she loved to entertain… But Mallory had started out with a scandalous pregnancy of her own. She'd only discovered she was pregnant after her boyfriend dumped her for her best friend, and she'd been working a nanny job and trying to hide her growing belly so she could keep her health insurance. Barrie wasn't in the dark about how Mallory's marriage began. Neither of her children were biologically Mike's, and yet they still had a family that gave Barrie a little stab of envy. It was the love in that home, and husband or not, maybe Barrie could give her child something similar. Not every family was traditional.

Barrie parked on the side of the drive, hoping she wouldn't get blocked in. If she got tired, she wanted to be able to leave without too much hassle. The house was lit up with Christmas lights, inside and outside. As Barrie moved up the front walk, she could hear music. Mallory appeared in the window, and she waved, then disappeared again.

"Barrie!" The front door burst open and Mallory shot her a grin. "I'm so glad you made it. Get in here."

Barrie hugged her friend at the front door, and when she came in, Mike was waiting to take her coat. He was dressed down in a pair of khakis and a Christmas sweater, but he was a good-looking guy, and even sweaters that were supposed to be tacky looked good on him.

"Let's see it," Mallory said, standing back.

Barrie felt her cheeks flush, but she took off her jacket and Mallory sighed in contentment. "Mike, she's gorgeous, isn't she?"

"You look great, Barrie," Mike said with a grin.

Katie was dressed in a little golden party dress, and Beau had already managed to get something chocolate smeared on his button-up shirt. The kids came over to give Barrie a hug, and she made the rounds saying hello to the guests who were already there—Mike's partner, Tuck, and his wife, Shana, the youngest two of their four children, and an older couple who were neighbors that lived on the same rural road. She was glad she looked good tonight—she needed this. There was no hiding this pregnancy, so she might as well rock it.

"How are you feeling?" Shana asked. "This is the fun part of pregnancy."

"Fun?" Barrie shook her head. "I'm still adjusting to *being* pregnant."

Shana's eyes glittered as she smiled back. "Enjoy this. You look beautiful, by the way. Mallory's been gushing about this dress, and she was right...wow! You're lucky that the maternity shop opened up. I'm half tempted to have another baby, just so I can shop there! No more catalog maternity shirts for me—"

"Oh, yeah?" Tuck's golden brush of a mustache quivered with humor. "You want to put a fifth one through college?"

Tuck and Shana bantered about the idea of another baby, and while Barrie smiled at their humor, she wasn't in the same position that Shana was in, either. This was harder alone. Mallory caught Barrie's eye across the room, and her friend pointed toward the kitchen.

"I'm just going to see if I can give Mallory a hand," Barrie said, excusing herself. "And if my vote counts, five is a nice round number." She winked at Tuck, who jokingly rolled his eyes, and she crossed the room toward the kitchen, where Mallory waited.

"So, how did lunch with Curtis go?" Mallory asked once they were safely alone. "You didn't call me."

Barrie chuckled. "You were busy getting ready for the party. And it was—" She sighed.

Mallory's expression softened. "Oh, Barrie. I could see the way he looked at you—which is why I threw you at him and ran away. I figured you might have some unfinished business."

"Our business is fifteen years old," Barrie replied. "Some things don't change, and we're both aimed in different directions. My life is here, and he's selling the building I'm leasing and heading out to Wyoming for his own business venture. This is…a pit stop."

"Plans might change," Mallory said.

"Whose?" Barrie spread her hands. "I'm barely holding things together here! I'm not following him anywhere! And as for him, he has nothing to his name besides that building. He has no choice but to sell."

"You aren't mad about it?" Mallory asked with a frown.

"Oh, I'm mad. It's just complicated." Barrie smiled ruefully. "What can I help you with?"

"The cheese platter."

They went to the counter. Mallory pulled some blocks of cheese from the fridge and passed Barrie a knife. Barrie put her cell phone on the counter and set to work.

"So, was I terrible to leave you with him like that?" Mallory asked.

"No, no…" Barrie opened one of the packages and began to slice. "The thing is, we still have that connection, and I don't know how to describe it. I remember why I fell for him so hard."

"Hmm." Mallory took a different block of cheese and used another knife to slice through the plastic. "How much longer is he here?"

"I don't know. He's leaving after the sale, which has to be finalized Christmas Eve. He offered to teach me how to make those shortbread cookies."

"He knows how?" Mallory asked in surprise.

"He took a class to impress some woman." Barrie shrugged. "And I know it sounds nuts, but learning how to make those cookies like my mom used to make… It would help. I want to be the cookie baker for my child, too. Mom's cookies were…"

They were perfect. They were comforting. They could be whimsical and fun. They were an expression of her love, and of all the traditions that Barrie could pass down from her mom, this one was lodged deep in her heart.

"Are you going to do it?" Mallory looked up.

"I shouldn't." Barrie sighed. "It's a kind offer, but spending time with Curtis is toying with my emotions and I know better than that. We always did have this really strong attraction that overrode our rational thinking. I miss feeling like that—desired, excited... But I'm too old for this crap, Mal."

Mallory laughed and turned back to slicing cheese. "No, you aren't. You're never too old for romance."

"I'm too old to risk it all on a guy I can't trust to follow through," she retorted. "And a baby ups those stakes."

"That is true." Mallory got a platter out of a cupboard, and they started to arrange cheese slices around the edges. "This makes your Christmas a whole lot harder, doesn't it?"

"Yeah," Barrie agreed. "It does."

It reminded Barrie of what she didn't have this Christmas. Her mom, that sense that everything would be okay so long as Gwyneth was there with some timely advice...and Curtis. Every single Christmas since Curtis, she'd felt a little stab of nostalgia for the life she'd wanted so very badly.

"What are you doing this Christmas?" Mallory asked.

"Dinner with my dad," she replied.

"Next Christmas, everything will be different," Mallory said, pointing meaningfully at Barrie's belly.

"I'm glad for that," Barrie confessed. "My baby will

be here, and I'll finally have someone to make Christmas for again."

"Again?" Mallory eyed her quizzically.

"Slip of the tongue," she replied. She didn't feel like explaining that one; it would only make Mallory feel sorry for her, and Barrie was tired of pity.

"Christmas with kids is fun," Mallory said. "They get so excited for Christmas morning, and the little things mean the world to them. Like pancakes for breakfast and decorating cookies… It's for them, really. Not us."

"Well, I'll start seeing Christmas through a child's eyes very soon," Barrie agreed. "And I'm looking forward to it. Nothing will be the same, and I think that's a good thing."

Except Barrie felt like she needed a little Christmas magic in her life. Most of the excitement might be for the kids, but she still needed the warm glow that Christmas brought—the warmth of hearth and home, the hope of love to come. Christmas reminded her of the good in the world, and she wasn't ready to let go of that.

Barrie's cell phone rang, and she put the knife down to answer the call. It was Betty's number.

"Betty?" she said, picking up.

"No, it's me." Curtis's voice was low and close, and she closed her eyes for a moment.

"Hi," she said.

"I'm sorry to interrupt," Curtis said, "but we've got another sick calf. Should I call Dr. Berton and give you the night off?"

"No, no, I'll come." Barrie licked her lips and shot her friend an apologetic look. "How bad is it?"

"I'm not sure this calf will make it," Curtis said. "Just hoping for the best. If you could get here as fast as possible—"

"Yes, I'm on my way." She had rubber boots, an extra farm coat and her vet bag in the back of her truck—she never left home without them. She hung up the phone and Mallory looked at her expectantly.

"Sick calf," Barrie said. "I'm sorry, Mal, but I can't afford to give up any calls to Palmer right now."

"I get it," Mallory replied. "Thanks for coming for a bit, at least. You look amazing."

Barrie chuckled. "Thank you for insisting I buy this dress. You're a good friend."

She gave Mallory a squeeze and then headed toward the living room and the front door. Some new guests were arriving, and Barrie stepped to the side, allowing herself to blend in to the chatter and good humor for a moment.

This was the kind of home that Barrie had been trying to build back when she'd been married to Curtis—the love, the fun, the sense of purpose in being a family. This was the ideal, but it worked only if both partners wanted it more than anything else. Love wasn't enough. That was where she'd gone wrong last time.

"You're leaving already?" Mike said when Barrie reached for her coat.

"Emergency call," she said, holding up her cell phone as if it were proof. "There's a sick calf. I'm sorry. Merry Christmas, Mike."

"You, too, Barrie." Mike helped her get her coat on. "And happy New Year if we don't see you sooner."

Barrie stepped into the winter cold, the chatter and cheery Christmas carols from the party melting into the scene behind her. The sooner this Christmas was over, the better. Life would be a whole lot easier once the pressures of the holidays were past.

Chapter 13

Curtis had transported the calf from the field to the barn, but it hadn't been an easy feat. This was no newborn cow—and a weaned calf couldn't be moved without a cattle trailer. It was weak and had hardly been able to walk from the trailer into the barn, so by the time Curtis had the animal settled, he wasn't sure whether it would pull through or not. He hoped so—he hated it when the cattle suffered.

But Barrie was on her way…

An image of her rose in his mind, but this time it wasn't the young wife with the sparkling eyes. It was the more mature Barrie he'd rediscovered this December. She was still stunning, and stubborn, and capable of tying him up into knots for years to come. Maybe it was because she'd never trusted him to provide for her back when they were married, but he found himself fantasizing about coming back to Hope when he had a financial investment he could stand on, proving he'd been capable and getting her to look at him in a different way. He wanted her respect, but more than that, he wanted her to know she could be safe with him.

The barn door banged shut and he turned to see Barrie coming inside. She passed the stalls and headed down the aisle toward him. This time, it wasn't her pregnancy that took him by surprise, but the party dress she wore under an unzipped winter coat. It swirled around her knees in a silken wave of wine-red material. The top of the dress curved smoothly around her plumped bust, and one porcelain hand rested on the top of her belly, the other carrying her black vet's bag. She walked briskly in a pair of rubber boots—a strange mix with her carefully coifed hair and immaculate makeup, and he couldn't help but grin.

"What's with you and your entrances?" he asked.

A smile curved Barrie's lips. "I was at a party, if you must know."

"Yeah? Is there a distraught date left behind?" he quipped, and as the words came out, he realized that he cared about that detail. A lot.

"Wouldn't you like to know." She stopped when she reached him, her blue gaze meeting his easily. "Which stall?"

Curtis stepped back and she scanned the calf in the stall beside him, her expression sharpening. He could see the professional in her taking over, and he felt mildly in awe of her as she slipped into the stall and put her bag down in the hay. She tucked her dress up underneath her as she crouched to inspect the animal. He couldn't help but wonder if treating sick cattle in party dresses wasn't so unheard of in her world. She worked quickly, checking the calf's temperature and its eyes. She pulled out a syringe and a bottle of medication.

"You were right to get me down here," she said, still facing away from him as she worked. "But I have a feeling this one's a fighter."

"I didn't notice in time," he said.

"It happens." Her tone was distracted, though, and when she finally rose and turned toward him, her expression wasn't reassuring. "Time will tell," she said, answering his unspoken question.

"Yeah." He nodded slowly. Sometimes that's all they could do—wait it out. "Thanks for coming."

"It's my job." That's what she'd told him the first time he'd seen her walk into this barn, but her gaze softened.

"You look fantastic, Barrie."

She peeled off her gloves, folding them into an inside out ball. "The gum boots complete the look," she said wryly.

"They kind of do. I don't know…gum boots always suited you."

She leaned against the rail, her gaze fixed on the calf. Then she glanced over at him. "How did you picture yourself at this age, Curtis?"

"You mean back when I was an idealistic kid?" he asked.

"Something like that."

"Well, for one, I was never terribly idealistic," he

replied. "But I guess I saw myself as a little more established by the time I was pushing forty. What about you?"

She'd hit her mark, he had no doubt. Look at her—gorgeous, successful in her own career... She was silent for a moment.

"I didn't see any of this," she said quietly. "The baby, the difficulty in running a practice on my own, being alone."

"Well, I guess twenty-year-olds don't tend to look at the practical side of running a veterinary practice," he conceded. "And as for being alone... Barrie, I'm pretty confident that you've got a lineup of admirers."

Barrie shook her head. "I cling to some image I conjured up when I was too young to know what real life was even like. And it's ridiculous—I know that—but I do. I was confident what success looked like back then, and I've arrived in a lot of ways, except it doesn't look the same now that I'm here."

"Your practice, you mean..." He wasn't sure what she was getting at.

"It's more fragile than I thought." She shrugged. "I didn't know how easily I could lose it."

That one stung—would she really lose everything because she had to find a new location for her clinic? He could argue that she wasn't as stable as she'd thought if she was so easily toppled, but this wasn't about defending himself right now.

"I'm sorry, Barrie." He sighed. "How will you do this? I mean, even if your clinic could stay put—what was the plan with the baby?"

Barrie shook her head. "I'm in a tough spot. My dad is still working full-time, and my mom is gone. I'd have to cancel my emergency services, which would be a pretty big hit. I'd need childcare during my regular hours, which can get expensive, but I thought I might be able to sort something out with Mallory. Still, keeping my practice open would be tight."

He could see the glimmer of determination in those blue eyes, though. "You want this bad."

"I've worked for *fifteen years* toward this, Curtis." A tendril had fallen free, and she pushed it away from her cheek. "I dreamed of being a vet as a kid. This isn't just a job, it's a passion." She sighed. "But I never saw myself dropping my newborn off with someone else and walking away for eight hours."

"It's no one's first choice," he agreed.

"I never saw myself as a single mom." She licked her lips.

"You're a planner," he said. "So you're hard on yourself."

"It's more than that," Barrie said. "I wanted to do this the traditional way—be married first, be able to stay home with my kids when they were small. I had a few ideals about starting a family, too, you know."

"Yeah, I remember those." Barrie always had a sense of the right way to do things and the wrong way. His first instincts had invariably fallen on the wrong side of that.

"You aren't the only one who had to juggle a few expectations," Curtis said after a moment. "I'm not exactly proud to be the guy who aged out of bull riding.

I wanted to come back to Hope as the conquering success, not the broken-down cowboy."

"You made adjusting your expectations seem a whole lot easier."

"Did I?" He sighed. "Maybe I hid it better."

She looked up, her eyes brimming with sadness, and before he could think better of it, he scooped up her hand in his. She didn't pull away, and he gave her fingers a squeeze.

"Losing you—" He should keep his distance—he knew that—but he found himself leaning closer. "I told myself if I stood firm—" He cleared his throat. "This isn't just residual feelings from back then. You and I— we've got something. Still. Again, maybe. But we've got something."

She pulled her hand back, and his heart sank. Every single day after he'd left, he'd had to talk himself out of calling her, going back... But his pride wouldn't let him. Love her or not, she didn't see him as a man who could protect her, and he hated that. But staying away hadn't allowed him to heal quite so well as he'd hoped, because the minute he saw her again...

"Ever consider working as the vet for a stud farm?" he asked softly.

Barrie shot him a sharp look, then frowned. "Curtis, I'm having a baby."

"I'm sure there would be childcare options in Wyoming, too."

She shook her head. "I need my community now more than ever. I need my dad, too. And he needs me. I can't just up and leave. Besides, if I take a break from my practice, I need to be here to start back up again—stay in people's minds as a valid option in veterinary care."

"I'm asking you to come permanently," he said.

"And if it didn't work between us professionally?"

There she was—all logical and planned out again. She was already putting in a backup plan. It wasn't that he resented her ability to navigate life, but she certainly didn't see a newly purchased stud farm as a viable option for her own career. Good enough for Curtis, maybe, but not for her.

"If you're already looking at making a change—"

"I'm not—not completely." She sighed. "I've worked too hard for what I've got here, Curtis."

"I worked hard, too," he said with a shrug. "But I'm not afraid to face a change."

She licked her lips, and pain flickered deep in her eyes. "You proved that when you left."

"I didn't mean—" he began. "I'm not talking about when we ended things."

She turned away from him and looked at the calf resting in the hay. Curtis would always be the loser who'd walked out on her, wouldn't he? He could go make a raving success of that stud ranch, and if she saw him again, she'd still see the twenty-two-year-old disappointment who hadn't been able to stick it out with her. Maybe he needed to take his own advice and leave Barrie in the past, much as that might hurt. Because some things didn't change, including her distrust.

Barrie watched the calf for a couple of beats, her mind spinning. It seemed so easy for him—just change tack! He'd always been flexible that way. If one thing wasn't working, he'd pivot and try something else. Unless his heart was set on it, like bull riding. He'd never given up on that. Too bad that determination couldn't have stretched over to being a husband, too.

She sighed. "I hope it works out for you, Curtis."

"So that's it." His voice was low and resentful.

"What do you want from me?" she demanded, spinning back toward him. "You waltz back into town to sell my building, then offer me some job in Wyoming and get offended when I don't jump? I have a *life*, Curtis!"

"I know." His dark eyes met hers. "And I told you that I'm sorry about this sale. I'm just trying to offer something—"

"A guilt offering. A job. Throwing me a bone." Barrie's voice shook with emotion, and she eyed him resentfully.

"You only need to say no."

But this wasn't about the job offer. She didn't bounce like he did. She didn't pivot when things went wrong. She stuck with it. She dug in her heels. She stayed the course—that was who she was—and while it made life harder in some ways, it meant that the people who loved her could rely on her. Curtis wasn't made of the same stuff. Not when it came to relationships.

He wanted her to just roll with this, but she wasn't the kind of woman who went with the flow very gracefully. She'd tried that rather recently during a convention in Billings. Look where that got her.

"I regret it when I do things spontaneously," she said.

"Like marry me."

"Not everything is about you!" She flung up her hands. "Look at me! Pregnant! I took a chance on a one-night stand because I was lonely... This is where spontaneity got me!"

"So what happened?" Curtis closed the gap between them, his dark gaze drilling down into hers. "Who's the father, Barrie?"

She'd been so determined to keep this secret—take it to the grave if need be—but looking up into Curtis's familiar, brooding face, the secret was too heavy.

"A vet from Billings." The words came out with a bitter taste. "It was our wedding anniversary, and I was at a veterinary convention. I figured if I just kept myself busy that weekend, I wouldn't think about you, but... I met this vet in the bar, and we started talking. I was lonely, and miserable, and remembering how the one guy I'd loved with abandon had abandoned me...and I thought—I need to stop this. I need to take a chance again. So I did. The next morning, I overheard him on a phone call to his wife."

"Did you tell him you were pregnant?"

"Of course. I'm nothing if not proper. I contacted him and he begged me to go away. He was terrified his wife would find out."

"So you did."

"I'd rather do it on my own." She shook her head, tears misting her eyes. She hated this. She hadn't meant to cry—she hadn't exactly made her peace with being a single mom, but she'd very happily turned her back on the cheating louse she'd made the mistake with. She didn't want another woman's husband!

"It was our anniversary," she said, her voice barely above a whisper. "After fifteen years, you'd think I'd be over you…"

"Barrie…" Curtis slid a hand behind her neck and leaned his forehead down onto hers. She closed her eyes, struggling to get her emotions under control, but as she did, she felt his lips cover hers in a kiss filled with longing. His hands moved from her face down her arms as he stepped closer, his musky scent enveloping her. She'd missed this so much—the way her body reacted to Curtis, melted under his touch. He pulled back.

"It wasn't your fault," he said gruffly.

"Dammit, Curtis, it was!" She stepped back. "I was the idiot who slept with a stranger!"

Her stomach felt cold now that there was space between them, and she ran her hand over her belly protectively. She could accept her mistakes—she didn't need someone to let her off the hook.

"What am I supposed to do?" he demanded. "I can't support you here—"

"I'm not asking you to!" She shook her head, confused. "Why would you do that? This isn't your baby!"

"Because I still love you!" His voice raised to something between a growl and a shout, and she was stunned into silence.

"What?" she whispered.

"I never stopped, Barrie." He heaved a sigh and shut his eyes for a moment. "I… I saw you again, and it was the same as it always was. I can't help it. And spending this time with you just showed me how little has changed. You're the only one who's ever made me feel this way. In fifteen bloody years." His gaze met hers in agonized pleading. "I'd stop if I could…"

"Me, too," she breathed.

"Stop what?" Curtis stepped closer again, his obsidian eyes pinning her to the spot. "Stop what, Barrie?"

"Loving you."

His lips came down onto hers once more, but this time she kissed him back just as hard. Why did Curtis have to come back and upset her careful balance?

"Then let's try again," Curtis said, pulling back.

"How?" She touched her lips, plumped from his kiss.

"Come with me to Wyoming," he said. "We'll start fresh. We'll figure it out."

An impulsive choice—the same kind of impulsive choice that left her pregnant. She wasn't thinking straight right now—she needed reason and logic.

"I can't just leave," she said, shaking her head. "But you could stay here. We lived here once. We could start again—on home soil."

"Except I have nothing here but that commercial building," he replied. "And I can't make enough off your lease to keep myself, let alone the both of us. I can't support you here, Barrie. But I *can* support you in Wyoming. I know you have a hard time trusting that, but if you gave me the chance, I could prove it. I can provide for you and the baby."

And they were right back to the same place they'd been fifteen years ago. He couldn't stay, and she couldn't go.

"It's not the same, Curtis," she whispered. "I'm having a baby. It changes everything…"

"It doesn't have to—"

"It does!" Her voice rose in spite of her attempt to control it. "I can't just leave Hope."

"You can't trust me to take care of you," he concluded.

"I—" Was that it? Maybe. "I need more. I need my home."

Couldn't he understand? Tears welled in her eyes. She'd never loved a man like she'd loved Curtis Porter, but fifteen years hadn't changed enough between them. She had a child to raise and a career to build, and he wanted her to just wing it—hop in a truck with him and see what happened.

She couldn't stand here and do this again. She knew how this ended, and she couldn't think straight—not with him looking at her like that. Not with his body so close, his mouth hovering over hers, waiting for her weakness... She took another step back, trying to find a foundation she could trust.

"I'm not thinking straight. I need some space." Turning away, she picked up her bag and started toward the barn door.

"Barrie, wait—"

"No!" She didn't turn. "I can't do it again, Curtis. Love isn't enough. It never was."

And if she could have broken into a run, she would have. But her pregnancy made that impossible. So she strode toward the door, holding in her tears until she erupted into the frigid night. Hot tears spilled free as she hoisted herself into her truck and turned the key.

Curtis wanted too much. She'd given him everything

she knew how back when they were married, and it hadn't been enough to keep him. All she wanted right now was to get back home to Miley and cry this out.

Tomorrow was Christmas Eve. If she could just get past the holidays, maybe she could find her footing.

Chapter 14

Christmas Eve dawned bright and crisp. Curtis finished his chores and did a check of the livestock in the barn. The calf from last night hadn't made it, and Curtis's already heavy heart felt leaden in his chest.

He kicked the snow off his boots before coming into the mudroom. He could smell fresh coffee percolating in the kitchen and the aroma of fried bacon, but it did nothing to entice him this morning.

"That you?" Betty's voice filtered into the room.

"Yeah."

He hung up his coat and dropped his hat on a peg. Curtis emerged in the kitchen and his aunt gave him a grin.

"Merry Christmas, Curtis."

"It's only Christmas Eve," he said.

"Close enough." She pulled some bacon out of the pan, then shot him a quizzical look. "What's the matter?"

"The calf died last night."

She paused then nodded. "That's too bad. And the others?"

"They recovered," Curtis said. "So no need to call the vet in again."

"Barrie," Betty said. "No need to call Barrie, you mean."

Fine—Barrie. She'd made herself clear last night anyway. If she didn't trust him, then staying here was the right call for her. It was logical—couldn't fault her there, could he? He sighed.

"I need to get this sale finalized and head out, Aunty."

Betty nodded slowly. "And what about Barrie?"

"What about her?" Betty held the plate of bacon toward him and he waved it off. "No, thanks."

Betty cocked her head to one side. "So, just like that?" she demanded. "Off you go—heart in a vise?"

"I have an appointment with Palmer to sign the papers for the sale," he said. "You knew I couldn't stay beyond Christmas."

"I'm not worried about myself," she retorted. "I'll get by. I've got neighbors and…friends."

"Palmer. You can just say it," Curtis snapped, and he was rewarded with a faint blush in his aunt's cheeks.

"He's a friend," she said weakly.

"He's more than that, and you can admit it," he said.

Betty met his gaze with an arch look of her own.

"Fine. I'll admit that Palmer and I have gotten close, if you'll admit the same about Barrie."

"Does that help?" Curtis asked. "I'm in love with her still, and the real kicker is that she loves me, too. And it won't work."

"Why not?" Betty frowned. "I've seen the two of you together lately, and—" Betty shook her head. "There's got to be a way."

"She doesn't trust me." Curtis sighed. "She still doesn't trust me to take care of her, and now she's got a baby on the way and she's determined to stick close to Hope, where she feels in control."

"A baby does change things," Betty said softly.

"So she keeps saying."

But did it have to? He could help her—provide for them. Curtis could be a dad to that child! With Barrie by his side, they'd make that stud farm a success... together. He wasn't asking her to take a back seat, for crying out loud.

"I understand her fear, though," Betty said. "She's had a rough go of it. After you two got divorced, she worked her tail off going to school and supporting herself. There were a few guys who tried to get her attention, but she took your divorce really hard. They didn't really stand much of a chance."

"So it's my own fault," he clarified.

"Curtis, you don't understand." Betty sighed. "The town has been rough on her for this baby. It isn't fair, but you know how people can be. And she's right— she's about to be a mother, and she has to think about everything, not just her heart."

"I want to take her to Wyoming with me. Start fresh."

"And maybe she can't." Betty shook her head. "Why don't you stay here? I could use the help. I can't pay too well, but you'll have room and board. You'd have her. I'm already leaving the ranch to you when I die, but if you and I ran it together in the meantime... There's room for Barrie and the baby here."

"Aunty, I appreciate the offer, but I've got to provide for her properly. I have my pride."

Betty sighed. "Okay. I'm just saying that sometimes, it isn't about who is right and who is wrong—it's about who's going to fix it."

And he'd tried that—did his aunt really think that he hadn't?

"She's not looking for money," Betty said. "That's all."

Curtis rubbed a hand through his hair, then looked out the window for a moment.

"You think she's more worried about me standing by her?" he asked.

"You left her once already," Betty said. "She's about to have a baby, everyone is gossiping about who got her pregnant and she's still clinging to this place. Barrie's never been the materialistic sort. She's holding on because Hope is offering her something she can't refuse."

Something worth more than her pride. Something more than love. Something definitely more than money...

"Some call it control," Betty said. "But maybe she's just holding on for dear life."

The words sent a shudder through him. Was she less in control than she let on?

"You're a wise woman, Betty."

"Glad you noticed." She glanced at her watch. "Are you going to be late to sign those papers?"

Curtis grabbed his hat and pushed it onto his head.

"Do you have any butter?" he asked.

Betty eyed him skeptically. "In the fridge. Why?"

Curtis opened the fridge and pulled out a block. "I'll buy you more."

He headed for the door—he knew what he needed to do. He was going to fix this, once and for all, and if she'd have him, he'd never look back. Hope might be Barrie's safety net, but he intended to be her soft place to fall.

Barrie stood in front of the mixing bowl, her phone in her hand. She had the ingredients ready to try these shortbread cookies just one more time. She'd cried all night. Poor Miley had done his best to comfort her, and eventually just curled up next to her with his head beside her belly, big eyes fixed on her until she fell asleep, exhausted. She woke up to Miley in the same position.

Her dad had called that morning to wish her a merry Christmas. He was excited about their dinner that evening, and he let slip that he'd bought her some baby things. She'd tried to sound chipper for him, but he wasn't fooled.

"It's Curtis again, isn't it?" her father asked.

"What can I say? He's my weak spot."

"Sweetheart, you'll always have me," her father said quietly. "I'm here to stay, okay?"

"I know, Dad. Thanks."

"And come over early. We'll eat ice cream out of the tub like we used to when you were little."

That was tempting, and she'd agreed. But standing here at the counter, determined to make some edible cookies to go with that ice cream, her heart was aching. Barrie had fallen in love with Curtis again—and she'd known better. The baby squirmed inside her, and she put her hand on her belly. Tears welled in her eyes once more, and she put down her cell phone and covered her mouth with one hand. Why did she have to fall for him like this? Why couldn't her rational mind trump her heart this time around? She'd known where this would go—because it was exactly the same as last time. He wanted her to be different than she was, and she wanted the same of him.

Love wasn't enough.

An engine rumbled into her drive, and Miley barked a few times, ran in a circle through the kitchen, then put his paws on the counter to look out the window. He barked again. Barrie wiped her eyes. It was Christmas—someone was dropping by, and here she was, nursing a broken heart. She didn't want to be seen like this—not now.

"Miley, quiet," she said, but her heart wasn't in it.

She heard boots on the step outside, and then a knock. Miley dropped back to the floor and barked again. She had no choice—she was obviously home. She went to the door and before opening it, she looked out the window. Her heart sped up at the sight of that familiar cowboy hat, bent down to hide Curtis's eyes, but she'd know that jawline anywhere. What was he doing here? Hadn't they done this last night already? With a sigh, she pulled the door open.

"Hey." Curtis stood on the step, and as he glanced up, she could see the lines around his eyes.

"You look tired," she said, stepping back to let him in.

"I didn't sleep," he replied, then planted a block of butter on the counter with a thunk. "Let's get to work."

"What?" She shook her head.

He took off his hat and tossed it next to the butter. As his dark gaze met hers, she felt the tears rise again.

"I missed you," he said, his voice a low rumble.

"Me, too, but it doesn't change anything," she whispered.

"I'm not selling the building," he said. "Your clinic can stay put."

Her heart sped up and she looked at him uncertainly.

"What about your partner?" she asked.

"He can scrape up enough credit on his own, but it means I'm out of the deal."

"But what will *you* do?" she asked, shaking her head.

"I'm staying here," he said. "My aunt still needs help at the ranch, and I'm going to stick around."

"For how long?"

"For good." He brushed a hair away from her face. "Betty pointed something out to me—I've been trying to prove that I could provide for you, but this isn't about finances. This is about something deeper."

"What's that?" she asked, frowning.

"Cookies." Curtis bent down and caught her lips with a quick peck. "We're making some."

Her mind was still reeling with everything he'd just said, and she stared at him, perplexed.

"You made a home for us," Curtis said. "And I never appreciated that. So why should you trust me to appreciate it now?"

"Good point," she whispered.

"Well, I've got a proposal for you. Let's make that home together. You're right—this isn't 1950, and I make a good shortbread. So let's do this together. Let's put together a home, the two of us. I can't promise lots of cash, but I can promise I'll work my heart out to provide."

"So you're really staying…"

He ran his thumb over her bottom lip, then dipped down and kissed her softly. "There are a few things I'm really good at—" his lips curled up suggestively "—and cookies are one of them."

"Curtis, this is all very sweet, but—" The words evaporated on her tongue and his lips covered hers once more. He pulled her in close, and when he'd left her thoroughly breathless, he pulled back.

"I love you," he murmured. "And I want you to trust me, but I understand if you're going to need some time on that. Here's what I want you to do—start a rumor. Tell three people a secret and demand they tell no one."

"What secret?" she asked with a low laugh.

"That I'm the father." He met her gaze evenly.

"But you aren't."

"Don't care," he replied. "Tell them I am. Take away the mystery. Put me on the birth certificate and I'll financially support the both of you. That's how serious I am."

"And then what?"

"Then go out for dinner with me, and let everyone see how I dote on you…" His voice was low and tempting. "Because I'm going to be here, Barrie. I'm not leaving. I don't care how long it takes you to figure out you can trust me again. I'm not giving up."

"You're sure?" she whispered.

"I've never been more sure of anything in my life." He licked his lips. "I want to marry you again, Barrie. I want to raise your child as my own, and I want the whole town to see how happy we are together."

"You'll be running the Porter ranch?" she asked after a moment.

"Yup."

"And you'll be living there?"

"That's the plan."

So close, yet so far away. This house suddenly felt big and rattling. She swallowed. "Is there room for me?"

A grin broke over Curtis's face. "Betty already offered. I'm not asking you to take a back seat, Barrie. I'm asking you to do this with me. Take the time you need with the baby and then start up your practice again. In the meantime, I know we'd sure value your input around the ranch."

She nodded. "Okay, then."

"Yeah?" Curtis bent to catch her eye. "But if you're moving in, I want to marry you."

Barrie chuckled. "So proper."

"To the core." His lips hovered over hers. "I want a home with you. I want matching towels. I want kids who call me Daddy and get mad at me when I'm late. I want to tell people I have to talk to my wife before I agree to something. I want traditions and photo albums and goofy stories that we tell about each other. I want the whole package, Barrie, and for me, that includes the vows. Marry me again. Give me another shot. I'll make it my life's goal to make sure you don't ever regret it."

There would always be risk, but with Curtis, she felt like her heart could start to heal. He was back… but more than that, he'd come home.

"Yes," she said softly. "I'll marry you."

Curtis's lips came down onto hers, and her heart swelled to meet his. She'd never stopped loving him anyway—they might as well make it official.

Epilogue

Barrie lay in the hospital bed, her newborn daughter snuggled in her arms. A girl. She was still in awe… She had a baby girl! Looking down into that tiny face, she felt herself grow. She was a mother, and her life would be devoted to this tiny person for the rest of her days. She could feel it.

Curtis bent down and kissed her forehead, and Barrie raised her gaze to meet his.

"You were amazing," he murmured. "You're like a Viking."

She laughed softly. "I feel like I've been through a battle."

Curtis reached down and ran a finger down their daughter's cheek.

"Do you have a name picked out?" he asked.

"What about Gwyneth, after my mom?" she asked.

"It's perfect." Curtis was silent for a moment. "Can I hold her?"

Barrie shifted the baby into Curtis's arms. He held her awkwardly at first, but the tension started to seep out of his arms as his dark gaze fixed on Gwyneth's tiny, squished face. A smile tickled the corners of his lips, and then his chin trembled. Curtis swallowed hard. He was feeling it, too.

"Wow…" he whispered. "I'm a dad."

"Are we going to be exciting enough for you?" Barrie asked softly. "The domestic life might get a little boring."

"Nah." Curtis touched the baby's cheek with the back of one finger. "This isn't boring… I had fifteen years to chase adventure, and this—" His voice caught. "Babe, this is *everything*."

He sat on the edge of the bed, and Barrie slid a hand over his muscled forearm. She loved him so much, and she'd been afraid that he'd change his mind after his first proposal, but he hadn't. He'd been by her side this whole time, completely in love with her. She hadn't moved in to the ranch house with Betty yet. They were being old-fashioned, and enjoying their engagement a little bit. She'd move in after the wedding made it official. But Barrie had closed her veterinary practice for the short term. As soon as she could handle everything again, she'd reopen.

"So what do you say…" he said quietly. "You ready to set a date for the wedding?"

She nodded. "Yes. I think I am."

Curtis shot her a grin and eased the baby back into her arms. He dipped his head down and caught her lips tenderly with his. The kiss was soft and lingering. When he pulled back, he tucked a tendril of hair behind her ear.

"Good," he whispered. "'Mrs. Porter' always did suit you."

She laughed softly. "Yeah…it did, didn't it?"

Barrie looked back at tiny Gwyneth in her arms. She was so little, so perfect. Her eyes were shut, and her lips were pursed in her sleep… She was theirs. Curtis was right. This was absolutely everything.

* * * * *

Ann Roth lives in the greater Seattle area with her husband. After earning an MBA, she worked as a banker and corporate trainer. She gave up the corporate life to write, and if they awarded PhDs in writing happily-ever-after stories, she'd surely have one.

Ann loves to hear from readers. You can email her at ann@annroth.net.

Books by Ann Roth

Harlequin Western Romance

Prosperity, Montana

A Rancher's Honor
A Rancher's Redemption

Saddlers Prairie

Rancher Daddy
Montana Doctor
Her Rancher Hero
The Rancher She Loved
A Rancher's Christmas

Visit the Author Profile page at Harlequin.com for more titles.

A RANCHER'S CHRISTMAS

ANN ROTH

To cowboys everywhere and
the people who love them.

Chapter 1

Gina was rushing out to get herself another espresso before the upcoming meeting when her office phone rang. Knowing that it might be someone from Grant Industries, she lunged toward her desk before her assistant, Carrie, picked up. "This is Gina Arnett."

"It's Uncle Redd."

Of all times for him to call.

"Hi," she said. "I know I haven't phoned you lately, but I've been in a real crunch here, working on that holiday promotion for Grant Industries—the big retailer I told you about last time we talked. If they like the results from the campaign I've put together, they'll put me on retainer for them for the next year."

Plus she'd earn a fat year-end bonus, which she really, really needed.

She checked her watch. Still time to race down to the

coffee bar and get that espresso—if she hurried. "We're rolling out part two of our Holiday Magic campaign tomorrow, and you wouldn't believe how busy I am right now. Can I call you back tonight?"

"I need to tell you something, Gina," her uncle said in a solemn tone Gina had rarely heard. "I'm afraid it can't wait."

She frowned. "What's happened?"

Uncle Redd usually cut straight to the chase, and this time was no different. "Sometime during the night, your uncle Lucky had a heart attack. He's gone."

"Gone?" She sank onto her desk chair.

"I'm afraid so." Her uncle cleared his throat. "How soon can you get home?"

It had been almost seven years since she'd visited there. The last time had been for her mother's funeral. She remembered the long flight from Chicago to Billings and the shorter connecting flight to Miles City, followed by a forty-mile drive to Saddlers Prairie. Getting there would take the better part of a day.

"I'll need to check with the airlines and get back to you," she said. "When do you need me there?"

"As soon as possible. Seeing as how Thanksgiving is next week, we decided to hold the funeral right away. We scheduled it for this coming Friday—three days from now."

Funeral.

The news finally sank in. Uncle Lucky was dead. Their little family just kept shrinking. Gina's shoulders sagged.

"Do you need help with airfare?" her uncle asked.

"No, Uncle Redd. I'm thirty years old and I make a good living." Never mind that most of her credit cards were just about maxed out. Nobody needed to know that. "As soon as I book the flight, I'll call with my arrival information. Or would you rather I rented a car?"

"Waste your money like that? There's no need, honey. I'll be waiting for you at the baggage claim."

Uncle Redd made a choking sound, and Gina suspected he was crying. Uncle Lucky had been his last living brother and they'd been close.

Gina had also been close to him, had spent most every summer of her childhood at his Lucky A ranch. She teared up, too.

Lately, Uncle Lucky had been begging her to come back and visit, saying he missed her and needed to talk to her about something important. Now she'd never know what he'd wanted to say.

Why hadn't she made more of an effort?

She managed to tell her uncle goodbye before she hung up. She was sniffling and looking up the number for the airline on her smartphone when the com line buzzed.

"It's me," her assistant whispered. "Where are you? Everyone's here."

By everyone, she meant Evelyn Grant, the great-granddaughter of William Grant and Grant Industries' first female CEO. That she'd even come to the meeting showed how important this campaign was to her. She wouldn't like to be kept waiting.

There was no time to grieve. Gina wiped her eyes, grabbed her iPad and left for the meeting room.

* * *

Later that afternoon, Gina sat in her office with Carrie reviewing what needed to be done with each of their clients when Gina's boss, Kevin, knocked on the door. Wearing an elegant cashmere coat and scarf over his bespoke suit, he looked put-together, handsome and successful. Sure, he was a bit on the ruthless side and on his third marriage, but careerwise, Kevin was her kind of man.

Someday, Gina hoped to meet and fall in love with someone with her boss's drive and determination. "Carrie and I are just reviewing my client to-do list," she said. "What can I do for you, Kevin?"

"Are you sure you can handle the Grant campaign from Montana?"

This was the third time he'd asked her that question since she'd told him about her uncle's passing. "Absolutely," she repeated with a reassuring smile.

As the only member of her family under seventy, she would be expected to handle her uncle's estate, meet with the attorney and cull his papers and personal effects before Uncle Redd moved into the house and took over the ranch.

But that shouldn't consume too much of her time, and she was sure she would still have plenty of opportunities to focus on her job. "Anything I can't do from there, Carrie will take care of. She's been in on this campaign from the start and she's up to speed on everything. And don't forget that next week is Thanksgiving. The office is only open Monday and Tuesday. That means I'm really only out three days this week and two days the next."

Gina's assistant, who'd worked for her for the past six months and was only a year out of college, nodded enthusiastically. Like Gina, she dressed in stylish suits and great shoes. She was smart and eager to get ahead, reminding Gina of herself at that age—of herself to this day.

"I'm excited about this challenge," Carrie said.

Seeming satisfied, Kevin nodded and checked his Rolex. "I have a dinner meeting tonight with clients and I don't want to be late. I'll leave you two to hash over any details. What time does your plane leave, Gina?"

"Six a.m." Way too early, given that she'd probably get to bed around midnight tonight. But for more than a month now, she'd pretty much lived on sleep fumes. With the help of copious amounts of caffeine and plenty of chocolate, she'd managed just fine.

"You'll be back the Monday after Thanksgiving."

It was a statement, not a question. "That's right," Gina said.

She'd booked a return flight for that Sunday, giving her ten full days in Montana. That should be enough time to see everyone and straighten out her uncle's affairs.

"Give my condolences to your family, and have a good holiday."

It wouldn't be much of a holiday. "Thank you, Kevin."

Her boss left.

Gina hadn't spent Thanksgiving or any other holiday with her relatives since her mother had died. They would probably expect her to cook Thanksgiving dinner, which was okay with her. She enjoyed cooking but never had the time anymore.

"Um, Gina?" Carrie said, bringing Gina back to the task at hand. "I'm meeting some friends in a little while and I should get going."

"Right," she said. "Let's review day by day what's supposed to happen between now and when I return. We'll start with Grant Industries and then go over the other accounts."

"I'm ready."

Carrie didn't quite manage to stifle a yawn, which caused Gina to yawn, too. They were both exhausted, but she needed to know she could depend on her assistant. A lot was riding on this campaign.

"This is a huge responsibility, Carrie. Are you sure you can handle it? Because I can easily bring in someone else." Several of her colleagues, including her best friend, Lise, would do anything for the Grant account. But when Grant Industries had signed with Andersen, Coats and Mueller, Kevin had selected Gina to manage it, and she preferred to keep Lise away from her "baby."

Carrie perked right up. "I'm thrilled to have this opportunity to prove myself."

Gina smiled, relieved. After reviewing all of their clients' accounts, Gina shut down her desktop computer. "That's it, then. My uncle's ranch only has dial-up, but I found a hot spot for wireless so I'll be able to stay connected." She would have to drive about five miles into town to get internet, which was inconvenient but better than nothing.

"Seriously? No wireless?"

"Unfortunately not. My uncle was a rancher and

didn't use the internet much. I expect frequent reports from you on the Grant account and the rest of our clients. Numbers, feedback plus any ideas or concerns you have. That way I can keep tabs on everything and make sure nothing slips through the cracks."

"No problem."

"Great. You have my cell phone number. If you need me for anything at all, text me or call—day or night. Oh, and Montana is an hour ahead of us, by the way."

Carrie nodded. "Don't worry about a thing, Gina. I can handle this."

Gina hoped she was right. Her job and her creditors depended on it.

Dusk was falling when Zach Horton exited Redd's battered Ford wagon. Icy wind blew across the airport parking lot, and he clapped his hand on his Stetson to keep it from flying across the pavement. Time to switch to a wool cap.

Redd blew on his gloved hands and squinted at the cloud-filled sky. "Looks like it's fixing to snow tonight. Good thing Gina's flight is due to arrive on time. I sure appreciate you driving my old heap to pick her up."

The seventy-one-year-old was too shaken up by his older brother's unexpected death to drive the forty miles to the airport alone, let alone in the dark. "I'm happy to help," Zach said. "I've been hearing about Lucky's niece since he hired me. It's time I met her."

She didn't know it, but Lucky had left her the ranch. He wanted her to take it over. Correction: he wanted Zach to persuade her to take it over. "Where did she say to meet her?" he asked.

"In the baggage claim area."

"She checked bags?"

"That's what she said."

Zach shrugged. According to Lucky, Gina Arnett was a marketing whiz, steadily climbing the corporate ladder. She'd recently been promoted to assistant vice president at her company. The whole family was proud of her.

Zach was familiar with the type. Uptight, driven, goal oriented—he'd had his fill of women like her. He'd had his fill of corporate deals and one-upmanships, period.

He doubted Gina Arnett would want anything to do with the Lucky A and had told Lucky so. But Lucky had asked Zach to do everything possible to persuade her. The rancher had taken Zach in when he was a broken man, and Zach owed him.

There weren't many people he counted as friends, and losing Lucky hurt. He would sorely miss the old man who had taken him in and mentored him in ways his own father never had.

He and Redd entered the baggage claim area, which was noisy and full of passengers awaiting their luggage.

After a moment, Redd pointed to a woman across the way. "There she is."

In high-heeled suede boots and a stylish camel hair coat over pants, she looked pretty much as Zach had pictured her, though taller. Her light brown hair was parted on the side and hung almost to her shoulders in a straight, sophisticated style. With big eyes, full lips and an air of self-confidence, she was knockout beautiful. Lucky had neglected to mention that.

"Uncle Redd," she said, hugging Redd tight. Her eyes flooded before she squeezed them shut.

Feeling like a voyeur, Zach stood back and averted his gaze, giving them privacy.

Finally, Redd let go of her and wiped his eyes. "Gina, this is Zach Horton—he's the foreman at the Lucky A."

She raised her watery gaze to Zach. Makeup had smeared under her grief-stricken eyes. For some reason, that made his chest hurt.

He whipped off his hat and extended his arm. "Pleased to meet you."

She had delicate fingers and a firm grip, her skin soft against his callused palm. "I'm sorry about Lucky," Zach said, sounding gruff to his own ears. He cleared his throat. "He talked about you quite a bit."

"He told me about you, too. I remember how happy he was when he hired you several years ago. He was always talking about how much he liked and respected you. I loved him so much." Her eyes filled.

As the tears spilled over, Zach's throat tightened, pressure building behind his own eyes. He turned away and nodded at the conveyor belt. "Here come the bags. Which one is yours?"

"I checked three—two big and one smaller. They're red with cream trim."

She was staying what? Ten days? This wasn't a vacation, and little Saddlers Prairie had only one real restaurant. What did she need all that stuff for? Zach didn't miss the laptop peeking out from her huge shoulder bag. She must be planning to work from the ranch. He'd expected that.

Gina pulled the smaller of the three bags from the

conveyor belt and Zach grabbed the remaining two. Redd reached out to take one, but Zach shook his head. "Leave those to me."

"I'll take the other one, then." Redd pulled the smaller bag from Gina's grasp.

"Thank you both." She hooked her free arm through Redd's. They bowed their heads and made their way toward the exit.

Shivering, Gina tucked her cashmere scarf into her coat collar as she, Uncle Redd and Zach made their way toward her uncle's old station wagon. The icy Montana wind was every bit as biting as she remembered—not much different from Chicago in late November.

Snow flurries danced in the glow of the parking lot's perimeter lights. A few flakes could easily turn into a deluge, and she hoped they made it to the ranch while the roads were still passable.

"You sit in the front with Zach," Uncle Redd said, the breath puffing from his lips like smoke while Zach loaded the luggage into the cargo area.

Tired from lack of sleep and the long travel day, and feeling emotionally raw, Gina preferred to sit in the back and just be. "You take the front, Uncle Redd," she said. "I'm fine sitting in the back."

"That's where the dogs ride. You don't want to get dog hair on those pretty clothes."

He had a point.

Zach slammed the cargo door closed and headed toward the passenger side of the car. "Hop in," he said, opening the door for her.

He was big and muscular and movie-star good-looking, with a strong chin and wide forehead, and he was tall enough that even in boots with three-inch heels, she had to tip her head up to meet his gaze. She'd noticed his striking silvery-blue eyes halfway across the crowded baggage-claim area.

Despite her grief, and despite the fact that she was usually attracted to corporate-executive types, she was hyperaware of him.

What drew her most was the sorrow evident in his face. No one had expected her still-spry Uncle Lucky to die at seventy-four. His loss would no doubt be keenly felt by Zach and everyone in town.

She slid onto the bench-style front seat—Uncle Redd's car was that old. In an attempt to get warm, she hunched down and hugged herself.

Zach got into the driver's side with a fluid grace she hadn't expected of a man his size, shut his door and started the car. "Once the engine warms up, I'll turn the heat up high," he said.

As he rolled toward the exit, she glanced in the rear-view mirror at her uncle. "I've missed Sugar and Bit. Are they still inseparable?"

"Pretty much. You'll see them at the house. If you want, you can keep them with you tonight for company. Wish I had the room at my place, but I don't."

The thought of staying alone at Uncle Lucky's didn't bother Gina. "Thanks, but your dogs won't even remember me. I'll be okay by myself."

"Probably better off without them." Uncle Redd chuckled. "Bit still thinks he's human, and that always gets Sugar's goat. They're like an old married couple."

"Sort of like Gloria and Sophie?" Gina teased. Her

elderly cousins, widowed sisters, lived together and bickered constantly.

"Exactly, and almost as old in dog years. Bit's almost ten and Sugar just turned nine." Redd sighed. "We're all gettin' up there—present company excluded."

"Don't forget, I recently turned thirty," Gina said. "That's not so young."

Zach made a sound that could've been a laugh. "You're just a kid."

She scoffed. "You can't be much older than me."

"Four years. That may not seem like a big difference, but trust me, I've been around the block a lot more than you have."

"I'm not exactly naive," she argued.

"From where I sit, you're both still babies," Uncle Redd quipped from the back.

Gina shared a look with Zach, both of them acknowledging that today, they felt old and weary.

At last Zach cranked up the heat, and a welcome blast of warm air hit Gina. The highway was dark and deserted, with only the car headlights lighting the way. No one spoke. The combination of warm air, darkness, silence and exhaustion was impossible to resist. Gina's eyes drifted shut. She was almost asleep when Uncle Redd broke the silence.

"Gina grew up here."

Zach glanced at her, his face shadowed in the dash lights. "Lucky said that after you graduated from high school, you left town."

She remembered that day well. Her parents had both been alive then, and excited about her future, yet sad to see her go. She'd been the opposite—desperate to leave Saddlers Prairie, get her education and start fresh in a big city. All her life, her parents had fought about money and struggled to make ends meet. From the time she was in grade school, Gina had vowed to leave town someday and find a high-paying job. She had no interest in ever coming back, except for occasional visits.

"She's the first one in our family to graduate college, let alone earn a master's degree," Uncle Redd said with pride. "She's a smart one and pretty, too."

"Uncle Redd!" Gina said, embarrassed.

"Well, you are."

She snuck a glance at Zach. His gaze never left the road, but his lips twitched, and she thought he might even crack a smile.

"Since the day she left she hasn't been back to visit but three times," Uncle Redd went on. "Once over Christmas break that first year in college and again when her dad—my oldest brother, Beau—passed that summer. After that, we didn't see her for another four years, when her mama took sick with pneumonia. Marie was forty-two when she had Gina. She and Beau had been married almost twenty years and didn't think they'd ever have kids. When Gina came along, they were over the moon. We all were. Of the three of us brothers, Beau was the only one to have a child."

"You don't need to bore Zach with all that," Gina said.

"I don't mind." Zach glanced at her. "I knew you were the only kid in the family, but Lucky didn't tell me the rest."

After another stretch of silence, Uncle Redd let out a loud yawn. Soon, soft snores floated from the backseat.

Gina glanced behind her. "He's out cold."

"I don't think he slept much last night." Zach rolled his shoulders as if he, too, were tired. "You're in marketing, right?"

She nodded. "I'm an assistant vice president with Andersen, Coats and Mueller."

"That's a big firm."

"You've heard of them?"

"I've read a few articles where they were mentioned. Do you like what you do?"

No one had ever asked her that, and she had to stop and think. "I love it."

That wasn't quite true. She loved the perks that put her in contact with the decision makers in big and small companies, and she liked the respect from her boss, colleagues, family and friends. "It's hard work, though. Right now, I'm in the middle of holiday campaigns for several clients." Her turn to yawn. "It seems like weeks since I've had a decent night's sleep."

Even without the holiday push, she couldn't remember the last time she'd slept through the night.

"Let me guess—you live on caffeine."

"And chocolate. Lots of both."

"And you enjoy living that way?"

"The chocolate part, for sure." She smiled. "Everyone knows that if you want to get ahead, you have to work long hours."

Although Zach didn't comment, Gina had the feeling he wasn't impressed. She wanted him to understand.

"Growing up, we had enough to eat and a roof over our heads, but we were poor," she said. "My maternal grandfather owned a farm equipment business, and when my parents married, he hired my dad to work for him. Then, when my grandfather died, my dad took over the company. For some reason it never did very well. My mother worked two jobs to pay the bills. I always wanted something better."

"That makes sense. So do you have the life you want?"

She was getting there. "I own a condo in an upscale high-rise and I drive a Lexus." Between the steep mortgage, car payments and credit-card bills, she never quite made ends meet, but that was her business. "I can eat out wherever I please and buy new clothes anytime I want. You draw your own conclusions."

"Sounds as if you're doing well."

A few moments of uncomfortable silence filled the car. Gina searched her mind for something else to talk about.

"Where are you from, Zach?"

"Houston."

"I thought I heard a bit of the South in your voice."

She was about to ask about his background and what had brought him to Saddlers Prairie when he turned on the radio. A Carrie Underwood song filled the air. And with that, the conversation was over.

Gina shifted so that she faced the passenger window. Giving in to the exhaustion weighting her down, she closed her eyes.

She didn't wake up until Zach shut off the engine and touched her shoulder. "Wake up, Gina. We're here."

Chapter 2

Zach gathered with the entire Arnett family, dogs included, in the living room of Lucky's house. They'd asked him to help play host to a steady stream of visitors, including the four members of the ranch crew and their families who stayed on during winter.

Lucky hadn't even been dead forty-eight hours, but that didn't stop the well-meaning townspeople. They brought food, offered solace and shared stories about the old rancher.

A cheerful fire danced in the fireplace, at odds with the occasion, and the little room was almost too warm. None of the Arnetts seemed to mind the heat or the company. Zach was grateful for the support and for their acceptance of him, no questions asked. It was a good thing because he wasn't about to air his dirty laundry to anyone. Only Lucky had known the truth.

From that first day Zach had drifted into town nearly three years ago, lost and broken, the people of Saddlers Prairie had welcomed him. Zach hadn't planned on staying, had only known that he needed to get out of Houston and start fresh someplace else. The big sky, rolling prairies and wide-open spaces of Montana had appealed to him, and the welcome mat in Saddlers Prairie had pulled him in.

In need of money—he was damned if he'd touch his bank account—he'd applied for work at the Lucky A. He hadn't known squat about ranching, but Lucky had taken a chance on him and offered him a job. Wanting the rancher to know what kind of man he was first, Zach had told him the whole sorry story of the commercial real-estate company he'd built and his subsequent downfall, sparing none of the ugly details.

Lucky had accepted him anyway and advised him to put the past behind him. Zach had done just that. He'd learned the ranching business and had soon become Lucky's foreman. The successful CEO he'd once been and the beautiful woman he'd been engaged to seemed like part of someone else's life.

Clay Hollyer, also a transplant and a former bull-riding champion who now worked as a rancher supplying stock to rodeos around the West, wandered toward Zach. His pretty wife, Sarah, pregnant with their first child, was at his side.

The couple offered their condolences. "What will you do now?" Clay asked.

The near future was a no-brainer. "Someone needs to take care of the ranch, so I'll be staying at the Lucky A for a while."

After that, Zach had no idea—except that he wanted to stay in town. His father and stepmother thought he was out of his mind for living in a trailer on a run-down ranch and working for peanuts when he didn't have to. But Zach had learned to draw happiness from the little things in life and, for now, he was content.

He glanced around for Gina. She was standing to the side of the fireplace, beautiful and animated as she chatted with people.

Make that he *used* to be content.

Now that Zach had met Gina, keeping his promise to Lucky and convincing her to hold on to the Lucky A seemed even more of a Sisyphean task than he'd thought. He seriously doubted that Gina would give up her career to run the Lucky A, but if he could at least convince her to keep the ranch in the family... That was what Lucky really wanted, for her to pass it down to her heirs—that was, if she had children one day.

She seemed so driven that Zach didn't know if she wanted kids. She sure was good with Bit and Sugar, though. The two dogs seemed wild about her, too. Bit, a Jack Russell, pranced around her, and Sugar, a white, sixty-pound husky, wagged her tail nonstop. Both of them hovered close and gazed at her adoringly, which said something about her.

Locals and transplants seemed to want to be around her, too. A group of women, some of whom she'd probably known growing up, surrounded her. Among them were Meg Dawson and her sister-in-law, Jenny Dawson, and Autumn Naylor, who were all married to ranchers, and Stacy Engle, who was the wife of Dr. Mark Engle, the sole doctor in Saddlers Prairie.

As engaged as Gina appeared to be, Zach noticed her yawn a few times. After spending the whole day traveling, she had to be exhausted. It had been a tough couple of days, and Zach fought the drowsies himself. Without thinking about it, he moved toward her. Her friends offered condolences to Zach before wandering off.

"You doing okay?" he asked, leaning in close to be heard over the noise in the room. He caught a whiff of perfume, something sweet and floral that reminded him of hot tropical nights.

"I'm managing. I found out from Stacy that you're the one who found Uncle Lucky yesterday. What exactly happened?"

Zach didn't like talking about it. "Lucky was supposed to meet me at the back pasture first thing in the morning. When he didn't show and didn't answer his phone, I came here, to the house, looking for him."

"And you found him still in bed. Uncle Redd mentioned that Uncle Lucky had a heart attack, but he didn't tell me about you finding him." Gina shuddered. "That must've been awful."

"Not the best way to start your day." Zach grimaced. "The only good part of it is knowing that Lucky was asleep when he died and didn't suffer. We should all be so lucky."

"Pun intended?" she asked, her mouth hinting at a smile.

"No, but what the heck." Zach grinned.

He liked Gina. He couldn't help himself. Not just because she was easy to look at. She also cared about her family and the people in this house. They seemed genuinely pleased to see her, and she acted as if the feeling was mutual.

She fit in well here. She *belonged*. Did she know how special that was?

"Do you ever see yourself moving back to Saddlers Prairie?" he asked, feeling her out.

"Are you kidding?" She let out a humorless laugh. "I'm staying through Thanksgiving, period. One week from Sunday, I'll be on a flight back to Chicago. I hope—"

"I'm glad you two are getting a chance to know each other," Gina's cousin Gloria said as she and her sister Sophie squeezed past several people to join the two of them.

Both gray haired with sharp, brown eyes, their faces looked so much alike, they could've been twins. That was where the resemblance stopped.

Gloria, bigger boned and taller than Sophie by a good four inches, patted his arm. "Isn't Zach wonderful?"

Sophie, who was two years younger than Gloria and soft around the middle, fluttered her lashes at him. "I hope you're getting enough to eat, Zach. There's a ton more food in the kitchen."

"I've had a plate or two, thanks."

"That's good." Sophie turned to Gina with a fond smile. "You're so thin, cookie. Did you eat?"

"I've been nibbling." Gina yawned.

Gloria gave her sister a dirty look. "You don't look too thin to me, sweetie. You're just right. Tomorrow will be a busy day. You have an early afternoon meeting with Matt Granger, Lucky's attorney. He'll give you a list of errands like you had had when your mother passed—stopping at the bank and so forth. You'll also want to make calls to cancel Lucky's health insurance and Social Security, any subscriptions he had and who knows what else."

Sophie frowned. "Don't burden her with all that now. She's exhausted, aren't you, cookie?" She grinned at Zach. "I call her 'cookie' because I could just eat her up!"

"You'll eat anything," Gloria muttered. "Land sakes, Sophie, she isn't a child anymore."

Used to the bickering, Zach glanced at Gina and saw her smother a smile.

"Now, now," Gina soothed, hooking her arms through her elderly cousins'. "Remember what's happened. And don't refer to me in the third person."

"All right, sweetie. Excuse us a moment, Zach." Gloria pulled Gina away from Sophie, speaking loudly enough that anyone within ten feet could hear. "What I was trying to say before *she*—" Gloria jerked her chin Sophie's way "—so rudely interrupted, is that tomorrow you'll be going nonstop, and you should probably get some sleep."

"We have guests, and I don't want to be rude."

"Yes, but you traveled all day, and it's an hour later in Chicago. People will understand, and they all know they'll see you again at the funeral. Zach and the rest of us will hold down the fort."

Sophie nodded. "We made up the guest bedroom you always use and put fresh towels in the bathroom for you." She lowered her voice. "Don't worry about Lucky's bedding. We disposed of it, so you won't have to. We wish you could stay with us, but we don't have the room. Unless you want to sleep on the living room couch…"

"I'll be fine," she said. "I think I will go upstairs in a minute."

After saying good-night to everyone and exchanging hugs and tears, she bent down to pat the dogs. They licked her and then trotted over to Uncle Redd.

"Thanks again for picking me up tonight," she told Zach. "I worried about Uncle Redd driving all that way, especially in the dark. I offered to rent a car, but you know how stubborn he is."

"Stubbornness seems to be an Arnett family trait." Zach's mouth quirked again, and Gina smiled. "If you can't sleep tonight and need company, give me a call. My trailer is just across the ranch."

"Good to know, but I'm so tired I'll probably fall asleep the second my head hits the pillow. Although if we didn't have a houseful of guests tonight, I'd take Uncle Redd's car and drive to the hotspot near the post office and check my email, just to make sure my assistant survived without me today." Gina yawned so hard, her eyes watered. "She hasn't called, so I guess she did. I'll call her in the morning."

Zach thought about telling her to blow off work and take care of herself instead, but he doubted she'd listen. He ought to know—three years ago, he'd been just like her. Probably even worse.

He nodded. "Sleep tight."

"And don't let the bedbugs bite? When I was a little girl, Uncle Lucky used to say that when I spent the night here. Good night, Zach."

He watched her trudge up the stairs, moving as if she was beyond weary. It was going to be a rough ten days.

Used to waking up early, Gina opened her eyes after a sound sleep. At first she had no idea where she was. It was still dark outside, but she could make out the faded curtains and old blinds pulled over the window and feel the lumpy mattress. She was in the small, plain guest-room she thought of as hers at Uncle Lucky's ranch.

But Uncle Lucky was gone.

Bleary-eyed but feeling oddly rested, she stumbled out of bed. The chattering of the guests downstairs had lulled her to sleep, and she had actually slept though the night. No tossing and turning, no waking up and wor-rying. Which was surprising, but Gina wasn't going to question her good luck.

She peered through the blinds. Sometime during the night, a few inches of snow had fallen. It wasn't enough to cause problems, but it blanketed the rolling fields in white.

Uncle Lucky's house was old and outdated, but thanks to storm windows and a working furnace, it was reasonably warm. So different from Gina's child-hood home, where winters meant shivering from the second she crawled out of bed until she climbed back in under the covers at night.

It wasn't exactly the Ritz here, but at least every-thing was in working order. Uncle Redd could move in without doing any repairs or updates, which would suit him fine. None of the Arnetts enjoyed spending money without a good reason. Gina had a very good reason for spending hers—to be successful, she had to look the part.

Still in a sleep fog, she padded to the bathroom. A shower helped shake out the cobwebs, and once she fixed her hair and applied makeup, she felt much better. Knowing she would be meeting with the attorney that afternoon and not wanting to have to change clothes later, she dressed in a cream cashmere sweater set and gray slacks, a stunning outfit purchased on credit at Neiman Marcus. Sliding her feet into her slippers, she headed downstairs.

Now that the visitors had all left, the little house was eerily silent. Much too quiet, but at the moment, Gina's main concern was coffee.

As a child, she'd spent every summer here, and she knew her way around her uncle's cluttered kitchen. Now cakes, pies and breads filled every spare bit of counter space, but some kind soul had cleaned up last night and run Uncle Lucky's portable dishwasher. Gina unhooked it from the faucet and wheeled it to its place against the wall, bypassing a stack of old newspapers that probably went back five years. Those had to go, but not just now. Coffee. She needed coffee.

Uncle Lucky had always preferred the no-frills stuff, and his coffeemaker was the kind that percolated on the stove and took its sweet time. Compared to the state-of-the-art coffee and espresso maker at Gina's condo, it seemed primitive.

Not that she made her own coffee often. In Chicago, she could run down the street and pick up an espresso at any number of places. But Saddlers Prairie didn't have many options. Barb's Café was nearly a five-mile drive from the ranch, and the Burger Palace, a fast-food place, was almost ten. Neither was open for business this early. She was stuck with Uncle Lucky's generic brand.

While the coffee brewed, Gina cut herself a thick slab of cinnamon-raisin bread. She popped it into the toaster and waited. Without Wi-Fi, she wasn't able to check her email and felt lost. She did have a text from Carrie. The rollout of the Grant Holiday Magic campaign had gone as smoothly as Gina had hoped, which was good news. Carrie didn't mention the other clients, and Gina assumed that all was well.

Her assistant's personal news was interesting. She texted she'd gone with friends to a bar after work on Tuesday and had met someone. He'd asked her to go out for dinner with him on Wednesday, and she had been about to leave for her date as soon as she fired off the report with the campaign's numbers. Gina would stop at the Wi-Fi hotspot and read the report later.

At least one of them was dating. Gina texted back a thanks for the info and asked about the dinner date.

She didn't need to talk to her assistant this morning, but she was used to being busy all the time, and the lack of rushing around and accomplishing things was unnerving. She dialed the office.

"Hi, Marsha, it's Gina," she told the receptionist. "Please put me through to Carrie."

"She hasn't come in yet."

Gina checked her watch. It was after nine in Chicago, well past time to start the workday. "Where is she?"

"Well, she had that dinner date last night. Maybe she stayed out late and overslept."

Not a good sign.

"Wait, I just remembered something," Marsha said. "On her way out last night, she mentioned something about stopping at some of the Grant department stores today. Maybe she's at a store right now."

Conducting a visual check. That made sense. Gina let out a relieved breath—and then wondered what she had been worried about. Carrie was a younger version of herself. As eager as she was to move up the corporate ladder, she wouldn't blow this.

"I've been thinking about you and your family," Marsha said with sympathy. "How are you doing?"

"It's not easy, but I'm managing," she said and gave Marsha a few details. "Will you have Carrie call me when she comes in?"

Gina disconnected and made a mental list of what she needed to do this morning. She would start with compiling Uncle Lucky's bank statements and legal documents so that she could take them to the meeting with the attorney. Her uncle's office was even more cluttered than the kitchen, and finding what she needed wouldn't be easy.

She also thought about the funeral tomorrow and all that entailed. Her family expected her to give the eulogy, which she'd started to write in bed last night. Gina didn't plan on taking up too much time because other people also planned to speak, but she still needed to hone her speech and practice it.

At some point she needed to sort through the old papers and junk her uncle had collected. And he'd collected piles of both.

Suddenly, she felt even more tired than she had yesterday. Last night, more than a few people had offered to help her with whatever she needed. After she sorted through everything, she would take some of them up on the offer and ask for help hauling things to the dump or the nearest charity bin.

For now, clearing out the clutter would keep her busy.

At last, the coffee was ready. It didn't smell very good, but beggars couldn't be choosers. She filled a chipped mug and searched the aging fridge for milk.

Casseroles, cheese plates and all kinds of food crammed the shelves. Thanks to the kind people of Saddlers Prairie, there was enough food in there to feed a small army. Even with Uncle Redd, Gloria and Sophie helping her eat it, there were enough meals to last until Thanksgiving.

She took her buttered toast and coffee to the table and sat down. Maybe Zach would help them eat some of this stuff.

Zach. Now there was a man. He was big and super good-looking—every girl's dream cowboy.

Gina frowned and reminded herself that she wasn't into cowboys. She liked ambitious men in well-tailored suits. She hadn't met the right one yet, but she had no doubt that, in time, she would.

The coffee tasted awful. If she hadn't needed the caffeine so badly she'd dump it down the drain. She was revising her eulogy and picking at her toast when someone knocked at the back door.

Pathetically eager for company, she jumped up and hurried to open it. Zach stood on the stoop, his face ruddy from the cold. Against the backdrop of the blue sky, his hair looked almost black and his eyes were the color of liquid silver. His heavy parka was unzipped, revealing a flannel shirt tucked into jeans.

"Morning," he said, his breath fogging in the cold air. "I finished the chores and thought you might want company."

How had he known?

"Sure." She widened the door. "Come in."

After wiping his boots on the mat he stepped inside, bringing a whiff of fresh air with him. "It's cold out there," he said, blowing on his hands.

"It's nice and warm in here."

As Zach shrugged out of his parka and hung it on one of the hooks along the wall near the door, Gina couldn't help admiring his broad shoulders, narrow hips and long legs.

He caught her staring. His mouth quirked and he raised his eyebrows.

It was a good thing she didn't blush easily. "I was wondering whether I should offer you coffee," she said. "Lucky's coffeemaker is older than I am, and this stuff tastes pretty bad. But there's plenty to eat if you're hungry."

Zach glanced at what was left of her toast. "That looks good."

"I'll slice some for you."

She started to stand, but Zach gestured for her to stay seated. "Relax—I'll get it myself. I met the woman who made that bread when she brought it by yesterday. Her name is Cora Mullins, and she went to grade school with Lucky."

He pulled a plate from the cupboard as if he was family. From the way Uncle Lucky had sung his praises, she knew he'd thought of him that way.

"May as well try the coffee, too," he said, grabbing a mug.

A few minutes later, he joined her at the kitchen table. He sipped cautiously. "Compared to the sludge Lucky makes—made—this isn't half bad."

He made a face that coaxed a smile from Gina. "Believe me, I tasted his coffee several times," she said. "I'm surprised I didn't sprout hair on my chest."

Zach's gaze darted to her breasts. Interest flared in his eyes and her body jumped to life. Maybe he wasn't her type, but she sure was attracted to him.

He glanced at her pad and paper. "Don't tell me you're working."

"I was trying to revise what I want to say at the funeral." She bit her lip. "But thinking about that makes me sad."

"Talk about Lucky's coffee. That'll get a smile out of everyone."

She hadn't thought of using humor. "Smiling through the tears—I like it."

Zach wolfed down the bread, obviously famished from whatever he'd been doing outside. "Before I forget, here's the key to Lucky's truck." He raised his hip and set the key and her uncle's rabbit foot keychain on the table. "He logged over a hundred and seventy thousand miles on it but maintained the engine beautifully. It runs great, but it's a stick shift and doesn't have power steering. Think you can handle that?"

She scoffed. "I learned to drive in that truck."

"No kidding! So Lucky gave you driving lessons?"

When she nodded, Zach shook his head and chuckled, a nice sound that brightened up the gray morning. "What's so funny?" she asked.

"The man was hell on wheels, pushing the truck so hard, it's a wonder he didn't burn up the engine he took such care with. I was picturing you with the pedal to the metal and the truck churning up clouds of dust. I'll bet Lucky got a big kick out of that."

"Especially when I pushed the speed up to sixty—which was about as fast as the old truck could go." She smiled at the memory. "I was fourteen, too young for a driver's license, but Uncle Lucky said I needed to learn in case of an emergency. He took me out on a few deserted roads where the sheriff wouldn't spot us and there were no other cars for me to hit.

"I spent most every summer with him while my parents worked at fairs around the state, trying to drum up business," she added.

"I'm surprised your dad didn't want to ranch."

"He, Uncle Lucky and Uncle Redd grew up on the Lucky A, but only Uncle Lucky stayed. Uncle Redd left to run the agricultural department of Spenser's General Store, and my dad went to work at my grandfather's farm equipment business. He said he liked getting paid regularly, but I don't remember that ever happening. But I mentioned that the other night."

"Yeah. That must've been tough."

"I was born into it, so I didn't know any better. But my parents did, and their money troubles definitely took a toll on their marriage." Gina didn't like to think of those times. "That's why I left home and why I work so hard at my job."

For no reason at all, her eyes teared up.

The concerned look Zach gave her only made her feel worse. "You miss him, don't you?"

She nodded and tried to blink back the tears. In vain.

"Uncle Lucky kept asking me to come back and visit," she said. "He said he had something to say to me in person. Now it's too late, and I'll never know what it was. Why didn't I make the time to come back?"

Chapter 3

Gina hunched her shoulders and wiped her eyes, and it was obvious that she was racked with guilt for not visiting while Lucky was still alive. She also seemed tormented over not knowing what he'd wanted to tell her. Zach knew, and this seemed a good time to enlighten her.

Even now she was beautiful, her eyes a soft green through the bright sheen of tears. She bit her bottom lip, and then freed it. Full again, it looked pink and soft and warm....

Zach tore his gaze away. He had a job to do, and he wasn't going to think about his strong attraction to her. She was mired in the corporate world and he wanted to stay as far away from that as possible.

He handed her a paper napkin to blow her nose. "Don't beat yourself up over what you can't change," he said, giving her the same advice Lucky had given him. "Your uncle knew you loved him, and that's what counts."

"But I'll never know what he wanted to talk to me about." She brushed crumbs from the tabletop into her hand and dumped them on her plate.

"I think I do."

"Oh? Tell me."

Her mouth opened a fraction, and from out of nowhere, Zach had the crazy urge to taste those lips. *Down, boy.* He raised his gaze and gave her a level look. "Lucky wanted to talk to you about his decision to leave you the Lucky A."

She blinked in surprise. "That can't be right. Uncle Redd is his brother. The ranch is supposed go to him."

"Lucky and Redd discussed it, and they both felt it should pass to you."

"But Uncle Redd never said a word about that over the phone or last night. I think you misunderstood."

Having sat in on the conversation, Zach shook his head. "I know what I'm talking about, but if you don't believe me, you'll find out when you meet with Matt Granger this afternoon."

"But I don't want this ranch," Gina said, looking stricken.

"All the same, it's yours."

"What am I supposed to do with it?"

Zach figured that was a rhetorical question, and in the silent moment that passed, he could almost see her mind work—and it worked fast.

"I guess I'll sell it," she said.

Not if Zach could stop her. "That's one option, but Lucky wants—wanted—to keep it in the family."

"Then he shouldn't have left it to me," she muttered, pushing her hair behind her ears. "I've had a lot of good times here, but I saw my uncle struggle every year. I know how hard it is to work from dawn to dusk, sometimes longer, all the while praying that Mother Nature behaves so that you can make a profit and survive another year. Sorry, but I'll pass."

She wore a stubborn look that reminded Zach of Lucky. With that and the defiant lift of her chin, Zach knew she'd made up her mind. Still, he had a promise to keep. "At least think about it for a few days. For Lucky."

"You're playing the guilt card. That isn't fair." Once again, she caught her lip between her teeth. "Even if I wanted to keep the ranch, and believe me, I don't, I don't see how that's possible. I live in Chicago. That's where my job—my life—is, and where I want to be. I'm a city girl now. Lucky's known for years that I wasn't coming back here."

"He left you the ranch anyway." Zach let the words hang there for a moment. "Ranching is good, honest work," he added.

"And for the most part, ranchers are good people—I know that. But it doesn't pay, not for the Lucky A. I don't have to look at my uncle's bank statement to know that he doesn't have two dimes to his name. He always struggled to keep his head above water. I decided long ago that this wasn't the life for me."

"Lucky used to talk about how you helped with the chores around here and how you enjoyed taking care of the animals and being outside."

"When I was little, I did."

Zach tried a different tack. "Can you honestly say you're happy with your life?"

"What are you, my psychiatrist?" she quipped, but she looked like a deer in headlights. "I'm a creative person, and I get to use that creativity in my work."

She hadn't answered the question, which in itself was an answer. "You didn't look like you were being creative when you walked off the plane last night," Zach said. "You looked ready to drop."

"I don't mind the long hours because it means that I'm successful and productive. And FYI, I happen to thrive on stress and a big workload."

Having been there, Zach understood. He also knew that that kind of adrenaline never resulted in long-term satisfaction. "So you enjoy life on the human hamster wheel."

"Sometimes it does seem like that, but... You couldn't possibly understand."

"Because I'm a ranch foreman." Stung, Zach crossed his arms. "You don't know anything about what I understand. You don't know anything about *me*." He considered explaining about the company he'd once owned, the things he'd done for the bottom line and the terrible price he'd paid. But that was his business. Besides, it was behind him now.

The starch went out of her spine. "That was rude, and I apologize."

Zach nodded. She angled her head and really looked at him. "You're right. I know very little about you, except that you're from Houston. There are ranches all over Texas. How did you end up at the Lucky A in Saddlers Prairie, Montana?"

"I needed a change." Which was all he was going to say. "You should know that I made a promise to Lucky that I'd convince you to keep the ranch."

"You're trying to change the subject. Don't tell me— you left Houston because you're a criminal." Her eyebrows arched and her eyes twinkled, lighting her whole face.

"Very funny. Nope." Not directly, anyway. In his own eyes, he was. The family of Sam Swain, the man who'd suffered a heart attack and died after Zach had forged the business deal that had undercut what he wanted, probably agreed. But Zach's family and fiancée at the time hadn't believed he'd done anything wrong— except when he'd sold his own company.

"You're going to have to break your promise to Lucky. I can't possibly—"

Not wanting to hear it, Zach held up his hands, palms out. "Just listen."

She sighed. "All right, but I've made up my mind."

"You no doubt know that people all over the country, maybe even the world, romanticize cowboys and ranching. Some even dream of living the ranching life. Why not indulge in that dream by offering a working vacation on a ranch?"

"You're talking about a dude ranch." She was tuned in now, her eyes bright and interested.

"Exactly. A few months ago, Lucky and I started laying out plans for turning the Lucky A into a working dude ranch. Imagine visitors staying for a weekend or as long as two weeks, paying for 'the ranching experience,'" he said, making air quotes, "and providing free labor. In return, the Lucky A supplies lodging, meals and expertise."

"Uncle Lucky thought that up?" Gina looked confused.

"Actually, I did, but Lucky jumped at the idea, especially after we penciled out the numbers. We'd have to update the bunkhouse and hire a cook, but if we brought in just twenty people a month between May and October, we'd break even."

"My uncle has never penciled out numbers for anything." Gina gave him a shrewd look. "Something tells me you haven't always been a ranch foreman."

"I've dabbled in a few other things. What do you think about the Lucky A Dude Ranch?"

"I have questions. These days, the crew lives in trailers. The bunkhouse hasn't been used for years, except for storage. Getting it in working order will take a lot of updating. Where does the money to make those improvements come from?"

"We penciled that out, too. The wiring and plumbing are in decent enough shape, but the building needs more insulation and a new furnace and air conditioner, plus paint and new fixtures. I can do everything but install the heating and cooling systems, which will save a bundle. The estimated cost will be roughly twenty to thirty thousand dollars."

"That's a lot of money."

Zach put up his hand, palm out, to silence her. "Lucky and I talked to the bank and they were willing to loan him half of that. If beef prices stay high, we figured he'd net the rest by spring. Once the business is up and running and profitable and the loan is paid back, we'll look into adding a couple of cabins."

Gina stacked her mug on top of her empty plate. "As intriguing as the idea is, you can count me out."

He'd expected this. "You say that now, but I'm not giving up." He scraped his chair back and stood. "Thanks for the coffee and toast. Before I forget, the combination to your uncle's safe is his dad's birthday, April 5, zero four zero five one nine. I'll let myself out."

He left her sitting at the table.

That afternoon, Zach, Curly and Bert, two of the crew members, checked the water troughs that provided a steady supply of water to the cattle. Sometime during the night, the heater in the big water tank had failed and the water had frozen in the pipes. Thirsty cattle had ventured onto the ice at the river, which was slippery and dangerous. Pete, a mechanical whiz, was already at work repairing the heater.

Donning safety glasses, the three of them wielded shovels and pickaxes to break the stuff up in the troughs and remove it. Then, with the help of a blowtorch, they began to melt the water in the pipes. For now the cattle would have the water they needed.

They were almost finished when Zach's cell phone rang. He pulled off a glove and slid the phone from his jacket pocket. He didn't recognize the number, but the 312 area code was Chicago's. Had to be Gina.

He'd been thinking about her pretty much nonstop since that morning. Everything about her both fascinated and irritated him. The cute expression on her face when she told him about the awful coffee she'd made, her pretty smile and the way her eyes had sparked when she defended her career. How her breasts had looked in that sweater.

Zach swallowed. He was way too attracted to her for his own good and was both pleased that she had his number and put out that she'd called.

Curly and Bert eyed him curiously.

"I better get this," he said. "This is Zach," he answered gruffly.

A slight hesitation. Then, "It's Gina. Is this a bad time to call?"

Did she have any idea of the knots she'd tied him up in? Yeah, it was a bad time. "I thought you had to meet with Matt Granger," he said, drawing raised eyebrows from Curly. He knew that Granger was Lucky's lawyer and realized who Zach was talking with. After hearing about her from Lucky for years, the crew had finally met her at the house last night.

"I'm supposed to meet him at three, but I can't find Uncle Lucky's bank receipts or other papers. I thought I'd find them in his desk, but they aren't there. Uncle Redd isn't answering his phone, and neither is Gloria or Sophie."

"Did you check the safe?"

"Um, I don't know where it is."

Why hadn't she asked him this morning? As much as Zach trusted the two crew members, he wasn't about to tell her within hearing range of them. "Hang on a sec." He muted his end of the line so she couldn't hear him. "I need to go to the house and help Gina with something."

"I'll bet you do," Bert said, giving him a sly look. "She's a foxy one."

Zach narrowed his eyes, and the burly ranch hand backed up a step. "No offense meant. What do you want us to do when we finish here?"

"Help Chet with loading the hay onto the flatbed. Make sure none of the herd has wandered off, and feed and water the horses. If you run into problems, give me a call."

Zach climbed into his truck and drove to the house.

Looking worried, Gina met him at the back door. "I had to call the attorney and reschedule for four. I can't find anything in the desk except junk. Uncle Lucky is—was—such a pack rat."

Zach eyed the four-foot-high stack of yellowing newspapers against the kitchen wall. "He sure was." He wiped his feet and stepped inside. "So you don't know where the safe is."

"I didn't even know he had one until you mentioned it this morning, and I thought… I assumed that the papers I needed would be in the desk."

"Let's go into Lucky's office." Zach followed Gina through the kitchen and down the hallway. She was wearing the same sexy sweater and pants as that morning, an outfit that had to cost a mint. Gina had a great ass and hips that swayed naturally and seductively.

By the time they reached the office, he was semi-hard and not happy about that. Turning away from her, he headed through the room, stopping in front of an oil painting of a cowboy astride a horse that hung opposite the desk. He lifted the painting off the wall and set it carefully down.

Gina's eyes widened. "For as long as I can remember, that painting has been hanging there. I had no idea it was hiding a safe."

"Now you know. This is where you'll find all of Lucky's important papers, including a copy of the will and our spreadsheet for the dude ranch."

"See, a word like *spreadsheet*—that wasn't part of my uncle's vocabulary."

"After we developed one, it was. Try the combination." Zach stepped back so that she could work the numbers.

She opened the safe and pulled out half a dozen folders. There was no room for them on Lucky's cluttered desk, so she stacked them on the desk chair. "Just look at all this stuff."

She was definitely unhappy about her uncle's filing system. A lock of hair had fallen over her eyes, but she didn't seem to notice.

"I wish I'd started earlier," she said. "I'm not going to have time to look through everything, so I guess I'll bring all these folders with me. Thanks for stopping what you were doing and showing me the safe, Zach. I don't know what I'd have done otherwise."

"Helping you out is part of my job."

She tugged at her sweater, drawing his gaze to her breasts. "I've been thinking about how we left things this morning. You meant a lot to Lucky, and he obviously trusted you. You're important to this ranch. My family and I need you here, Zach. You're not going to quit, are you?"

"I wouldn't do that. But you should know that I intend to honor my promise to Lucky. I'll do what I can to change your mind."

"Try away. It won't work."

With her chin up and the confident smile on her mouth, she was irresistible.

"That sounds like a challenge—and I always like challenges," he said, advancing toward her. "Did you mean that?"

"I... Did I mean what?"

"About me trying to convince you." Her eyes were the prettiest color, green with little flecks of brown and gold. "Did you?"

He brushed the silky lock back from her face and tucked it behind her ear. Her pupils dilated and he knew she felt some of what he did. She touched her lips with the tip of her tongue in what he recognized as a nervous gesture.

"I—"

He laid his finger over her soft lips. "Shhh." Tipping up her chin, he kissed her.

Zach's hands were cold from being outside, but his lips were warm. And very good at their job. Gina hadn't kissed anyone since she and Wayne had parted ways in June. Even in their first few months together, when there was some degree of passion between them, Wayne had never kissed her like this.

The kiss was firm, yet sweet and gentle, and something more she couldn't define. Whatever it was, she liked it. A lot. Zach smelled of fresh air and man and was every bit as hard and muscled as he looked.

His arms tightened around her, and she willingly sank against him. Another kiss followed, and another. Shifting so that she was even closer, he slid his tongue over hers. Gina felt his arousal against her stomach. Her nipples tingled and her panties were instantly damp.

She wanted to go on kissing him forever. Instead she pushed him away.

He looked every bit as stunned by the heat between them as she was. "You better go or you'll be even later for your meeting," he said, his eyes hot as he straightened her sweater.

"Right." She managed to close the safe and hang the painting with barely a tremble.

"You're a very convincing man," she murmured on the way to the kitchen. "But—"

"You're still going to sell."

She nodded.

By the time they reached the back door, she felt reasonably normal again. "Thanks," she said as she opened the door for him.

The corner of his mouth lifted. "For showing you the safe, or for those kisses?"

Both. "I'll see you later."

"No doubt. Have fun with the lawyer."

In a daze, Gina drove down the highway in Uncle Lucky's hulking truck. Traffic was light, but then in Saddlers Prairie it always was. Her mind wandered. She couldn't get over Zach's kissing her and how much she'd enjoyed it. In Uncle Lucky's office of all places.

Her uncle had only been gone a few days. They hadn't even held the funeral yet, and here she was fantasizing about the hunky foreman. What was she thinking?

That was the trouble—she hadn't thought at all. She'd simply reacted. Boy, had she.

Up in rancher heaven, Uncle Lucky was probably shaking his head, wondering if she'd lost her mind.

She had—temporarily. Zach Horton wasn't her type. Besides, she wouldn't be here long. Getting involved with him was a bad idea.

Involved? Gina frowned. Just where had that idea come from? So they'd shared a few kisses. Fabulous, bone-melting kisses, the thought of which, even now, made her lips tingle and her stomach flutter. They didn't mean anything and wouldn't happen again.

Though if Zach did kiss her again, she wasn't at all sure she'd stop him.

Her cell phone rang. Grateful for the interruption and eager to get her mind off Zach and his kisses, she set her phone on speaker mode and picked up.

"It's Carrie," her assistant said.

Gina started guiltily. She hadn't thought about work or Carrie since early this morning. "It's about time you called me back," she chided. "Where have you been all day?"

"Where do you think I've been?" Carrie sounded defensive.

"I called you early this morning—hours ago."

"The note from Marsha didn't say it was urgent. Did she tell you that I was at the office until almost nine-thirty last night? I was up before dawn this morning and worked from home. Then I stopped in at a few of the Grant stores so that I could get a visual to go with the numbers they've been sharing." She filled Gina in on what she'd observed. "I sent you an email with all the details. Did you see it?"

"Not yet, but I'll be checking soon." On the way back from the attorney's office.

Things seemed to be going well, and Gina smiled. "That sounds good, Carrie. I'm impressed with what you've done. I thought you were supposed to have dinner last night with that guy you met at the bar."

"Chad. Yeah, but it was too late for dinner, so we had drinks instead. We made a dinner date for this weekend."

Been there, done that. Getting ahead sometimes meant putting your personal life on hold. "I'm glad he's flexible," Gina said.

"Chad's an attorney—he understands long hours. That's one of the many things we have in common."

Everything Carrie said reminded Gina of herself and Wayne. When they'd first started dating they'd both thought they shared a number of interests. But after a few months, they'd realized that the only thing they really had in common was the desire to climb the corporate ladder. Neither of them had been upset when they'd parted ways.

"Have you had a chance to work on any of our other campaigns?" Gina asked. "Is there anything I should know about?"

She heard the sound of papers shuffling. "Oh, you know—the usual reports and phone calls. All the companies are anxious about their holiday campaigns."

Something in her voice put Gina on alert. "Is everything okay? If you need help, tell me now."

"I don't! It's super busy, but I'm handling it," Carrie assured, sounding extra perky.

Too perky. Gina's worry radar kicked up again. But then, like herself, her assistant thrived on deadlines and stress, so maybe the bubbly enthusiasm was for real.

"Look for an updated report on the Grant stores tomorrow," Carrie added.

"Do you think you could send it this afternoon? With the funeral tomorrow, I doubt I'll be checking email until the following day."

"I'll try. How are you?"

Gina didn't have to think long about that. She'd just been kissed more thoroughly than she could ever remember, by a man she had no business kissing, and already she wanted more. She was a confused wreck.

She shook her head. "At the moment, I'm driving my uncle's old four-speed truck down an all-but-deserted two-lane highway to his attorney's office."

"That doesn't sound fun. You take care of yourself and your family, and don't worry about me or work. Things are great here."

Gina disconnected, dismissed her concerns and went right back to thinking of Zach's kisses.

Chapter 4

Thanks to the meeting with the attorney, checking her email—and not finding the report from Carrie—and running some errands, Gina didn't return to the ranch until nearly dinnertime. She walked in the back door with her arms full. Her family was in the kitchen—Sophie and Redd getting out cutlery and dinner plates and Gloria putting one of the casseroles into the oven.

"You're finally back." Gloria lifted her cheek for a kiss. "What took so long?"

"Honestly, Glo." Sophie tsked. "Give the girl a chance to catch her breath."

"For goodness' sake, Sophie. It's a figure of speech, not a criticism."

Gina ignored the petty squabbling and set down her things. "I met with Matt Granger. Then I ran around, doing all the things he needed me to do. I also checked my email and stopped off at Spenser's to buy trash bags and boxes for when I sort through Uncle Lucky's things. Since you're all here…"

She leaned against the counter and crossed her arms. "You all knew Uncle Lucky left the ranch to me instead of Uncle Redd. Why didn't one of you say something?"

Her uncle and cousins exchanged looks. "We thought it might be better coming from someone else. I need a kiss, too," Sophie said, as if their keeping a secret from Gina was no big deal.

Obligingly, she kissed her cousin's wizened cheek.

"Were you surprised when Matt told you?" Uncle Redd asked, offering his cheek, too.

Gina kissed him, then straightened and frowned. "I would've been if Zach hadn't warned me."

"*Zach* told you?" Gloria's eyebrows shot up. "I didn't expect that."

"I'm thankful he did," Gina said. "I don't like surprises like that."

Sophie looked contrite. "We were afraid you'd be upset."

"That doesn't mean you should avoid the subject. How would you feel if I did that to you?"

Her uncle gave her a sheepish look.

"I guess we should have told you," Gloria said.

Sophie bit her lip. "Please don't be angry with us."

She looked so anxious that Gina kissed her cheek again. "I'll live. But from now on, please don't keep secrets from me."

"Understood." Uncle Redd eyed the folders she'd set on the counter. "What's all that?"

"Papers I took to the attorney. I'm going to put them

away and drop these trash bags and boxes in Uncle Lucky's office. I'll be back."

In the office, Gina removed the painting and opened Uncle Lucky's safe. She returned the folders and then searched for the packet the attorney had described. She found what she was looking for in the back corner of the safe.

She didn't have to fold back the layers of tissue paper to know what was inside—the watch Uncle Lucky had inherited from his father, who'd gotten it from *his* father. According to the attorney, for some time now, Uncle Lucky had thought of Zach as the son he'd never had and had asked that the watch be passed on to him. Gina knew that Zach would be touched.

Over his seventy-four years, Uncle Lucky had known his share of ranch hands. As far as she knew, he'd never grown as close to any of the others as he had to Zach. It was comforting to know that someone her uncle cared about had lived on the ranch these past few years.

She should've been here, too. Once again, her guilt stirred. Every year, Andersen, Coats and Mueller closed from December 24th through January 1st, and she could easily have flown home last year. Her uncles and cousins would have loved that.

Instead, she'd spent Christmas Eve at a party with Wayne. That night, he'd stayed over, but early the next morning, he'd left for a family get-together, and she'd gone to Lise's townhouse for brunch. She'd spent the rest of the day alone, filling the time with work.

This Christmas was bound to be even more lonely, but she wasn't about to come back here in a month.

She locked up the safe, placing the package in her purse.

When she returned to the kitchen, mouthwatering smells greeted her. Her stomach growled, demanding to be fed. Someone had set the table, and the family was seated around it. "That smells so good, and I am so hungry," she said, licking her lips.

"The casserole needs to bake at least another thirty minutes, so I'm afraid dinner won't be for a little while yet, but sit down and relax." Gloria patted the chair next to her. "Tell us what else Matt Granger had to say."

"You all know that Uncle Lucky wasn't exactly flush with cash. There's enough money in the bank to pay salaries and the bills for a few months but not much extra."

The next part was difficult, but Gina needed to say it. She cleared her throat. "Mr. Granger explained that even though Uncle Lucky left the ranch to me, I'm not legally bound to keep it. He said that what I do with the ranch is up to me."

"What do you plan to do?" Uncle Redd asked, but his resigned expression told her he already knew the answer.

"This is what I told Zach and Mr. Granger." Gina made sure to look each of her relatives in the eye. "I've had some wonderful times here, but I can't keep the ranch. I guess I'll put it on the market, hopefully before I leave town."

In the beat of silence that filled the room, Gina's family traded looks.

Sophie shook her head. "I'm afraid that won't work. You see, next Thursday is Thanksgiving, and Carole

Plett always closes her real-estate office for the entire week."

"Then I'll talk to her tomorrow. She'll be at the funeral, right?"

"Unfortunately, she won't," Gloria said. "I was at Anita's Cut and Curl this morning, getting my hair done for tomorrow. Carole happened to be there, too. Her daughter in Elk Ridge just had a little girl, Carole's first grandchild. As you can imagine, she's eager to get her hands on that baby, and since the real-estate business is slow this time of year, she decided to close up shop this afternoon. She's probably pulling into Elk Ridge just about now."

"That reminds me," Uncle Redd said. "We got a sympathy card from her today. She donated a big bouquet of flowers for the funeral."

"That was real sweet of her." Sophie looked pleased. "I was over at the church earlier today, making sure everything is ready, and those flowers look just beautiful."

So much for listing the property while she was in town. Gina sighed. "I guess I'll call her from Chicago."

"That's a real good idea, honey," Uncle Redd said. "It'll give you more time to think about whether you really want to sell."

"I don't have to think, I—"

Uncle Redd fixed Gina with a stern look she rarely saw, and the rest of her words died in her throat. "This land has been in our family for generations," he said. "It ought to stay in our family."

"He's right, cookie," Sophie said. "You should pass it on to your children—when you have them."

Gloria narrowed her eyes. "Speaking of children,

how much longer are you going to wait before you get married and start a family?"

Gina gave her a wry look. "Gee, Gloria, why don't you ask me something *really* personal?"

Undaunted, her cousin settled her hand on her ample hips. "I'm family. I can ask you anything I please. And don't try to put me off."

"Fine. At the moment I'm not dating—I just don't have time. You know how busy I am with work."

"What happened to Wayne?" Sophie asked. "He sounded like a nice fella."

"He is," Gina said. "But things didn't work out."

Hating the pitying looks on her cousins' faces, she added, "It wasn't a bad breakup or anything. We realized we didn't love each other and that we didn't have a future together. We parted on good terms." She shrugged. "I promise you that someday I'll get married and start a family. But it won't be for a while."

"But you're thirty years old." Gloria frowned. "You should already be married and settled down. Why, when I was your age, I'd already been married and widowed."

Gloria's husband, Harvey, had died in Vietnam and she'd never recovered. As far as Gina knew, she hadn't dated since.

"Tony and I tried to have kids." Sophie gave her head a sorrowful shake. "But I kept losing them early in the second trimester."

"My first wife couldn't get pregnant at all," Uncle Redd said. "The second one said that taking care of me was enough and my third had had her tubes tied. If this family is to continue, it's up to you."

The constant pressure to marry and have babies never

stopped. "Hey, this is the twenty-first century. I'm still young and I have a career, remember? I love what I do, and I'm darn good at it. That's why I was promoted to the assistant vice-president position last spring."

"And we're all real proud of you," Uncle Redd said. Sophie and Gloria nodded enthusiastically. "But couldn't you hold on to the ranch?"

Gina hated to disappoint her family, but they needed to understand. "Who's going to pay the ranch crew's salaries when the money runs out? Even if I paid them with my own funds, and I'm not going to do that, we all know that sooner or later, the ranch will need even more cash to stay afloat."

She wasn't about to confess that despite her large paycheck, keeping the creditors off her back kept her virtually broke. She was too humiliated. "Besides, I live more than eleven hundred miles away," she went on. "How could I possibly run the ranch? And don't tell me I should move back here. I have a good job in Chicago, and I like living there."

A stony silence met her words.

"Times are tough," Uncle Redd said. "There's no guarantee you'll be able to sell the Lucky A."

Gina hoped he was wrong. "Well, then—"

A knock at the door cut her off. Relieved at the interruption and wondering who had come to pay their respects, she jumped up. "I'll get that."

She opened the door and found Zach.

"Hey," Zach said, wiping his feet on the mat.

"Hi." Gina looked surprised to see him—and a little confused. "I didn't expect to see you tonight."

"Your cousins invited me to dinner."

"And you're right on time, Zach," Gloria called out from the kitchen. "Don't just stand there heating up the great outdoors, Gina. Let the man in."

Gina stepped back. Her cheeks were flushed, reminding him of how she looked after he'd kissed her a few hours ago. Not that he needed reminding. He'd thought of little else since.

"You're just in time, Zach—the casserole will be ready in a few minutes," Gloria said. "If you haven't washed up, now's the time."

No one moved except Gina. Walking beside her toward the utility room, he smelled her perfume and the subtle scent of woman underneath. And wanted to taste her again. Just what he needed.

He stood back while she washed her hands at the big utility room sink. "You okay with me being here tonight?" he asked over the hiss of water.

"As long as you don't try to convince me to change my mind about the Lucky A."

He glanced at her sexy mouth. "I can't guarantee that."

Her eyes darkened. She quickly rinsed and dried her hands. She seemed flustered.

"Speaking of the ranch, how was the meeting with the attorney?" he asked as he lathered up.

"Thanks to you, I didn't get any surprises. I can't believe my family didn't say anything. I told them that I'm going to sell."

Zach turned off the tap and took the towel from Gina. "I'll bet that went over big."

"Not so much. I'm tired of thinking about what I

should and shouldn't do with the ranch. Could we please change the subject?"

If she was still thinking about it, then she hadn't made up her mind after all. Zach smiled to himself. "Sure."

"Did you know that Uncle Lucky left you a few things?"

"Me?" He couldn't imagine what, but he was intrigued.

She nodded. "I'll tell you about it after dinner."

He could live with that.

They returned to the kitchen. Zach couldn't help noting the sly looks on the faces of Gina's family. What were they up to?

"Zach, you'll sit next to Gina," Sophie directed a little too offhandedly.

So that was the game. They wanted to push him and Gina together. Gina closed her eyes for a moment and sighed.

Zach sat down to a bubbling casserole and thick slabs of homemade bread.

When everyone had filled their plate, Gloria smiled at him. "How was your day?"

"Busy." He told them about the broken heater in the big water tank.

"What happened there?" Sophie asked, pointing to the cut on the underside of his forearm.

"I got into a little argument with a barbed wire fence."

"Ow."

Zach had suffered worse. "It'll heal."

His plate was empty, but he was still hungry.

Gloria noticed. "Please, have more. You wouldn't believe how many casseroles we have to eat up."

He helped himself and dug in.

"Uncle Lucky left some of his things to Zach," Gina said near the end of the meal.

"Oh?" Sophie looked as intrigued as Zach.

Gloria and Redd leaned forward eagerly. "What did he leave you, Zach?"

"Gina hasn't said yet."

"Spit it out, girl," Redd ordered. "Before we all die of curiosity."

"I was going to wait until after the meal, but all right." Gina turned to Zach. "Uncle Lucky left you his horse, Lightning."

"Ah." Redd sat back with an approving nod. "Lucky loved that horse so. It's fitting that he'd want you to have her."

The horse was a beauty and as fast as her name. Zach was deeply moved. "I never expected that."

"There's more," Gina said. "You also get his saddle."

The handcrafted saddle had been one of Lucky's prized possessions. "Are you sure?" Zach asked.

Gina nodded. "He put it in his will."

"I remember when Lucky bought that," Sophie said. "It was the year all of us took Gina to the state fair in Great Falls." She smiled fondly at Gina. "You were about ten."

"I remember that! I was with Uncle Lucky when we stopped at the saddle maker's booth. He had a big, round belly that stretched his shirt so tight, I was sure all the buttons would pop off."

Her family chuckled. She had them all wrapped

around her baby finger. Zach could see why. With her eyes sparkling and that pretty smile on her face, she could charm a barn rat.

"As I recall, your daddy also wanted a saddle." Redd shook his head.

Gina's smile faded. "I remember that, too. My parents had a big fight over it. Mom wouldn't let Dad spend the money. They didn't speak to each other for days after that."

Zach absorbed the information with interest. Except for Gina, the entire Arnett family seemed to have the frugal gene. But Gina earned enough to buy whatever she wanted.

The family looked solemn now, their thoughts on that day long ago.

"I'm honored to have that saddle," Zach said. "I'll take good care of it. Every time I use it and whenever I ride Lightning, I'll think of Lucky."

Redd nodded. "Now that's real nice. I know that wherever Lucky is right now, he's grinning like a son of a— Like a fool."

"He left you one more thing," Gina said. "I put it in my purse in the other room." She went to get it.

Lucky had already given him more than enough. Zach frowned.

When Gina returned, she handed him a tissue-wrapped package. "This is for you."

Zach had no idea what it could be.

"Is that what I think it is?" Gloria asked, her hand over her heart.

He carefully unwrapped the package. A moment

later, he held up a gold pocket watch that looked well used.

Redd nodded. "That watch belonged to our grandfather and then to my daddy."

"Then it should be yours," Zach said.

"Lucky was the oldest son, so it went to him. I got Granddaddy's gold cufflinks. Lucky wore that watch for special occasions. You'll need to wind it to make it run, but it still keeps perfect time. Next to that saddle, it was his most prized possession. He was supposed to pass it to his son. You were the son he never had, Zach, and it's good that he wanted you to have it."

Over the years Zach had received his share of expensive presents, but no one had ever given him such a meaningful gift. He swallowed thickly. "I will cherish this watch forever."

Gina and her cousins teared up, and Redd cleared his throat and wiped his eyes. "You're a fine young man, Zach Horton."

He hadn't always been. Without Lucky, he might still be lost. Dearly missing his friend, Zach curled his fingers around the watch.

"You'll need to get yourself a chain for it, Zach," Redd said. "Put it in your pocket for now so you don't lose it."

"I wouldn't want to break it."

"You won't."

Zach slipped the watch into his hip pocket. In the trailer where he lived there wasn't a place to display it, but he intended to find one.

Gina stood to clear the table and rinse the dishes, and Zach loaded them into Lucky's portable dishwasher.

"Who wants coffee?" Sophie asked.

"Coffee?" The expression on Gina's face was priceless.

He couldn't stem his laughter, and she laughed, too. Sophie frowned. "What's so funny?"

"I made a pot of Uncle Lucky's coffee this morning," Gina said. "Zach knows how terrible it was—he had a cup."

As soon as Gloria heard that Zach had been here that morning, she smiled. Sophie looked pleased, and Redd looked like the Cheshire cat.

They weren't exactly subtle.

"I promise you that this coffee will taste much better," Sophie said. "I brought over a different kind and I scoured Lucky's coffeepot from top to bottom. I don't think the poor thing has been cleaned in a decade."

"I never even thought of that. Okay, I'll give it a try." Zach shrugged. "If you're game, so am I."

"I'll get some of those chocolate-chip cookies Mrs. Yancy dropped off yesterday," Gloria said. "They're delicious."

"Shouldn't we save them in case someone stops by?" Gina asked.

"We won't have any guests tonight. They're all waiting for the funeral tomorrow."

In no time, Zach and the Arnetts were enjoying cookies and decent-tasting coffee.

"You're right—this is good," Gina said. "I think I'll have a second cup. Anyone else?"

Zach and the others shook their heads.

"Careful or you'll be up till all hours," Redd warned.

"That's okay. I have work to do."

"Why don't you take the night off, cookie?" Sophie patted her hand. "You look so worn out."

"I am pretty tired." Gina said, massaging the space between her brows.

"You need rest so that you can be strong tomorrow."

"You're right. Forget that second cup of coffee. I'll go to bed early."

An image of Gina in bed filled Zach's mind. He pictured her in a black satin teddy that revealed all her curves. He imagined slowly peeling the garment off her body and making her forget all about sleeping...

He caught himself and shut down his thoughts. Lucky had just died. Gina was grieving, and so was Zach. He shouldn't be thinking about sex.

What kind of man was he, lusting over Lucky's niece when he was supposed to be focused on convincing her to keep the ranch?

She wasn't even his type. He steered clear of women like her. Steered clear of getting involved, period. Getting involved meant questions, and he wasn't about to explain his past to Gina or anyone else.

They were arguments he'd repeated to himself several times today. That didn't stop him from fantasizing about her.

"You're frowning, Zach." Sophie looked concerned. "I thought you liked Mrs. Yancy's cookies."

"They're great." Forcing a bland expression, he helped himself to a few more. "I was thinking about the funeral."

Gloria let out a weighty sigh. "It's on all our minds."

"What time is the service?" Gina asked.

"Ten-thirty." Redd stacked his mug on his empty dessert plate. "But we don't know how long it'll last—that will depend on how many people share stories about Lucky."

Zach expected to hear a whole lot of those. Most everyone had counted the rancher as a friend.

"As soon as the service ends, there will be a reception in the church's rec room," Gloria said. "Then the five of us will come back here and scatter Lucky's ashes."

Gina gave a solemn nod.

Nothing about it sounded easy. Tomorrow was guaranteed to be a long and difficult day.

Chapter 5

On the day of the funeral, Gina woke up feeling sad and heavy. It was early and still dark outside, and she flipped on the bedside-table lamp. Before she even got out of bed, she checked her phone. There were no messages.

She speed-dialed Carrie's cell phone. The assistant didn't pick up. Instead of leaving a message, Gina hung up and called the main office line. "Good morning, Marsha. Will you put me through to Carrie?"

"Of course, but you'll get her voice mail. I haven't seen her yet this morning."

It was almost nine in Chicago. "That's two days in a row," Gina muttered. On this of all days, her assistant was the last person she needed to worry about.

"I wish I knew where she was," Marsha said, and Gina pictured the forty-something secretary giving her head a disapproving shake. "Is there something I can do to help?"

"If you're not too busy. She was supposed to email me a report yesterday, with updates on the various campaigns for each of my clients, but I didn't receive it. I won't have access to email today, but if you can find the report, I'd love to know what the numbers are."

"Let me put you on hold and see what I can find."

While Gina waited, she opened the closet and pulled out the outfit she'd packed for the funeral. At the time, the black suit and gray blouse had seemed appropriate. But now that Zach had suggested using humor, she wished she'd brought something less somber.

On a whim, she plucked a green holly-sprig pin with red berries from the jewelry she'd tossed into her carry-on. The holiday season didn't officially start for another week, but she didn't think anyone would mind.

"You'll never guess what I found in Carrie's office—Carrie herself," Marsha said when she returned to the phone. "She was asleep at her desk. Apparently she worked late last night and dropped off. She was pretty upset when I woke her and she realized what had happened. She's going home to shower and change clothes, and she asked if she could call you with the numbers later."

"Poor Carrie." Gina felt bad for her assistant. She thought about asking one of her colleagues to step in and take some of the load off Carrie's shoulders, but she didn't have time to explain and review the details just now. "Just make sure she emails that report sometime today, and ask her to call me this afternoon. I should be able to talk by four Montana time at the latest."

"I'll be thinking of you. There is one more thing you should know. Some of your clients called yesterday, and I'm not sure Carrie returned their calls."

Andersen, Coats and Mueller had built their reputation on quality service and excellent results, which meant seeing to the client's every need—which included returning calls promptly.

Growing more concerned by the minute, Gina frowned. "Would you email me the messages? Then please call and let the clients know where I am, and tell them that I'll contact them first thing on Monday morning."

Her stomach in knots, she disconnected. If her assistant flaked out on her, they were both in a world of trouble.

But she couldn't worry about any of that right now. Setting her work troubles aside, she turned her focus on the day ahead.

As funerals went, Lucky's wasn't half bad, Zach mused as he piloted Redd's station wagon and the Arnett family back to the ranch. Redd's was the only car big enough to seat five adults. The ranch crew followed behind the wagon, a melancholy contingent of cars and trucks that would leave Zach and the family to scatter the ashes on their own. The afternoon was overcast and cold, and Zach figured they were in for another snowstorm. He hoped it held off until the family dispersed Lucky's ashes.

It had been an emotionally draining day. Sophie and Gloria slumped on the bench seat up front, and in the back, Redd and Gina stared out their respective windows.

Zach patted Lucky's watch, which was attached to his pants by the chain he'd found at a jewelry store in the next town. Wearing the watch somehow helped. He glanced in the rearview mirror. As if Gina felt his stare, she turned from the window and solemnly met his gaze. Her eyes were red and swollen. Tears had washed away her makeup and her lipstick had worn off long ago, but she didn't need cosmetics to look pretty. She was what Lucky would have called a natural beauty.

"How're you doing?" he asked softly.

She squared her shoulders. "I'm okay."

As he drove down the highway toward the ranch, he thought about her funny yet poignant eulogy. She'd touched him and everyone else, and sniffling sounds had filled the little church.

She'd dressed for the occasion in a black pantsuit with a festive pop of color on the lapel and high, black heels that made him wish she were wearing a skirt so that he could look at her legs. His grief didn't stop him from wanting her, and apparently he wasn't the only one. More than one male in attendance had checked her out.

"I just thought of something," Gloria said as they neared the ranch. "At least three inches of snow are on the ground and the earth is frozen solid. How are we supposed to scatter Lucky's ashes?"

Sophie's fingers worried the straps of her purse. "Maybe we should hold on to them until the spring thaw."

"Months from now?" Redd snorted. "By then, Gina might have sold the ranch."

Sophie and Gloria swiveled their heads around to eye her.

With her lip firmly between her teeth, she dug in her purse for a tissue, setting off a flurry of tears and nose blowing.

Zach cleared his throat. "Lucky loved the river. We could scatter the ashes there."

"But it's frozen," Gloria said.

"Not at its deepest points. We'll find a place where it isn't." Zach turned up the gravel driveway, passing under the Lucky A Ranch sign that hung under an iron arch spanning the entrance. As he turned toward the house, the caravan of vehicles behind them blinked their lights and headed for their respective trailers.

"Save your good shoes and take my car over to your trailer, Zach," Redd said as Zach pulled up close to the back door. "Get changed and we'll see you back here shortly."

Zach nodded and escorted Gloria and Sophie to the door.

When he returned to the house, he left the engine running, headed up the steps and knocked on the door.

They were all waiting for him. Gina had changed into jeans, winter boots and a body-hugging pullover sweater the color of whipped butter.

After everyone was in the car and buckled up, he headed slowly toward the river. "The ground is good and hard. I should be able to drive almost to the riverbank."

The ranch hands had offered to do all the afternoon

chores, giving him the rest of the day off. In the distance, cattle huddled together around fresh feed the crew had just delivered. Snow flurries swirled through the air. If they wanted to beat the harder stuff, they'd best get moving.

A scant few yards from the water, Zach pulled to a stop. The wind had kicked up and the icy air stung his face.

He took hold of Sophie and Gloria. Gina grasped Redd's arm. She'd traded her expensive coat for a burgundy-colored down jacket and scarf and a stylish hat that protected her ears.

Standing at the riverbank, she frowned. "The entire river looks frozen to me."

"Not out there." Zach pointed to a dark patch of water at the widest part of the river, a few yards away.

"But that's halfway across. It can't be safe."

He nodded. "Trust me, the ice is thick. It'll hold us."

"All five of us? Are you sure?"

"If I weren't, I wouldn't have suggested bringing the ashes out here. I wouldn't put you or anyone else at risk."

Gina shot a worried glance at her cousins and Redd. "Maybe they should watch from here."

"That seems wise," Redd said. "It isn't that I don't trust your judgment, Zach. But at our ages, we can't risk slipping and falling."

"That's right." Gloria moved closer to Redd and Sophie. "We'll say our goodbyes from here. What about you, Gina?"

"I want to do this." Gina turned her impossibly big eyes on Zach. "You'll come with me?"

A snowflake clung to her eyelashes. He had the urge to kiss it away, but instead he nodded and took the urn from her.

She hooked her hand through his arm, and he swore he felt her warmth through her fur-lined glove. They made their way cautiously across the ice. Less than a foot away from the sluggish water that was on the verge of freezing, he pulled her to a stop. "We'd best not go any closer."

Gina nodded and, with her teeth, tugged off her gloves. She shoved them into her pockets and took the urn from Zach. She opened it and held it up. "Goodbye, Uncle Lucky. Be at peace," she said over the wind.

Beautiful words that would've meant more if she was keeping the ranch. Zach silently pledged to continue trying to convince her.

From the riverbank, Gloria and Sophie called out their own final messages, and Redd added, "God speed."

"Goodbye, friend," Zach murmured, his chest tight with feeling.

He and Gina shared a long look filled with mutual loss and grief. Then with a thrust of her arms, she sent Lucky's ashes flying. They mingled briefly with the snow before dropping quietly into the water.

Silent and solemn, she handed the empty urn to Zach. Her hands were red, and she tugged on her gloves with clumsy fingers. He knew how cold they were. His own face was numb, and he regretted leaving his woolen ski mask at the trailer.

Gina hooked her arm through his again and they made their way toward the bank. Snow was coming down hard now, and the sky had grown steadily darker. Zach guessed it was after four. Gloria, Sophie and Redd headed for the car and piled into the backseat.

"At least one of you should ride in the front with Zach and me," she said as Zach opened the passenger door.

"We don't mind sitting back here together." Redd winked.

It was clear that they wanted Zach and Gina to get together.

Now, there was a match doomed before it even started.

Regardless, today they'd shared something neither of them would ever forget.

As soon as the engine purred to life, Zach turned the heat on full blast.

"That feels good." Gina held her hands in front of the vent.

She practically hugged the door. Even so, Zach was as keenly attuned to her presence as if she was sitting close.

She pulled off her hat and he caught a whiff of her flowery perfume. His body stirred. This was getting old.

"I don't feel the heat yet." Gloria stomped her feet and rubbed her hands together. "It's beastly cold. I wouldn't be surprised if we all had frostbite."

"The way we're all bundled up?" Sophie harrumphed. "You're so melodramatic, Glo. You should've gone into acting."

At the house, Gina exited while Zach helped her cousins.

The empty evening stretched before him, as gray

as the sky. He wanted to join the family, but he'd been with them all day and didn't want to intrude any further. "I'll leave you to it," he said, shoving his hands into the pockets of his parka.

"Leave us to what?" Sophie's lips quirked.

He shrugged. "You probably want time alone, with just the family."

"Nonsense," Redd said. "You're as much a part of the family as the rest of us. But I happen to have an ulterior motive—I was hoping you could whip up some hot toddies to help us get warm. I'm still thinking about the ones you made last year during that stretch of subzero weather. Best I ever tasted."

Gloria grasped Zach's arm. "You heard the man. Please stay."

"All right." Zach held the door for everyone.

Inside, Gina studied him with a thoughtful expression. "Hot toddies aren't exactly the kind of thing people our age drink," she said. "Where did you learn to make them?"

"In a different life." An easy life of wealth and luxury Zach had once taken for granted. Life at the Lucky A was harder and leaner, but in the three years since he'd sold his company and taken a job here, he didn't miss much of what he'd given up. He was certainly happier.

"Did you own a bar or something?" Gina asked while her cousins dug out the ingredients for the drink.

"In a manner of speaking." He hung up his coat. "When you were fourteen, Lucky taught you to drive. When I was that age, my father taught me to mix drinks.

He thought that if I played bartender during the parties he liked to throw, I'd be too busy to get into trouble."

"Did it work?"

"Let's just say, I learned to sneak my drinks when no one was looking. It was a great gig—until I got caught."

Sophie tsked, Gloria covered a smile with her hand and Redd grinned and said, "I'll bet your daddy whupped you good."

Looking amused, Gina arched her eyebrows. Her cheeks were pink from the cold, and for the first time all day, her eyes were bright and filled with humor.

"I got a stern lecture, which was probably worse than any spanking," Zach replied with a deadpan expression.

As he'd hoped, they all laughed. He joined in. After the weighty day, laughing felt good.

As soon as Gina hung up her coat and tugged off her boots, she moved toward the stairs. "I'm going to make a few calls. I'll be down in a little while."

Zach shook his head. She couldn't even take the full day off for her uncle's funeral—a needed reminder that he wasn't interested.

"Damn you, Carrie," Gina muttered as she sat on the bed and checked her phone messages.

Out of respect for her family and the funeral, she'd left her phone in her room today. At some point this afternoon, Carrie had called with an update and numbers. Unfortunately, she'd repeated the same information she'd already shared. And she didn't mention the client calls she'd failed to return.

She was exhausted, but Gina also suspected that despite Carrie's assurances that she could handle the temporary responsibilities she was saddled with, she wasn't ready.

Gina thought about telling Kevin, but she wasn't ready just yet. She definitely needed to ask one of her colleagues for help. As busy as they all were, they wouldn't appreciate having to take on more work. Carrie wouldn't like it, either, but she obviously couldn't handle the workload by herself.

Marsha had also called with the names and numbers from the past two days' calls and let Gina know she'd contacted them.

Outside, darkness had fallen. Gina checked her watch. The funeral, reception and spreading the ashes had taken longer than she'd imagined. In Chicago it was after five and the Friday before Thanksgiving to boot. The office was already gearing down for the holiday and upcoming short workweek, and Gina doubted that anyone would be there now. All the same, she left a message for Carrie.

She also tried Carrie's cell, but her assistant didn't pick up. Well, she had that dinner date tonight. Gina left a message that ended with, "First thing Monday morning, you and I need to talk. Expect my call at nine a.m. Chicago time."

Having done all that she could for now, she stood. She caught a glimpse of herself in the mirror. Somehow, her makeup had disappeared, and she looked all washed out. If only she'd realized sooner. Wanting to look better for her family, and yes, for Zach, she freshened up her makeup and ran a comb through her hair. There.

She looked better, but between the funeral and worrying about Carrie, she felt as if she'd been through the wringer.

Needing the comfort of her family and Zach, she headed downstairs to rejoin them.

Chapter 6

A roaring fire crackled in the fireplace, as if this were a normal November evening at the Lucky A. It wasn't. Uncle Lucky had been a huge presence in Gina's life, and his passing left a big hole in her heart. That he wasn't here to tease her and make her laugh put a definite damper on things, but Zach and her family were good company.

Having consumed one of his delicious hot toddies before dinner and two glasses of wine with the meal, she was finally relaxed. Zach and Uncle Redd had brought up a set of old TV trays from the basement and they'd eaten in front of the fire, polishing off a whole casserole, most of a chocolate cake and two bottles of wine—with numerous toasts to Uncle Lucky.

Uncle Redd set down his cake plate and patted his belly. "That was real tasty," he said, stretching and yawning. "It's been a long day, and I'm ready to go home." He gestured at Sophie and Gloria. "Get your coats, girls."

Too full and comfortable to move just yet, Gina scrutinized her uncle from her chair. "It's stopped snowing, but there are at least a few more inches on the ground. The roads are sure to be slippery, and you've had quite a bit to drink. Plus it's dark. Why don't you stay here? There's room for all of you."

Uncle Redd shook his head. "We'll do that at Christmas. I can't leave the dogs alone overnight. I'm not driving more than a few miles and I could do it blindfolded, so the dark isn't a problem. Besides, I only had the one hot toddy and half a glass of wine, and you saw how much food I put away tonight. I'm as sober as I was when I got up this morning."

He shot a wry look at Sophie and Gloria, who'd helped Gina and Zach drink the wine. "I can't speak for your cousins, though."

The women glanced at each other and giggled. Slightly drunk herself, Gina smiled.

In no time, everyone was in the kitchen, Gina and Zach helping the older ones into their coats.

After all they'd been through today, Gina felt very close to her family. She hated to see them go and dreaded spending the night alone in the house. But she wasn't going to admit it.

"Will I see you tomorrow?" she asked after she hugged and kissed each of them.

Gloria shook her head. "Probably not, honey. Saturday is the day Sophie and I do our house cleaning. Besides, you'll be sorting through Lucky's papers and things, and we'd probably just get in the way. Why don't you come to our house Sunday night for dinner? We'll plan our Thanksgiving meal." She smiled at Zach. "It goes without saying that you're invited again this year— both for Thanksgiving and Christmas."

"I appreciate that," Zach said. "Count me in."

Without Uncle Lucky, both holiday celebrations were bound to feel dreary. Gina half wished she could come back at Christmas.

Redd opened the door to leave. "Don't stay up late, you two." Winking, he closed it behind them.

"They couldn't be more obvious about pushing us together." Gina shook her head in disbelief. "I love them all dearly, but sometimes—make that a lot of the time— they drive me crazy."

"They aren't so bad."

"That's because they're on their best behavior when you're around. You should hear them nag and question me about when I'm going to get married. They're worried that if I don't get married and have kids soon, the Arnett family line will die out."

"What do you tell them?"

"That I'm barely thirty and I have plenty of time. I'm not even dating right now."

"Too busy working?"

"That, and I'm also picky."

"Let me guess, you're looking for a CEO to come along and sweep you off your feet."

She laughed. "He doesn't have to be a CEO as long as he's ambitious. My family doesn't understand at all."

Zach was silent and his expression was unreadable. Gina wished she knew what he was thinking. "Men don't have the same kind of pressure as women," she added.

"Sure we do, but in different ways. You have a choice of whether or not to make your name in the world. We don't have that choice."

"Your family puts that kind of pressure on you?"

"Every man's does."

"And you're rebelling."

For a moment he looked puzzled. Then his eyes narrowed a fraction. "You mean because I'm a ranch foreman. You're a white-collar snob." He snorted and headed back to the living room.

She was offended. "I am not! I just… You're really smart, Zach. What you said about Uncle Lucky at the funeral today was eloquent and moving. You have all this potential, and…" By his grim expression, she saw that she'd only made things worse, and she let the words trail off.

"You're wondering why I don't do what you do? Put in eighty-hour workweeks chasing after the next deal? That's an empty life I don't choose to live."

None too gently, he began to stack the dessert plates.

She'd really hit a sore spot. "You're going to break something, Zach."

He set down the dishes and slapped the folding TV tables shut. "I'll take these back to the basement."

"I can do that later."

Tight-lipped, he hefted the five folded tables and strode toward the kitchen.

Those tables were heavy, yet he toted them as if they weighed nothing. Gina followed him, jogging to keep up. In the kitchen, she shot around him to open the basement door and flip on the lights down there.

His footsteps thudded down the wooden steps, each one sounding like a scold. Feeling terrible for insulting him, she chafed her arms.

Uncle Lucky's portable dishwasher was still hooked up to the kitchen faucet from after dinner. The cycle was finished, and she unhooked and wheeled it to its place against the wall.

She was about to put the clean dishes away when she heard Zach come up the stairs.

Her heart pounded. Twisting her hands at her waist, she met him at the top of the steps. He looked surprised. "What's wrong?"

"I just— Don't be angry, Zach."

"Damn straight, I'm mad. I don't like being judged, especially when you know nothing about me."

She was wearing flat ankle boots tonight, which gave him a height advantage of at least four inches. Looming over her with a dark expression, he was intimidating, but she met his gaze. "Not for lack of asking. You won't tell me anything."

"My past is my business. It's over and done with, and I don't talk about it." He crossed his arms as if daring her to say one more word about the subject.

Frustrated, she offered something of an apology. "I won't bring up your past again, all right? But don't blame me for making assumptions. They're all I have to go on."

That didn't make him any happier, and she threw up her hands. "You should probably just go home," she said, hating the thought of his leaving like this, of being alone for the rest of the evening.

"I'll stay until the dishes are done. You empty the dishwasher and I'll bring in the stuff from the living room."

"That'd be nice. Thank you."

Not in the best of moods, Zach turned and headed back to the living room. Of all the nights to have words with Gina. He didn't want to argue with her or leave things unsettled. The second he'd caught sight of her in the airport baggage claim, he'd known they were as mismatched as a cowboy boot and an expensive pump.

The problem was that every time he saw her, he wanted her more.

He shouldn't have kissed her yesterday, but he wasn't sorry he had.

The plates clattered loudly as he stacked them. Then he remembered Gina's warning to be careful. He collected the utensils and glasses with more care and brought them to the kitchen.

Gina was putting away the clean silverware and acknowledged him with a curt nod.

Time for an apology. He set the dirty dishes in the sink and waited for her to look at him. Her wary expression tugged at something in his chest. "Look, I don't want to fight with you," he said.

"I'm so sorry for what I said—what I implied." She swallowed loudly, her eyes filled with remorse. "That was rude and completely uncalled for."

"It was, but I overreacted. We've both been through a lot, especially today, and feelings are raw."

"It isn't just losing Uncle Lucky." She bit her lip. "I'm worried about things at work."

"Ah." She kept reminding him that work was her main priority, and he kept forgetting. Unable to think of a decent reply, Zach shook his head. "I'll grab my coat and let you get back to it."

"Tonight I don't want to do anything remotely work related," she said. "I don't even want to think about my job, but I'm so stressed out that I can't help it. Carrie, my assistant, isn't doing what she promised. She's supposed to take up the slack and handle the accounts while I'm here. I've only been gone three days, and already she's fallen behind. My clients expect blue-ribbon service. I can't risk losing them because of her."

Zach understood. "Ask a colleague to step in and help."

"I'm going to have to," she said. "But everyone is trying to clear off their desks before Wednesday, when we close for the long Thanksgiving weekend."

"Have you talked to your boss?"

"Not yet." She sighed. "It's a bit of a mess. My assistant and I both assured him that she was up to the responsibility. He isn't exactly the compassionate type and I worry that he'll question my ability to manage. Even if I do find someone to step in, I'll have to take the time to explain what needs to be done. Which means I'll be stuck spending more time on work when I'd rather focus on the things I need to do here before I leave. Like sort through Uncle Lucky's papers and his personal effects and figure out what to keep and what I can toss. How am I supposed to get it all done?"

"Winter is a slow time for ranchers. I'll do what I

can. Other people have offered to help, too. We can't sort through Lucky's papers for you, but we can get rid of the newspapers and old magazines and clean out the basement. You just need to ask."

"Thanks. I'll sort everything out and let you know." She gave him a small smile. "Sorry for dumping on you like that."

"No problem." Zach felt for her. "I remember when my grandfather died. My family put what we didn't want or need immediately into storage. It was years before anyone looked through that stuff. You already have Lucky's financial papers. You could go through the rest of his things some other time."

That stubborn look crossed her face. "I don't want to put it off, Zach. I don't think Uncle Lucky would want me to." She pulled the last of the cutlery from the open dishwasher and put it away. "I feel bad enough that I didn't come home more often while he was alive. The least I can do is take the time and care to sort through his things now."

Her shoulders slumping, she fiddled with the knob on the silverware drawer and avoided his gaze. She was easy to read. Guilt was weighing her down.

Having been there himself, Zach knew how heavy that load was. He moved toward her. "Letting the guilt eat you alive won't do you or Lucky any good," he said. "Like he used to tell me, don't beat yourself up over things you can't change."

Her curious expression told him that she wondered what he'd beaten himself up about. But Lucky had been the last person to hear about that, and Zach was not going to revisit his sorry past ever again.

"My uncle gave you good advice, but I don't know that I can follow it."

"If I did, you can. You look like you could use a hug," he said, surprising himself.

He opened his arms, and she walked into them.

Without her heels, she barely reached his shoulder. As strong a woman as she was, her bones were fine and delicate. Zach tucked her against the hollow of his shoulder and rested his chin on the top of her head.

After a few moments, he felt the tension drain out of her, felt her relax. Perfume and the womanly scent underneath filled his senses. "That's much better."

Closing his eyes, he kissed her head. She wriggled closer, her softness teasing his body to life.

Now who was tense? Zach loosened his hold on her and started to back away.

"Don't go." Hanging on tight, she looked up at him, her green eyes round and pleading. "I need you tonight. Kiss me, Zach."

All day he'd wanted to do exactly that—and more. But wanting her was wrong for them both, and kissing her was dangerous.

He should walk away now, while he still could. But she laced her arms around his neck and pulled him down, and he was lost.

Her lips were sweet and eager. He slid his tongue inside her mouth and explored. He sat her on the cutting board top of the dishwasher and stood between her long legs.

One kiss blended into another, each one burning into him. His body went hard with desire. Wanting to taste more of her, he ran his lips down the column of her neck. She liked that, especially when he nibbled the place where her neck met her shoulder.

Mindful of the tiny gold hoops in her ears, he gently tugged her earlobe with his teeth. She liked that, too.

Hands on her hips, he scooted her forward and moved in closer. Big mistake.

She stiffened. "No, Zach."

What was he doing? He was supposed to convince Gina to keep the ranch, not fool around with her.

He straightened and stepped back. Gina hopped down from the dishwasher and tugged her sweater over her hips. The soft wool stretched tight across her breasts.

Zach swallowed. "It's time for me to go."

He grabbed his coat and let himself out.

Upstairs, Gina stared at herself in the bathroom mirror. With her slightly swollen lips and her flushed cheeks, she looked as if she'd been thoroughly kissed.

And she had been. Closing her eyes, she replayed the thrill of Zach's demanding mouth on hers and the way his strong arms had felt around her.

She'd enjoyed his kisses all too much, had wanted more. Which was exactly why she'd stopped him. She wasn't into casual sex, nor was she about to get involved with Zach—even if he was intelligent and not at all the hard cowboy she'd first thought. She wanted a man with the drive and ambition to be more than a ranch foreman.

None of that stopped her from thinking about him.

His father had taught him to mix drinks so that he could bartend at parties. That didn't sound blue-collar. Did Zach's parents have money? Had he attended college? Why had he left Houston, what had brought him to Saddlers Prairie and why was he working as a foreman on Uncle Lucky's rundown ranch?

Gina was beyond curious, but Zach was so closemouthed about his past that she doubted she'd ever learn the answers from him.

That wasn't going to stop her from trying to find out more. Surely someone in Saddlers Prairie could tell her what she wanted to know. She would ask around and see what she could find out.

Chapter 7

There was nothing quite like waking up gradually in bed on a Saturday morning. After rising before dawn pretty much seven days a week for months, lazing about felt luxurious.

Yawning and stretching, Gina let her thoughts wander. Naturally they homed in on Zach. Everything he'd done yesterday, from giving a eulogy at the funeral to spreading Uncle Lucky's ashes to spending the evening with her family, had been above and beyond and proved what a great guy he was.

But he was a rancher, and his life was tough. Gina wanted an easier life, with a regular paycheck, raises and bonuses.

Which meant that Zach wasn't the guy for her.

But the way he made her feel when he kissed her...

She went warm and soft inside. She wanted more in spite of herself.

No, she firmly told herself and sat up.

It was time to get up and get to work on the house. She would start sorting through Uncle Lucky's things, beginning with the contents of his desk.

After showering and dressing, Gina headed downstairs. While her cinnamon bread toasted and the coffeemaker percolated, she turned on her phone.

To her relief, Carrie had texted, letting her know she'd emailed the report Gina wanted and that she would wait for Gina's call Monday morning.

"That's more like it," Gina murmured. She was relieved and decided that for now, she wouldn't bother any of her colleagues with the request to help her assistant.

As she loaded her breakfast dishes into the dishwasher, she couldn't help remembering the kisses she and Zach had shared right there last night. Unbidden heat flooded her, and she wanted him again.

Exasperated with herself, she turned her back on the dishwasher and considered making plans to go out tonight and do something to take her mind off Zach.

Saddlers Prairie didn't offer much of a nightlife, but she needed something to fill the evening. Not that she didn't have plenty to keep her busy right here. It would be nice to get out, though, even for a little while. She needed to write thank-you notes to those who sent cards and flowers, so she could drive over to Spenser's and pick up some nice note cards and some chocolate. Then she'd check out the TV guide and look for a movie. And, what the heck, she'd check her email today after all.

What a fabulous Saturday night she had planned.

Armed with trash bags and boxes, Gina started for Uncle Lucky's office.

She was halfway down the hall when her cell phone rang. She glanced at the screen and saw that Autumn Naylor was calling. Autumn was a year older than she was, but they'd attended the one-room Saddlers Prairie grade school together. Both had been dirt poor and they'd developed a friendship of sorts.

"Hey, Autumn," she said, smiling.

"Hi, Gina. That was a nice service yesterday."

"I thought so, too. We were all glad to see you and your family."

Autumn and Cody had an adorable little girl and four foster sons they were raising at Hope Ranch.

"I know this is last minute," Autumn said. "But Cody and the boys are seeing a movie in Red Deer tonight. April goes to bed at seven, and I have the whole evening to myself. I'm throwing a pizza party, no guys allowed. You know everyone who's coming, either from school or the funeral, and I'd love for you to come. That is, if you can spare the time. I know you have a lot on your plate."

Gina jumped at the invitation. "I'll be working on the house all day, but I'm free this evening. What should I bring?"

"Nothing, but since the Pizza Palace is on your way here, it'd be great if you picked up the pizzas for me. I'll call and put them under my name."

"Sure," Gina said.

"Great. See you tonight."

Pleased to have something fun to look forward to, Gina hummed as she sat down at the desk.

Having done a cursory search through the drawers the other day, she didn't expect to find anything worth keeping. They contained packages of never-used pens and pencils, paper clips and sticky notes—enough to last years. Her thrifty uncle had always preferred to buy his supplies in bulk. She would donate them to the school, she decided as she filled a box.

She made short work of all but the fat bottom drawer, which was crammed with ancient-looking folders containing old bills and statements dating back decades.

Who knew why her uncle saved all this stuff, or why he kept his current statements in the safe. Not that it wasn't entertaining to see what groceries had cost twenty-five years ago. Otherwise, it was worthless.

She was tossing the folders into a trash bag and thinking about taking a coffee break when a yellowed folder label caught her eyes. It read *Beau and Marie* in faded ink. Her parents.

Curious, she opened the folder, which was thick with papers. At first she wasn't at all sure what she was looking at, but seeing her parents' signatures here and there filled her with nostalgia. Her father's sense of humor and self-deprecating laugh had often lightened up the most difficult times, while her mother's canning and baking skills had kept their stomachs relatively filled. And despite working two jobs and preserving food, she'd somehow found the time to make many of Gina's clothes—outfits that often rivaled the store-bought items the other girls wore but sometimes fell far short.

Even after all these years, Gina still missed them—but not the hard life they'd endured.

At the bottom of the file she found papers that made

her widen her eyes and suck in a breath. Bankruptcy papers.

The one on top noted that shortly after her birth, her parents had declared bankruptcy.

Stunned, she sat back in her chair. No one had ever told her about this. Not a whisper, even after both her parents had died.

Something else her family had kept from her. It had happened a long time ago, so what was the big secret?

Of course, bankruptcy wasn't good; Gina got that, but she was family. She deserved to know! Fuming, she set the folder aside, stood and stalked into the kitchen. Next time she saw her relatives, they were going to hear about this.

Over a cup of reheated morning coffee, she thought about her parents' bankruptcy some more. Knowing about it explained a lot. Her mother's constant worry about money and her tight hold on the family purse strings, and her father's grudging acceptance that his wife controlled the checkbook.

They'd had a legitimate reason for their money problems. Thanks to a recession and hard times, the farm-equipment business had all but failed. To supplement the family income, her dad had started an equipment-repair business, which had brought in some cash. Both her parents had put in long hours, leaving Gina to fend for herself at home.

Another unsettling part of the whole thing was that, despite her own large paychecks and fat year-end bonuses, she also struggled to make ends meet.

In that way, she wasn't so different from her parents. That was upsetting. She wasn't like them. She wasn't!

Too restless to sit still, she carried her coffee to the window and stared out at the snow-covered backyard and the rolling pastures beyond.

The snow turned everything into a winter wonderland. But nothing could hide the hard-scrabble life her uncle and parents had lived. Gina's life was much easier, and she had the condo, high-end car and closet filled with beautiful clothes and shoes to prove it. Yes, she struggled to pay the bills, but her bonus would help her catch up.

Skating so close to the financial edge was nerve-racking, something she didn't want to think about right now. She pushed the thought away and stared at the back pasture and the herd of cattle lumbering toward an old flatbed, where four men tossed heavy bales of hay onto the ground.

Was that Zach? He was too far away for Gina to be sure, but... No, that was him. As the tallest man, he stood out. Even in a bulky winter jacket, she recognized his long, muscular, jeans-clad legs.

From out of nowhere, a sigh escaped her. She was relieved that for the moment he was out of reach and glad she had plans away from the ranch that evening.

With any luck, she could avoid Zach for a while and rein in her unwanted feelings.

Man, it was cold. Standing in the north pasture, Zach stomped his numb feet and glanced at the wintry blue sky. It didn't look like snow, but in Montana, you never knew. Between the bitter cold and ice and the seasonal downtime at the ranch, Montana winters were a bitch.

Not that any of the ranch hands complained. They

were glad for the work and used their free hours to spend time with their families and visit the friends they had little time for during the rest of the year. Next week, Pete, Bert and Chet would take off for the Thanksgiving holiday, while Zach and Curly had Christmas Eve and Christmas Day off.

When the truck bed stood empty, Zach whipped off his hat and wiped the sweat from his forehead with his coat sleeve. "That's it for today."

Chet and Pete whooped and made for the truck.

Curly Gomez, wryly nicknamed for his bald head, hung back. He and Zach had become friends of sorts and often spent their Saturday evenings hanging out together. They headed for the barn on foot.

"What's on the agenda tonight?" Curly asked, his breath puffing from his lips like smoke.

Anything that would take his mind off Gina. After a hard evening last night—*hard* being the operative word—Zach needed to keep his distance.

The wanting inside him just wouldn't quit. It had been a while since he'd scratched that particular itch, and he figured it was time to change that. "I'm thinking we grab a pizza at the Pizza Palace, then drive up the highway to Sparky's." The bar just outside town was a good place to hook up with a willing woman.

Curly grinned. "Pizza, beer and ladies—I'm game. It's your turn to drive."

Zach nodded. "I'll give you a call when I'm ready to go."

The Pizza Palace was busy, but then it was a wintry Saturday night in Saddlers Prairie. Zach and Curly were in a booth and about to dig into their extra-large pizza when Curly leaned across the table toward him.

"Don't look now," he said under his breath, "but the dark-haired woman at the table to your left is checking you out."

"Yeah?" Zach took a big bite out of his pizza and surreptitiously glanced around. The woman was about his age, with long hair, full lips and big breasts—just his type. She gave him a friendly smile.

Oddly, aside from a spark of attraction, he didn't feel much interest. Unsmiling, he nodded at her and returned his focus to his dinner.

"What'd I tell you?" Curly said with a go-get-her smile.

"She's okay."

His friend's jaw dropped. "If you don't think she's hot, you need glasses."

She was hot enough. Unfortunately, Gina was the woman Zach wanted.

Frowning, he reached for a second slice and glanced at the door as it opened. Gina walked in.

Of all people. A certain part of his body woke up. He swore under his breath.

Curly glanced over his shoulder. "That's Gina."

"Yep."

"She's a real class act. I wonder what she's doing here?"

"She must want a Palace pizza."

"Well, it is one of the finest pizza joints around." Curly's mouth quirked. "The *only* pizza joint around."

She'd spotted him. Zach nodded. Looking a little uncomfortable, Gina headed uncertainly toward the table.

"Hello, Curly," she said, wearing a bright smile that faded when she turned her gazed to Zach. "Hi."

They shared a long look fraught with meaning. They hadn't seen each other since last night. In the twenty-four hours since then, Zach had done more than his share of fantasizing about exactly what he wanted to do with her next time they were alone. Not that there would be a next time.

Tell that to his body. A fresh wave of desire hit him; it was so strong that he got hard just sitting there. Lucky for him, the booth hid his lap.

Curly shot a puzzled look at both of them. "Uh, you want to join us?"

Just what Zach needed—the company of the woman he was better off avoiding.

"Actually, I'm here to pick up an order," she said. "If it's not ready, I'll sit down for a minute—if it's okay with you, Zach."

It was so not okay, but he shrugged. "Sure."

While she was gone to check on the order, Curly raised his eyebrows. Ignoring him, Zach helped himself to another wedge of pizza.

Moments later, Gina returned to the table. "My pizzas are still in the oven. The guy at the counter will call my name when they're ready."

"You ordered more than one, eh?" Curly said. "Is your family coming over tonight?"

Gina shook her head. "They're for a party at Autumn Naylor's house."

"Hope Ranch." Curly nodded. "I've been in that house. It's nice and big, perfect for a party."

Zach pictured people milling around, some of them

no doubt trolling for available women. The thought of a bunch of single men scoping out Gina bothered him. "Who else will be there?" he asked, narrowing his eyes.

She looked surprised by the question. "Friends from high school who are home for Thanksgiving break and a few other people."

Curly laughed. "Cody's cool. I'll bet he wouldn't mind if Zach and I crashed his party."

Gina smiled. "But Autumn would. This is a girls-only party. Cody isn't even invited."

Zach relaxed. "Did you get a lot done at the house today?"

"I did." She wouldn't meet his eyes, whether because of those kisses last night or something else, he wasn't sure. "But there's still much more to do."

"Naylor," a teenage boy called out.

"That's my order." Gina jumped out. "I'll see you later."

Zach followed her with his eyes. He couldn't help it. Her camel hair coat bustled around her legs as she hurried to the pickup counter, all corporate and businesslike. He imagined she moved that quickly all the time at work.

Carrying four large boxes, she moved more slowly toward the door. Several men checked her out. Two started to rise to hold the door for her.

Zach slid out of the booth and beat them to it. The scent of fresh-baked pizza all but drowned out her scent, but he swore he caught a whiff of her perfume.

"Thanks," she said with a quick smile.

"No problem. You and your girlfriends have a good time tonight."

"We will. You, too."

Curly didn't say a word until the door closed behind her and Zach returned to the booth. With a wink, he leaned toward Zach. "She's interested in you."

Zach shook his head. "She goes for the corporate-executive type."

"A woman's eyes don't lie, man. Every time she glanced your way, they lit up."

So that he wouldn't have to reply, Zach bit off a huge chunk of pizza.

"I saw how you watched her when she wasn't looking," Curly went on. "Why are you even talking about going to Sparky's tonight when what you want just walked out the door?"

Zach glanced out the large front window. He could see Gina piling the pizza boxes in the passenger seat of Lucky's truck, her thick coat hiding her hips. All the same, he was aroused. He tore his gaze away and cleared his throat. "Maybe I don't want to be interested in her."

"Doesn't mean you aren't."

"She's not my type."

"Come on, man. She's beautiful and a lot hotter than the brunette at the other table. By the way, as soon as she saw the way you looked at Gina, she left."

Curly's plate was empty. "You finished?" Zach asked. When his friend nodded, he said, "Me, too. I changed my mind about that beer. I'm ready to call it a night."

"It's only seven-thirty, man. Let's grab a pitcher at Sparky's like we talked about."

Zach didn't feel like it anymore. "When we get back, you go on without me."

"Suit yourself. But it's gonna be one lame Saturday night for you."

Chapter 8

Feeling like a giant bundle of exposed nerves, Gina set the pizzas on the passenger seat of the truck. She could feel Zach looking at her—or was she imagining things? On the way to the driver's side of the car, she glanced furtively through the front window of the Pizza Palace. He was frowning at Curly, almost as deeply as he'd frowned at her when she'd walked through the door.

He'd been less than pleased to see her tonight, and apparently he was still unhappy. Gina hadn't exactly been thrilled to see him, either. She pulled out of the parking lot and turned onto the highway. She hadn't expected to see him for several days and hadn't been prepared for the powerful effect his mere presence had on her.

The heat and naked need on his face had stirred her own desire. It was a good thing he hadn't unleashed his smile. Because if he had, she'd probably still be sitting in that booth, wanting him.

Which was startling in itself. No man had ever made her feel like that, turning her on with just a look.

Out of all the available men in the world, why did she have to want Zach Horton?

Refusing to think about him anymore tonight, Gina turned on the radio. The toe-tapping music from the bluegrass country station reminded her of Uncle Lucky, and she suffered a wistful pang. He'd loved bluegrass. At the same time, the delicious smells of freshly baked pizza filled the truck, making her mouth water. Better to salivate over food than Zach.

In what seemed like no time, she was rolling up the long gravel driveway of Hope Ranch. Although she'd never been there before, even when it had been known as Covey Ranch, she was aware that Hope Ranch was far more successful than the Lucky A.

That was obvious by the big house alone. Light blazed from every window on the main floor and across the wraparound porch, making for an impressive sight.

A good half dozen cars were parked in a large turn-around near the house. Gina parked the truck there. Cradling the pizza boxes, she climbed the steps and crossed the porch. She rang the doorbell with her elbow.

Autumn opened the door with a smile. "I'm so glad you're here," she said, relieving Gina of the pizzas. "Thanks for picking these up."

Gina stepped into a wide entry. She shrugged out of her coat and hung it in the coat closet. In the adjoining great room seven women sat before a roaring fire. Three were friends she'd lost touch with after high school and the other three had been at the funeral. She didn't know the slightly older woman.

She needed this night, catching up with old friends and getting better acquainted with new ones. She needed to relax and push Zach, Uncle Lucky's death and her work worries from her mind.

The women smiled and called out greetings, and immediately Gina felt at home.

"Cocktails and appetizers are on the side table," Autumn said. "Help yourself. I'll stick these pizzas in the oven to stay warm. I'll be right back."

By the time Gina poured herself a glass of wine and found a seat on the massive sectional sofa that faced the fireplace, Autumn had returned.

She reintroduced everyone. "You remember Sarah Hollyer, Meg Dawson, her sister-in-law, Jenny, and Stacy Engle. They were all at your house the other night and at the funeral. Next to Stacy is Joan Tyee, who you haven't met. She's a close friend of mine." Autumn grinned. "When I took the housekeeping job here, I was an awful cook. Joan saved me by teaching me how to make a few things. If she hadn't, I probably wouldn't have been here long enough for Cody to fall in love with me."

"Not true." Joan's eyes sparkled. "He was in love with you the second you walked into the house."

"Joan's husband, Doug, is foreman here at Hope Ranch," Autumn said. "He's really great with our foster sons."

Gina wondered what it was like, being a foreman's wife. "Do you also work at the ranch?" she asked Joan.

The woman shook her head. "I'm an office manager

for an insurance company in town. I also have two little ones at home—and as you can see, baby number three will arrive in a few months."

Joan bracketed one side of her mouth with her hand, as if about to reveal a secret she didn't want others to hear. "I'm almost forty-two," she said with a wry expression. "And this pregnancy came as a complete surprise. Doug and I are thrilled, of course."

A special glow lit Joan from the inside. Gina almost envied her, which was odd. She was so not ready for motherhood. Maybe after she was promoted to vice president—provided she met her Mr. Right.

Joan went on. "Dr. Mark assures us that everything is normal, for which we're grateful. But after this one, I'm getting my tubes tied."

Everyone laughed.

When Meg, who was sitting next to Gina, got up to chat with someone across the room, Sarah Hollyer took her place. "I've been wanting to ask you something."

Assuming she had some marketing questions, Gina smiled. "Fire away."

"What do you think of Zach?"

Taken off-guard, Gina struggled for an answer besides, *He's a great kisser.* For the life of her, she couldn't come up with anything else. "What do you mean?" she finally said.

"I met him a couple years ago, when I interviewed him and Lucky for an article I was writing about ranching in eastern Montana. Your uncle made me laugh, but Zach really impressed me with his smarts. I think he's a great guy and really good-looking. Not as handsome as Clay, but a close second."

"Uncle Lucky had quite a sense of humor," Gina said. "And you're right about Zach. He's a good man." Maybe Sarah could tell her something about him. "What do you know about his background?"

"Only that he's from Texas and has been here about three years."

"I remember when he stopped at the clinic for a tetanus shot a few months ago," Stacy said. "Every woman in the room was fanning herself. A gorgeous guy like that... It's a wonder some lucky woman hasn't snapped him up."

Gina didn't like that idea at all. Frowning, she stood. "I need more wine."

When she returned to her seat, a woman named Dani, who'd been in several of Gina's high school classes, angled her head toward her. "I hear you live in Chicago and that you're the assistant vice president at a big marketing company. What's that like?"

Finally, a subject Gina could sink her teeth into. "The job or Chicago?" she asked.

"Both."

"My job is pretty demanding, but I love the challenge. Chicago's great—it's big and vibrant, and there's always something to do."

"Wow," Dani said. "I'll bet they have great stores there."

"Every chain you can think of, plus a lot of great boutiques. It's a shopper's paradise. And the restaurants are amazing."

A lively discussion followed. Gina was enjoying herself. She loved the hustle and bustle of Chicago, but these women made Saddlers Prairie seem pretty darn great. Already she felt closer to them than she ever had to Lise or any of her other colleagues at Andersen, Coats and Mueller.

As for friends outside of work, she didn't really have any. And whose fault was that? She'd been so busy working that she hadn't taken the time to cultivate real friendships.

"I'm ready to eat," Autumn said. "Help me with the pizzas, Gina?"

Gina followed her into a spacious, state-of-the-art kitchen. "Wow," she said. "This is a far cry from the places we lived when we were kids."

"I know." Autumn grinned and pulled on oven mitts. "Sometimes I have to pinch myself to make sure my life isn't a dream. And I'm not talking our bank account or this house. I found the love of my life. With Cody, I'd be happy living in a shack."

Gina wasn't sure she believed that. "You've been poor. You know you'd be worrying about how to pay the bills and feed yourselves."

"What I mean is, the house and money are just icing on the cake. Let's put these in the dining room."

As Gina helped arrange the pizzas on the dining room table, she mulled over Autumn's words. She'd never considered that love could matter so much more than money, and she certainly hadn't seen that with her parents. She wondered if they'd enjoyed each other's company before the bankruptcy.

"Dinner is served in the dining room," Autumn announced in a fake British accent that had everyone chuckling.

"Yay!" Stacy pushed herself up and rubbed her

rounded belly. "You'd think that with this baby squishing my stomach, I'd never feel like eating. But, no, I want to feed my face all the time."

Fresh laughter broke out.

The lighthearted conversation was exactly what Gina needed. She relaxed as she hadn't in forever, and for a while she forgot all about Zach and the sad event that had brought her back to Saddlers Prairie.

The pizza was gone and everyone was sipping tea and enjoying brownies still warm from the oven when Autumn sat back and glanced at Gina.

"So are you dating anyone in Chicago?"

The conversation around the table stopped as everyone waited for Gina's reply. Now, that was being put on the spot, Gina thought.

"Not since my boyfriend and I broke up over the summer," she said. "The truth is, I've been too busy to even think about meeting guys. Once things slow down at work, I'm sure I'll start dating again." She crossed her fingers and, without intending to, held them up for all to see.

Autumn looked sympathetic—the last thing Gina wanted. "Don't worry about me," she said. "I'm happy."

But was she really?

"I used to think I'd never get married," Sarah said. "I certainly didn't see myself in Saddlers Prairie. Yet here I am, living on a ranch with the best husband in the world and the mother of year-old twins. I've never been happier."

She sounded a lot like Autumn.

Except for Gina, all the women were married with children, and they nodded and smiled. She felt like the odd girl out. Yet she also felt accepted and liked by everyone. Not for her work accomplishments but for who she was right now. She wasn't used to that. It felt...different, in a good way.

Not long after dinner, the party wound down. At the door, Autumn hugged her. "It's been great seeing you. I wish you'd think about coming home again for Christmas."

Gina had thought she didn't want to, but now she actually considered the suggestion—for all of five seconds. No, she decided. She needed to stay in Chicago and work.

Next year, for sure.

Gina spent Sunday cleaning out the basement. She stopped in time to shower and change before heading to dinner at Sophie and Gloria's. By the time she parked in front of their little house, she was hungry and grouchy. Scooping up a cake—the last of the desserts brought to the house by people paying their respects—and her parents' bankruptcy folder, she made her way to the front door. Tonight, she wanted answers.

She knocked before opening the door and stepping into the modest living room. Wonderful smells greeted her, and she sniffed appreciatively.

"There's my favorite niece." Seated in the recliner, Uncle Redd waved. "Is that a cake?"

"Your only niece," she corrected, placing her things on a chair and hanging up her coat. "And yes, it's a cake."

Her uncle frowned. "You don't look happy. Rough day?"

"Actually, I accomplished quite a bit." She had the bulging trash bags to prove it. "But no, I'm not very happy. Follow me into the kitchen and I'll explain why."

In the small kitchen, her cousins were working their magic.

"Hello," Sophie called out, tipping her cheek up for a kiss. "Dinner's almost ready."

Gloria nodded. "Grab an apron and dress the salad."

"Not until we talk."

"But dinner's almost ready," Sophie said.

"It can wait." Gina gestured at the kitchen table. "Sit." She jerked her chin at Uncle Redd. "You, too."

"Oh, dear," Gloria muttered. "What is it this time?"

"First, you neglect to warn me that instead of Uncle Redd inheriting the Lucky A, I am. I thought the secrets were behind us, but I was wrong." She slapped the thick folder on the table so that they could all see it. "I can't believe you all didn't tell me about my parents' bankruptcy."

Uncle Redd scratched the back of his neck. "It was a long time ago, honey. Before you were even born."

"According to the paperwork, I was a few months old."

"Same difference. By the time you were big enough to understand, your folks had put it behind them. What would have been the point of opening that old wound?"

"The point is, they're my parents. Bankruptcy is a huge thing, and I should've been told."

"You know now, and what good has it done?" Gloria shook her head. "You're all upset."

"I'm angry, but not because of the bankruptcy. Because of the secrecy around it."

"Your parents were ashamed—we all were," Sophie said.

Uncle Redd nodded. "We've never been rich, but we always pay our way. It's a matter of pride. That bankruptcy was the first time anyone in our family faced financial ruin. And in such a public way. Beau and Marie wanted to protect you from the shame."

In a public way? "You're saying that people in Saddlers Prairie knew?"

Her uncle nodded. "By law, *The Saddlers Prairie News* is required to print a statement as a notice to creditors. That's a requirement of anyone declaring bankruptcy. You can imagine the humiliation."

In a town the size of Saddlers Prairie, Gina definitely could. The truth was, bankruptcy was humiliating, period—even in a bustling city the size of Chicago. She was beyond thankful for her upcoming bonus.

"I never heard even a whisper about it from anyone in town," she said.

"Why would you? It was no one's business."

"But news travels around here like wildfire."

"Yes, and then it dies down."

"Tell me how it happened."

Uncle Red rested his arms on the table. "Beau wasn't frugal like Lucky and me. He had a reckless streak and liked to spend money."

"He used to say that if you spend like you're rich, then you'll be rich," Gloria said. "He claimed that was how he got your mama to look at him and her daddy to bring him into the farm-equipment business."

Gina nodded. "He was dressing for success." When her family gave her blank looks, she explained. "In the corporate world, looking and acting successful is key to real success. People treat you differently and doors open that would otherwise stay closed."

"Beau may have taken over the business, but he wasn't anything like a corporate executive," Uncle Redd said. "He spent his paycheck on trips to Vegas and things he didn't need. A big truck, a fancy car for Marie, a new color TV and whatever else caught his fancy."

Gloria made a face. "As you can imagine, on Beau's salary that didn't work out so well. He opened a few credit cards and got him and Marie into a real financial pickle. Back then, he handled the finances. Marie had no idea that they were living on credit. She thought they were doing real well, and Beau did everything he could to keep her believing it. After they declared bankruptcy, she closed all the credit-card accounts and took over the budget."

"So that's why Dad had to ask Mom for any money he wanted to spend," Gina said.

"Uh-huh." Uncle Redd shook his head. "Beau didn't like that one bit, but it was either toe Marie's line or hit the road, Jack."

"Were they ever happy together?"

"Until your mom found out about the financial mess he'd gotten them into."

No longer angry, Gina sighed. "If I'd known all that, I would've understood my parents a whole lot better." Though her life wouldn't have been any easier.

"Are we finished here?" Gloria asked. "Because I'd like to eat sometime before midnight."

"Okay, but first, are there any other secrets I should know about? If so, please tell me now. I don't want to come across papers someplace and get sucker punched again."

Her relatives looked genuinely thoughtful for a moment. Then they glanced at each other and shrugged.

"None that I can think of," Uncle Redd said.

Sophie shook her head. "If something comes to me, I promise I'll tell you."

"Girl Scouts' honor." Gloria held up her hand in a three-finger salute.

"If you don't, I'll never trust any of you again." Gina grabbed an apron from a kitchen drawer. "Now I'll dress that salad."

Chapter 9

At eight o'clock sharp Monday morning—nine o'clock Chicago time—Gina called the office.

"Good morning," Marsha said in her cheerful voice. "How are things in Montana?"

Gina thought of Zach and the old and new friends she'd made. "Not bad, considering."

"All ready for Thanksgiving?"

"No, but I will be." With Sophie and Gloria's help, she'd put together a grocery list for the holiday. After she cleaned out Uncle Lucky's bedroom today, she would head to Spenser's and buy the needed ingredients. "How about you?"

"Haven't started yet. I'm awfully glad we're closed on Wednesday. I need that day to buy groceries and cook. I imagine Carrie told you she's sick?"

"Sick?" Gina echoed.

"She just called in—I assumed she'd talked to you first. She has the flu and a bad case of laryngitis. I could barely hear a word she said. She won't be in today, and I doubt she'll be in tomorrow, either."

Gina had checked her email before going to Gloria and Sophie's the night before and had seen Carrie's report and an email that had been upbeat and relieved her worries. But now... The fact that her assistant hadn't contacted her was both puzzling and worrisome.

Especially with a busy day scheduled. She rubbed the space between her eyes. "Meetings with Evelyn Grant and another client are set up for this afternoon, and I'm going to need help. Who's in the office?"

"Everyone but Carrie and Kevin. He's out for the day with potential new clients. The rest are all in back-to-back meetings, but Shirley and Jon should be finished around three. Shall I buzz one of them?"

Both colleagues worked as hard as Gina, and she doubted they had time to step in. "Never mind," she said. "I'll call the clients and set up phone meetings instead."

"All right. If I don't talk to you again before Thursday, happy Thanksgiving. We'll be awfully glad to have you back next week."

Irritated, Gina speed-dialed Carrie's cell phone. She didn't expect her assistant to pick up, and of course, the woman didn't. "I'm sorry you're sick," Gina said when voice mail kicked in. "But we still need to talk before Thanksgiving. As soon as you feel better, give me a call—even if you have laryngitis."

She spent the next hour making calls to clients and apologizing for not returning calls the day before. They all knew about Uncle Lucky and seemed surprised that she was calling instead of Carrie. Explaining that her assistant was ill, Gina set up phone meetings for the following morning.

Then, channeling her frustration with Carrie, she attacked Uncle Lucky's bedroom.

Stacks of old catalogs filled one wall. Sweating and muttering, Gina hefted trash bags of J.C. Penney and farm and agriculture catalogs downstairs.

"What were you thinking, Uncle Lucky?" she muttered as she shoved the heavy bags outside.

They joined a mound along the back of the house—a big, ugly pile of black plastic against the snow. Hating the sight, Gina decided to burn their contents in the bin near the barn. Right away.

Then she would drive to Spenser's and pick up the groceries for Thanksgiving and another box of trash bags. She would check her email, too. After that, she might even stop at Barb's Café and treat herself to dinner.

Using one of Lucky's old Jeeps to trundle from pasture to pasture, Zach kept an eye out for stranded or lost cattle. He preferred riding horses, but with the temperature somewhere south of twenty degrees, it was too damn cold. He was out of the car, battling the harsh wind and tramping down a gully to reach a misguided heifer, when he smelled smoke.

He squinted at the white plume, which looked to be coming from someplace near the barn. When he'd checked in with the crew earlier, no one had mentioned burning any trash today. That left Gina.

The heifer lowed mournfully, and Zach turned his attention to her. She'd wandered onto the icy gully bed and couldn't get across it.

He slipped and slid toward her. "Easy there," he said. Hands on her rump, he grunted and shoved, forcing her forward until her hooves found purchase. She trotted up the slope of the gully. Panting and sweating, he followed her out. When they both reached flat ground, he gave her rump a thwack. She loped off toward the rest of the herd.

One down and hopefully zero to go.

Ready to resume his search for lost cattle, he climbed into the Jeep, pulled off his gloves and cranked up the heat. But instead of heading for the back pastures, he drove toward the barn. Toward Gina.

Though acres separated them, she was easy to spot. Her burgundy jacket added color to the gray afternoon. Zach steered toward her. He hadn't seen her since running into her at the Pizza Palace Saturday night. They'd both been uncomfortable, and he figured they should probably talk. This was as good a time as any.

As he neared her, he noted the jeans hugging her long legs. Legs that fueled his fantasies and kept him up at night. She was hefting a fat black bag, one of a pile nearby. Hearing the Jeep, she paused and shaded her eyes against the winter sun. She wasn't wearing a hat or a scarf. In this weather? What was she thinking?

He watched her dump the contents of the bag into the bin. The paper caught quickly, wind fanning the flames high and whipping her hair across her face.

Braking to a stop, he exited the vehicle, shoved his

hands into his jacket pockets and tromped across the snow toward her. "That's a lot of trash bags."

"You have no idea."

"You're supposed to ask for help."

"I wanted to do it myself."

She couldn't seem to keep still. She walked around the fire, fiddled with her gloves and pulled up her jacket collar. Her cheeks were red with cold. Zach could think of a few great ways to warm her up, all of them involving getting her naked and under the covers. He swallowed. "Where's your hat?"

"I left it at the house. I meant to grab a scarf, but I was distracted and forgot."

"I've got an extra wool cap in the Jeep. It isn't fancy like your hat, but at least you'll be warm."

"Great—thanks."

He retrieved the navy cap and handed it to her. She pulled on the cap so that her ears were covered. She looked cute.

"That's much better. I'll give it back later." She held out her gloved hands to the fire.

"Keep it until you leave. We need to talk about the other night," he said.

"You mean at the Pizza Palace?"

"I was thinking about a different night." The night he'd kissed her until his body was on fire. "You'll be seeing a lot of me while you're here, and I want us to be comfortable around each other."

"I'm okay, Zach. I wanted what happened."

He had to ask. "Do you want it to happen again?"

"I don't know." She poked at the fire, stirring the

flames higher. "Right now, I don't know much of anything."

She looked like she needed a friend. "You want to talk about it?" he asked.

"You might be sorry you asked."

She gave a wry smile, coaxing a smile from him. He scooped up a trash bag and emptied it in the bin. Fresh flames crested the metal walls. "I'll take that risk."

"Okay, but don't say I didn't warn you," she began. "I set up a phone call with my assistant for this morning, but she's sick with the flu. She can't help that, but she didn't even bother to let me know. I found out from the office receptionist. I think she's avoiding me, and I wish I knew why."

Zach should've guessed that this was about work. "Maybe she's afraid of you."

"The way she's been acting since I left, she should be. I can't get a hold of her, and we've been communicating mostly through texts. It's almost as if she's ducking me." Gina looked indignant. "In the six months since I hired her, she's always worked as hard as I do. She's ambitious, too, and seemed more than eager to take over for me for a few days. I wish I knew what she's up to."

"Maybe she thought she was ready for the responsibility, but she isn't. Or she's having boyfriend or husband problems and it's interfering with the job."

"She's single, and she's always been focused, no matter what. She wants to get promoted. We're a lot alike that way. Right now, she doesn't even have a boyfriend. But come to think of it, Friday night she did have a date with someone new." Gina rubbed her chin, leaving behind a smudge. "I wonder if she caught the flu from him."

"You'll find out when you get back next week. You'll straighten things out then."

"Let's hope. I can't afford to have anything else fall through the cracks." Her eyes were round and shadowed. "I really need her to pull her weight."

"What fell through the cracks?"

"Appointments with two clients—one of them a huge account. I set up phone meetings with them for tomorrow, which isn't ideal, but it's better than nothing. The problem is I don't have time for that right now. There's still so much to do with the house. I haven't emptied Uncle Lucky's closet and dresser or sorted through either of the guest bedrooms, and I have less than a week to get it done." She emptied a bag into the fire.

"Sure you don't want help?"

"You still have plenty to do. Anyway, this is something I should do on my own. Thanks for listening. There really isn't anyone else I can talk to."

"No problem." To keep the fire going, he dumped another bag onto the fire. "Lots of newspapers and magazines here."

"And old bills that go back decades. I found this stuff everywhere—stacked on shelves in the basement, in Uncle Lucky's office and in his bedroom..." Gina shook her head. "I knew he was a pack rat, but I never guessed he was this bad."

With a frown bracketing her mouth, she looked worn down, even more exhausted than when she'd stepped off the plane.

"Did you find anything worth saving?" he asked.

"Something that might change your mind about holding on to this ranch?"

"You don't give up, do you?"

He made a face and she laughed, which was what he'd wanted.

Zach grinned. "Seeing you crack a smile eases the pain of your decision."

A moment later she sobered. "I wish... It's too bad you don't have the money to buy the Lucky A."

Her words just about knocked him to his knees. Not even Lucky knew that he had money—a great deal of it. It sat untouched in an investment account and had since Zach had sold his company for a hefty sum. He'd given away half of the profits but wasn't sure what to do with the rest. He didn't intend to use the money for himself.

"Even if I did, I'd never buy this place," he said. "Lucky willed it to you, and he meant for you to keep it."

"Yes, I know." Her eyes took on a stubborn glint and she set her jaw. "I'm not going to change my mind, Zach."

As determined as she seemed, he wasn't about to give up. "You never did say if you found anything in those papers."

"As a matter of fact, I did." She kicked at the snow. "Lucky kept a folder that belonged to my parents. I discovered that around the time I was born, they had declared bankruptcy. I had no idea—no one ever told me." She frowned. "I don't understand secrets like that."

Zach did. Some things were best kept from others. "Every family has skeletons in their closet," he said.

"Yes, but do they keep those secrets from their own flesh and blood?"

Thanks to the internet and the local paper, Zach's family and anyone who read the business pages knew about his mistakes. He shrugged. "I guess that depends."

"Maybe. At least now I know why my mother was so tightfisted."

She angled her head a fraction, and he knew she was going to ask him something.

"Did your parents fight over money?"

As an insurance executive, Zach's father earned more than he could ever spend, and his mother's trust fund made her independently wealthy. "No, but they fought about everything else." Remembering the constant volley of criticism and accusations, he winced. "They divorced and remarried each other twice before they both moved on to other partners. My father is still with his third wife, and my mother just married husband number four."

"And I thought my childhood was rough."

"I got used to it."

"I always wished I had a brother or sister, especially when my parents fought. Do you have any siblings?"

"A brother, and yeah, as kids, we leaned on each other quite a bit."

"Is he still in Texas?"

Zach nodded. "He and his wife live in Houston."

"I'll bet you miss him."

"We're not close anymore." Not since Zach had sold his business and walked away from his life of luxury. Jim thought he was crazy. The entire family did, and except for obligatory phone calls on holidays, they rarely touched base.

Gina opened her mouth, no doubt to ask him something else.

Wary, he eyed her. "What's with the questions?"

"I just think we should get to know each other better."

She already knew more about him than most people in town. Zach let his eyes travel lazily over her. "After the other night, I'd say we're starting to get to know each other pretty well."

Her red cheeks flushed redder still. "You know what I mean." She didn't ask him anything else, which was what he'd intended. "I need to finish this and get to Spenser's." She emptied two trash bags into the bin, one on top of the other, jumping back when the flames flared up. She almost bumped into Zach.

"Careful." He caught her in his arms.

She'd knocked the hat cockeyed. With cold fingers, he tucked her hair back and straightened the cap, tugging it gently over her ears. "There."

His fingers lingered on her soft skin.

"Your hands are cold," she said.

"I took off my gloves when I got you the hat." Zach dropped his arms to his sides. He longed to kiss her—and more. But any of the ranch hands could be nearby. Already Curly suspected that something was going on between Zach and Gina, and Zach didn't want him or the other men catching sight of anything that would cause them to talk.

The shed where Lucky stored tractors and other heavy equipment was only a few yards away. "I want to show you something." Zach caught hold of Gina's hand and tugged her forward. "It's important."

"What is it?"

"It's important," he repeated.

"Is it okay to leave the fire?"

With the ground covered in snow and no trees within fifty feet, there was no danger of a spread. He nodded and tugged her toward the shed.

Moments later, they stood on the far side of the building, out of view of prying eyes.

Gina looked around and frowned. "I don't see anything here except snow. What did you want to show me?"

"It's this way."

Never taking his eyes from her, he backed her toward the siding. The curious look on her face quickly changed to something altogether different. Pure yearning.

When she was trapped between the shed and him, he placed his hands on either side of her head and kissed her.

She hesitated briefly, and then let out the soft little moan that drove him wild, placed her gloved hands around his neck and pulled him closer. Or tried. Thanks to their bulky coats, they barely touched.

That didn't stop Zach from catching fire. He wanted to drag her to the nearest bed, get naked and bury himself in her warmth. But that wasn't a good idea. Reluctantly, he broke the kiss.

"Let me know if you want help with the house," he said.

Nodding, she stood where she was, against the wall, flushed and dreamy eyed, and watched him walk away.

Chapter 10

One down, one to go, Gina thought as she hung up from a phone meeting Tuesday morning. The next call, to Evelyn Grant, was scheduled for an hour from now. With so much to do before leaving town, she wasn't about to waste a minute. She decided to empty Uncle Lucky's bedroom dresser and closet, which shouldn't take long.

Aside from well-worn jeans and flannel shirts, he didn't have a lot. Most of the clothing was ready for the rag bin, but a few items were in good enough condition for charity. She set those aside, along with his boots, which were in decent shape. His old Stetson sat on the shelf above the clothing rod.

At the sight of the battered hat, Gina's eyes filled. She couldn't part with that, so she set it aside, along with two photos. In one, she was about eight and seated on

Belle, a gentle old workhorse, while a young-looking Uncle Lucky grinned by her side. The other was of her uncle and Zach on the roof of the barn, replacing the roof. Obviously mugging for the photographer, they held up tools and grinned against a cloudless blue sky.

In a white T-shirt and faded jeans, Zach looked gorgeous. A man didn't come by those biceps and flat belly without engaging in serious physical labor.

He was pretty serious about kissing, too....

Gina went all soft inside, caught herself and raised her chin. Zach wasn't what she wanted, and she was not going to kiss him again.

Setting the hat and photos aside, she reached for an ancient shoe box on the shelf. Men's dress shoes—she didn't remember her uncle ever wearing those. But the box weighed too little to contain shoes, and she heard the familiar rustle of papers inside.

"Oh, dear God, not more to sort through," she muttered.

Dreading what she'd find, she pulled the lid off. The box was filled with letters. A whole stack of them, addressed to her uncle in neat, feminine script Gina didn't recognize.

The top envelope showed a faded postage stamp marked Red Deer, a town about forty miles away. The date was some thirty years ago, when she'd been a newborn and Uncle Lucky was in his mid-forties.

Curious, she sat down on the floor with the box, opened the envelope and slid out a folded, multiple-page letter.

The faint scent of rose perfume filled her nostrils.

That and the *My Dearest Lucky* greeting had her eyes opening wide.

Apparently her seemingly celibate uncle had once had a girlfriend.

"Well, well, Uncle Lucky." Wanting to know more, she went straight to page three, where the letter ended with, *I can't wait until next Saturday night. Love, Corinne.* Beside the signature was a hot-pink lipstick imprint. "Corinne with the sexy lips," Gina murmured, smiling.

She'd never heard her uncle mention anyone by that name, but then he'd never mentioned a girlfriend, period.

According to the postage-stamp dates, her uncle had received weekly letters from Corinne for three years. Wanting to know why the letters had stopped and everything in between, Gina found the first letter and started reading.

Corinne had sent a thank-you for the birthday flowers Uncle Lucky had brought her on her twenty-seventh birthday. She'd been quite a bit younger than he.

She wasn't a great writer, but her stories about the animals treated at the large veterinary clinic where she worked made for entertaining reading. Corinne's insights and feelings about Uncle Lucky made the letters even more interesting, and Gina read them all. The last one, written shortly before Corinne's thirtieth birthday, broke Gina's heart. Corinne wrote that she was tired of waiting for Uncle Lucky to propose and ended the relationship.

He could've married and had kids. Kids that would

be Gina's age and would probably have wanted to keep the Lucky A. Instead, he'd died childless and alone.

With a heartfelt sigh, Gina set the box aside. Suddenly she remembered. The phone meeting with Evelyn Grant! She'd completely forgotten.

She grabbed her phone and called Ms. Grant's private line. "Evelyn Grant," said the crisp voice.

Gina swallowed. "Good morning, Ms. Grant, it's Gina Arnett. I, uh, I'm running a little late today, and I apologize. But I'm ready now and—"

"A *little* late? We scheduled our meeting for nearly an hour ago."

Having never forgotten something so important in her life and never let anything come between her and her clients—especially this one—Gina felt both terrible and embarrassed. Her face burned with humiliation. "I'm so sorry. Do you have time now?"

"Kevin and I have already spoken."

That was not good. As if on cue, Gina's other line buzzed impatiently. Kevin, the screen read. He would have to wait.

"Again, I am so sorry," she said. "What can I do to make this up to you?"

"Don't blow me off ever again."

The phone clicked harshly in Gina's ear.

Groaning, she buried her face in her hands. Not ready to face Kevin, she phoned her favorite Chicago florist and ordered the most expensive Thanksgiving flower bouquet available to be sent to Evelyn Grant immediately.

Then, biting the bullet, she called her boss and apologized.

Kevin's disapproving silence screamed in her ear.

"I sent flowers," she added lamely.

"That doesn't make up for what you did. Grant Industries is one of our biggest clients, Gina. They represent substantial fees for us. Someone else could've taken over the account while you're out, but you insisted that you and Carrie could handle it. What's going on with her? Since you left she's hardly been at the office. You should've let me know she was falling short."

He'd trusted Gina to do her job and she'd let him down.

"If we lose the account because of your mistakes…" Kevin let the incomplete threat hang in the air.

Knowing she was in trouble, Gina winced. "You have my word that I'll make this up to you and Evelyn Grant."

"You'd damn well better."

"I'll be in the office bright and early Monday morning, and everything will be fine," she assured him.

"It had better be."

In other words, her job was on the line. Kevin wasn't the most understanding boss. She'd seen people fired for less.

He hung up, the click of his phone sounding ominous—exactly like Evelyn Grant's.

Early on Thanksgiving Day Zach turned up the Lucky A driveway, the twenty-pound tom turkey he'd picked up from a rancher in another town tucked safely on the passenger seat of the truck. He looked forward to the great meal and the relaxing day ahead, but first there were chores that needed doing. He also needed to change clothes. Which was why he planned to drop off the bird at the house and come back later.

He was near the parking area by the back door when his cell phone rang. He glanced at the screen. It was his brother, Jim. Zach hadn't spoken to him since May, when he'd called to wish Zach a happy birthday.

He braked to a stop. "Hey, Jim."

"Hey," his brother said. "Happy Thanksgiving."

"Back at ya. When are you and Susan taking the kids to Dad and Ava's for Thanksgiving dinner?"

"Four. I'll bet you're eating with the Arnetts again, watching a bowl game and enjoying the good company."

Jim sounded envious. "That's right." Zach wasn't going to say anything, but the words slipped out. "It won't be like last year, though. Lucky had a heart attack last week. He didn't make it."

"That was unexpected."

Zach cleared his throat. "Yeah."

"I'm sorry. So your Thanksgiving will be as dismal as mine."

Zach snorted. "I seriously doubt that."

"You're probably right. What are you going to do now that Lucky is gone?"

He wasn't about to explain about his promise to Lucky or about Gina. "I'll be here at the ranch for a while, tying up loose ends."

"Are you coming home, then?"

"I'm already here. Saddlers Prairie is my home now."

"Compared to Houston, that little burg has nothing to offer. Come back, Zach. It's time to stop punishing yourself for something that wasn't your fault."

"I'm not punishing myself." Anymore. "A man can

change, and I did. I'm a rancher now. Why can't you and the rest of the family accept that?"

"Because you have an MBA from Harvard, and you built and ran a successful commercial real-estate business. That's why."

"A business I sold."

"For a hefty profit, and I respect that. People buy and sell businesses all the time. Start a new enterprise. Hell, ranches are businesses, too. If you bought one and ran it, I might understand. But you're working for someone else, and all your smarts and know-how are going to waste."

They'd hashed through this umpteen times. Zach was in no mood to do it again. He snorted. "You sound more like Dad every day."

"Don't play the Dad card on me. You know I want you to be happy."

Zach thought about his life on the ranch, the hard physical labor and the feeling of accomplishment at the end of the day. "I am," he said. "Send my love to Susan and the kids."

"Conversation over—I get the message. Susan and the kids send their love back. You going to call Dad and Ava and wish them a happy Thanksgiving?"

Zach glanced at the lit kitchen window, which was all steamed up from whatever the family was cooking. He wanted to get in there, drop off the turkey, do his chores and hurry back. "Maybe later."

In a far darker mood now, he pocketed the phone, plucked the turkey off the seat and stepped onto the back stoop. He wiped his feet and knocked before opening the door and stepping into the kitchen. "I'm here to drop off the turkey. Where do you want it?"

"You're just in time," Gina said. She was standing at the stove, stirring something. "My cousins are making the stuffing now."

In a plaid bib apron, she looked like a glamorous cooking show host—if you didn't count the forced smile and circles under her eyes. Looked as if she still wasn't sleeping well. Probably worried about something job related.

She wasn't the only one. Sunday morning she was leaving, and Zach still hadn't managed to change her mind about the ranch. He needed a plan, but hadn't come up with one.

"Ladies." He nodded at Sophie and Gloria, who sat at the table, each chopping vegetables on portable cutting boards.

Sophie patted her hair and smoothed the bib of her own apron, as if wanting to look her best for him, and Gloria offered a flirtatious smile that would probably knock a seventy-something guy off his feet. Behind them, Gina shook her head, as in, what can you do with these two?

Zach couldn't stop a grin.

"Before you give that bird to Gina, show him to us," Gloria said.

Zach held the turkey up for her inspection.

Sophie nodded approvingly. "You picked out a nice fat one. What does he weigh, twenty pounds?"

"A little over."

"You did good, honey." Gloria smacked her lips. "We'll be eating leftovers for days."

"If that's a problem for you, I'm happy to help out," Zach teased, feeling better by the moment.

"You know you're invited back for leftovers, just like always," Sophie said.

The Arnetts were so different from his own family, who left their chef to cook and never shared the leftovers. "I'm counting on it. It already smells good in here."

"It should—Gina's been working for hours, making pies, sweet potato casserole and cranberry sauce," Sophie said. "We already told her that you're the official mashed potatoes and gravy expert."

Zach nodded. "That's why they invite me back every year."

Gina laughed, and a genuine smile lingered on her lips. Zach exhaled in relief and realized he'd been waiting for that.

"After Redd dropped us off here, he went to get the chestnuts," Gloria said. "But he'll be back soon. He'll want to roast them over the fire and watch the game with you."

"Then I better finish my chores, go home and clean up and come right back."

"As Thanksgivings go, this one ranks right up there with the best of them." Uncle Redd gave Gina a fond look. "It's great to have you here in the bosom of our family, honey."

"It's good to be here." Gina meant that. Surrounded by family and Zach made it easier to set aside her worries about work. "I just wish Uncle Lucky were with us."

"Oh, he's here." Gloria glanced around and smiled. "I can feel him."

Her sister sniffed. "Don't be ridiculous."

"I *do* feel him. If you don't, then I feel sorry for you."

"Well, stop."

"Girls, girls," Uncle Redd said. "We're celebrating Thanksgiving, remember?"

Gina glanced at Zach. Eyes twinkling, he shrugged.

She couldn't help laughing. "Now it sounds like the Thanksgivings I remember so fondly."

"Sure was a good meal." With cheeks that matched his name, Uncle Redd patted his round middle. "You girls outdid yourselves today, and Zach, those mashed potatoes and gravy were your best yet. Only trouble is, there's no room left in this belly for pie."

Gina chuckled along with everyone else. She'd laughed a lot today, and she felt good.

Sophie pushed her chair back. "I'd suggest a walk, but it's too cold and slippery out there. Let's digest awhile before we think about dessert."

"You all relax and I'll clean up," Zach offered. In a sports jacket and khakis, he looked handsome. He slipped out of the jacket and rolled up the cuffs of his oxford shirt. He'd eaten as much as Uncle Redd, but unlike her uncle, his cheeks weren't flushed and his belly was still flat.

"I'll help," Gina said, rising.

Gloria frowned. "You've been working all day, honey. Redd, give Zach a hand. Moving around will help your stomach settle. When you two finish, Sophie and I will make the coffee and cut the pie. For now, we

girls are going to enjoy the fire in the living room."
She stood and beckoned Gina and Sophie to follow her.

"That Zach is a keeper," Gloria said when the three of
them were seated around the fireplace. "If only there'd
been a man like him when I was your age...."

"Harvey was a fine man, Gloria. So was my Tony."

"I know that, Sophie—I'm just trying to make a
point." With a devilish look on her face, she gave an
exaggerated nod toward Gina.

They expected a rise out of her, but the best she could
manage was a shrug.

"You don't seem your regular self, cookie," Sophie
said. "All this sorting through Lucky's things has worn
you out."

That was partly true, but Gina was also worried sick
about her job. If Evelyn Grant asked to work with someone else in the firm, or worse, decided to leave Andersen, Coats and Mueller...

But no, Gina wasn't going to think about that now or
share her uneasiness. Zach, her family and her friends
in Saddlers Prairie all thought she was riding high, and
she wasn't about to tell them otherwise.

"Or maybe you're not ready to go back to Chicago
just yet?" Sophie went on. "Your visit certainly has
flown by."

"Land sakes, Sophie, don't go sending her off early.
It's only Thursday, and she's here until Sunday morning."

"I know that, Gloria! All I'm saying is that I'll hate
to see her go."

"Excuse me, but I'm right here," Gina said. Tired
of their bickering, she hastily changed the subject. "I

found something interesting the other day that I want to show you—after we've all had our dessert and coffee."

"I hope it isn't another secret we supposedly kept from you," Gloria said. "But then, I don't think there are any more of those."

Sophie smiled. "On that, dear sister, we agree."

Chapter 11

Redd set down his pie fork and blew out a breath. "My mouth wants more, but I can't eat another bite. What'd I tell you about Gina's cooking, Zach?"

"She's great." Zach sat back, rubbed his belly and grinned. "I'm in the same boat."

After finishing his chores this morning, he'd sucked it up and called his father. The stilted conversation had been worse than the one with Jim, but then he'd expected as much. He'd come to the house in low spirits, but his mood had quickly done a one-eighty.

"I'm glad you liked the meal." Gina smiled. The shadows in her eyes had completely faded, and she looked as relaxed as Zach felt. "I like to cook but never get much of a chance at home." She glanced from Zach to her uncle. "You two say you're full, but I've seen the way you eat," she teased. "In a few hours, you'll be hungry again."

"Watching football always makes me hungry." Redd raised a hopeful eyebrow at Zach. "Ready for another game?"

"No way, Jose." Gloria shook her finger at him. "One game per holiday, remember? Besides, Gina wants to share something with us—something of Lucky's she found the other day," she added, looking pained.

"Dear Lord above." Redd put the back of his hand to his forehead. "Don't tell me she's uncovered another *secret.*"

"It *is* a secret, of sorts." Gina pushed to her feet. "Wait'll you see the box I found in Uncle Lucky's closet."

"Box?" Gloria frowned. "That sounds intriguing."

Zach thought so, too, but he was more fascinated by the length of leg he glimpsed as Gina climbed the stairs. He'd never seen her in a skirt until this afternoon. Her calves were every bit as shapely as he'd imagined. She was wearing hose and he wondered if she wore a garter belt or maybe thigh highs.

He itched to run his hand up her leg and find out. His body stirred, and he nearly groaned out loud.

Redd and the cousins were shooting him curious looks, and he realized he was staring at Gina as she disappeared up the steps. He tore his gaze away and stood to clear the dessert dishes.

"Leave those," Redd said. "Let's sit by the fire and wait to see what Gina found."

When Gina returned, she set an open shoe box on the coffee table.

"Those are letters." Redd squinted at the pile. "Who are they from?"

"A woman named Corinne from Red Deer. According to the letters, she and Uncle Lucky were involved for three years."

Gloria and Sophie exchanged baffled looks, and Redd shook his head. "I never heard of any Corinne. Lucky would've said something."

"I read every letter," Gina said. "He and Corinne were definitely involved."

Not once in the three years Zach had known Lucky had the old rancher been with a woman, but he'd enjoyed looking at and talking about them. Zach was glad that at one time his friend had done more than talk.

"I certainly never guessed," Sophie said.

"Nor did I." Gloria shook her head and chuckled. "And all this time, I worried that he was a closet homosexual."

Sophie looked shocked. "Gloria!"

"Well, the man never dated or any of the other things men are prone to do. You know what I mean, Zach."

About to sip his coffee, Zach choked. He shared a look at Gina, and they both bit back laughs.

Half an hour and another piece of pie later, Redd yawned. "I'm ready to go home and sleep off this meal. Girls?"

Sophie and Gloria looked equally sleepy. They both nodded.

"We'll be back tomorrow night for leftovers," Gloria said. "Of course you'll join us again, Zach."

He glanced at Gina, waiting for her okay. She nodded. "I'll be here," he said. "The roads are pretty icy tonight. Let me drive you in my truck."

Redd frowned. "I can't leave my car here. How would I get it in the morning?"

"No problem," Gina said. "I'll drive it to your house. Zach can follow me in his truck and bring me back. If that's okay with you, Zach?"

"Sure."

She gave him a look that warmed him from the inside out and filled his head with fantasies straight out of high school—making out in the dark truck and fooling around. It wasn't gonna happen, but it sure was fun to think about.

After escorting Sophie and Gloria up a treacherous walkway and safely into the house, and then dropping off Redd and his car, Zach was alone with Gina.

"I'm glad they're all home safe," she said as he pulled away from Redd's place. "The roads really are bad tonight. And the walkway here and at my cousins' place… I worry that someone will slip and fall."

Zach shared her concern. "I'll stop at both houses in the morning and scrape and salt the walks and front steps."

"Okay, but we both know that the snow and ice will only come back again."

"True, but at least they'll be able to get to the house for leftovers."

For a few moments they rode along in silence, with only the headlights lighting the dark highway. Aware of black ice, Zach made his way cautiously toward the ranch.

"My family is something else," Gina said as they crept along.

He wasn't about to risk taking his gaze off the road, but he sensed she was smiling. He shook his head and grinned. "They're characters, all right, but good people."

"And yet so irritating. The bickering between Sophie and Gloria drives me crazy."

"I'll take them over my relatives any time. My family is too stiff and formal to bicker, but they excel at sarcasm. Every holiday meal is like a competition." Just talking about it put a bad taste in Zach's mouth. "I used to get indigestion without taking a single bite of food."

"That doesn't sound fun."

"I'd rather have a root canal."

"But you talk to them on holidays?"

He nodded. "Some things you have to do. I don't miss being there."

"I don't miss being in Chicago, either."

She'd never said that before. Zach tore his gaze from the road to glance at her. "I thought you were anxious to get back."

"I am, but I really enjoyed celebrating Thanksgiving with my family."

Zach considered the Arnetts family. But they weren't, not really. He was on his own. Driving in the darkness, he felt truly alone—or would have without Gina beside him.

"I had a great time today, too," he said.

"I needed the break."

"You've been working hard."

"Not hard enough."

Her bitter tone surprised him. He figured she'd talk about it, but she flipped on the radio instead.

In no time, he drove under the Lucky A sign.

"Are you hungry again?" Gina asked when he pulled to a stop at the back of the house.

"I could eat. You?"

"I hate to say this, but yes."

She looked so pained about that that Zach chuckled.

"Why don't you come in and have some leftovers?" Gina said. "There'll still be plenty for tomorrow and the day after that."

Not relishing returning to his trailer just yet, Zach readily agreed.

Inside, he added another log to the fire. He helped Gina unload the dishwasher and put away the clean dishes.

"Now I'm getting really hungry," she said. "Let's make turkey and cranberry sandwiches."

"We can use the dinner rolls for bread."

"You liked those?"

He nodded and licked his lips. She laughed again, making the day that much more perfect.

Sitting side by side on the sofa, they dug in, the fire crackling merrily.

"Do you know why Corinne broke things off with my uncle?" she asked after a while. "She wanted to get married, and he wouldn't commit. I think that's so sad. He could've had a child—someone besides me to inherit the ranch."

She almost sounded regretful. Zach couldn't help but wonder if she was beginning to have second thoughts about selling the ranch. He wasn't about to push her by asking. "Some guys just aren't wired for marriage," he said.

"What about you?"

He shrugged. "I was engaged once."

"Really?" she said, clearly surprised. "What happened, if you don't mind my asking?"

The man who'd bought the Horton Company from Zach had started dating his ex-fiancée. A year later, they'd married. Gina didn't need to know about that—she'd only ask questions Zach wasn't going to answer. "She didn't like the direction my life was taking and married someone else," he summarized.

The sharp look she gave him could've cut glass.

"What?" he said.

Gina smoothed her napkin. "Was it because you were a ranch foreman?"

"There's nothing wrong with what I do, but back then, I didn't even know what a ranch foreman was."

"Where did you work?"

"It's not important. Turns out, I like being single."

Zach saw that she had more questions. Before she could voice them, he asked one of his own. "What about you, Gina? Are you a commitmentphobe?"

"Not at all, but I've been so busy working that I really haven't had time to date. I thought things might work out with my last boyfriend, but it turned out that we didn't have much in common. We didn't have great chemistry, either."

"You and I have chemistry." Zach took her plate and set it aside. "Lots of it."

When he leaned in for a kiss, she didn't stop him. One kiss wasn't enough—for either of them. He was already hard and aching, but then, just looking at her aroused him.

He cupped her soft, full breasts. He brushed his thumbs over her nipples and felt them sharpen, heard her suck in her breath and release it in a sweet, low moan.

He wanted to hear that again. Wanted her under him, begging for more. He unbuttoned her blouse. She was helping him get rid of it when he heard the landline ring.

Gina frowned. "Who'd call at ten-thirty on Thanksgiving—and on the landline? Nobody uses that except my family...." Face paling, she shrugged back into her blouse and jumped up. "Oh, God, I hope nothing's wrong."

She hurried to the kitchen, buttoning the blouse on the way. Zach was right behind her.

Reaching across the counter, she snatched up the phone. "Hello? Uncle Redd—hi. Is everything okay?" She sent Zach a worried look. "You think you're having a *heart attack?*"

Please, not Redd, too.

"Did you call Dr. Mark?" She listened. "That's good. I'm relieved that the medics are on their way. You wait for them and don't move an inch. Zach and I will be right over."

By the time she hung up, Zach had his coat on and his keys in hand.

Some five hours later, Gina let out an exhausted yawn and tucked Uncle Redd into his own bed. "I'm awfully glad you only had indigestion. No more overindulging, okay?"

He gave a sheepish nod. "A fifty-mile round-trip drive to Flagg Memorial hospital in Elk Ridge is no fun, especially late at night. Sorry I bothered you and Zach."

She glanced at Zach, standing back out of the way. His eyes were hot and his expression intense, and she knew he was remembering what they'd been doing when her uncle's call had come in.

Zach's mouth on hers, his hands... If not for the interruption, she might have done something she regretted. "That's okay, Uncle Redd. You get some sleep, all right? Zach and I will be back in the morning to check on you and clean your walkway."

"Okay, honey. I still get to come to dinner tomorrow night, right?"

"Of course, but you're only allowed a small sliver of pie. Sleep tight." She kissed his whiskery cheek.

She and Zach left. "I'm sure relieved he's okay," he said as he pulled away from the curb.

So was Gina. "I'm glad I was here for him. Can you imagine going through all those tests alone? Sophie and Gloria don't drive in the dark, and I wouldn't want them to." She'd phoned her cousins several times, first to tell them what was happening and later with the results of the tests. "I don't ever want to be away again during a family emergency."

"If and when something happens, the only way you can be sure of being here is by moving back to Saddlers Prairie," Zach said.

He was right, but she was happy living in Chicago. "You don't quit, do you?"

"As the poet said, 'I have promises to keep.'"

"I'm not going to live here, but I do intend to visit

more often." She would come back in the spring to check on the ranch—if it hadn't sold by then—and again next Christmas. Though the thought of celebrating a family Christmas somewhere besides the Lucky A was unbearably sad.

At almost 4:00 a.m., it was already Friday. Only two more days until she flew back to Chicago. She would miss everyone, including Zach. Especially him.

Want to or not, she liked him. A lot more than she should.

She was silently chiding herself for letting him kiss her and more when he pulled up close to the back door and set the brake. With country music softly playing on the radio, he kissed her—a long hot kiss that erased all rational thoughts and left her aching for more.

He pulled back. Reluctantly, she opened her eyes.

"Sleep tight, Gina," he said in a low, throaty voice that stroked her like a caress.

Her whole body quivered. "You, too," she managed, doubting that she'd calm down enough to sleep for a long time.

Chapter 12

Zach's alarm went off Friday morning, waking him from an erotic dream involving him and Gina and a big, rumpled bed. His body was hard and pulsing, and he groaned—both from fatigue and from waking up to the reality of a double bed with only him in it.

He wanted to fall back to sleep, but Chet, Pete and Bert were gone over the holiday and this was Curly's morning to sleep in. Someone had to get up and do the chores. Grumbling, he padded into the bathroom for a shower and shave. After a quick breakfast, he headed for the barn. Snow swirled around him, stinging his face. It was still dark and he couldn't see the sky, but the air felt wet, heavy and cold. They were in for a big snow.

To his surprise, Curly was waiting for him in the barn, a steaming mug between his hands. "I didn't expect to see you up this morning," he said.

"Couldn't sleep. How was your Thanksgiving?"

Zach thought about all that had happened yesterday—the laughter and the great meal, kissing Gina and more. Redd's worried call had interrupted them before things went too far, and he was both relieved about that and frustrated. "Good and not so good," he summarized.

He explained about the trip to the hospital. "Gina and I didn't get back until almost four in the morning."

"Huh." Curly gave a knowing nod.

"Huh, what?"

"It's that look on your face. Things between you and her must be heating up."

Not about to share any details, Zach shrugged. "Like I explained before, she's looking for a different kind of guy. Anyway, she's leaving Sunday."

"I wouldn't be so sure about that. The weather people are forecasting a bitch of a storm. We're talking a mammoth blizzard."

Of all the weekends for a storm—and for Bert, Pete and Chet to be away. Zach swore. "We'd best start getting the cattle fed and into the west pasture, where the trees will give them more shelter."

Moving the stock took a while. They didn't finish until after midafternoon. Not long after they'd fed and stabled the horses, the wind picked up and the snowfall grew heavier, until Zach could barely see his own hands. With the cattle sheltered and fed for now and the horses cared for, it was time to head inside.

"Let's keep in touch," Zach said. "Have your walkie-talkie handy in case our cell phones go out. And stay warm."

Curly nodded and moved quickly toward his trailer, disappearing in the thick snow.

Zach turned toward the house. Toward Gina.

Not long after lunch, cupping the landline to her ear, Gina peered out the window and frowned. "Yes, Uncle Redd, it's coming down hard." So hard she couldn't see beyond the back stoop, let alone the barn. She guessed that Zach and Curly were taking care of the cattle—a huge job for only the two of them, made worse by the heavy snow.

"They're saying this will be the blizzard of the century," her uncle said.

Gina hoped they were wrong. She needed to fly home on Sunday, both to get to the office and to get away from Zach.

"It goes without saying that your cousins and I won't be over for dinner," Uncle Redd went on.

"I'll miss you, but I'm glad you're staying safe at home. Do you have enough to eat?"

"Plenty. If you need anything, don't forget that Zach is close by."

Forget? The man hadn't been out of her thoughts since she'd first opened her eyes this morning.

"Don't worry about me," she said. "I'll be fine."

"Well, I better let the dogs out to do their business while they can still get there. Call you later, honey. Or you call me."

"Will do. Love you."

With no family dinner to look forward to, the rest of Gina's day loomed heavily ahead. She hoped Zach was still planning to stop by for leftovers.

At the thought of seeing him tonight, she let out a dreamy sigh. She certainly wouldn't object to another evening of kissing and more....

"No," she firmly told herself. She couldn't.

If she were smart, she'd uninvite him to dinner, but that would be rude. She would tell him up front that there would be no kissing or anything else tonight. That made her feel safer.

If she could just stop thinking about him...

She needed to keep busy, which wasn't a problem because she still needed to clean out both of the bathrooms. She decided to start with the smaller one on the main floor.

Like all the other rooms in the house, the bathroom was cluttered with old magazines. In the linen closet she found enough towels and soap for an army. The packaging on some of the soap looked decades old, and she guessed that years ago, her thrifty Uncle Lucky had bought a case or two on sale—just as he had all those unopened office supplies. Which made her both smile and shake her head.

She decided to share the supplies with Zach and the other hands. What they didn't want, she would donate to charity. She was nearly finished, wondering whether Zach was hunkered down in his trailer or outside battling Mother Nature, when she heard a knock at the back door.

With the weather as bad as it was, it couldn't be anyone except Zach. Her heart thudding, Gina smoothed her hair, hurried to the kitchen and opened the door.

The eaves over the stoop provided some shelter, but snow coated Zach's wool face mask and coat.

"You look like a yeti," she teased, beckoning him inside.

He wiped his boots on the mat. "It's damn cold." Instead of moving into the kitchen, he stopped just inside the door. "I should tie a rope between the door and the barn so that I can find my way there later—unless you threw it away."

She shook her head. "I've been focused mostly on papers and the worthless junk Uncle Lucky saved. Whoever buys the ranch might want it and some of the tools down there. I'll get the rope."

Gina hurried down the wood steps. Moments later, rope in hand, she returned to the kitchen. "When you finish tying it, come back. I'll make a fresh pot of coffee."

He was gone awhile, so long that the coffee finished perking and started to cool. Gina was beginning to worry when he entered the house again, bringing a gust of cold air with him.

She shivered. "Perfect timing—the coffee's ready."

"Good. I need something hot."

Zach met her gaze, and her desire for him flooded back.

He pulled off his gloves, removed his boots and then shrugged out of his coat. He wore faded jeans and a thick sweater over a plaid flannel shirt.

Gina glanced out the window. "It's snowing so hard. How can you even see out there?"

"That's why I wanted the rope. I'd guess a good two feet and counting have accumulated so far. With the wind, some drifts are twice that size. And it's only been a few hours since the storm began. It's a good thing Curly and I got the cattle moved and fed."

She knew that cattle ate and drank a great deal and had to be fed and watered daily. "How will you feed them tomorrow?" she asked as she filled two mugs.

Cupping his hands around the warm ceramic, Zach carried his coffee to the table and sat down. "We'll use the plow and tractor to deliver the feed." He tasted his coffee. "While I was out there, I did some thinking. This house is much closer to the barn than my trailer. Curly's trailer is close, which is good, but he doesn't have room for me. For the sake of the cattle, I should bunk here tonight—if that's okay with you."

Zach here, all night? The very thought was unnerving, but he was right about the barn. "With two empty bedrooms upstairs and one down here, there's plenty of room, so why not?" She sat down across from him. "But no more kissing or anything else."

"I've been thinking the same thing," he said, but the heat in his gaze didn't match his words.

Her anxiety must've shown, for his mouth quirked. "Don't worry, I'll behave."

Part of her was relieved. At the same time, she also wanted him to ignore her hands-off rule. Feeling as if the devil sat on one shoulder and an angel on the other, she gave a jerky nod.

"I'll take the bedroom down here tonight."

That they would sleep on different floors felt somehow safer. Gina let out a breath. "Great."

"Great," he repeated. "Have you spoken with Redd today?"

She nodded. "A little while ago. He's fine, but with

the storm, he won't be here for dinner tonight. Neither will Sophie and Gloria, and we have so many leftovers. I wish I'd given them each a plate to take home last night, but I assumed they'd be here."

"Don't worry, I'll help you get rid of the extra food." His eyes twinkling, Zach licked his lips, making her laugh.

Then she sobered. "It's a good thing the storm held off until today. Otherwise, Uncle Redd would never have gotten to the hospital and we'd all be worried sick about him." The thought made her shudder.

"He's fine," Zach said. "That's what matters."

Gina bit her lip. "I worry, though. Both my dad and Uncle Lucky had heart attacks that killed them. Uncle Redd could be next, and I'm not ready to lose him."

"Don't court trouble. If it were me, I'd schedule a physical and get him checked out."

"I'll nag Uncle Redd about that. Not that he'll listen to me."

"I'll back you up."

They lapsed into comfortable silence, like longtime friends. Or an old married couple.

Married? Gina frowned. They weren't even dating. Even if she lived here, they would never go out. They wanted different things.

She glanced out the window over the sink, where snow was rapidly accumulating on the windowsill. "How long is this storm supposed to last?"

"Days. The people on the radio are calling this the blizzard of the century."

"Well, I'm going to hope for the best," Gina said, crossing her fingers. "Big winter storms in eastern

Montana aren't exactly rare, and it's a sure bet that as soon as the snow stops, the transportation people will clear the roads. By Sunday, everything should be fine."

"I wouldn't count on it."

She couldn't be stuck here! She needed to prove herself at work. "This is a really crucial time of year for my clients, Zach. I have to get home."

"Fine, but you can't control Mother Nature. Your boss knows that. He'll understand."

Under normal circumstances, maybe, but with her recent screwups and Kevin already upset, Gina had her doubts. She didn't even want to think about Evelyn Grant.

The storm had to stop, and soon. She closed her eyes and prayed for a miracle.

"Look what we did tonight," Zach said, gesturing at what was left of the turkey and trimmings. "We made a huge dent in the leftovers. Sophie, Gloria and Redd would be proud."

He waited for Gina to laugh or at least crack a smile, but the corners of her lips barely lifted. Come to think of it, she hadn't eaten all that much. She seemed nervous, really uptight.

Zach looked her straight in the eyes. "I said I wouldn't make a pass at you tonight, and I won't."

"I know." The smile she attempted fell short.

"Well, something sure has you bothered."

Resting her chin on her fist, she gave a glum sigh. "I told my boss I'd be in the office Monday morning. I want to be there, *need* to be there, but I'll probably be stuck here."

With those words, Zach knew with a sick certainty that she would never change her mind. No matter what he did or said—and because of the promise to Lucky, he wasn't about to give up—she wasn't going to hold on to the ranch.

"You really hate being here," he said.

"It's not that bad. But there's so much to do at work, and without Wi-Fi, working from here is difficult at best. I have to get to the office, where I have easy access to the internet and can run over and see my clients at any time."

Been there, done that. Only after quitting the rat race had Zach realized that most of what he'd once considered important was meaningless busywork. He doubted Gina wanted to hear that, but he could change her perspective.

"What's the worst that could happen if you stay here a few extra days?" he asked.

"Probably nothing." She toyed with her fork. "I just… There's a lot on my plate right now."

"Which your capable assistant can handle. Tell her to shape up and get it done."

Gina gave an uncertain nod. "If I can ever reach her."

"Hey." Zach tipped up her chin. "You can't do anything about it tonight, so you may as well relax."

"I'll try." She took a deep breath, exhaled and then rolled her shoulders.

"Feel better now?"

"A little. I talk to you about my worries, Zach. Why don't you talk to me?"

He frowned. "About what?"

"Anything. Your family, your past."

This was why he avoided relationships. "I told you about my family—we don't get along. As for the past, it's over and done with, so why rehash it?"

"Because it's interesting. I want to know where you used to work and what you did for a living. Why are you so closemouthed about it?"

"Because it's none of your damn business." Zach crossed his arms and set his jaw.

"All right." Gina threw up her hands. "Forget I asked."

Ready to do exactly that, he stood. "Let's get this mess cleaned up. You clear the table and I'll wash the dishes."

They worked well together and finished in no time. Now what?

With hours left before bedtime and no fooling around on the agenda, the rest of the evening stretched out like an empty highway.

Zach thought of something to do that was both fun and safe. "Now and then, Lucky and I used to play board games," he said. "How about a game of Scrabble and a couple beers in front of the fire? We can set up the card table."

Gina perked right up. "I used to play with Uncle Lucky, too. I haven't played a board game for ages. I put those games in the giveaway pile and was going to take them to the charity box at the church. I'm glad I haven't had time."

Ten minutes later, Zach was sitting across the folding table from Gina, with two bottles of beer and the Scrabble board between them and a dictionary and score pad within easy reach.

They chose letters, and then drew to see who went first. Gina won that. Without hesitation she spelled the word *socks*.

"That's a double score for me—twenty-two points," she said, looking pleased with herself.

Zach was impressed by her speed. As the game progressed, she grew more animated, and at last the tension that had been with her for hours faded.

Her vocabulary, competitive spirit and wit dazzled him. With the sparkle in her eyes and the flush of excitement on her cheeks, she was stunning.

Beauty, brains and a great sense of humor—talk about a lethal combination. Zach wanted her more than ever. He wanted to kiss the smug look right off her face and make her forget all about their word competition, but he'd promised not to go there.

He narrowed his eyes. "You never said you were an ace Scrabble player. You're beating the pants off me."

"That I am," she crowed. "I love to win."

"Who doesn't?" He spelled out a thirty-pointer.

"Not bad, Horton." She clamped a pen between her teeth, reminding him of a gambler with his stogie. "Would you care to bet on the winner of this game?"

Chuckling, he shrugged. "You're on. If I beat you, you have to make me breakfast when I get back from my chores in the morning. If I lose, I'll cook for you."

"Deal—and FYI, I like my eggs over easy." She reached across the table and they shook on it.

Things got serious then, both of them concentrating. By the time they were down to four tiles each, Gina was ahead by eight points.

After studying the board, she sighed. "All I can do

is use my *t* and *h* to make *the.* That's four more points, giving me a twelve-point lead, minus two points for my last two tiles. Which means I win. Yes!" She pumped her fist in the air.

"Not so fast. I still have a few usable tiles left." Zach went for a triple word score. *"Kiss,"* he said with glee. "That's twenty-four points, minus two points for my last tile. I'm the winner."

"By twelve points. Darn you." Gina attempted a forbidding frown, but her laughing eyes ruined the effect.

The urge to pull her close grabbed Zach hard, and it was all he could do to stay in his seat. He scooped up the tiles and returned them to the letter bag.

Oblivious, Gina settled the lid on the box. "What time will you be back for breakfast, and what do you want to eat?"

What he wanted had nothing to do with food. "Surprise me. I don't know how long I'll be. That depends on what Curly and I find once we're out there." He stood, went to the window and looked through the drapes. "It's still coming down fast and hard."

His own words had him thinking about hard, fast sex. If he didn't get away from Gina soon, he'd break his promise for sure. He turned from the window. "I'd best get some rest."

Though as restless as he was, he'd be lucky to fall asleep anytime soon.

"I'll get you some sheets and blankets."

Gina disappeared down the hall. Zach folded up the table and chairs and pulled himself together.

When she returned, he took the bedding from her. "Tonight was fun."

"Yeah."

For a few long moments they simply stared at each other.

By the soft look in her eyes, Zach swore she wanted him to kiss her. But she glanced away, cleared her throat and headed to her room. "Well, good night."

"Night." His unwitting gaze settled on her lush behind until she disappeared at the top of the stairs.

Chapter 13

Gina awoke to an utterly silent house, courtesy of the snow insulating the world from normal sounds. Had it finally stopped?

She hurried out of bed and peered through the blinds. The thick curtain of falling snow gave her the answer.

The storm was still raging.

Wonderful. It was after seven and Zach was probably out with the animals. Gina didn't envy him that job.

Standing under a hot shower, she thought about last night. Zach had kept her laughing. He was smart and funny and a competitive player, and she'd enjoyed spending the evening with him. A little too much.

She was starting to care about Zach—a lot more than was smart.

She wanted a man with drive and ambition, she reminded herself. And though she knew a fair amount about him now, he wouldn't answer her questions about his past. What was he hiding? Whatever it was, it couldn't be good.

Her heart didn't seem to care.

Dressed in jeans and a warm pullover, she headed downstairs.

Zach had already made coffee. Grateful, she poured herself a cup and then peered out the kitchen window, hoping to catch sight of him. Gina saw only the driving snow.

Even with the rope connecting the barn and back door, navigating through the deep snow wouldn't be easy. How would Zach ever find the cattle, let alone make his way back? She began to worry.

To keep herself occupied, she wandered to the living room and flipped on the TV. Newscasters predicted record snowfall and warned people to stay inside.

In the kitchen again, she rummaged through the refrigerator and considered what to make for breakfast. Then she thumbed through the phonebook and found the number for the airport. A recording announced that it was closed and all flights were canceled until further notice. The bus station had shut down, too.

With a heavy sigh, she sat down at the table and called her family.

After brief conversations with each of them and assurances that she would check in later, she hung up. Her next call was to Kevin. She hated bothering him on a Saturday morning, but this couldn't be helped.

"It's snowing here, too," he said after she updated him. "But nothing like where you are. What are your chances of getting here in time to go to work Monday?"

"From what the weather forecasters say, zero." The storm wasn't her fault. All the same, she felt guilty.

"When do you think you'll be back?"

"I wish I knew. This blizzard is supposed to last for days."

Kevin was silent a moment. "Make sure you get Carrie in line. Otherwise, she's toast."

"Believe me, I will." Gina wasn't about to explain to her boss that she hadn't spoken with her assistant in more than a week. She was ready to fire Carrie herself. "What do you want me to do about Evelyn Grant?"

"Bring in Lise."

Gina preferred to keep the account to herself, but she knew her friend would do a good job. "I'll call her today."

"You do that. Keep in touch."

As soon as Gina hung up, she dialed Carrie's cell number. After four rings, her assistant answered. "Hello?" she mumbled, sounding sleepy.

"I woke you," Gina said. "Are you still sick?"

"Not anymore. Hang on a sec."

Carrie covered the phone. Gina couldn't make out what her assistant said, but she definitely heard a man's voice.

"I'm back," Carrie said. "Did you get the email I sent yesterday?"

"I didn't get a chance to check." Tired as she'd been from her late night at the hospital, Gina hadn't even thought about email. "As of last night, we're in the middle of a blizzard. The airport is closed, and I could be stuck in Montana for days. I expect you to pull your weight at work. That means returning calls to any client who asks for me, and no more coming in late."

"All right." Carrie sounded sulky. "I just wish you'd read my email."

"What did it say?"

"I'd rather you read it."

Now Gina was seriously worried. "Thanks to this blizzard, it may be a while before I'm able to drive to a place where I can access Wi-Fi. You may as well tell me now."

Carrie hesitated and then let out a resigned breath. "Something amazing happened to me, Gina. I've fallen in love with Chad, and he's in love with me."

Gina wasn't sure what she'd expected, but it wasn't this. "But you barely know him," she said.

"I know him better than you think. When I came down with the flu last Sunday, he took care of me. We've been together every day and night since."

Six whole days. Gina suppressed a skeptical snort. "Great, but you can't just blow off our clients because you're in love with some guy you just met."

"Chad isn't just 'some guy,'" Carrie fired back, indignant. "He's the one—my soul mate. I had Thanksgiving dinner with his family, and he came to my parents' for dessert. They adore him, Gina. We're already talking about marriage and starting a family."

As incredulous as Gina was—who fell in love that quickly and stayed in love?—she almost envied her assistant. "Not just yet though, right?"

"No, but meeting Chad has changed everything. I realize now that a career in marketing isn't for me. I want a less stressful job, where I don't have to work such long hours or take my work home with me. That way, Chad and I can see more of each other."

Gina picked her jaw up off the floor. "But he works long hours, too," she said.

"That's true, but he enjoys what he does. I don't."

"You could've fooled me—you sure acted like you did."

"Because I thought I wanted to be like you. But I'm not you, and I need more in my life than just work."

Not sure whether to be flattered that Carrie had wanted to be like her or insulted that her assistant thought she had no life, Gina frowned. But Carrie was right. Without work, Gina had no life. Which was kind of pathetic but also necessary if she wanted to get ahead. "But you're on the fast track at Andersen, Coats and Mueller," Gina argued. "You want to move up in the company, don't you?"

"I thought I did, but I was wrong."

Wondering if the flu had addled Carrie's brain, Gina shook her head. "This job is the chance of a lifetime, Carrie. Don't throw away your future on an impulse. In a few days you're going to wake up, and I would hate for you to regret this."

"I don't think I will. The truth is, I've been thinking about switching jobs for over a month."

"You never said anything. You jumped at the opportunity to take care of my clients while I was gone and assured me that you could handle the responsibility. The day after I left, you worked so hard you fell asleep at your desk and didn't wake up until the next morning."

"That was awful."

"I'm sorry you had so much to do, but when I get

back your workload will lighten up substantially. In the meantime, Evelyn Grant needs attention and so do our other clients. I'm counting on you, Carrie, to do what you promised and give the clients what they want and need."

"Yeah, okay. When did you say you'll be back?"

"As soon as the airport reopens. I'll keep you posted. I'm going to call Lise and ask her to step in and help with Grant Industries."

Her assistant sounded remarkably cheerful about that. So different from a week and a half ago.

Gina's temples began to throb, threatening a bear of a headache. After digging through her purse for the aspirin bottle and taking two tablets, she phoned Lise.

"Can you help me out?" she asked after explaining the situation.

"Kevin specifically asked for me to work with Evelyn Grant? That's so cool. I assume I'll also get part of the bonus from the account?"

Gina hated to give up a penny of that hard-earned money, but she didn't have much choice. "Absolutely. The hard-copy records are in my file cabinet." She gave Lise the password to access the information online.

"I've never experienced a blizzard," Lise said when the business part of the conversation ended. "What's it like?"

"Pretty, but a little scary." Especially with Zach still out there. Gina glanced anxiously at the window. "I just wish my uncle had installed Wi-Fi here."

"I don't blame you. If I had no internet and was stuck on a ranch in the middle of nowhere, I'd go nuts. How do you keep from losing your mind?"

If it wasn't for Zach, Gina knew she'd be pacing the house. "It isn't so bad," she said.

"Let me guess—you've met a sexy cowboy and he's keeping you company."

Her friend must be a mind reader. "Something like that."

"Mmm, that sounds intriguing."

The back door opened. With the wind howling at his back, Zach stomped his feet on the mat and stepped inside. Relief flooded her. His coat, gloves and face mask were coated in snow, but he was safe.

"I have to go," she told Lise. "I'll call you again soon."

"You better. I want the whole scoop on your cowboy."

By the time Gina disconnected, Zach had stripped off the face mask and gloves. His coat and boots followed.

"You made it back," Gina said.

"Thanks to the rope from the barn to the house. Visibility out there is near zero, and the snow is deep. Curly and I made half a dozen trips between the barn and west pasture to feed all the cattle."

"That sounds like a lot of work."

"Yep. I'm sure glad Pete fixed the water heater and the cattle have the water they need. Otherwise, we'd be in big trouble." Zach's stomach growled. "What's for breakfast?"

"How about a cheese omelet, bacon and toast? Sit down and I'll bring you a fresh cup of coffee while you wait."

Zach grinned. "I'm sure glad I won the game last night."

Gina put her hands on her hips. "Those are fighting words, Mr. Horton. Care for a repeat tonight?"

"Sure. Or we could try a different game. Lucky kept several on hand."

"Let's stick with Scrabble."

The blizzard continued throughout Monday and Tuesday with no signs of easing up. Zach and Curly spent hours feeding the cattle and checking the water supply and did what chores they could in the barn. Mostly they holed up in their respective shelters.

Avoiding the half-mile trek to the trailer and back every day was a relief, but staying in the same house as Gina was tough. Zach wanted her more every day, and keeping his hands to himself was torture.

He did his best to steer clear of her when he could, and they settled into a routine of sorts. Zach spent part of his day doing chores, and Gina continued to grapple with her job responsibilities and sort through Lucky's stuff. Zach helped her pack boxes destined for charity and fill bags with trash. Soon trash bags accumulated in the hallway, until there was hardly room to pass by.

Evenings, they took turns cooking dinner and then played various board games, with the loser making breakfast for the winner.

After dinner on Wednesday, the snow finally tapered off.

"Look at that." Gina pointed through the window on the kitchen door. "We can actually see the moon tonight."

Standing behind her, Zach inhaled her sweet scent. He was close enough that he could brush her hair aside, lean down and nuzzle her neck.

He stepped back and cleared his throat. "The roads should be cleared in a day or two."

"Just in the nick of time—the freezer is nearly empty. I wonder when the airport will reopen and when I can go home."

Soon, Zach hoped. He was enjoying Gina's company far too much and was tired of being in a constant state of arousal. He looked forward to going back to his trailer.

"Sometime this weekend, I'd guess," he said. "This is probably my last night in the house. We've played every board game here. What'll we do tonight?"

It was a loaded question because what he wanted was to fool around. But he'd promised to behave, and he would keep his word if it killed him. Which it just might.

Looking as if she'd read his mind, Gina swallowed and tugged the hem of her sweater over her hips. "They're showing one of my favorite movies on TV tonight. We could watch it."

"Which movie is that?"

"It's a Wonderful Life."

Zach remembered the film. "I haven't seen that since I was a kid. Sure. We'll make popcorn. Too bad we finished the remainder of the beer last night."

"We're out of wine, too. I could make hot chocolate."

"Then I really will feel like a kid again."

Gina checked her watch. "The movie starts in twenty minutes. I'll make the popcorn and cocoa right away."

"I'll light the fire."

By the time she brought in the refreshments, the fire was crackling and Zach had the TV turned to the right channel. He took the cocoa mugs from her and set them on the coffee table.

Gina wandered to the picture window and opened the drapes. Moonlight lit the snow and stars glittered in the sky. "What a beautiful evening," she murmured.

And a beautiful woman staring into the night. Zach considered joining her at the window, but he didn't. Best to stay out of reach of temptation. "You don't see all those stars in Chicago," he said, taking his mug to the armchair. "Too much light pollution. If you lived here on the ranch—"

"Don't start that again." She sat down on the sofa. "You can't reach the popcorn all the way over there."

She had a point. Wary of sitting too close to her, he settled into one end of the sofa. Gina stayed at the opposite end. Now they both had to stretch to reach the popcorn.

The movie started. Zach watched for a while but soon got sidetracked by Gina. Looking intent and entranced, she leaned slightly toward the TV screen and silently mouthed much of the dialogue, right along with Donna Reid, Jimmy Stewart and the other actors.

During an ad, he muted the sound. "Just how many times have you seen this movie?"

"At least a dozen, maybe two."

"Seriously?"

"I told you, it's one of my favorites."

He chuckled and shook his head. "You're an *It's a Wonderful Life* junkie. I'd never have guessed."

"I love most every Christmas movie. I love Christmas, period."

Then why did she spend the holiday in Chicago year after year? Her work, Zach figured. She wanted to stay close by in case one of her clients needed her.

"You've been saying you want to spend more time with your family," he said. "Why don't you come back this year? You'd make them very happy."

"Because when I finally leave here, Christmas will be less than two weeks away. It seems silly to fly home, then turn around and fly all the way back. Besides, I've already been here almost a week longer than I expected. I need to stay in Chicago, but I'll come back in the spring to tie up any loose ends at the house. Next year, I'll definitely be here for Christmas."

"Okay. Winter is a bad time to try to sell property around here. You may as well hold off on putting the Lucky A on the market until you come back next spring."

She kept insisting she was going to sell, but a few months down the road she might change her mind.

"You have a point, but I—" She broke off, snatched the remote from the coffee table and turned on the sound. "The movie's starting again."

Once again, she turned her attention to the TV screen.

Zach had trouble getting into the story, mainly because he couldn't concentrate on much besides Gina. He was too fixated on watching her lick her lips after she sipped her cocoa or swallowed a mouthful of popcorn. He couldn't help but imagine her tongue on him. With her every breath, her breasts rose and fell.

She was so damn sexy, and sitting a couple of arms' lengths from her ranked up there with the most difficult things he'd ever done. He seriously considered returning to the armchair, but he stayed where he was and fought a battle with his growing desire.

When Jimmy Stewart kissed Donna Reid for the first time, Gina glanced at him, her lips looking full and lush. "That's just about the most romantic kiss ever."

Her cheeks were flushed from the heat of the room and the tiny gold flecks in her eyes reflected the fire. She looked warm and inviting and irresistible.

But it was the longing on her face that did Zach in. She wanted him.

A certain part of his body began to rise. "We can top George Bailey and Mary Hatch anytime. But I made a promise not to kiss you, and I won't break it without your okay."

"Break it, Zach." She slid across the cushions, toward him.

He muted the TV and did what he'd been aching to do for days. Pulled her into his arms and kissed her.

She tasted of popcorn, cocoa and passion.

He'd missed this, wanted to go on kissing her, but after a few minutes, he reluctantly broke contact. "How does that compare to the kiss we just saw?"

"I'm not sure." She twined her hands around his neck. "Could we try it again?"

"I see no problem with that."

He kissed her again, and heat sizzled between them. That kiss blended into another and another. Zach forgot to think. Eager to touch her, he cupped her breasts.

With a pleased, purring sound she pushed her ample

softness against his palms. He brushed his thumbs over her nipples and felt her shudder. His hands shook, he wanted her so badly.

He wanted more. A lot more. Somehow he managed to pull back. "This is dangerous," he said, breathing hard.

"Shhh." Gina pulled him down for another kiss.

He eased her back so that she lay against the sofa pillow. With her light brown hair spread across the pillow, her eyes closed and desire tinting her face and neck, she was beautiful. The most beautiful woman Zach had ever known.

He slipped his hands under her sweater and pushed it up so that he could see her. Her stomach was warm and smooth. She wore a lacy, white bra that plainly showed her dusky pink nipples, the points stiff against the lace.

Blood roared through his head. He unhooked the front clasp, pushed the bra aside and ran his tongue across one nipple.

Whimpering, Gina slid her restless hands under his shirt and up his back. Zach tasted the other breast. Her nails scraped lightly over his back.

His body was on fire, and his erection throbbed and demanded release. He was reaching for the button on her jeans when his elbow connected with the coffee table. It hurt like hell.

"Damn it."

"What happened?" Gina asked, looking slightly dazed.

"Bumped my funny bone." And a good thing he had. What was he doing?

He fastened her bra and tugged her sweater down.

"Are you okay?" Gina asked.

Her lips were lush and swollen from his kisses and her normally smooth hair was tangled and sexy. Zach wanted her more than he'd ever wanted a woman. But he wasn't right for Gina, and she wasn't right for him.

He was starting to care. Hell. He was so not okay.

He grabbed the remote. "Everything's fine."

She nodded and glanced at the TV screen. "We missed the end of the movie."

"That's okay. We know it has a happy ending."

At his sarcastic tone, she frowned. "You don't believe in happy endings?"

"Only in novels and movies." Zach flipped off the TV.

"That's sad."

He slanted her a look. "I'm a realist. How many couples with happy endings have you seen in real life?"

"I can think of several right here in Saddlers Prairie. Autumn and Cody Naylor, Jenny and Adam Dawson, Megan and Drew Dawson, Mark and Stacy Engle. Clay and Sarah—"

"Yeah, I get it. Some people do have happy endings."

But not Zach. He was alone, just as he wanted to be.

"You think I'm looking for a relationship with you," she said.

"Are you?"

"Of course not! I'm leaving in a few days." She tucked her hair behind her ears. "I'm not some naive girl, Zach. We kissed and you unfastened my bra. It was really nice, but that's all."

There was a lot more between them than that, and they both knew it.

And he needed space, needed to tamp his feelings down and keep them there. He stood. "I need to be up early. I'm going to turn in."

She nodded. "Who's making breakfast tomorrow?"

"I'll fix myself something before I leave. I'll be extra busy the next few days, clearing pathways around the ranch and catching up on chores I haven't been able to do. I probably won't see you again before you leave."

"Oh—okay." She glanced at her hands and then offered a bright smile. "Good night, Zach, and thank you for everything."

Chapter 14

By Friday the airport had reopened and the roads were finally clear enough to drive. Gina wanted to leave the next morning, but due to the blizzard and a glut of passengers, she couldn't get out until Sunday. As soon as she booked her ticket, she called her family.

"Hi," Gloria said.

"Good morning, cookie," Sophie chimed in from the extension phone. "I'll bet you're glad the roads are open."

"I am. I just got my ticket home. I leave Sunday morning. Let's have one last dinner together tomorrow night."

"That sounds lovely, but you don't want to cook on your last night in town."

"Actually, I've pretty much emptied the refrigerator," Gina said. Zach could take whatever was left. "I was thinking we could eat at Barb's Café." It was the only restaurant in town besides fast-food places. "My treat. Tell Uncle Redd to meet us at your house. I'll pick you up there and drive his car."

"You and Zach can sit in the front seat," Gloria said, her voice coy.

They all knew he'd stayed at the house during the blizzard. Gina wasn't about to feed their speculation frenzy. "Zach and I haven't seen each other in a few days." Not since the night of those melting kisses.

It was a relief not having to face him and having the house to herself again. At least that's what she told herself.

The truth was, she missed his company. She missed him.

Which was why she wanted to hurry back to Chicago and immerse herself in work.

"What do you mean, you haven't seen each other?" Sophie asked.

"I've been busy with my work and the house, and he's had a lot of ranching chores. I'm sure he's fine."

"After he stayed with you and made sure you were safe, that's all you have to say?"

"What do you expect me to say?"

Gloria snorted. "For a smart woman, you sure are thick sometimes. Zach cares about you."

"Of course he does. I'm Lucky's only niece. Now, what time should I pick you up?"

"Tell me you invited him to dinner."

"No, I didn't. This is a family dinner."

"And Zach is like family."

They were impossible. "You know what I mean," Gina said.

"I know what you *sound* like. You're avoiding him."

Which was true, but then, Zach was avoiding her, too. He seemed to think she wanted more from him than she did. Gina did have feelings for him, but she wasn't about to let them out. He wasn't the right guy for her. "Why would I do that?"

"I'm not in the mood for guessing games, Gina. What did you and Zach argue about?"

Would they never quit? "Oops, gotta run. See you tomorrow night."

Uncle Redd's line was busy when she tried to call him, so she called Carol Plett, the Realtor.

"This is the slowest time of year," Mrs. Plett said. "It's best to wait until January."

"Could you at least come look at it?" Gina asked. "I'm flying back to Chicago Sunday and would like to settle things before I leave."

"Unfortunately, I'm just about to leave for Elk Ridge to see my new little granddaughter. The blizzard kept me away from her last weekend, and I miss her. I've been in Lucky's house many times and I know the ranch well. I'll draw up the listing papers and send them to you."

When Gina hung up, she tried Uncle Redd again. This time, she reached him. "Meet us at Gloria and Sophie's at five-thirty," she said after inviting him to dinner.

"It's a date. Gloria says you and Zach had a fight."

Her cousin hadn't wasted any time passing on her suspicions. "That's not true," Gina said. "What's wrong with wanting a meal alone with my family? Hey, will you drive me to the airport Sunday morning? My plane leaves at eight, and we'd have to leave around five-thirty."

"At that hour it's still dark out, and you don't want me driving all that way in the dark. Besides, I don't get up as early as I used to. Why don't you ask Zach— since you two aren't in a fight? He gets up early, so he won't mind."

Gina was sure he would. If only she could call a cab. Unfortunately there were none in Saddlers Prairie. She thought about asking Autumn or one of the other women she knew for a ride, but they all had families and she didn't want to impose.

She sighed. "I don't have much choice, do I?"

Despite having been plowed, Saturday night the roads were coated with black ice. Returning from dinner at Barb's, Gina piloted Uncle Redd's sedan at well below the speed limit.

In the passenger seat, Sophie smiled. "Tonight was wonderful fun—and so yummy. I've always enjoyed the food at Barb's."

"Home cooked is better, though," Gloria said from the backseat.

Sophie sniffed. "I know that, Gloria, but eating out is about more than just the food. It's nice to be waited on and let someone else cook. Best of all, there are no dishes."

"And Sugar and Bit get the bones—a real treat for them," Uncle Redd added. He was sharing the back with Gloria.

After working on the house all day and carting a truckload of donations to the school and church, Gina had needed to get out and had enjoyed the evening with her family—bickering and all. "You know you could eat there every week, if you wanted," she said.

"Waste all that money?" Uncle Redd snorted.

Sophie nodded. "He's right. We don't have the kind of income you do, cookie. Living on Social Security and a small pension doesn't leave much for extras."

"Sophie!" Gloria scolded. "We may not have Gina's business smarts and financial resources, but we're comfortable, and you know it. Thank you for treating us, Gina."

"Yes—thank you, cookie."

Gina would've died if they'd realized how broke she was. She smiled. "It was my pleasure."

Gloria leaned up and touched her shoulder. "We're really going to miss you."

Uncle Redd and Sophie murmured agreement.

"I'll miss you, too," Gina said. Along with everyone else in Saddlers Prairie—her friends and, most of all, Zach.

"I wish you'd come back for Christmas," Uncle Redd said.

Lise had invited Gina over for brunch again, which was something to look forward to, but the rest of the day was bound to be lonely. "I've already been here for nearly a week longer than I planned," she explained. "I can't afford to take any more time away. But I'll be back in the spring, and I promise I'll be here for Christmas next year."

With any luck, by then the Lucky A would be sold.

Her heart wrenched at the thought, and not just because there would be no more Christmases there.

She was beginning to think she should keep it. Which was ridiculous. The ranch would never be profitable, not without a large infusion of cash she didn't have. She needed to sell and would put it on the market in January.

"Someone ought to live in that house and take care of it until it sells," Uncle Redd said. "Zach should move in."

Gina hadn't thought of that, but it was a good idea.

A block before she reached Gloria and Sophie's house, she slowed way down. "It's slippery out there. I'm going to walk you two inside. Uncle Redd, you can wait in the car."

Gloria waved off the suggestion. "Nonsense. Why, only a few hours ago Zach came by and cleared and salted our walk—just as he promised he would before the blizzard. I wasn't going to tell you this because you said you didn't want him to come tonight, but I invited him anyway, as a way of thanking him for all that he does. He couldn't make it."

Gina was relieved about that. She wasn't great at pretending to be relaxed and happy when she wasn't. If Zach had come tonight, fooling her family wouldn't have been easy. It was bad enough that she would see him tomorrow.

"For the last time, we're not fighting—he's taking me to the airport in the morning, remember? I'll ask him about moving into the house then." As soon as he dropped her off and drove away, she would push him from her thoughts—and her heart. "Tonight I wanted to have dinner with just us," she added.

"Well, I missed him," Sophie said. Gina pulled to a stop in front of the house. "What time is your flight?"

"Eight a.m. We'll leave the ranch at five-thirty."

Gloria opened her door. "Wait for me," Gina ordered. Taking care not to slip, she headed around the car.

"I don't need any help." Gloria's mouth tightened, but she allowed Gina to take her arm. "Have a safe trip home, and call to let us know you made it."

"No matter what time you get in," Sophie added, grasping hold of Gina's other arm.

As they made their way slowly toward their front door, Gloria shook her off. "The walkway is just fine, Gina. I'm not a doddering fool. I'm quite capable of—"

Her words died as she lost her footing and slipped. Gina grabbed for her, but it was too late. Her cousin fell hard on the walkway.

Gina covered her mouth with her hands. "Are you okay?"

"I skinned my palm and twisted my ankle, but I'm all right."

As Gina extended her arms to help her cousin to her feet, Uncle Redd exited the car. "Let me give you a hand," he called out.

The last thing Gina needed was for him to slip and fall, too. "It's okay," she called out. "Please wait in the car."

"I'm fine," Gloria insisted.

Pulling a two-hundred-pound woman to her feet was no easy task, and Gina grunted with the effort. Gloria leaned heavily on her and limped slowly forward.

Gina frowned. "You're in pain."

"I'll live."

"Maybe we should call Dr. Mark," Sophia suggested, looking worried.

"I'm not going to bother the poor doctor on a Saturday night. I'll clean my palm, ice the ankle and take two aspirin, and everything will be fine. Go on now, Gina. Drive Redd home and drive yourself back to the house so you can get a decent night's sleep."

"You're sure?" Gina asked as Sophie opened the front door. "Let me come in and take a look at your ankle."

"You're not a doctor, and I don't need a nursemaid."

Her cousin set her jaw and Gina knew that arguing was pointless. "Okay." She hugged both her cousins. "I'll miss you both so much."

"Us, too, cookie," Sophie said. "Don't forget to call when you get home."

Antsy to leave, Gina was up and dressed early Sunday morning. As she sipped coffee and waited for Zach, she glanced around the kitchen. Without the clutter, it looked bigger. A couple of coats of paint and some new curtains would do wonders for it.

Would she be able to stay there this spring, or would new owners already be living in the house?

Saying goodbye to the place where she'd spent many happy weeks every summer of her childhood made her heart ache, and she half wished she could stay. Which was ridiculous. Her life was in Chicago, and she could hardly wait to get back to work. Back to the comforts of her own apartment. Wi-Fi, a great music system and a flat-screen TV. Entertainment and good restaurants within walking distance. She filled a Thermos with the coffee she'd made and washed out the pot. And really good coffee.

Footsteps thudded on the back stoop, followed by a knock. Zach.

He was freshly shaved, wide-awake and so handsome that her heart lifted at the sight of him.

"Morning," he said in a gruff voice, sounding as if they were his first words of the day. He wiped his feet on the welcome mat and stepped inside. "Ready to go?"

"Almost. I want to ask you something."

That earned her a wary look.

"Don't worry, I wouldn't dream of prying into your past."

His eyes narrowed a fraction. He didn't like that. She hurried on. "I was talking with my family last night, and we think that you should move into the house until it sells. It's not good for it to be empty." But it was more than that. For reasons she couldn't define, she needed Zach to stay here.

"I cleaned out most of Uncle Lucky's junk and the fridge is empty," she went on, "but the towels, linens and kitchen things are still here."

She sucked in a breath and waited.

"Sure, I'll stay here."

Overcome with relief, she exhaled. "That's great."

Her gaze collided with his. The warmth she saw there confused her and made her want to cry. Uncomfortable, she held out the Thermos. "This is for you to drink on the way to the airport."

"I could use more coffee. Why don't you hold on to it while I load your bags into the truck?"

When the last suitcase disappeared from the kitchen, Gina shut off the light. She thought about locking the door, but as far as she knew, Uncle Lucky had never locked up. She left it as he would have. It was still dark outside, and now the house was dark, too.

After buckling up, she handed Zach the keys to the house.

He pocketed them and pulled out of the driveway. "I'm ready for some of that coffee now."

"Sure." Gina opened the Thermos and filled the cup.

He was quiet for a while, sipping and keeping his eyes on the deserted highway.

Tension filled the truck, not much different from the night they'd met. But so much had happened since then. She couldn't leave things like that.

"Zach, I—"

"I don't want—"

They spoke at the same time.

"Go ahead," Zach said.

"You first."

He nodded. "I left a little abruptly the other night. I… It wasn't anything you did. I enjoyed being with you—all of it."

His eyes were warm again, and she all but melted. "Me, too."

The next stretch of silence was far more relaxed.

"Shoot," she said. "I left the hat you loaned me in the house. It's in the coat closet."

"Okay. How was the dinner with your family last night?" he asked.

"Fine, until the end of the evening. I was helping Gloria up the walk, but you know how independent she is. She shrugged me off and, of course, slipped on black ice. She twisted her ankle. I was able to get her inside, but she wouldn't let me examine her ankle. She promised to take a couple of aspirin and ice it. I think she'll be okay."

"She's tough. What's on your agenda when you get back?"

"If my flights are on time—please, God—and I get home at a decent hour, I'll probably stop at the office and get ready for Monday. I'll be touching bases with all my clients and visiting a few in person." Starting with Evelyn Grant. If she'd even see her. Gina had spoken with Lise several times. She and Ms. Grant seemed to be getting along well, but Gina wanted the woman to give her another chance.

"I'll bet the people you work with will be glad to see you back."

"I'll be glad to see them, too." Except for Carrie. According to Marsha, she'd been coming to work on time but leaving at five o'clock sharp. Employees at Andersen, Coats and Mueller rarely left at five, and it was obvious that her heart was no longer in the job. Either she was going to quit, or Gina would have to let her go.

"I've been wondering, Zach. When the ranch sells, where will you go?"

"Maybe you'll keep it and I won't have to go anywhere."

"Very funny. I can't keep it. How many times do I have to tell you that?"

"Hey, I'm just doing what I promised Lucky I'd do."

She couldn't help admiring him for his persistence. "You should've been in sales," she teased. "You're great at refusing to take 'no' for an answer."

"But not so hot at closing the deal."

"Not this deal. So what are your plans for after the ranch sells?"

"Haven't thought much about that yet."

Of course he hadn't. Which just underlined how different he was from Gina.

Suddenly her cell phone rang. Before 6:00 a.m.? She pulled it from her purse and glanced at the screen. What she saw worried her.

"It's a call from Flagg Memorial Hospital." She bit her lip. "Don't tell me Redd had another attack of indigestion. He needs to get that physical." Zach shot her a worried look before she answered. "Hello?"

"It's Sophie."

"Hi, Sophie. What are you doing at the hospital?" Gina asked. "Before you answer that, I'm putting you on speaker so Zach can hear."

"Hi, Zach."

"Hey, Sophie."

"We missed you at dinner last night. In case Gina didn't tell you, Gloria slipped on black ice and twisted her ankle on our own walk. She skinned her hand pretty bad, too, trying to break the fall. It's not your fault, though. You did a fine job clearing off the snow and ice. I guess Gloria found a patch you missed."

"But she swore she was all right," Gina said. The sun wasn't close to rising, and outside it was still pitch-black. She frowned. "You shouldn't drive in the dark,

Sophie, especially on the slippery roads. Why didn't you call and let me come get you?"

"Because you have a long travel day ahead of you, and you needed your rest. But don't worry, cookie, I wasn't about to drive. I called Uncle Redd instead."

"He isn't supposed to drive in the dark, either," Gina said. "That's why Zach is driving me to the airport instead of Uncle Redd." She realized that her uncle was just as invested in her getting together with Zach as her cousins.

Zach shook his head. "Tell us what's going on, Sophie."

"Gloria's hand is pretty banged up, and X-rays showed that her ankle is broken. They're keeping her in the hospital for a few more hours. She's sleeping right now, which is a blessing, if only because she's stopped complaining."

Despite the seriousness of the situation, Zach's lips quirked. Gina couldn't stifle her smile, either.

"When we get her home, she's supposed to stay off her foot and rest her hand for a few days," Sophie went on. "Can you imagine? Gloria hates for other people to take care of her."

"No kidding," Gina muttered.

"The nurse says she'll need crutches, but with her poor hand, how is she supposed to use them?" Sophie sighed. "I just wish we had an extra bedroom downstairs so she could sleep on the main floor. Hold on." She covered the phone for a moment and then returned. "I have to go—someone else needs to use the phone."

"Call us back," Gina said, wishing her cousin owned a cell phone.

"If I can. Have a safe flight."

"Bummer," Zach said when Gina disconnected.

"Oh, man, a broken ankle. I could've taken Gloria to the hospital last night, only she insisted she was fine. I don't see how Sophie will be able to take care of her."

"She's an Arnett, and Arnetts always manage," Zach said. "That's what Lucky used to say."

Manage or not, Gina couldn't leave her family, not like this. Praying that Kevin would understand, she glanced at Zach. "Please take me to the hospital."

Chapter 15

Zach was more than a little surprised by Gina's request to go to the hospital. Just as he was starting to relax. Keeping his distance the past few days hadn't been easy, and knowing he was taking her to the airport and wouldn't see her again for several months had been a big relief.

But now… "Are you sure?" he asked. "Your flight leaves in ninety minutes."

"I wasn't around for Uncle Lucky. I'm not going to make that same mistake again. I'll have to fly out later."

He gave her a sideways look. "Will your boss be okay with that?"

"He'll have to be."

Zach wasn't okay. He understood about Gloria, but he wanted Gina far away, out of temptation's reach.

Thirty minutes later, he and Gina were headed down

the hospital hall toward Gloria's room. Even before they reached the room, he heard Gloria's querulous voice. "I want to go home."

"You know we have to wait for the doctor to discharge you," Redd replied.

"That's right," Sophie said. "Be patient."

"Don't you boss me around, little sister."

Gina rolled her eyes at Zach. "They don't sound any different than they always do."

Pasting a smile on her face, she entered the room. "Hi, Gloria." She bent over the hospital bed and kissed her cousin's cheek.

Not wanting to interfere, Zach hung back.

Instead of seeming glad to see her niece, the older woman glanced from Gina to Zach and frowned. "What are you two doing here? You should be on your way to the airport."

"I've decided to stay for a few more days," Gina said. "Until I know you're okay."

Sophie looked relieved, but Gloria's lips tightened. "Of course, I'm okay. It's not like I'm dying. How are you, Zach? We missed you at dinner last night."

"So your sister said. How's that ankle?"

"I'm on pain meds and I feel pretty good. I just wish people would stop fussing over me." Gloria wore a stubborn look that reminded Zach of Gina. "I want to go home."

Her younger sister let out a fed-up sigh. "Yes, you keep telling us that. You—"

Redd quickly cut in. "Once we leave, we have a bit of a problem. Glo needs crutches, but with her sore hand she'll only be able to use one."

"I'm afraid that's true," Gloria admitted. "But I'll make it work."

Zach had his doubts. She wouldn't be able to get around easily. As independent as she was, she wasn't going to like that.

Suddenly Gina's stomach grumbled.

Gloria raised her eyebrows. "Skipped breakfast, did you? You better head on down to the cafeteria and get yourself something to eat."

"But I just got here," Gina said. "I don't want to leave you, except maybe to talk to the doctor."

"There'll be time for that after you've eaten. You must be hungry, too, Zach. Both of you—go. And bring us back something. Hospital food is dismal, and we're all running on empty."

"What would you like?" Zach asked.

"A cinnamon roll or doughnuts would be nice." Sophie looked hopeful.

"Not for me." Redd rubbed his chest, as if remembering his bad case of indigestion. "I better stick with a bagel and jam."

"That reminds me," Gina said. "You need to schedule a physical."

Moments later, Zach and Gina entered the empty elevator. He smelled her perfume. His body stirred and he wished to hell that Gloria had never slipped and that Gina was on a plane that would take her away.

"Gloria seems in decent spirits," he said.

"As argumentative as ever. This isn't going to be fun for her—or any of us." She tapped her finger against her lip. "Gloria needs a place to sleep where she doesn't have to climb the stairs. I'm thinking she should stay at the ranch and sleep in the downstairs bedroom."

"Good plan—if you can convince her. I'm happy to continue staying in my trailer." Which would help him keep his distance. If he had to see Gina, he would make sure he wasn't alone with her.

The elevator dinged and opened its doors on the lower level and they stepped off.

"I'm going to call my boss now," Gina said. "I'll meet you in the cafeteria."

Zach was selecting a variety of bagels and sweet breakfast treats when she joined him.

"Did you talk to your boss?" he asked.

"He didn't answer, so I left a message. That's a lot of food."

"We're a bunch of hungry people."

"We better get back upstairs and feed my cousins before they bicker to death."

"Please give me the remote," Gloria said. It seemed to be her umpteenth demand since Gina had helped her to the living room sofa. "Then I want some tea. I have tea bags in my purse."

Gina handed her cousin the remote. "I'll go heat up the water and add tea to the grocery list."

She headed for the kitchen, wishing her family would hurry back. Zach had taken Sophie to get her car and pack some of Gloria's belongings. Uncle Redd had gone home to feed Sugar and Bit.

Gina microwaved a mug of water. She brought the mug, a tea bag from her cousin's purse and a bowl of sugar to the living room. Busy channel surfing, Gloria took one sip and then yawned and set the mug down. "I think I'll take a nap."

"But what about your tea?"

"I'll drink it later."

Gina nodded. "I'll get you a blanket." When she returned with a quilt, Gloria was snoring away, her foot propped on a pillow on the coffee table.

After tucking the cover around her, Gina tiptoed out. She needed to drive to Spenser's and stock up on groceries, but she wasn't about to leave Gloria alone.

She was sitting at the kitchen table, making a grocery list, when her cell phone rang. It was Kevin.

Before answering, she closed the door between the kitchen and hallway.

"That's too bad about your cousin, but we need you at the office," Kevin said after she explained the situation.

"I know, and I really want to be there, but this can't be helped. She's in a lot of pain and her sister can't care for her by herself."

"There are nurses and licensed caretakers for that sort of thing."

True, but if Gina so much as mentioned hiring someone to take care of Gloria, her cousin would have a fit. "For now, it's best that I'm here," she said. "Just give me a few more days."

"You said the same thing when you were stuck in the blizzard. That was bad enough, but there was nothing you could do about it and I understood. But this... I don't understand. If it was something life threatening, sure, but it's a broken ankle." Kevin made a disapproving sound.

Gina wasn't about to explain that she felt guilty for

neglecting her relatives. "She's family, Kevin, and she's old. She needs me."

"Your clients need you, too. Maybe you've forgotten them."

"I've worked for you for nearly seven years. You know I'm not like that. I'll call them in the morning and explain, and I'll be back as soon as I possibly can. It won't be long, I promise."

"This elderly relative of yours isn't going to heal quickly. You could be gone weeks."

Gina hoped not, but unfortunately, Kevin was likely right.

She was silent a moment too long. He harrumphed. "You need to get your priorities straight."

"Work is my priority, just as it always has been."

"I'm beginning to doubt that. Christmas is only two and a half weeks away. You stay in Montana and use the time to think about what you really want."

"But—"

"I've always liked you, Gina, but I don't think you fit at Andersen, Coats and Mueller anymore."

"You're firing me?" Her heart nearly stopped. "But I'm on track to be your next vice president."

"Things change. Lise has been handling Grant Industries quite well, and Evelyn requested that she take over the account. I was going to talk to you about that tomorrow, but you're not coming in. I'll parcel out the rest of your accounts to our other associates."

Gina swallowed around her suddenly dry throat. "But I'm sure that if I talk to Carrie, she'll—"

"We both know that Carrie isn't working out. Since you won't be here to fire her, I will."

"I understand." She bit her lip. "What about my year-end bonus?"

She needed that money to pay her current bills.

"You'll get your salary through the end of the year, and you can cash out any vacation time you haven't taken. I don't think you've earned your bonus."

She couldn't bear to think of what would happen without it. Creditors would hound her to death. She might even go bankrupt. Humiliation for what could be made her feel sick. She refused to be like her parents.

"I'm not just talking about Grant Industries," she argued, emboldened out of desperation. "I brought in several new clients this year and earned quite a bit of money for the company. I deserve to be compensated."

"You almost cost me the Grant account. No bonus, Gina, but if you want to come back, you can take Carrie's job." Kevin disconnected.

In shock, she gaped at the phone. Kevin had never been the most compassionate man. His main interest had always been the bottom line. How many employees had come and gone because they fell short of his expectations? Gina had always produced. She'd prided herself on earning his trust and had never imagined she would one day join their ranks.

After putting in all those years of hard work and loyalty, it hurt. Now what was she supposed to do, and what would she tell her family and friends here in Saddlers Prairie? They all thought she was a rich and successful marketing professional, and she couldn't bear to lose their respect.

What to do, what to do? Her mind working furiously, she prowled around the kitchen. Finally she came up with something. She would explain that she'd decided to stay through December so that she could take care of Gloria and spend Christmas with her family.

Footsteps thudded across the back stoop, and she barely had a moment to compose herself. Sophie, Uncle Redd and the two dogs crowded through the door.

And, oh, dear God, Zach. Why did he have to be here now, when Kevin's words had barely sunk in? More than anyone else, Gina couldn't bear for him to know the truth. She wasn't sure why she needed him to believe she was successful, but she did.

Forcing a cheerful expression, she held a finger to her lips and kept her voice low. "Gloria's asleep in the living room."

Avoiding Zach's gaze, she bent to pet the dogs as they licked her face.

"Gina?" Zach said.

He sounded concerned. Realizing she was frowning, she quickly smoothed her expression. "Yes?"

"Where do you want me to put these suitcases?"

"Just leave them in here. When Gloria wakes up, I'll move them."

"One of those is mine," Sophie said. "I don't like staying alone in that house."

With Sophie here, too, Gina would have to pretend she was happy all the time. Wonderful. "That's fine," she said brightly. "There's certainly room for you. What about you, Uncle Redd?"

Her uncle shook his head. "I'd rather sleep in my own bed. But the dogs and I will stay for dinner tonight."

"Will you join us, Zach?" Sophie asked.

"Sorry, I can't."

That was a relief—she wouldn't have to pretend quite so hard at dinner. "Now that you're here to keep an eye on Gloria, I'm going to drive to Spenser's and pick up some groceries," she said.

"I'll follow you out." Zach shot her a questioning look and reached for the doorknob.

He was going to ask her what was wrong. Great, just great. Gina shrugged into her coat and grabbed her purse. In an effort to forestall any questions, she turned toward her cousin and uncle. "You should all know that while you were gone, I talked with my boss. I've decided to stay here through the holidays."

Redd grinned, and Sugar and Bit wagged their tails and yipped with excitement.

"That's wonderful, cookie." Sophie laid her palm over her heart. "I know your uncle Lucky is smiling down at you. He'll be downright euphoric when you put up the Christmas lights and a tree."

Something was wrong. Zach couldn't put his finger on exactly what, but Gina looked shell-shocked.

"Are you sure you want to be here for three more weeks?" he asked as he shut the back door behind them.

"This way, I'll be able to spend Christmas with the family and do a few more things at the house before the Realtor lists the property."

"Your boss is okay with that?"

Instead of meeting his gaze, she pulled the key to Lucky's truck from her purse. "I decided to use up some of my vacation time."

"But this won't really be a vacation. You'll still be working with your clients."

She seemed to find the keys fascinating. "I'm going to let people at the office handle my clients."

She was a workaholic, she wouldn't meet his gaze and nothing she said made sense. Zach gave her a sideways look. "Tell me you're not doing this out of guilt."

"Partly. Look, I don't want to be away from Gloria for long—I better get going."

She left him scratching his head, wondering what was really going on.

Chapter 16

Zach was heading out to pick up a few things Curly needed to repair the tractor motor when he spotted Gina—climbing a ladder. For the past few days he'd mostly avoided her, only stopping by the house to briefly visit with Gloria and Sophia. Knowing she was within easy reach and would be for the next few weeks was killing him. Just as it had before.

He couldn't avoid her now. Wearing the same navy cap he'd loaned her weeks ago and her burgundy jacket, she was making her way up with strands of Christmas lights looped over one shoulder. Was she nuts?

He braked to a stop, strode straight to the ladder and gripped the base.

"Do you know how dangerous this is?" he said. "The ground is icy. The ladder legs could slip and you could fall."

"I'm being very careful," she replied. "I made sure to pack the snow around the—"

The lights fell from her shoulder and sailed down, barely missing his head, and the ladder jerked to the side. If he hadn't been here to grab on to it, Gina would've tumbled twenty feet down.

He shuddered to think of that.

"You climb down *now*," he ordered, the close call making him sound brusque.

The second her feet touched the ground, Zach pulled her around and gripped her shoulders. His hands shook a little. "Don't you ever do anything that crazy again!"

In the weak winter sun, her widened eyes looked especially green and reflected his own fear. She swallowed. "I'm sorry. I don't know what got into me. Trying to do everything myself, I guess."

"You and your aunt Gloria," he muttered. "Next time, ask for help."

He wanted to both shake her and kiss her until they forgot her near accident. But that would be as reckless as her solo climb up the ladder. Besides, her nosy cousins were peering out the kitchen window.

He let her go and then scooped the lights from the snowy ground. "I'll put these up. You hold the ladder."

Gina didn't argue.

By the time he finished he was calm again. "Let's see if they work. Go ahead and turn them on."

Moments later, twinkling lights outlined the roof of the house.

"They look so pretty," Gina said. "And to think that I only decided to put them up to get out of the house for a while."

"Let me take a wild guess—your cousins are getting on your nerves."

"Ya think? They went at each other nonstop while I put up the tree this morning and I really needed a break. I've run out of errands that will get me out of here, and I've visited my friends so often that their kids are beginning to think I'm family."

"Is Gloria feeling any better today?"

"A little. She's determined to use the crutches despite her sore hand. She's anxious to go back to her own house, but I can't see her getting up and down the stairs for a while yet. It sure would be nice to have the house to myself. Between Gloria's demands and complaints, Sophie's nonstop chatter and their constant bickering, I'm about to lose my mind."

Zach could just imagine. He glanced at them through the window, and they smiled and waved.

Gina followed his gaze and frowned. "Did you see that? Gloria just threw us a thumbs-up. I think she's pleased to see us talking. The way she, Sophie and Uncle Redd keep singing your praises, it's obvious what they want. Oh, brother."

"They never have been subtle."

Even though her cousins were out of hearing range, Gina lowered her voice. "If you can think of anything else to get me out of the house, let me know."

Zach had some interesting ideas, but what he wanted was off-limits. "Maybe you should talk to your boss about working from here after all, and save your vacation days for something fun."

She all but recoiled. "I don't think I'll do that."

She didn't offer an explanation and Zach wasn't

about to press her for one. As curious as he was, how she spent her time here was none of his business.

He shrugged. "If you want, you can give me a hand with some of the chores." Not that he needed help this time of year.

"Sure. What do you have in mind?"

"Bert just let the horses out to pasture. Their stalls need mucking out, and someone needs to bring them in again and brush and feed them."

Cleaning stalls was no fun, and he expected her to turn down the offer. Instead she jumped on it. "I used to muck out the stalls for Uncle Lucky. I'll do it right now."

"Seriously? You must be desperate."

She shot a quick look at the kitchen window and winced. "More than you'd ever guess."

Gina's identity had been tied up in her job for so long. Without clients and projects to fill the days, she felt purposeless and restless, like a ship adrift at sea. She was also worried sick about her finances.

Caring for the horses was a godsend. The gentle animals didn't judge her, and their blatant bids for attention made her laugh and took her out of herself. She'd convinced Zach and the other ranch hands to let her take care of them every day.

Often someone else was in the barn, mending harnesses, oiling saddles or loading the flatbed with hay for the cattle. Zach was always with one or more of his men, and she never saw him alone.

He was friendly but distant, which was safer for Gina. It was better that way. But she missed his warmth and their conversations.

Nine days after Gloria's accident, on a cold, clear afternoon, Gina was standing on a rung of the wood corral fence, fretting about money and watching the horses frisk about, when Zach joined her.

"Need help bringing in the horses?" he asked, stepping up next to her.

She shook her head. "They're having such a good time that I decided to leave them out a while longer. They're fun to watch."

A few of the animals nickered and started toward Zach. He grinned. "They can be real hams."

Gina nodded at Lightning. "Do you think he misses Uncle Lucky?"

"Sure he does, but he seems to like you."

"He likes you more." The horse all but ignored her in favor of Zach. "They all do."

"They know I have treats." He pulled a baggie of sliced apples from his pocket. "Take some."

Gina placed an apple slice in her palm, held out her arm and clicked her tongue. "Come here, Lightning." The horse gently took the apple from her and chuffed his thanks.

"Do that every day, and he'll love you forever," Zach said.

She didn't remind him that she wasn't going to be here forever.

When the apples were gone, he stepped down, his boots crunching on the hard snow. "Let's bring them in now."

Gina opened the gate and the horses trotted toward the barn.

Compared to the frigid air outside, the barn felt

warm. The smells of hay, horses and leather reminded her of her childhood and filled her with nostalgia for those days. Days she'd gladly left behind years ago—or so she'd thought. Now she actually enjoyed being here.

When had that happened?

Zach helped her brush the horses. While they worked, he seemed at ease, and they talked as they had before the tension between them had become like a wall.

"I need your help," she said as they hung up the brushes.

"Don't tell me—you want to string lights around the barn roof." Zach's lips twitched, and for the first time in days, she laughed.

"No, but this *is* about Christmas. There are only nine shopping days left, and I don't have any idea what to get Redd, Gloria or Sophie."

"Being here is enough."

"Besides that. I'd like to give them each something they really want." Nothing too pricey. Gina really had to watch her spending now. "I'm planning to drive to Elk Ridge tomorrow to go shopping, and I'm open to ideas." The town had a mall with several decent stores.

Zach didn't even hesitate. "I know something that doesn't require driving or shopping. Keep the Lucky A."

The longer Gina was here, the less she wanted to sell. But with her money troubles, she couldn't even entertain the thought of holding on to the ranch. She needed the proceeds to pay down her debt. "I'm putting it on the market in January—you know that."

"Then Elk Ridge, it is. I happen to be heading there in the morning to pick up a part for the tractor. Let's carpool."

She could easily take Uncle Lucky's truck, but the way it guzzled gas... "Okay, but I have no idea what I'm shopping for, and I could be a while."

"No problem—I need to pick up gifts for my family, too. We'll leave right after the morning chores and get an early start."

At the door of the barn, Zach plucked something from the hat he now considered hers. "Straw."

"Why does that not surprise me? I probably stink like the stalls."

He leaned in and sniffed. "I smell horse and hay but mostly flowers. I like that perfume."

"It's very high-end stuff called eau de shampoo."

They both smiled. He glanced at her mouth and sobered. Gina recognized that intense look. He was going to kiss her.

Although her mind warned her that that was dangerous, every cell in her body strained toward him.

Zach cupped her face between his roughened hands and kissed her, and she felt as if she'd finally come home. Grasping his shoulders, she leaned into his solid body.

One kiss wasn't enough and neither of them pulled away. All the passion and feeling Gina had stuffed down deep inside bubbled up.

Sometime later, breathing hard, Zach rested his forehead against hers. "You don't taste like horses, either."

"That's a relief."

His silvery eyes shone with feeling. A warm glow started in her heart and spread through her. She wanted Zach, but what she felt was so much more than desire.

She was falling in love with him.

That scared her. She knew what she wanted—a meaningful career, a life free of financial struggle and a man who was as driven to succeed as she was. Zach wasn't that man.

There was only one solution—to fall out of love with him.

Oh, that wouldn't be easy. Impossible, as long as she was there and seeing him all the time. She may as well enjoy what time she had left with him. When she got back to Chicago, she'd lick her wounds, find a new job and move on.

She made a show of glancing at her watch. "I better go inside and make sure Gloria and Sophie haven't murdered each other."

Zach opened the barn door and gestured her out. "I'll see you in the morning."

Zach hated Christmas shopping and usually did most of it online. But after picking up the tractor part, he decided to join the hordes of frenzied shoppers at the mall. After depositing the gifts he'd bought for the Arnetts in his truck, he sat down in the crowded food court to wait for Gina.

Gina. She was never out of his thoughts. He hadn't meant to kiss her yesterday, had fully intended to stick to his self-imposed distance. But she'd looked into his eyes with so much feeling and yearning that he hadn't been able to stop himself.

The passion in her kisses had nearly knocked him to his knees and erased his already shaky resolve to stay away from her. He no longer cared that acting on his desire was dangerous. His every waking thought was of making love with her. Soon.

Spotting her across the way, he waved. A smile bloomed on her face, and she strode toward him.

"Success!" she said, setting her bags down and sliding into a chair across the table.

Her cheeks were pink with excitement and her eyes sparkled.

Drawn into her web of happiness, Zach grinned like a love-struck fool. "I found what I needed, too," he said. "How about a quick bite before we head back to the ranch? I'm running on empty."

Gina laughed. "Of course you are."

While they dined on mall fare, he asked Gina what she got her family.

"Uh-uh." She shook her head. "You'll have to wait until Christmas morning. Show me what you got yours."

"Can't—I had them sent. I bought a Nerf basketball set for my nephew and a Play-Doh kit for my niece."

"They'll love those."

"That's what the clerk who sold them to me said." He shrugged. "They get so much stuff they probably won't even notice."

"Of course they will—you're their uncle. What did you get your dad and stepmom?"

"The usual—a fruit basket. I always get my mother perfume and I give my brother and his wife gourmet chocolate."

Gina didn't comment. She didn't have to—her frown spoke volumes. He shrugged. "Hey, at least they won't return that stuff."

"Ah, they must be difficult to please."

"In every way. My father thinks I'm wasting my life."

Now why had he told Gina what he hadn't even shared with Lucky? She angled her head, curious. Ready to rebuff any questions, he sucked in a breath.

She surprised him and said nothing. That was good. Real good, but instead of feeling relieved, he wanted to tell her about the mistake that had changed his life.

Which gave him pause. He didn't talk about that.

Besides, right now she seemed relaxed and happy, and he didn't want to ruin her mood. Deep down, he suspected she might side with his family, believing he'd done nothing wrong and that he was out of his mind for giving up his old life. Zach couldn't handle that kind of condemnation, not from her.

He stacked their plates and stood to carry them to the trash. "It'll be dark soon. We should head back or your family will start to worry."

"They won't worry. They'll speculate, wondering what we're doing together."

Her laughter brought a smile to his face. Once again, he relaxed. By the time he pulled onto the highway, the sun had set.

Gina settled back in her seat. "Thanks for this. I really needed to get away for the day."

"No problem."

"Are you going to the Christmas party at the Dawson Ranch Friday night?" she asked.

"I go every year."

"Good, then you can help with Gloria. She'll have a fit if she misses it. What's it like?"

"Noisy and crowded, but fun. Everyone in town is there."

Neither of them spoke again. The warmth and darkness of the truck felt private and intimate. As Zach steered the truck toward home, he realized that he wasn't ready to go to the ranch just yet. A few miles from the Lucky A, he pulled into a deserted lot and braked to a stop.

Gina frowned and glanced at the snow-laden, empty fields illuminated by his headlights. "Why are we stopping here?"

Leaving the engine idling and the heat on, Zach leaned across the bucket seats and kissed her the way he'd wanted to all day.

Pulling away, he shrugged out of his coat and climbed over the console to join Gina in her seat. She shed her coat, too. They reclined the seat back as far as it would go and made out like teenage kids, touching each other everywhere and breathing hard.

After a while, dangerously close to losing control, he pulled back. "I want to make love with you, Gina, but when I do, it will be in a bed, not here in the truck."

"We could go to the house, but Sophie and Gloria are there. Let's go to your place."

The modest trailer wasn't the custom-built, five-bedroom home Zach had once owned, but there weren't any hotels in Saddlers Prairie, and it was the best option. He nodded. "After the party."

"All right." She leaned up and kissed him, a kiss filled with passion and promise.

Hard and aching, he returned to the driver's seat and headed for the Lucky A.

Chapter 17

"Your cell phone is ringing," Sophie called out from the kitchen, where she and Gloria impatiently waited for Zach to take them to the party at the Dawson Ranch. Uncle Redd had hitched a ride with his next-door neighbor.

On her way downstairs, Gina frowned and hurried into the living room, where she'd left the phone. She knew at a glance that it was a from the credit-card company, reminding her that she was over her limit and late on a payment.

A payment she couldn't afford to make until her paycheck came in next week. After that check, she had one more coming, plus her vacation pay. What would she do then?

Flooded with shame, she silenced the call and stuffed the phone into her purse.

"Who was that?" Gloria asked.

"Sales call."

"Six days before Christmas? You'd think those people would give it a rest. You look very festive in that red
sweater, by the way."

"Thanks." She hadn't brought any Christmassy outfits with her and would have liked to buy herself something new for tonight. But with her money situation,
that was out.

"Your hair is pretty, too. I've never seen it swept up
that way. Zach will like that." Sophie gave her a knowing look.

In the three days since the trip to Elk Ridge, her
family had doubled the sly looks and bold comments
without the slightest encouragement from Gina or Zach.
She'd barely mentioned Zach's name, and he hadn't
stopped by the house.

But she thought constantly of him and what they
would do together at his trailer later tonight. She was
playing with fire but couldn't make herself stop.

Zach knocked at the door, and she let him in. His
appreciative gaze flitted over her sweater and pleated
skirt. "I like that outfit."

Her heart rate bumped a few notches. "Thank you."
She took in the dark green sweater that lovingly hugged
his broad shoulders and the black dress pants that em-
phasized his flat belly and narrow hips. "I like what
you're wearing, too. Green is nice and festive."

His eyes warmed, filled with promise for the night
ahead. "Red and green—you two look like a matched
set," Gloria quipped. "You can admire each other more
later. Let's get to that party."

Zach turned his attention to her cousins. "You both look beautiful. Let's go."

He helped everyone into their coats. When he reached for Gloria's arm, she sniffed. "Now that my hand is better, I've gotten pretty good with these crutches. I can do this myself."

"Yes, ma'am." Zach held up his hands and stepped back, far enough to give her space but close enough to catch her if she slipped. "After you."

Tonight he was driving one of the ranch Jeeps, which was roomier than his truck. Gloria sat up front so that she could stretch out her leg, and Gina and Sophie sat in the back.

Over the past few weeks, Gina had been at the Dawsons' house a few times for evening get-togethers with Jenny, Meg and other friends. She loved everything about the family home, which was generations old and spacious enough for the Dawson brothers and their families, yet warm and comfortable.

Gina hadn't seen the tree, though. Standing in a corner in the great room, it had to be eight feet tall and was bright with lights and ornaments. Men, women and children filled every room on the main floor with conversation and laughter.

Gina helped Gloria sit down and made sure she had food and drink. Then she filled a plate for herself, taking it with her while she greeted friends.

People she hadn't seen since the funeral and hadn't had much of a chance to talk to told her how pleased they were that she was staying through the holidays. Some asked about her work and praised her for doing so well. Feeling like a big fake, she smiled and pretended her life was as cushy and great as everyone believed.

Her conscience ate at her. Sooner or later, she would have to tell them the truth. The thought of losing the respect of Zach, her family and friends bothered her so much that she barely touched the food on her plate.

With the sixth sense that seemed to kick in when Zach was near, she could tell that he was watching her. Standing across the room, he raised his eyebrow. Gina managed a smile. He jerked his head toward a hallway, signaling her to follow him. When they met there, he pulled her through a closed door that turned out to be the powder room.

He shut the door, backed her against it and kissed her. Gina's money troubles melted away. She forgot she was broke, forgot she was in a bathroom at a Christmas party. She forgot everything but Zach.

Still kissing her, he cupped her breast and pushed his thigh between her legs. She moaned into his mouth.

"That's just a sample of what I want to do with you later," he said, nuzzling her ear. "Let's see if we can't get your cousins out of here soon."

Impatient for Gina to arrive, Zach checked his watch for what had to be the dozenth time. It had been nearly an hour since he'd dropped her and her cousins off at the house. She'd wanted to wait until her cousins were safely in bed before coming back to Zach's.

Suddenly he heard the old truck rumble to a stop in front of the trailer.

He opened the door and gestured her inside. "Hey."

"Hi." She hesitated a moment, almost as if she feared crossing the threshold.

He tried to see the trailer through her eyes. He'd tidied up and changed the sheets and towels, but no amount of cleaning could change the fact that his place was small and shabby, something he wouldn't have set foot in back in Houston, let alone live in.

Not ideal for a woman used to the finer trappings money bought. Sometimes Zach missed the luxury and comfort he'd once taken for granted, but at least here his conscience was clear.

He helped her out of her coat and hung it on the hook on the door. She'd taken her hair down but was still in her party clothes, a snug sweater, a short, pleated skirt and sexy heels that made her great legs look impossibly long.

He gestured toward the sofa, which was half the size of the one in Lucky's living room and a lot saggier. "I opened a bottle of wine."

"I barely sipped my glass at the party. How did you know?" She sat down. Her skirt rode up, revealing a nice length of creamy thigh. "I didn't think Sophie and Gloria would ever go to bed," she said, sipping from her glass. "I felt like a teenager, waiting for my parents to fall asleep so I could sneak out."

Zach joined her and sampled his own glass. "We should've just told them you were coming over."

"Give them even more ideas about us? No, thanks."

He slipped his arm around her. "I want you to know that I'm clean."

"Me, too." She gulped her wine.

"Nervous?"

"A little. I'm not sure why."

Zach was pretty sure the trailer and his blue-collar job had something to do with it. If he were smart, he'd tell her that this was a bad idea and he'd changed his mind.

He wanted her too much for that. "I know a great way to relax you." After setting both their glasses on the coffee table, he directed her to turn around so that her back faced him.

He began to knead her shoulders. She was small and delicate boned.

"That feels good," she murmured, bowing her head.

Her tense muscles quickly softened until she was leaning into his hands. Brushing her hair aside, Zach kissed the crook of her shoulder and felt her shiver. "Better?"

"I'm putty in your hands."

"Just wait." He tugged her sweater up and massaged her slender back. Her skin was soft and smooth.

Her breathing quickened, growing jagged as he unfastened her bra and cupped her breasts from behind.

With a soft moan, she arched into his hands. Her nipples hardened to sharp points.

How he wanted her. Hungry, his body pulsing, he turned her to face him, pulled her sweater over her head and got rid of his own.

Her breasts were full and taut.

"You are so beautiful."

Tracing her nipples with his finger, he thrilled to her shudder of pleasure. Moving from one nipple to the other, he followed his finger with his tongue until she was restless and panting and he was in danger of losing control.

"I don't want to make love with you on this old couch," he said and pulled her up.

He led her into his bedroom. The double bed took up most of the space. Gina stepped out of her heels and unzipped her skirt. It pooled at her feet, leaving her in thigh highs and bikini panties. "You look hot," he said.

She gave him a smile as if she was well aware of that and started to peel off the stockings.

Zach stopped her. "Leave those on."

"You like them."

"Very much. But the panties can go."

As she stepped out of them, Zach quickly shed his pants and boxers. They were both naked, both studying each other. Her womanly body awed him.

She stepped into his arms. His—for tonight.

She was smooth and soft and warm, and she fit perfectly against him. Kissing her, he backed her to the bed and eased her down. He slid his hand between her legs. She was wet and hot.

Zach groaned, and his body demanded release. Dear God, he wanted to be inside of her.

But not just yet. Kneeling between her thighs, he parted her folds and explored her most sensitive place. A sound that was half moan, half sigh filled the air.

She shifted restlessly, caught hold of his ears and tugged him closer. Moments later, she climaxed. When she relaxed and went still, he kissed her inner thigh, her stomach. Claimed her mouth.

She reached between them. If she touched him there, he would lose it.

"Easy." Clasping her wrists, he pushed her onto her back. "Are you ready for more?"

"Yes. This time, inside me."

He sheathed himself. In one thrust he entered her.

She was slick and hot and tight, and she felt so damn good. Wanting to take it slow, Zach closed his eyes and for a long, tortured moment didn't move.

But Gina hugged his hips with her thighs and clenched her muscles around him and he forgot all about going slowly. She began to make sweet sounds that signaled her climax was near.

On the brink himself, Zach thrust fast and deep until the world disappeared. Together they exploded in blinding pleasure.

Later, drained and utterly satisfied, he collapsed beside her.

Gina let out a satisfied sigh. Zach kissed the top of her head. She smelled like her flowery shampoo and sex, a heady combination. "I'm glad we finally did that," he said.

"Mmm, me, too." She kissed his ribs and snuggled close.

Soon her breathing eased and he knew she was sleeping.

He cupped her hip. Murmuring, she moved closer. His chest was full, and he knew that what he felt for Gina went way beyond the fantastic sex they'd just shared. But he'd already known that.

As special as she was, she was straight out of his old world, driven by money and success. Like his family and his ex, she wouldn't understand why he'd left that life behind. For sure he wasn't about to open himself to that by explaining about his past.

Any kind of relationship beyond sex was doomed to fail.

Uneasy, he stared at the ceiling and wondered what he was doing. *Relax,* he told himself. *Gina doesn't want a relationship with me, either.* This was about sex—nothing more.

He drifted off to sleep.

Without intending to, Gina had fallen asleep in Zach's bed. Before she even opened her eyes, she could tell that he had drifted off, too. The room was dark, but light from the other room spilled in and she could easily make out the fake wood walls, decor from an era long past. The watch Uncle Lucky had left him ticked softly on the knotty-pine dresser. There wasn't room for any other furniture.

Zach's entire trailer was smaller than Uncle Lucky's kitchen and living room combined—barely big enough to accommodate one person.

How could he stand living here?

In his sleep, he cupped her bottom possessively in his big hands. Fresh desire flooded her. Never mind where he lived—she wanted him to touch her like this forever.

But she wanted more than that—a lot more. She wanted Zach to have a good job and a future, wanted to know about his past. She wanted the security of her job at Andersen, Coats and Mueller and her year-end bonus.

Unfortunately, what she wanted was the opposite of what she had. If only…

Beside her, Zach stirred. He was awake and aroused.

His fingers slid between her legs, spreading heat through her and erasing her thoughts. He kissed her passionately, and she forgot about everything but the here and now.

Some time later, she smiled up at him. "That was even better than the first time."

"The best way in the world to wake up. Makes you wonder why we wasted so much time getting here. We should have done this weeks ago."

"I'm not wired that way." She traced the planes of his face. His cheekbones and regal nose, his strong chin and jaw. His eyelashes were longer than any man had a right to.

Such a handsome face. With an inward sigh, she admitted to herself that want to or not, she was completely in love with him.

He opened his eyes and stared into her soul with a tenderness she hadn't seen before. He cared for her, but he didn't really know her.

Didn't know that instead of a being the successful marketing executive he thought she was, she'd lost her job and everything she'd worked for. Worse, she was in a huge financial bind.

She was a complete fraud.

Tell him, her conscience whispered. The very thought terrified her. And have him change his mind about her, look at her with the same disgust she held for herself? She couldn't bear that.

"You okay?" he asked.

No, and it was best to change the subject. "I was thinking about how little I really know about your past."

His expression shuttered. "You said you wouldn't ask again."

He didn't trust her, and her heart recoiled. She grabbed gratefully onto the feeling. Better to feel hurt than guilty. "I changed my mind. What are you hiding from me?"

Stony faced, he sat up. "It's late."

Gina sat up, too, pulling the covers with her. "So you can do the most intimate physical things with me, but you can't share your personal stuff." Add utter hypocrite to her list of flaws.

"What we just shared was pretty damn personal. I care about you, Gina, but this is as personal as you're going to get from me." He rose from the bed and put on his boxers.

"I'll leave as soon as I'm dressed." Holding the blanket around her like a protective shield, she retrieved her clothes. "Where's the bathroom?"

"Down the hall, to your left."

"Go back to sleep," she said. "I'll let myself out."

Zach didn't argue.

Fifteen minutes later, feeling more alone than she could ever remember, she tiptoed into the house and made her way up the stairs.

Chapter 18

In need of a friendly ear, Gina called Autumn the following day and invited her to lunch. "Let's meet at the Pizza Palace," she said.

"Love to. Hold on while I see if one of the boys can watch April." Seconds later, she was back. "It'll have to be a quick lunch. I can meet you at twelve, but I have to be back by one."

Shortly before noon, Gina found an empty booth and sat down to wait for her friend.

It wasn't long before Autumn slid in across from her, her cheeks flushed from the cold. "What a great party last night."

"It was."

A teenage girl took their orders. When she left, Autumn smiled. "You and Zach are seeing each other while you're in town, huh?"

"I'm not sure." Gina bit her lip. "That's one of the reasons I called you. I really need to talk to someone."

"What's the matter?"

"It's pretty embarrassing. You won't tell anyone, right?"

"Not even Cody."

Satisfied, Gina lowered her voice. "Zach and I made love last night."

"The way you were looking at each other at the party, I'm not surprised." Autumn frowned. "You don't seem happy about that. Was the sex bad?"

Still glowing from their lovemaking, Gina shook her head. "It was wonderful. But Zach doesn't trust me. He's told me a little about his family, but he won't talk about his past—where he worked, what he did there and why he left Houston. I can't help but wonder what he's hiding."

Autumn nodded but didn't comment. She listened without judgment, which was exactly what Gina needed.

Gina wasn't going to share her own secrets, but once she started talking, her troubles spilled out and she unloaded everything—her strong feelings for Zach and why they scared her, her job situation and her money troubles.

"Here I am, questioning Zach for not telling me about his past, when my own life is a total sham," she finished. "Pretty pathetic, isn't it?"

Autumn shrugged. She didn't seem nearly as disappointed in her as Gina had imagined. "Stuff happens."

The waitress delivered their food. As soon as she moved away from the table, Autumn went on. "The job thing isn't your fault."

"No, but my financial situation is."

"You can fix that. Trust me, I know—I was in the same boat when I went to work as Cody's housekeeper. You'll get another job and everything will be fine." Autumn dug into her lunch.

Having eaten little since long before the Dawson's party, Gina was famished. For a few minutes she and Autumn both concentrated on eating.

"I'm not sure what to do about Zach," she said when she finally came up for air. "Should I trust him?"

"You're the only one who can answer that. What does your heart tell you?"

"I'm in love with him, and I think he cares about me, too."

Autumn nodded thoughtfully. "Maybe if you trust Zach enough to share your problems with him, he'll open up to you."

Gina had never considered that.

"It all boils down to what you want," Autumn said as they finished the meal. "What do you want, Gina?"

She'd been mulling that over since Kevin had suggested she think about it. "I'm not sure," she admitted.

"You'll figure it out. I hate to cut our conversation short, but I have to get back."

They paid and walked out to their cars.

Before they parted ways, Gina hugged her friend. "Thanks for listening."

"Anytime. Let me know what happens, okay? And merry Christmas."

On the drive back to the Lucky A, Gina thought hard about what she wanted.

Only weeks ago, her dream had been to make vice

president at Andersen, Coats and Mueller and go on climbing the ranks from there. The commonsense part of her wanted a good job in marketing and the potential to advance. But her heart wanted Zach, and fighting with her heart was a losing battle.

Autumn was right—if she wanted a relationship with him, she needed to be honest. The very thought terrified her. He might not be as easygoing about her situation as Autumn had been. Gina would have to tell her family, too.

She swallowed. Could she risk the humiliation of admitting she'd been living a lie?

She wasn't sure she was brave enough.

Falling for Gina was about the stupidest thing Zach had ever done, and over the next few days, he called himself ten kinds of fool. He steered clear of her. She didn't try to find him, either.

His one consolation was that they seemed to be of the same mind. Neither of them wanted a relationship. That was a relief—or so he told himself.

On Christmas Eve day he was in a foul mood. Hard work always helped take his mind off his problems, but he'd worked over Thanksgiving. For the next two days, Pete, Bert and Chet were responsible for doing all the chores.

Early that afternoon, Redd phoned him. "Merry Christmas. The dogs and I just arrived at the house. We're spending the night. The usual friends and neighbors will be stopping by later this afternoon, and we want you here."

Zach was in no mood to spend the holiday with the

Arnetts, particularly Gina. He doubted she wanted to see him, either. But her family expected him there. "What time?" he asked.

They settled on three o'clock—an hour away.

Zach was wandering around the small trailer, waiting for the time to pass, when someone knocked on his door.

Grateful for the distraction, he opened it. To his surprise, Gina stood on the stoop.

He drank in the sight of her. "Redd called a little while ago. I said I'd come at three. What are you doing here?"

"Merry Christmas." She fiddled with her glove and tried to smile. "May I come in?"

Wondering what she wanted, he shrugged. "Sure."

He moved back so that she could step inside.

Zach looked wary and tired, as if he hadn't been sleeping. Gina wasn't sleeping well, either. There was too much to think about, too much at stake. Weighing the risks of honesty versus continuing to live a lie had consumed her, and she couldn't sleep or eat, let alone enjoy the Christmas festivities.

She was so miserable that Gloria and Sophie had stopped bickering, uniting to shower her with pitying looks. Even Sugar and Bit avoided her, slinking past with their tails between their legs.

Her conscience was eating her alive. If she didn't do something soon, she would make herself sick.

It was time to tell the truth.

Zach took her coat and hung it on the hook. "You want coffee?"

At the moment, she couldn't put anything in her

stomach to save her life. "No, but I would like to sit down."

He gestured toward the little table in his miniscule kitchen. They sat, their knees almost touching.

"If this is about the other night…" He cleared his throat. "I shouldn't have let you leave like that."

"We both said things." She wasn't sure exactly how to begin, so she spoke from the heart. "I know you care about me, Zach, and I have feelings for you, too. Strong feelings. But I need to tell you something, and… Well, I'm pretty sure that once I do, your opinion of me will change."

Any wariness vanished under a quizzical look.

"When Gloria broke her ankle and I called my boss, he was pretty unhappy that I wanted to stay here," she said. "In a nutshell, he gave me a choice—either leave the company or come back as an assistant." The idea was so repugnant that she shuddered. "I can't do that. He's not going to give me my year-end bonus, either, and you have no idea how badly I need it."

Afraid of what she'd see in Zach's eyes, she looked down at her hands. "I'm in real trouble. I can't pay my bills, and collectors are starting to call. I have one more paycheck and my vacation pay coming. After that…" She swallowed around a lump of fear. "I may have to declare bankruptcy. I didn't think I was anything like my parents, but I guess I'm like my dad. He spent money he didn't have to impress people, and I did that, too."

There. It was out.

Her cheeks burning with humiliation, she forced herself to meet Zach's gaze. To her surprise, she saw only warmth.

"Back up to the part about your feelings for me," he said. "I'm a lowly ranch foreman."

"I know, and go figure. I've been thinking about your past. I don't understand why you're hiding it from me, but the truth is, I already know everything I need to about you. You're a good man with a big heart—that's what matters."

The last part was the hardest to say, and she cleared her throat. "Now you know that I lied about my life. If you don't… If you're not interested in me anymore, I understand."

"Because your jackass boss fired you and you have money problems?" Zach shook his head. "Those things don't matter to me. I'm still crazy about you."

Gina couldn't quite believe her ears. "Even if I have to sell the ranch to pay down my bills?"

Across the table, he caught hold of her hands. "That'd be a real bummer, but even then."

She was so overcome that her eyes filled. "Zach Horton, I love you."

"Yeah?" A smile started at his lips and spread until his eyes lit up and crinkled at the corners. "I love you, too. Come here, and I'll show you just how much."

Zach pulled her close and kissed her, and nothing else mattered.

Later, when she was lying naked and sated in his bed, her cell phone rang. "I better get that." She pulled out of his arms and glanced at the screen. "It's Gloria. I told her I was going out, and I'm sure she wonders where I am."

"Tell her you're with me."

"I will."

When she hung up, she reached for her clothes. "It's time to go to the house."

"We still have a lot to talk about," Zach said.

"We'll have to save that conversation for another time. Please don't say anything to my family about my job or finances. I'm not ready to tell them."

"I won't say a word."

Chapter 19

Later that evening, after the guests had consumed the Christmas Eve meal and headed home, and Gloria, Redd, Sophie and the dogs were safely asleep, Zach sat on the sofa with his arm around Gina. Only the fire and the Christmas-tree lights lit the room.

"What a beautiful tree," she said, snuggling close.

"You're beautiful." He kissed her, her soft sigh wrapping around his heart.

Gina loved him. He felt good about that and awed that she'd been honest with him. It hadn't been easy for her to tell him about losing her job or her money worries, but she'd told him all the same.

Her courage inspired him, and before he left the house tonight, he intended to bare his soul to her. She deserved to know the kind of man he used to be. Like his family, she might not understand why he'd chosen to give up his old life, might think he was crazy. She could decide she didn't want him, after all. Dread knotted his gut.

"Zach? You're frowning."

"Am I?" Not quite ready to tell her, he forced a light expression. "I think your family's onto us."

"You mean because they made sure we sat next to each other at dinner and turned in early so that we could be alone?" Gina rolled her eyes. "I should never have told them we were together when they called this afternoon."

"Are you going to tell them about your job?"

"Yes, tomorrow. I'm not looking forward to that."

"They're still going to love you," he said.

He only hoped that Gina would still love him when he shared his past.

"They're going to be shocked. They're so proud of me, and I hate letting them down."

"They'll get over it."

"Will they?" She tried to smile. "I feel lost, Zach, and I will until I find a new job. Plus, they think I have all this money. I need to tell them, but I wish I didn't."

"Hey." He smoothed her hair back and smiled into her worried eyes. "You're one of the bravest, strongest people I know, and you can do this."

"Brave and strong. I've never thought of myself as either. Thank you for that." She leaned up and kissed him, a gentle press of the lips not meant to incite passion.

Yet the hunger between them simmered in the air.

Gina checked her watch. "It's getting late and we both need to get some sleep. I wish you could stay here tonight, but with my family in the house..."

"Yeah, that'd feel weird."

Zach needed to go soon, but first it was time to come clean. "Before I leave, there are some things you need to know about me." He let go of her, leaned forward and stared at his hands. "I don't like to talk about my past, but it's time I explained."

Gina sucked in a breath and went still.

"I used to own my own company. Horton Real Estate was a commercial real-estate corporation. I worked long hours and lived for deals and profits, and my company thrived and grew. I met my fiancée when she came to work for me. We lived in a big, custom-built home and owned three cars. Money, love, success—I had it all and should've been happy. But I wasn't. I thought the answer was to cut bigger and better deals.

"A man named Sam Swain owned a choice section of land I coveted. I dreamed of developing it into a premiere shopping mall. Swain wanted to leave it undeveloped and deed his acreage to a land trust."

This next part was hard, and Zach paused and studied the calluses on his palm. Gina reached for his hand, silently offering support. Unable to look at her just yet, he laced his fingers with hers and went on. "I wouldn't let it go. I wined and dined his family, his accountant and his lawyer. I wouldn't let up. Soon everyone Sam trusted, especially his wife and kids, was pressuring him nonstop to take the money and sell. He finally signed off on the deal, but it broke his heart. Literally. Not long after I took possession of the property and broke ground, he dropped dead of a heart attack."

Emotion clogged his throat and he swallowed. "Sam Swain is in his grave because I put him there."

Gina opened her mouth, but he signaled that he wasn't finished. "His death changed me. I no longer wanted to run the business or cut deals. I sold the company and donated some of the proceeds to the land trust Sam favored. My family ridiculed me for that. They still think I'm crazy. Losing their support was rough, but at least my fiancée stood by me."

He gave a humorless laugh. "Or that's what I thought at first. I was mistaken. She broke off the engagement and decided to stay on at the company. A year later she married the man who bought it from me.

"That was around the time I left Houston. I wasn't sure where I wanted to go or what I wanted to do. After drifting for months, I ended up in Saddlers Prairie. I didn't know anything about cattle, but Lucky took a chance on me. He taught me about ranching and showed me how to find joy in simple things like a hard day's work. He advised me to learn from my mistakes and move on." He managed a smile. "I'm still working on that one."

Finished, he bowed his head.

Gina pulled her hand from his, cupped his face and turned his head toward her. "Sam Swain's death wasn't your fault, Zach."

They were the same words his family had repeated countless times, only hers held no scorn. In Gina's eyes he saw only love.

"You're a good man, Zach Horton. That's why I fell in love with you." She smiled. "Even though I fought it tooth and nail."

Zach's heart swelled in his chest. "That's one battle I'm glad you lost."

He kissed her without holding anything back. A long time later, he reluctantly broke away. "I should go." He took her hand and pulled her to her feet.

She loved him, but he wasn't sure love was enough. If she accepted him as he was, he would give her a Christmas gift she would never forget. If not... Well, that just might kill him.

At the back door, he turned to her. "We have..." So much was riding on her and what she wanted, and his voice shook. Zach stopped and cleared his throat. "We have a lot to talk about. I know you want a high-flying corporate executive, but I can't be that man ever again. If you want a future with me, you have to be okay with that."

He left her standing in the door.

There was so much to think about, and Gina couldn't sleep. Zach loved her and she loved him.

But was love enough?

She no longer had a big salary to keep her afloat, and neither did he. She didn't want to make the same mistakes her parents had made—she didn't want a marriage plagued with money worries.

Zach had suffered dearly for Sam Swain's death, which hadn't been his fault. His guilt over that made Gina love him all the more. Everything made sense now. His comments about the rat race and his seeming disinterest in the corporate world.

Living a hectic, competitive life hadn't made him happy. It didn't make her happy, either. Nor had her big salary, expensive clothes and nice condo.

If she set aside her money problems, she wouldn't miss her job at all.

That was such a revelation that Gina could no longer lie in bed. She rose and slipped on her robe. Uncle Lucky had taught Zach to find joy in the little things. Why couldn't she do the same? Peering out the window, into the darkness, she noted how the snow caught the moonlight, making the moon twice as bright. The fields sparkled with light.

Such a beautiful ranch and a perfect Christmas Eve night. She could almost imagine Santa and his sleigh flying through the sky.

She smiled with joy. So this was what finding pleasure in little things felt like.

Still grinning, she crept back downstairs. The fire was low but she heard the sizzle of the dying embers. The sound delighted her, and plugging in the Christmas-tree lights only increased her happiness.

She plunked down onto the sofa and, for a while, she simply enjoyed the sights and sounds. Then she thought about other things that made her happy. Not what, *who*.

Zach.

He'd made her laugh countless times and always brightened her day—even when she was mad at him.

Regardless of what he did for a living, life with him would always be blessed with love and joy.

And just like that, Gina let go of her need to be with a man driven to succeed. She let go of her own need to climb the corporate ladder.

It was an odd feeling, trusting that she was good enough to have love and friendship no matter what she did for a living. She would need time to get used to that.

Her debt was an awful burden, and the thought of

declaring bankruptcy made her sick to her stomach. She didn't want to do that and needed a new job—soon.

Sometime before dawn, she stumbled upon the solution to her problems. She could hardly wait to share it with Zach and her family.

She tiptoed into the office, wrote a note and wrapped it in Christmas paper. After adding a ribbon and printing Zach's name on the gift card, she slipped it under the tree beneath the other presents.

Humming and feeling strangely energized, she danced up the stairs to shower and dress. Downstairs again, she made the coffee and started the Christmas breakfast casserole.

It was baking in the oven when her family entered the kitchen. Minutes later, Zach showed up.

"Merry Christmas, Zach. I thought about what you said last night, and I'm fine with you—just as you are."

Zach's eyes looked suspiciously bright. Gina's eyes filled, too. Without the least bit of embarrassment or nervousness, she pulled him down for a kiss.

When they broke apart, the expressions on her family's faces were priceless.

After breakfast, Uncle Redd pushed his chair back. "Let's take our coffee into the living room and open our presents."

It was time to tell her family the truth.

"If you'd all wait a minute." Gina stood and gestured for her family to remain at the table. "There's something I need to tell you."

Wanting Zach's support, she glanced at him. Without hesitation he joined her, grabbing hold of her hand.

Gloria and Sophie gave her knowing looks, and

Uncle Redd beamed. They obviously thought that this was a romantic announcement of some kind. They were in for a disappointment.

"This isn't easy for me to say," she said, "and my timing sucks."

They looked concerned now. Zach gave her hand an encouraging squeeze and her story spilled out.

"You don't know this, but a couple of weeks ago my boss fired me," she said, strangely eager to get the words out. "But that's not all. I'm in debt and teetering on bankruptcy. I know how embarrassing that is for you. I'm so ashamed and so sorry to ruin your Christmas this way."

For once, Gloria was speechless.

Sophie clutched her chest. "Oh, cookie, that's terrible."

"We'll be all right, honey," Uncle Redd said. "But what will you do?"

"I'll answer your questions after we open our gifts."

"Now?" Gloria frowned. "This is serious. Don't you want to talk about it?"

Sophie glared at her. "She just said she will later. It's Christmas, and she doesn't want to think about her problems right now."

"Well, I do."

The sisters glared at each other.

"Girls, please." Uncle Redd shook his head. "Like Sophie says, it's Christmas. Can't you knock it off for a while? If Gina wants to open presents now, so do I."

Her family all looked fondly at her.

Nothing had changed. They felt for her, but they still loved her, just as Zach had said.

She could hardly wait for them to open their gifts.

They headed into the living room, Zach holding her hand until she pushed him into a chair and handed out the presents.

Her family loved the things she'd picked up at the mall. Sophie loved her new earrings and Gloria wrapped herself in her new sweater. Uncle Redd was pleased with his kidskin gloves and Sugar and Bit seemed delighted with their new chew toys.

Gina opened the gift they'd all chipped in to buy her. "Red cowboy boots. I love them! Thank you all."

They gave Zach a display case for his watch.

"What a lovely Christmas," Sophie said.

"Wait—there's something else under the tree." Gloria pointed to the last gift. "It's a skinny little thing. What is it?"

"That's for you, Zach—from me." Gina retrieved the gift from under the tree and handed it to him.

He unwrapped the paper and read the note she'd written. He looked incredulous. "You're not selling the ranch."

"That's right." She smiled. "That's my real present to you all. I'm not sure yet how I'll keep it going, but, Zach, I hope you'll stay and help me. As soon as I get back to Chicago, I'm going to cut up my credit cards and trade in my Lexus for a practical car I can afford. I'm going to sell my condo, too. I'll use some of the proceeds to pay down my bills and the rest to pay your salary. Will you stay?"

"Where will you be?" he asked.

"I'm going to drive right back here and move into this house. I've decided to start my own marketing/

PR business. I'm good at what I do, and I know I can make it work."

Gloria wiped away a tear, Redd cleared his throat and Sophie bawled like a baby.

"I think they like the idea," Zach said. "I sure do."

"So you'll stay on?" Gina asked.

"That depends on what you think of my Christmas gift to you." He pulled an envelope from his pocket and handed it to her.

As Gina read Zach's card, her jaw dropped, just as he'd imagined it would. He grinned.

"Do you mind if I share this with my family?" she asked. He shook his head. "Zach has offered to buy half the ranch so that we're equal partners." A puzzled frown filled her face. "How can you afford that?"

"I have some money in the bank, money I haven't touched in a long time." He hadn't known what to do with the proceeds from the sale of his company. Now he did. "I figure that with your marketing smarts and my business know-how, we'll get the dude ranch up and running in no time." He grasped hold of Gina's hands. "If things work out the way I hope, we'll be much more than business partners."

He wanted to go on, but emotion clogged his throat. He had to swallow and clear it several times. "What do you say?"

Gina's eyes filled with warmth and love. "I feel like I'm in a fairy tale. Yes, Zach, I'll be your partner in every way. Merry Christmas, everyone."

* * * * *

SPECIAL EXCERPT FROM

H HARLEQUIN®

SPECIAL EDITION

Despite lying on her résumé, Amanda Lowery still manages to land a job designing Halcyon House for Blake Randall—and a place to stay over Christmas. Neither of them have had much to celebrate, but with Blake's grieving nephew staying at Halcyon, too, they're all hoping for some Christmas magic.

Read on for a sneak preview of Jo McNally's
It Started at Christmas...,
a prequel in the Gallant Lake Stories miniseries.

"Amanda, I didn't mean to upset you. I don't ever want to do anything that scares you."

She sucked in a deep, ragged breath, looking so terribly lost and sad. Her eyelids fluttered open. She stared straight ahead, talking to his chest.

"You don't understand, Blake. There are days when... when everything scares me." Her voice was barely above a whisper. His heart jumped. He thought of that first day, when she ended up unconscious in his arms.

Everything scares me.

She'd kicked her shoes off earlier, and in her bare feet the top of her head barely reached his shoulders. He put his fingers under her chin and gently tipped her head back.

He wanted to kiss this woman.

Wait. What?

No. That would be wild. He couldn't kiss her. Shouldn't. But how could he not?

Her hair tumbled off her shoulders and down her back in golden curls. Before he knew it, his free hand was slowly twisting into those curls. She didn't pull away. Didn't look away. He lowered his head until his face was just above hers. He felt her breath on his skin. She smelled like citrus and spice and blueberries and red wine. Her lips parted and she stared at him with her enormous eyes.

"I swear I don't want to scare you, Amanda. But… may I kiss you?" His voice was a raw whisper. "Please let me kiss you."

His words came out as a plea. He'd never begged for anything before in his life. But here he was, begging this sweet woman for a kiss. Ready to drop to his knees if that was what it took. He heard his father's voice in his head, mocking his weakness. That was when he started to straighten, started to come to his senses. Then he heard her whispered answer.

"Yes."

Was there any sweeter word in the world? Adrenaline surged through his body, and his hand tightened in her hair. His eyes opened to meet those two oceans of blue. Dangerous blue. Deep enough to drown in.

She was frightened, but she was trusting him. And that realization scared him to death.

Don't miss It Started at Christmas… *by Jo McNally, available December 2019 wherever Harlequin® Special Edition books and ebooks are sold.*

Harlequin.com

Looking for more satisfying love stories
with community and family at their core?

Check out **Harlequin® Special Edition**
and **Love Inspired®** books!

New books available every month!

CONNECT WITH US AT:

Facebook.com/groups/HarlequinConnection

ReaderService.com

**ROMANCE WHEN
YOU NEED IT**

HFGENRE2018

Don't miss *Stealing Kisses in the Snow*,
the heart-tugging romance in

JO McNALLY's

Rendezvous Falls series centered around
a matchmaking book club in
Rendezvous Falls, New York.

As Christmas draws ever closer, so do Piper and
Logan. Could these two opposites discover that all
they want this Christmas is each other?

Order your copy today!

Looking for inspiration in tales
of hope, faith and heartfelt romance?

Check out **Love Inspired**® and
Love Inspired® **Suspense** books!

New books available every month!

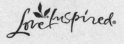